ALIEN CLAY

Praise for The Final Architecture

"Enthralling, epic, immersive, and hugely intelligent."

—Stephen Baxter

"Adrian Tchaikovsky: king of the spiders, master worldbuilder, and asker of intriguing questions. His books are packed with thought-provoking ideas (as well as lots of spiders; did I mention the spiders?). One of the most interesting and accomplished writers in speculative fiction."   —Christopher Paolini

"Adrian Tchaikovsky's *Shards of Earth* is one of the most stunning space operas I've read this year.... Tchaikovsky's world building is on glorious display as he throws all manner of spaceships, creepy aliens and strange technology into a delicious sci-fi soup. It's dense, it's funny, it's exciting, it's touching and it's perfect for someone looking for a space opera built on a grand scale."   —*BookPage* (starred review)

"Dazzlingly suspenseful.... Tchaikovsky's intricately constructed world is vast yet sturdy enough to cradle inventive science, unique aliens, and complex political machinations. With a mix of lively fight scenes, friendly banter, and high-stakes intrigue, this is space opera at its best."
—*Publishers Weekly* (starred review)

"Tchaikovsky writes space opera on a grand scale, creating a massive, complex, vividly realized future environment.... He guides the reader through this endlessly intriguing universe with a rock-steady sure hand. Fans of space opera should leave the book in breathless anticipation of the second installment in the trilogy."   —*Booklist*

Praise for Adrian Tchaikovsky

"A refreshingly new take on post-dystopia civilizations, with the smartest evolutionary worldbuilding you'll ever read."
—Peter F. Hamilton on *Children of Time*

"*Children of Time* is a joy from start to finish. Entertaining, smart, surprising, and unexpectedly human."
—Patrick Ness

"Brilliant science fiction and far-out worldbuilding."
—James McAvoy on *Children of Time*

"This is superior stuff, tackling big themes—gods, messiahs, artificial intelligence, alienness—with brio."
—*Financial Times* on *Children of Time*

"Packed with ingenious ideas.... Classic widescreen science fiction."
—*New Scientist* on *Children of Time*

"An enormously interesting and well-drawn SF novel that asks some tough questions and makes interesting extrapolations."
—*SF Signal* on *Children of Time*

"A timely warning about the dangers of artificial intelligence and super weapons in the hands of unscrupulous powers."
—*Guardian* on *Dogs of War*

BY ADRIAN TCHAIKOVSKY

SHADOWS OF THE APT

Empire in Black and Gold
Dragonfly Falling
Blood of the Mantis
Salute the Dark
The Scarab Path
The Sea Watch
Heirs of the Blade
The Air War
War Master's Gate
Seal of the Worm

ECHOES OF THE FALL

The Tiger and the Wolf
The Bear and the Serpent
The Hyena and the Hawk

THE FINAL ARCHITECTURE

Shards of Earth
Eyes of the Void
Lords of Uncreation

Guns of the Dawn

Children of Time
Children of Ruin
Children of Memory

The Doors of Eden

Alien Clay

ALIEN CLAY

ADRIAN TCHAIKOVSKY

orbitbooks.net

Orbit
Hachette Book Group
1290 Avenue of the Americas
New York, NY 10104
orbitbooks.net

First U.S. Edition: September 2024
Originally published in Great Britain by Tor, an imprint of
Pan Macmillan, in March 2024

Orbit is an imprint of Hachette Book Group.
The Orbit name and logo are registered trademarks of
Little, Brown Book Group Limited.

The publisher is not responsible for websites (or their content)
that are not owned by the publisher.

The Hachette Speakers Bureau provides a wide range of authors for speaking events. To find out more, go to hachettespeakersbureau.com or email HachetteSpeakers@hbgusa.com.

Orbit books may be purchased in bulk for business, educational, or promotional use. For information, please contact your local bookseller or the Hachette Book Group Special Markets Department at special.markets@hbgusa.com.

Library of Congress Control Number: 2023952535

ISBNs: 9780316578974 (trade paperback), 9780316578981 (ebook)

Printed in the United States of America

LSC-C

Printing 1, 2024

To Everyone Fighting The Mandate

DRAMATIS PERSONAE

Selected personnel of the Labour Colony on Imno 27g, informally known as "Kiln." Under the authority of Earth's Governmental Mandate:

Staff

Commandant Terolan
Doctor Nimell Primatt—Bioscience team leader
"Feep, Foop and Fop"—Bioscience researchers
Vessikhan—Archaeology team leader
Ylse Rasmussen—former Science team leader
Mox Calwren—engineer
Suiye—Security lieutenant

Labour

Doctor Helena Croan—Dig Support team leader
Professor Arton Daghdev—Dig Support
Ilmus Itrin—Dig Support
Parrides Okostor—Dig Support
Marquaine Ell—Dig Support, intended
(Acceptable Wastage)

Clemmish Berudha—General Labour
Armiette Graisle—General Labour
Alaxi—General Labour

Vertegio Keev—Excursions team leader
Greely—Excursions
Hakira—Excursions
Yeremy—Excursions
Okritch—Excursions

Shoer—General Labour
Frith—General Labour

Booth—Maintenance

PART 1
LIBERTÉ

1.

They say never start a story with a waking, but when you've been hard asleep for thirty years it's difficult to know where else to begin.

Start with a waking, end with a wake, maybe.

Hard asleep is, I am informed, the technical term. Hard, because you're shut down, dried out, frozen for the trip from star to star. They have it down to a fine art—takes eleven minutes, like clockwork. A whole ship full of miscreants who are desiccated down to something that can…well, I was about to say survive indefinitely, but that's not how it goes, of course. You don't *survive*. You die, but in a very specific flash-frozen way that allows for you to be restarted again more or less where you left off at the other end. After all the shunting about that would kill any body—the permanent, non-recoverable kind of kill—who wasn't withered down.

They pump you full of stuff that reinflates you to more or less your previous dimensions—you'll note there's a lot of *more or less* in this process. It is an exact science, just not one that cares about the exact you. Your thought processes don't quite pick up where they left off. Short-term memory isn't preserved; more recent mental pathways don't make the cut. Start with a waking, therefore, because in that instant it's all you've got, until you can establish some connection to older memories. You know who you are, but you don't know where you are or how you got there. Which sounds terrifying but then let me tell you what you're waking up into: actual hell. The roaring of colossal structural damage as the ship breaks up all around you. The jostling jolt as the little translucent bubble of plastic you're travelling in is jarred loose and begins to tumble. A cacophony of vibration coming through the curved surface to you: the death throes of the vessel which has carried you all this way, out into the void, and is now fragmenting. There's a world below that you know nothing about, not in your head right then. And above you are only the killing fields of space. The fact there's a below and an above shows that the planet's already won that particular battle over your soul and you're falling. The oldest fear of monkey humanity, the one which makes a baby's rubbery hands clench without thought. Such a fall from grace as never mankind nor monkey imagined.

All around you, through the celluloid walls of your prison, you see the others too. Because it can't be hell without fellow sinners to suffer amongst. Each in their own bubble sheared away from the disintegrating ship. Faces contorted in terror: screaming, hammering on the walls, eyes like wells, mouths like the gates of tombs. You'll forgive the overwrought descriptions. I am an ecologist, not a poet, but mere biology does not suffice to do justice to the appalling sight of half a hundred human beings all revivified at once, and none of them understanding why, even as *you* don't understand why, and the vessel coming apart in the wrack, and the world below, the hungry maw of its gravity well. Oh God! The recollection of it makes me sick to my gut. And of all things, in the midst of that chaos, to remember *I am an ecologist*.

4

Out in space where there isn't even an ecology. Was there ever a less useful piece of self-knowledge?

Some of us haven't reawakened. I see at least two bubbles whirl past me in which the occupant remains a dried-out cadaver, the systems failed. Acceptable Wastage is the technical term, and that's another unwelcome concept to suddenly have remembrance of. For there are always some who don't wake up at the far end. They tell you it's the inevitable encroachment of entropy over so long a journey. Maybe it is. Or maybe those who don't wake up are the most egregious troublemakers. It's hard to recognize anyone when their skin is stuck to their skull without the interposition of familiar flesh, but I think I see my old colleague Marquaine Ell go whirling past. She's been shipped all the way out here from Earth, even at the minimal expense they've boiled the process down to, yet they might as well have just thrown her into the incinerator for the same effect.

With the reminder of that minimal expense comes another piece of knowledge. Another couple of my neurons renewing a severed acquaintance, bringing understanding that's relevant but unwelcome. That this is *intentional*. It's no traumatic wreck of the Hesperus. Not a bug but a feature. Sending people into space used to be expensive, and for people anyone cares about it still is. You're encouraged to keep them reliably alive in transit, with actual medical care and life support and sporadic wakings to check on their oh-so-delicate physical and mental wellbeing. And, saliently, you're encouraged to arrange a means by which to bring them *back* home again, their tour of duty done. Big expensive ships that can do complicated things like refuel, slow down, speed up, turn around.

But if all you want to do is deliver some felons to a labour camp on a remote planet, because it's literally cheaper and easier than sending machines to do the same work, then you don't ever have to worry about them coming back. Because they won't. It's a life sentence, one-way trip. More unwelcome revelations fall into my head, even as my head, along with the rest of me, falls into the pull of Imno 27g.

I should be beating my newly revivified fists against the inside of my bubble, except it's whirling round and round, having dropped out of the disintegrating ship, and the world below is growing in size. The void has become a sky, yellow-blue. Can you have a yellow-blue? Not on Earth, but this is Imno's sky. Blue for the oxygen the planet's biosphere has pumped into the atmosphere as a by-product of its metabolic pathways, just like on Earth. Yellow for the diffuse clouds of aerial plankton. Or they're yellow-black, actually, because of their dark photosynthetic surfaces. Blue-yellow-black should not be a colour, and of all things it should not be the colour of the sky.

We fall. At some point the chutes open: filmy transparent plastic, already biodegrading from the moment it contacts atmosphere. Like the ship, it's designed to last the minimum possible period of time to do its job. The ship, that unnamed plastic piece of trash which was printed as a single piece in Earth's orbit, no more than a one-shot engine and a pod to hold us all like peas. An egg-case, perhaps. Designed to carry its corpse-cargo across space to one of the current "Planets Under Activity," as the Mandate's Expansion department terms it. To carry us to Imno 27g, then break apart in the upper atmosphere. Fragmenting into pieces even as the one-shot medical units resuscitate its cargo from cadaver to screaming lost souls tumbling to our doom. While some of us don't get the wake-up, others who do won't survive the descent. Doom is what we're all going to, sure enough, but it's less drawn-out for some than for others. My bones jar as my chute deploys, and while I see others similarly wrenched from the teeth of the ground, I also see the handful whose chutes have failed drop away. Still screaming, as they remember just enough to know they're about to die all over again.

I don't die from not waking up, and I don't die falling from the edge of the atmosphere either. I'm not written off on the ledgers as Acceptable Wastage. They have to work out very carefully the precise level of expense that's necessary, and the precise percentage of failed deliveries—meaning dead people—this entails. Because who wants to spend a single cent more than you have to when you're shipping convicts off to die in a distant world's work camp? People who've gone against the system and are now going to pay their dues permanently, for the rest of their lives. People like me. I hear the figures later: twenty per cent Acceptable Wastage. If that sounds like an absurd loss of investment, then you don't know the history of people shipping other people against their will from place to place.

They put manoeuvring jets on the pods. Little plastic things. One shot. As I fall—it seems to take so long!—I see them fire. Each one discharges its blast of bottled gas and destroys itself in the process. If that allows me to land where I'm supposed to, then good. If I end up somewhere distant from the work camp then they aren't going to waste the work-hours it would take to retrieve me. I'll die trapped in my bubble or outside it, because Imno 27g is full of things that will kill you. Especially alone and with only half your head together. Not that there has ever been anything in my head that would help me survive on this alien world.

But that doesn't happen to me either. I come down with everyone else, those of us not covered under the Wastage provisions, around the same place, where they're waiting for us. The camp's commandant has sent out the heavy mob, just in case we somehow managed to form a revolutionary subcommittee on the way down. On seeing the riot armour and guns—the "minimally lethal" public order pieces I (now) recall from Earth, which only kill you an acceptable proportion of the time—I remember there *had* been a revolutionary subcommittee I was part of. Not, obviously, on the ship, because we'd all been flash-frozen corpses. And not on the way down, because we'd been far too busy screaming. But back on Earth, before they'd infiltrated our network, tracked our contacts, arrested everyone we knew for a discounted friends-and-family betrayal, I had actually been part of the problem, so I'd earned this. Back on Earth I had been stubbornly proud of the fact, too. In the prison attached to the space port, in the cramped orbital quarters, I had known that, yes, I was going to be deported to the camps, but at least I'd tried to do my bit, even a lowly academic like me.

Right now, after plummeting to this doom, then seeing the death-squad-slash-welcoming-committee, I regret it all. If a political officer magically manifested, offering a pardon if I signed a confession, I'd reach for the pen. Much unlike the song, I regret every one of my life choices that has led me to this point. It's a moment of weakness.

My bubble deflates around me. I have a fraught minute of fighting it off to stop the clammy plastic suffocating me before they cut me out. They have a special tool for doing this, like a heated knife. I gain a shallow, shiny slash along my thigh to testify to their general lack of care wielding it. One more person becomes Wastage when they're the last to be cut free and by then it's too late. All within tolerance, you understand. And that's it. We're down. I look up into an alien sky.

2.

I want to be still, but they won't let me. We stumble and sway and try to make words happen with numb, clumsy tongues. The heavy mob grab us and shake us, shoving us about. Not so much physically moving us as just Lesson One in How Things Are Going To Be from now on. A heavy hand on my shoulder, a little formal handshake that makes my teeth rattle. And all the time I'm scanning the faces of my fellow damned souls. My mind keeps skipping and I can't even remember why, but then it comes back to me. Marquaine. Marquaine was on the same ship. Was part of the same consignment of expendables. My friend, my colleague, my fellow hell-raiser and political delinquent. It can't have been her face I saw, dried to her skull and whirling away into the abyss up there. That can't be the end of such a brilliant mind, a celebrated career, a *friend*. I stagger into the others, gabbling, slurring. I paw at them, but every face is a stranger. She's not here. She died like we all did, back in Earth's orbit when they desiccated us, and her promised resurrection never came.

Marquaine Ell had been in the next cell to me, in the port holding facility, and we'd been able to talk through the wall. There'd been a knack to it, once you worked out that the scratched point in the wall hid a bubble in the structure that carried sound through. The whole place wasn't much better constructed than the fragmentation barge they were going to ship us out on. If you put your ear and jaw to that one point in the wall where the scratches were, you could hear the person in the neighbouring cell if they put their mouth to the matching point on their side. The scratches were there from prisoners before us who'd found this out and had the fellowship to think of those who would come after. To save us fumbling about for the right spot. After all, it wasn't as if anyone in those cells would be there for long. I think about them now: some prisoner on the very cusp of being shipped off on the barges, perhaps about to become Acceptable Wastage in turn, finding some way of marking the wall just to help a person they'd never meet and would never know. Just because of the one thing they'd very definitely have in common with that successor: being enemies of the Mandate, enough to be deported off-world.

Marquaine was in the next cell to me both physically and ideologically. We were perpetrators of sibling unorthodoxies, even though she hadn't, to my knowledge, become involved with the harder-edged layers of resistance I had. The subcommittees and everything that entailed. That was me, the soft-handed academic, deciding to stick it to the Mandate. Trying to be more than an armchair agitator. And yet we were put in neighbouring accommodation waiting for the barges. That, more than anything else, told me I'd been taken up just for my scholastic misdemeanours and the other stuff had never made it into my file.

We had both been rising stars in the same field, and were about the same age. There'd been a conference, up on one of the big luxury orbitals, where Marquaine and I, and another colleague, Ilmus Itrin, had been inseparable: the Three Musketeers. We'd talked out-of-doctrine science over the fancy tea set they'd printed out for us, loudly enough to twitch the ears of our respective faculties down on Earth. The grasp of the Academic Mandate had seemed loose right then, and we believed in the freedom of knowledge and the inevitable triumph of reason. As the rigid scientific orthodoxy looked like it was finally in full retreat, we were spinning out all sorts of ideas in our fields. Xenobiology was the hot topic, after all. Humans had set foot on other worlds, and on some of those worlds there had been life of a sort. It seemed inevitable that the next probe would yield the Big Discovery we all knew must be out there.

Ten years before that, when I was a student, it had all been very different. Orthodoxy was like a hand at your throat. If we had anything to say that didn't fit within the narrow spaces between those clenched fingers it was whispered in secret. Unredacted textbooks got passed hand to hand like the samizdat novels that they were constantly arresting people for printing. The first discovery of extraterrestrial life had thrown Academic Mandate into a spin. What if we inadvertently discovered a reality that didn't match the dogma? Horrors! Except, over time, it all fell within tolerance. The looked-for upheaval to our understanding of the universe never happened. No aliens turned up to break our laws of physics, or demonstrate there was a better way to run your civilization than the way our authoritarian overlords did. So over the years, it felt like the grasp of orthodoxy relaxed. Enough for Marquaine, Ilmus and me to say the unspeakable over good coffee and printed strawberries, up at the Nineteenth Conference on the Further Prospects of Life.

With Mandate officials one table over, hunching their shoulders and pretending not to hear. They were yesterday's men, we knew. We were the future.

Now I'm in the future and it's not what we thought. That iron hand was just shifting its grip. Maybe relaxing to see which parts of its contents would wriggle the most, so it could apply properly targeted pressure.

Let nobody tell you the Mandate isn't patient. Here I am, thirty years from Earth, and it's still all part of the long-term plan. They gave us enough rope, and the purges only started after every loudmouth malcontent had been given a chance to identify themselves. Or else for the Internal Investigations office to flip enough people to ensure that even the close-mouthed dissidents were accounted for too, on someone's little list. They actually missed me the first time, when they picked up Ilmus and most of the others in my small circuit. Me and Marquaine and a handful of other survivors were left, like isolated teeth in a jaw jollied up by the police in the interrogation suite. We wept for the decimated faculty, for the great minds who had been spirited away. In private, we mopped our brows and were thankful it wasn't us. And we dared to believe that Internal Investigations was fallible. Maybe there were even sympathizers amongst their ranks. Why couldn't *we* infiltrate *them* for a change? Except it wasn't like that. They were just giving us more rope in case we could fashion them some additional nooses. So we went into hiding. We wore new identities as effective as fright wigs and false noses held on with string. We tried to work out who'd sold our friends to Investigations. We wouldn't make it so easy for them, we told each other. We'd spot the spooks and the informers. We wouldn't break.

But everyone breaks, and there are far too many informers

to spot them all. They got me before Marquaine, and in our neighbouring cells at the port holding facility she never asked me if I'd sold her out, in the end. If she broke. She didn't want to hear the answer. I was the last person on Earth she was going to talk to besides the deportation staff. So we danced around it and spoke of other matters. Earth matters. The last chance for a lot of things.

And now I have seen every surviving face and none of them is hers. My glimpse up above in the wrack of the barge was exactly what I thought. She's dead. Or rather, she never came back to life. One of the most incisive minds of our time has become no more than Acceptable Wastage. And I, all unworthy, am still alive on an alien world.

Here's a brief primer for the incurious.

Humanity had journeyed to eleven exoplanets at the point in time when they packed me off. As in, actually set foot on them. Unmanned missions had been to...I think the last count was seventy-eight. The sixty-seven lacking that human footprint were either still under committee review, relegated to automated exploitation, or simply canned as not being worth another look. There's a lot of rock in the near reaches of the galaxy. Of those eleven we'd been to, nine had produced life of their own, while the other two were rich in mineral deposits and situated problematically enough that a human hand on the tiller was necessary. And how glad I am, even though I've just seen How I Might Have Died played out in a variety of ways, that I haven't been assigned to any of those. Shipped out to be a cog in a mining operation on an airless toxic rock somewhere. Not that the presence of life necessarily means air or a lack of toxins.

Life, though. Nine worlds with life of some kind, out of seventy-eight surveyed. That might sound disappointing to you, but to a xeno-ecologist like me it's fantastically exciting. My predecessors in the field were very worried the number might turn out to be zero out of seventy-eight, or out of any number you cared to mention. That would have been appalling. We'd have all been out of a job for starters.

Six of the nine living worlds have nothing on a macro-cellular scale. And I'm not talking about *cells* necessarily, not like Earth has. But the life on these is composed of individual units too small to see with the naked eye, perhaps forming colonies or randomly aggregate communities like coloured crusts at the edges of deep-sea vents. Or building lumpy, unimpressive reefs that are basically just stacked graveyards of past minuscule generations. So, three worlds out of seventy-eight had actually produced life on a scale familiar to a child of Earth. Again, it'll sound disappointing to you, but it's bloody amazing to me. *Three*, out of only seventy-eight. The galaxy abounds with life!

I hadn't *visited* any of those worlds until now. Because there were two lists of academics who were chosen to go on a trip to the outer worlds. One was composed of individuals in good ideological standing with the Academic Mandate, and I have never kissed enough ass or compromised enough scientific principles to be on that. The other list was composed of those who had transgressed, danced their way through the show trials without actually being executed, and then been deported on the one-way fragmentation barges. Which I have in fact just had my solitary ride on.

It could have been worse, I decide, as I stand here and get my first look at this new world.

Quite aside from the possibility of mining rocks or studying alien germs for the rest of my abridged life, I understand that another of the three worlds, Imno 11c, or "Swelter," has a mean temperature of eighty-four degrees centigrade in the temperate zone, and is geologically active enough that the air's mostly smoke. The life there, by all accounts complex and fascinating, exists in slow migration along deep-sea vents, in a lethargic ecology powered by geothermal energy. It's basically snails all the way down, or at least blobby mollusc-looking things with shells made from the heavy metals the critters need to get out of their systems to avoid being fatally poisoned. Getting fatally poisoned is, I am led to believe, the second most common cause of death amongst the labour camp workers on Swelter, after catastrophic pressure-crushing accidents, because the seas are very deep and water is very heavy.

In contrast, the relevant moon of the third planet, Kaleb 3p, or "Tartrap," is really fucking cold. And dying from being really fucking cold is, I understand, de rigueur there. It orbits a gas giant out in the far reaches of that overpopulated system and only tidal heating from its parent planet prevents it from freezing solid. It has seas of liquid hydrocarbons and a complex ecosystem built up of exotic chemosynthesis. Everything there is very big and very slow, so much so that we don't know how most of the species actually produce little big slow aliens because none of them have got round to it in the several decades since human researchers arrived there. In contrast, Imno 27g, my new home, is a paradise.

It does not feel like a paradise, not to any of us. We stand there, still in the crinkly paper one-pieces they put us in when they froze us and shipped us out. The clothes, if that's even the word for them, are already falling apart. We end up holding disintegrating handfuls in front of our relevant bits, pinning the wretched garments together at shoulder and hip like we're at the galaxy's cheapest toga party. It's cold too. I know, intellectually, that it's morning and 27g has a serious diurnal temperature swing that means we'd be sweating buckets by noon and then freezing by dusk. And the air smells of burning. I also know, intellectually, that this is from by-products of the local photosynthetic pathways. The fact that we can smell what the air is like is already one up on either Swelter or Tarpit, because if you take a deep breath of the atmosphere on either of those you'll end up dead in short order. So I am very, very lucky indeed. I have seventy-seven potential problems but being on Imno 27g isn't one of them.

(For the avoidance of doubt, and for the slow students at the back, Imno is the Astro-discovery Mandate program that revisited this star system. It was the 27th one the program renamed under the new conventions, and this world I have just put my feet on is the sixth out from the star. We don't call it that, of course. We call it Kiln, and back on Earth I assumed this referred to the temperature fluctuations, but I was wrong. Kiln had a secret that nobody back at Mandate HQ had been telling. It's easy enough to bottle up information after all, when it takes thirty years for word to get back to Earth, and there's only one state-controlled channel.)

Our bubbles have burst around a cleared field, artificially flattened and still with machine tracks all over it. The welcoming committee are keen to get us into the camp proper—we can see the familiar chainlink and hard-plate walls of it rising into a grimy plastic dome, a real taste of home. The deportation camp Marquaine and I were held in was made of just the same stuff. I do my best to take a look beyond, because it's an *alien world* and, fine, it's the alien world I'm going to die on, but you have to be curious, surely. Right then I assume they're going to just have me digging holes and cleaning privies, never to emerge again, so I want to see the Great Outdoors at least once.

There's a forest. They've cleared a hundred metres of space between it and the camp's walls, but I catch a glimpse of it before they hustle us inside. They're not exactly trees and not exactly plants, honestly, but the basic physics of solar collection produce a convergence with those, even if they've started with very different building blocks. And the essential stuff of Kiln's biology is carbon-hydrogen-oxygen, as well as those familiar building blocks like amino acids, which can form entirely of their own accord without any actual life present at all. Life on Swelter and even Tarpit has an overlap with Earth, and Kiln even more so. But still very alien. Incompatible. Reaching the same ends by different means. The "trees" look like chonky vases crowned with a great rosette of black petals, twenty metres across in some cases. There's no dendritic structure at all—no branching from bough to branch to twig, the pattern that repeats ad infinitum in Earth biology, from trees to the passageways of the lungs. Here there are just those big bulbous tuber trunks and the extravagant whorl of enormous leaf-petal-sail things that are the photosynthetic surfaces. They're almost black, eating as much light as they can, not even greenness escaping them. The swollen trunks are yellow-orange, only slightly different in colour to the dusty burnt-looking ground. We see no motile life in that first brief snatch of Kiln, though it is out there. The cleared ground keeps it at bay, at least during the day, at least long enough for us to walk across it. Then they get us inside the camp's fence, kicking the laggards and beating us with gun butts. Most of the others are only too glad just to get under cover, away from the alienness. It's me who dawdles, staring. It's me who takes the blows on my back and shoulders. Not even properly professional brutality; there's almost an edge of hysteria to it. There's a distinct sense of hurry, with plenty of mirror-visor helms glancing at the treeline.

They next herd us into an enclosed chamber just within the gates, leaving us there and gassing the fuck out of us. Something eye-watering and acrid sears my throat and stings my skin. It goes on for a good three minutes, which I know because I'll go through it plenty more times, and eventually I just count the seconds. Everyone is given a solid lungful of the stuff. When it's done, one of my fellows, a woman, is on the ground wheezing, gasping, clutching at her throat. She's dead even before our guards come back in, or else they were politely waiting for her to die before they returned. Just to save themselves the trouble of not helping her in person, rather than not helping her remotely. It was an allergic reaction. I'm told about half a per cent of people can't take the decontamination. So at least my odds were pretty good when it came to this particular death.

I mean, honestly, I've survived so much by now, I should be feeling immortal.

But I'm not feeling immortal. I don't think I ever felt quite so mortal in my life. I remember how it had been in the justice camp, waiting for my trial. I was so bloody defiant.

The principled scholar in opposition to the fascist regime. Let them do their worst! I would stand on the scaffold and spit in their eye. Except it hadn't been the scaffold. My execution is going to take place over years of privation, light years from home. Whatever the minutiae of the desiccation process, I suspect in most cases defiance doesn't survive rehydration.

They finally let us out of the airlock, the decontamination chamber, and we see what's under the camp's dome.

The usual, of course. The local earth bonded into mock-crete and shaped into low, unlovely buildings. I can instantly tell you which is the labourer dorm, which is the workshop and infirmary—or maybe the infirmary-slash-research facility (it's always reassuring when the science needs sick people on hand as a ready resource, yes indeed). I see the expected network of gantries, towers and upper residences, where the staff and guards live, and from which privileged vantage point they can look, spit and, if need be, shoot down at we lesser beings. They'll have the communications and control up there, their link to the satellites and whatever orbital infra-structure's in place for Kiln. They'll have the lifeline to Earth. After all, they're due to go back someday unlike us. But all of this is just home cooking from my perspective, and not what I'm interested in. Because the camp buildings make a ring, and what they make a ring around are...

For a brief moment I think the central structure is made up of dead trees, because the walls of it are of the same rounded shape. My second assessment is that they're fossils, based on the stony-looking spires rising past those broken-vase structures—spires like upright leaves with regular projections, now weathered and broken off. Gigantic fossils of an earlier age of this alien world. There's only so long I can kid myself, though. Only so long I can keep these prodigies trapped within the realm of bio-ecology.

These have been *made*. They are buildings, or the ruins of them. Kiln once boasted a civilization, and the shape of some of these ruins looks enough like the pottery ovens of old Earth to give the planet its name. We've not just found another iteration of life here, we've found other *minds*. And three complex ecologies out of seventy-eight worlds is one thing, but one other intelligent species in the whole universe cracks all our assumptions wide open. For a moment I forget that I'm a prisoner because my mind has just been freed.

The guards muscle in before I can assess it further, and march me off to go before the commandant. I haven't been in the camp five minutes and already it seems I'm in trouble.

3.

I'm still clutching my paper rags to my privates as they shunt me up the gantry stairs, which is a recipe for barked shins and grazed knees and leaves me precious little modesty by the time I get to the top. As though they've driven me up there just so I can exhibit my wretched physique to all and sundry. I'm trying to ask questions, which they're not interested in answering, unless you count physical violence. Which, in my experience to date, has a certain finality as a conversational gambit.

"What did I do?" I demand, and by the second time it's more pleading and begging. There aren't many good reasons to be hauled off to see the big man. And I can't see why they'd need to make an example of someone right now, given all the varied examples that our delivery method provided us with, but that's the only thing I can think of. They're going to dangle me from the scaffolding just to make sure everyone else is sufficiently educated as to the way things are run around here. A final irony, the career academic ending his life as a lesson.

When I'm shoved into the complex of buildings up there, I frantically reassess my expectations. Torture, perhaps, or a little recreational beating. Maybe it's in the guards' contracts that they get one out of each shipment for their personal diversion. After all, their lives must be short of entertainment otherwise. I look for the thumbscrews and the electrodes, the big truncheons and the easily washed-down floor.

The lead guard cuffs me about the head and then rips the last of my tatters away. I brace myself for the latest, maybe the final piece of oppression I'm to receive from these faithful servants of the Mandate.

The Mandate's business is control. If the Mandate didn't want to go to space, it's not as though there'd be some interstellar underground railroad ferrying dissidents out of their jurisdiction. If the Mandate didn't care about extrasolar life then it could destroy and bury the data from the probes which had gone to Swelter, Tartrap and Kiln and the rest. It's not like your friendly local revolutionary subcommittee would launch its own competing space research program using bottle rockets and string.

So: cover up all evidence of extraterrestrial life, then. Say it's all star stuff but none of it organized in a particularly energetic way, so everyone can go back to their textbooks and forget about little green men, thank you very much. Except, of course, the Mandate never has the degree of control it wants. Word gets out. It always does. Little cells of interfering academics like yours truly would end up poring over the details and know that *Something was Out There* that the Mandate didn't want us to know about. Simply uncovering that much would be a morale-boosting victory for us and, from that statement, I think you can truly see how trivial we all were, in the greater scheme of things.

Perhaps because the bureaucrats and tame scholars of the Mandate were equally trivial in their outlook, they wanted to deny us even that miserable triumph and so didn't cover anything up at all. The data arrived and was duly released. Life in the universe! Worthy of study! We academics raised our voices in a clamour, demanding action. Or, rather, we didn't because, by the time the announcement was made, action was already under way. Every world out there with life was getting a labour camp and a science team, along with mining concerns and the like, exploiting concentrations of rare elements. It's only really the rare elements, you understand. There's no point in bulk shipping the common stuff over a distance of light years. It costs too much to ever make back your stake and you may as well just do something similar within the solar system.

Cost is, of course, the problem. You might ask why the restrictive, oh-so-narrow-minded Mandate is spending its valuable resources shipping people like me off to Kiln to go look at aliens. And, yes, the simple threat of *Behave or we'll deport you to an alien world by the absolute cheapest and nastiest way* has some use as a stick to threaten people with, but it's not as though the Mandate is particularly short of sticks. Why look at aliens at all?

Because, as I said, the Mandate's business is control.

I don't mean that they're worried about a Kilnish invasion fleet, or they want to turn the snails of Swelter into colonial slaves, or anything like that. I mean philosophically. The Mandate was very keen on building a detailed model of the universe. From subatomic to universal, they wanted a text-book explaining how it all fits together. And that sounds suspiciously creditable, to an impressionable scholar. The Mandate is big on academia. Plenty of scholars live happily in their ivory towers, writing papers politely refining one another's critiques. Big on the arts, big on the sciences, especially big on humanities and philosophy. What's not to like?

From my point of view, what's not to like is how they have their methodology absolutely backwards. The Neo-Cientifico doctrine looks powerfully sound on the face of it —all that investigation, and understanding our place in the universe through detailed study of those other worlds. But after a while you work out that they're *starting* with our place in the universe, and the goal of all that work is to draw some nice straight lines from *what we've found* to *what it means*. And woe betide you if that's not where the points on your graph are leading.

Trivial, like I say. And our academic quibbles, those of people like Ilmus and Marquaine and me, are all equally trivial. But such trivialities got us all deported into space the cheapest way and Marquaine didn't survive the trip.

Except... what I just saw today. The ruins on Kiln. *That* was a bit more than trying to prove the undersea life of Swelter was equivalent to this or that stage of Earth's prehistory, or show how the sluggish metabolic pathways of Tartrap fit the ideas enshrined by past luminaries of biochemistry. The stakes went up after what they'd found on Kiln, and I realize now they really can redact the data if they try hard enough, because not a whimper of it had found its way to our debating rooms back on Earth.

In that room, the brutal servants of the Mandate give me new clothes to replace the flaking paper envelope they sent me into space with. Real clothes, weirdly antiquated. Not that Mandate styles vary much over time, given how much they value conformity, but the height of the stiff collar, the way the cuffs clip about my wrists like manacles, rather than buttoning back, is old-fashioned. The overlap of the jacket, fastening all the way across the left breast, almost under the armpit, is that faux-military style of two generations ago. The way formal clothes looked when they'd sent Commandant Terolan and his expedition out here. An unintentional statement about the ideology of space travel.

Earth is crowded. The solar colonies are at economic capacity. Yet you'll notice that when I was talking about why to send us out here to study, I didn't even mention sending us out here to *live*. It isn't deportation to "the colonies" out beyond the solar system. Just the labour camps, serving specific industrial or studious purposes. There *are* colonies, but only within the solar system, and even then, tightly limited and regulated. Keeping someone alive on half-habitable Mars is expensive. Keeping someone alive on Titan, or in the sky factories above Venus, is murderously expensive. Why not colonize the exoplanets, most especially halfway-congenial Kiln? Places where we can walk under the sky without instantly freezing, burning or suffering explosive decompression? Surely the Mandate, global superstate that it is, wants its space empire?

Let the clothes tell the story. Here on Kiln, the Mandate is a century out of date. I imagine Commandant Terolan sitting up there in the antique uniform of his day, a man on the far side of middle age who'll be getting on the boat in ten, fifteen years to go home for a state-sanctioned retirement. Going home to an Earth he won't recognize despite the Mandate's best attempts to halt time and control progress. Even the "perfect state of governance" shifts in a thousand little ways. Thirty years have passed on Earth since they sentenced and sent me away. If there was a revolt here on Kiln it would take thirty years for word of it to get back home and another thirty, plus mustering and prep time, to send a response. In which time who knows what would have happened at either end of that ridiculous thread of whispers? The Mandate isn't interested in spreading humanity throughout the galaxy, not even to our nearest neighbouring stars. Clenching their fist around the solar system is enough of a test of their authority; freezing time by redacting history and monitoring every little act and reaction. Allow people to set up in living, breathing colonies across the vast interstellar gulfs and you've de facto lost control of them. You've created not dependants but rivals. And so the work camp on Kiln—like all of its siblings on other worlds—is something different. Nowhere anyone's going to call home. Something locked down and militarized and given over to a ruthless ideologue the Mandate knows they can rely on. I picture him, brutal, slab-faced, not a new thought in his head save those that come in by official decree. A monster given sovereignty over monsters, who in turn have sovereignty over we prisoners. In my new outfit, I am braced to enter the lair of the beast. The guards give me no choice about it, shoving me onwards. And so I enter the presence of Commandant Terolan.

He doesn't look so bad, honestly. Balding, sideburned, a style as oddly quaint as the outfits we're both in. Sitting there at the far end of a plastic table as his flunky serves us dinner. Actual dinner, spun out of an actual food printer, just like Momma used to make. Raising his white cup with a twinkle, he invites me to join him in the traditional toast, "The Continuing Mandate of Humanity!" And I do join him, of course. I can be anyone's hypocrite if it gets me fed.

"You may ask the question," Commandant Terolan says, as

I drink. I watch him warily, because maybe this is one of those loyalty tests so beloved of middle managers who want to play the petty tyrant over their underlings. Maybe the question is, in fact, forbidden, and I may *not* ask it. Recognizing that fact would show my compliance with orthodoxy, or otherwise I'm a dissident. Given I've been shipped out here for unorthodoxy and dissidence then maybe that makes me, what? Dissident squared? A dissident's dissident? The man who cleans the privies, anyway, or goes in to fix the nuclear reactor wearing a paper apron as protection.

So I don't ask until, "Ask," he prompts. All genuine civilized charm as he sips from his delicate cup.

It's not as if the question hasn't been burning in me ever since I saw that strange structure, and eventually I can't keep it in, even if I want to. The words pour out of me thusly: "Who built those ruins?"

"Good," Terolan agrees. "Who. Not *what*. Orthodoxically correct. I was hoping I could find a use for you here, Professor Daghdev." He's obviously listened to the pronunciation audio that came with my permanent record, eliding the middle "g" the way everyone in the prison service hadn't, on the rare occasions they'd even cared I had a name.

"I know you, of course. It's a small field," Terolan says. As I was only a student when they sent him out here, he must mean he receives the *Approved Academica* with each fresh delivery from home, and has been keeping tabs on the xenoscience sections. Not exactly surprising for a man sitting on what he has here. I have a mad moment when I wonder if my entire arrest was triggered at his behest, just to put me at his service. But no. I earned my sentence. Besides, he'd have had to have sent the order back when I was sitting my first exams. We were both no strangers to longevity treatments, but nobody's that patient. The camp did have a standing order out, though, I discover later, for any academic of appropriate credentials who fell into the prison service. An order that had been sent from Kiln back when the first research chief here started going off the rails, which had arrived on Earth just in time for my fall from grace. Maybe that also meant a few borderline cases, the mildest of the unorthodox, like my friend Ilmus, had been nudged over the boundary into "deportation" just because there was an explicit request for them. Someone back home probably got a nice little bonus for every scholar they sent on a one-way space mission.

"Eat," Terolan invites. I've just reached the "very, very hungry" stage of post-revivification, so I do. It's good. The camp commandant and his senior staff eat as well on Kiln as the faculty did back at the Panoptic Academy.

"Earth proteins, I take it?" It's partly an attempt at a joke, ho ho, partly a genuine worry after I've already peristalsed my first mouthful.

"We experimented with the alternative," Terolan tells me. "Unsuccessfully. I can show you the results if you like." The twinkle is still there but it's frozen, become a sharp-edged shard of glass. I'm being reminded of our relative stations, just in case the sharing of bread gives me any delusions of companionship. "Professor," he goes on, the iron fist back in its glove without obvious transition, "I would appreciate your professional opinion and assistance with the quandary this world presents us. You are in a position to render a considerable service to human science and knowledge. If that was ever important to you."

"It was," I get out, around a mouthful. "It is."

"Not so important that you didn't get yourself sent here," Terolan says, as his man comes over to top up his cup. He swills it, peering in with a divinatory air. "The food is reclaimed biomass," he says. "It's all so maddeningly close, and yet you couldn't eat it as it is. There's no going out to bag an alien for the pot. Except...eventually you could, and that...becomes problematic. No..." A reverie comes over him that excludes me. A tantalizing trail of half-spoken breadcrumbs that peter out maddeningly in the middle of the forest, leaving me...where?

At the mercy of the wolves, is where, but the twinkle has returned to his gaze again and I understand it's at least four parts an act. He wants me to be curious and to be worried, and to be *his*. Luring me into collaboration with him by the hooks of my profession, as well as my understanding that my fortunes are entirely his to hoist or cut loose.

"You know what they call this place, of course."

"Imno twenty-seven gee," I pronounce fastidiously. The proper, formal name. No dissidence here, no sir.

"And?"

I shrug inwardly. Who am I kidding, exactly? "Kiln."

"Kiln," agrees the commandant. "And something was baked here, Professor. There are dozens of these settlements, or monuments, or shrines, across this part of the planet. Small, similar but not identical. Evidence of a widespread common culture. They were built by a process we can't quite understand, but most definitely raised artificially, no natural phenomena. The work of sapience. There are records of past study and doubtless you'll be granted access. You've seen what we have out there, and you're thinking...actually, why don't you tell me? What are your first impressions, Professor Daghdev?"

I blink lazily over it to give myself thinking time. Sounding out my inner scholar and trying to work out *what* those impressions are, and then whether I want to be candid about them with this man. But they're so meagre they're not worth dissembling over.

"It looks simple. Small scale. So it must have been small groups or very small builders." I'm thinking some level of early-human development as an analogue—pre-agricultural maybe, or just in the transition. Or I'm thinking termites.

"What if I told you there was drainage, signs of higher- and lower-status chambers based on interior space. Evidence of a stratified civilization with all that must inevitably require —surely law, philosophy, consideration of their place in the universe?"

I nod cautiously. Because big and small chambers, drainage, even air conditioning for when it gets hot, are all termite things too. Wouldn't it be a grand joke if everyone was writing erudite sociology papers on what turned out to be a glorified colony insect, or Kiln's nearest equivalent. Commandant Terolan reads it in my face and smiles condescendingly.

"Quite," he says. "And if I told you they had a power network, except we don't know what it was actually powering."

"Source?"

"Solar."

Life cracked solar power on Earth billions of years before we made the first artificial panel, and I nod cautiously again but don't say anything smart in case it cuts dinner short before the dessert trolley is wheeled in. Once more Terolan reads me, sure enough, and his smile widens.

"There's writing too, Professor Daghdev. Not translatable, obviously, but writing, decoration, art. For the first time, evidence of true thought evolved on another planet, in another solar system entirely. The greatest discovery humanity has ever made, waiting to be announced across the Mandate the moment we actually have something more than weak speculation to announce. Because where are they now? Our best guess is nobody's lived here for a thousand years, but there's no sign of war or deliberate destruction. The only damage can be put down to time or our own study methods."

My heart, my mind, they race! *Writing?* I don't believe it. A lot of things can *look* like writing, especially if you're desperate enough to find it. There are fossils called graptolites so named because they look like alien cursive scrawled in the ancient rock. I maintain my veneer of diplomacy, wondering if he's baiting me. "There are a lot of reasons a settlement can be abandoned. Or a whole region."

He nods as though I've passed another test. "Geo survey suggests the planet was wetter back then, that we're in a relative ice age right now, with the polar oceans frozen over, the forests shrunken. But this... We've compiled a bestiary of the life on this world, and you'll get to see those files too, of course. It's only a fraction of what's out there, but it's ... nothing that might have built this. A whole world, yet nothing that could look you in the eye and know you. Nothing that isn't just a beast, even if it's an alien beast. Where did they go, Professor? We haven't even found the *remains* of anything that could have built these places. No precursors. No stone flakes and axes. Nothing that could ever have evolved into a sapient builder species, or devolved from it. We haven't found the tools they used either, and in that absence we can't even understand *how*. Do you understand me?"

He's standing now, making the table creak where he leans on it. I look into his pouchy face and see an unexpected earnestness. They'd sent out a Mandate man, but a scientist, too. When Commandant Terolan takes the slow boat back to Earth he wants to have findings to present, a solution to Kiln's mysterious, vanished civilization.

"I am very glad you survived transit," he tells me. "I'd hoped there would be two of you here with me. The other didn't make it, which is always unfortunate. The journey to Kiln is dangerous." Spoken with the assurance of someone for whom it hadn't been. The *other* had been my friend, colleague and comrade, and these mealy words from Terolan are Marquaine Ell's eulogy. She deserved better. "Kiln is dangerous too," he adds as an afterthought. "The turnover amongst the regular labour force is high. Contamination is a constant problem." Back home that means coming into contact with dangerous ideas. Out here I understand a more biological connotation.

"You're threatening me." I've finished the meal by now, drained my cup, and feel I can roll the die a little.

"Professor Daghdev," the commandant tells me, "you are a convicted dissident and heterodox thinker. You have been sent to the extrasolar camps. Because they know, back home, what our situation here is, you were diverted to one of the least lethal destinations within human reach. But Kiln will still kill you, sooner or later. It kills them all, the Labour. It's what the Labour is for. It's what you're for. But in recognition of the assistance you can provide, I am offering you the opportunity for it to be *later*." He claps his hands and his people appear to clear the table. The guards are there to clear me off too, hoisting me out of the chair. A flunky takes the chair even as my backside leaves it and I decide they will feed it into the incinerator so not a trace of me might remain to trouble the commandant. Perhaps they'll scrub me from the air, too.

"I hope that we will have many conversations in the future," Terolan tells me. "I look forward to hearing your theories once you have had a chance to study both the ruins here, and the local ecology. An unparalleled opportunity to practise your discipline. How your colleagues back home must envy you." Again that damnable twinkle, inviting me to chuckle genially as the guards virtually hold my feet off the ground. Ignoring the fact that those colleagues I had who were loyal enough not to be shipped out in the fragmentation barges are retired or even dead of old age by now. "For now, I will have my people show you to the labour dormitories and the life that the less privileged here enjoy. I find that tends to focus people a great deal. A few days' thinking time. Obviously a proud and idealistic opponent of everything the Mandate stands for would require that." He stares me right in the eye, pretending to tremble a little at the terrifying academic with his dangerous theories. "I won't even ask you to formally recant your heterodoxies, Professor. That will simply sit implicit between us once you become a contributing member of our community here."

They take me out of his rooms, down from the elevated reaches where the masters of the camp live. They remove the clothes they'd given me, strip me naked, then beat me a little when I try instinctively to resist them. Just a little, nothing that would disable. A very precise and courteous brutality, like an hors d'oeuvre of broken glass served on a silver tray. They next give me a coarse one-piece jumpsuit of artificial fibre over paper underwear. One guard has a syringe-bolt-gun affair and they tag me, shooting a metal bolt in over one collarbone in a sudden and incapacitating spike of pain. The collar of my jumpsuit buttons neatly to it, as though the whole thing is simply to dissuade me from running naked into the woods should the urge take me. It's a tracker, I understand. My clothes and my implanted tag, constantly talking to the camp's admin system, telling them where I am and what my vital signs are doing. Right then, with the pain and the shock, they're spiking hard enough that I hope I'm giving some monitoring snoop an aneurism.

4.

Ah, the life of a privileged academic! I'm not being ironic here, given I've just had a metal bolt shot into my collarbone. I'm thinking about the actual life I actually had, not long, but also several decades, ago. Before the first big purge.

There are some old fortune-telling cards that turn up every so often in backroom junk sales, or passed hand to hand between collectors of occult and banned artefacts. Not the sort of thing you'd expect a hard-line Cientifico like me to have seen, but when you dabble with radicals you meet all sorts. Plenty of different and utterly opposed groups have an interest in bucking against the Mandate back home. Every so often circles coincide. The subcommittees overlap to plan some joint operation or share resources. It almost never works. You spend so long staring at your own people for signs of faltering, how can you be expected to trust some pack of fetish-fondling spiritualists? I remember leafing through a deck of those cards, though. Didn't think much of it at the time, save that the art was very fine—they were antique, or at least lovingly reproduced from an earlier age of more baroque tastes.

There was this one card that recurred to me later, when I understood how things had actually been every day of my dissident life. A carefree youth with a dog, dancing about on the edge of a cliff and utterly clueless about it. That was us, we academics playing at revolutionaries. Putting forward our unorthodoxies because everyone *knew* the Mandate didn't care enough to slap us down. Pushing the envelope of acceptable thought with our purely theoretical treasons, pretending they were important while we knew the Mandate knew we were only boffins farting about, and who really cared outside the pages of the journals? Except it turned out they *were* important. When we told each other excitedly this was our way to loosen the Mandate's intellectual grasp from within, someone was listening and taking names. When we told each other we were serious revolutionaries, some of us actually were, sliding into practical action while maintaining the veneer of a weekend dissident.

And then suddenly there were boots kicking in doors, forcing some of us to flee, while others didn't get the chance. The brute squads swooped in with their jackboots and dawn raids. Marquaine and I, tipped off before we could get far enough down the list, abandoned our tenured rooms, our books and our institutions, and went on the run. Throwing ourselves on the mercy of all those contacts we'd previously disdained because our genteel academic revolution had been the only right way to do things. And, of course, they caught us anyway, because here I am on Kiln, but we dodged the first wave of arrests and deportations, winning ourselves almost an entire extra year on Earth.

For all that year we wondered who it had been. Because that's how it always goes. Someone is taken in, and steamed in the interrogation suite until they crack. They give over the names, exaggerate the crimes, what was said and done, because by then they're desperate to have something to sell, to buy their life back. Or else someone had been through that transformative process long before, conducted secretly enough that none of their fellows ever knew they'd been turned. Someone in those meetings, listening to every bold word of treason. A poison in the heart of the subcommittee. Or there were several someones. You hear stories of when seven out of ten people turned out to be on the Mandate payroll in one form or another, including the leaders. All that effort just to trap a few witless fools who'd never have strayed if not for the prearranged inducements of professional traitors. After Marquaine and I escaped the first cull, of course everyone we turned to was thinking the same thing, when they actually took our calls. *Was it you? Are you unsound?* And the moment you ask that question about anyone, then the answer always becomes *Yes*. Nobody trusts you. Your ongoing good fortune itself becomes incriminating.

So the various reactions I meet when they chuck me in the Labour Block aren't really surprising.

Ideally I'd have wanted a closer look at those central ruins before my comeuppance, but now is not the time for me to recommence my career as a serious academic! *Now* is the time I'm hunched about the crippling pain of the bolt, while a pair of Terolan's bully boys half shove, half carry me across the compound. From under the dome, the sky appears more brown-grey than blue-yellow-black, I note inanely. The light is weird, but not as weird as it was outside. It's more like Earth's sun through the smoggy air of the industrial districts I went to ground in. Ah, home!

I have a blurred view of those big kiln-like structures looming over us—three storeys high at least, with the broken-off, fronded vanes even higher between them. I gibber something about looking at them, but it's not really scientific enquiry that motivates me. Just a desperate thought that if they stop hauling me around so energetically maybe it wouldn't hurt as much. And I have a presentiment of what I'll run into the moment they leave me alone with my peers. Because like I say, I'm used to the looks you get the moment you catch a break. On the run, amongst the gutter dissidents, you do your best to look as wretched as possible. Not because someone stronger will take anything you have if you flaunt it, though that happens, but because everyone's eyes will say *Who did you sell to buy that?*

I've just been to dinner with the commandant. They very publicly took me from the line to give me this special treatment. Terolan wasn't just buying me with a drink and a snack, he was making sure I was spoiled goods for anyone else. I know I'm going to get a kicking the moment the guards leave me alone, and make absolutely zero friends amongst the Labour. That was his intent as much as the carrot-and-stick routine. If he wants his tame scholars to help him solve Kiln's academic quandary, then he doesn't want to share them with anyone else.

I'm making such a fuss that my escort is forced to pause a few seconds beside the ruin. More to change their grip than to indulge me. I stare up at the impossible things. These alien works. Built. Incontestably, intelligently built. Supplied with power too, Terolan said. A network of communities (were they?) spread over the planet. A civilization (was it?) reduced now to just dry relics like this.

Think about human history. We've gone up and down more than once. Drought and cooling events hit Earth's past too. It's easy to see how a thronging society can collapse if you've expanded to agricultural capacity in the warm period, then a little ice age comes along and you've got the same number of people but only a quarter of the food. Except it isn't as though humanity became *extinct* after the Bronze Age Collapse. We muddled on, just fewer of us, in less complex societies, for a while. And even in those places where everyone bailed on the region and went elsewhere, we weren't tidy-minded enough to clear away all our own bones and tools and things to frustrate future archaeologists.

So where were the remains of the kiln-makers of Kiln?

I admit, given they've just bolted a staple through my clavicle, most of this erudite speculation comes post facto, but I like to think at least the germ of the question is there in my pain-racked brain at that moment.

The Labour Block is a low, flat-roofed building, with one side of it made from clear plastic so nobody has privacy and the sun's your alarm clock. There are cameras inside, too, but I'm used to living under surveillance. Welcome to the Mandate! I'm absolutely certain the inmates know exactly which corners and edges aren't visible, and how keen the audio receptors are, all that. Not even for the purposes of holding a good revolutionary subcommittee but just for basic, everyday living.

Inside, the centre of the space is taken up with hard plastic slabs assembled as tables. Later I'll discover there's a whole changeover routine morning and evening, and those slabs also serve as the beds once you slot them into their wall mounts. I'm dumped down next to one of these mounts, just a moulded slot in the wall. There're about three hundred of them, lining the long space of the Labour Block. My new home.

The badge they plug in over my particular niche, as well as the bolt they drove into me, identify me as 2275. By this time the pain has dulled enough for my mind to think through the unpleasant implications of that label.

They don't reuse numbers, I divine, and they have a maximum operating capacity of three hundred in this, the sole labour dormitory. And I'm very aware they don't ever send the Labour home; there's no end to someone's sentence after they deport you to the extrasolar labour program. I have a brief, bleak moment of wondering where the grave-yard is for those who've been used up before me to further the Mandate's researches here on Kiln. Then I reassess the logistics of deep-space supply and understand I've not been bleak enough. Nobody is going to bury the dead on Kiln. One corner of the Labour Block is a reclamation unit, to make sure none of those useful Earth-made molecules go to waste. Organic chemistry is incredibly versatile, after all. The majority of the elements in your body are the same as in the plastics that come out of an all-commodities printer. The clothes and plates, the chairs and blunt cutlery, it's all at least partly reclaimed people. As is the food. A narrow spur of the dorm interior runs down the unit's side with slots so we can feed scraps and used goods in. The big slots for bodies are on the outside, not to spare our feelings but just for practicality.

Later I'll understand that, putting our society's hideous pragmatism aside, there's another reason nobody has dug out a little cemetery plot outside the dome, with headstones and dates and "Taken from us so young." The incompatibility between Kiln and Earth biology is a bridgeable gap. It reaches for us. It would have uses for our dead.

I notice there are surprisingly few people in the Labour Block right now. Except of course it's towards the end of a work day so people are working, while the main body of my admissions class are being shown the ropes of their new professions. I've missed induction. I don't fit. It seems I have a precious hour or so of rattling around the dorm before Kiln closes on my every hour like a vice. I try to spend it lying on the floor in agony but the score or so of people who are there come over to look at me, and possibly give me the aforementioned kicking early.

"He's for Excursions?" asks one of them. That sounds jolly, I think I might like an excursion. Straw hat, bucket and spade on the sunny beaches of Kiln. Maybe life here won't be so bad after all. I'm quite disappointed when one of the guards grunts, "He's Dig Support." That sounds like actual *work*.

I don't particularly notice the guards leaving, but when they're gone, I'm left with the muttering. I know it without having to look at any of the mutterers. It's distrust, distilled down to the sound of human voices. I hoick myself up until I'm in a sitting position with my back to the wall, the better to ward off the blows. The score of my fellow Labour are standing round me, a loose and distant crescent, not the boots-incoming close knot I might have expected. They look lean, tough and ugly. They are people who have survived Kiln thus far, which is as much of a survivor as you can ever get, what with two thousand dead since the camp first set up.

One of them finally comes closer, bending over me. I flinch back and he says, "Get your hand off your bolt, you twat," without much actual rancour. When I do he reads out what's stamped on it. "Twenty-two seventy-five Daghdev," pronounced wrongly, but if I start correcting people now I'll never stop until someone punches me in the mouth. I squint at him. He's a solid, grey-haired man, the oldest here, and older than me. There's a lot of pockmarks and scarring under one eye and down his cheek, as though he once had some bad skin condition which ended up with something being lasered out of him. His bolt swims into focus: 1611 KEEV.

1611. That makes him one hell of a survivor. And he's going to be important. We're going to get to know each other, me and 1611 Keev. But all that's in my future. Right then, Keev just grunts. I'm not Excursions, so he has nothing to teach me. I learn later that he and his team, the people there, have just come back from doing their job. They have one day in the dorm until they need to go and Excurse again. But I won't share the perils of their lot. I'm not one of them. More, I'm Dig Support who, I will soon learn, Excursions view as soft-handed class traitors born with a silver trowel in their mouth. But the anticipated kicking doesn't materialize. Keev would probably even have helped me up if I'd been interested in doing anything other than lying on the ground in a foetal position. 1611 Keev has survived this long because he doesn't give a damn about factions, feuds, informants or enemies, or anything other than living one more day at a time on Kiln. Right then, he is not my friend, but he's not interested in being my enemy. It's not something he feeds off; he has no ideology. So the whole kicking, spitting and finger-pointing can wait an hour or so until everyone else turns up to find me there. In which time I've got over the worst of the pain and pulled my wits together.

Then they arrive: more Excursions, as well as Domestics, Maintenance and, in the midst of them, my own tribe of miscreants, the elite scum everyone else resents.

I brace myself for the muttering, and it most certainly comes. Some of them just want to take it out on the fresh meat because entertainment's scarce on Kiln if you're Labour. Some have heard from others in my batch that I was given the special treatment. I'm an object of suspicion. Doubtless I'll find my bed short-sheeted (there are no sheets) and poisonous spiders in my boots. (There are no spiders. There are worse things than spiders.)

There are a lot of tough-looking bruisers amongst that company, all of them with more than enough suspicion to come at me. One in particular, in fact, meets my gaze with a definite *I know what you did* sort of stare. What saves me from a truly professional kicking from the hoi polloi is my academic credentials. By which I don't mean the natural respect of the working man for the professional scholar, but that the academics already present have very personal grudges and push to the front of the line. Honestly, it's like a faculty reunion in here, since the Kiln camp has those standing orders to secure any halfway-qualified dissident for its unique research needs. So it's not just that there are lots of eyes on me, it's some sets in particular. A knot of people shove almost eagerly through the crowd with the sort of fascinated horror you'd get at public executions. Familiar faces, my fellow Dig Supporters. I meet the gaze of Ilmus Itrin, my colleague, my friend, who was never a revolutionary, just a nonconformist on a personal level. Who wasn't quick enough when they came for us, and ended up on the boat before mine. I meet the gaze of Parrides Okostor, those hawkish features now half-hidden behind a bristling beard. Back before it all went sour, he and I had sat side by side at every subcommittee meeting. Devotees to the cause of undermining the Mandate, because it seemed like a consequence-free game at that time, in those salad days before the purges began. There are others, too. Names I don't know, names I've heard or seen on papers, but faces I recognize. Luckless students of fallen masters or enfants terribles murdered in the crib. It's a small fishbowl, back home. The Venn diagram of academics in fields related to mine who've also been politically or criminally incautious has limited overlap.

I look particularly to Ilmus again but they're hanging back. My oldest friend and they won't even look at me. Parrides isn't so shy. His angry stare asks the question I've been primed for since leaving Terolan's quarters. *Was it you?* And I want to have it out right there. To jump up on a table and orate to the whole Labour Block, aided by a presentation with 3D models, graphs and a thorough bibliography, everything I've done between then and now, ending with when they finally kicked down *my* borrowed door and sent me here. I want to establish, through the exercise of scholarly logic and beyond a shadow of a doubt, that it wasn't *me* who shopped us all, back then. Who dragged Ilmus down, even though they'd never so much as handed out an inflammatory pamphlet. Who had them haul Okostor out from mid-lecture, the eyes of a hundred prim little students widening in horror as the Enforcers muscled in and dragged him off. He'd fought, they said. He actually decked one of them, broke his hand against the armour plate but still floored an enforcer.

Ilmus is slender and willowy, and if they were the one going for me I'd have been able to hold them off until I could get some words out. Parrides Okostor was always a big man and the labour camp has made him hard too. He's had an extra eleven months of Kilnish hell compared to me, and quite reasonably wants to know if I bought that extra time on Earth with his name passed to a Mandate interrogator.

My mouth crams with words as he shoulders towards me. All my proofs and protestations stand ready. Yet I can't. The opportunity doesn't come, and there's nothing I could say that would establish my innocence sufficiently anyway. That's how they always get you. Everyone has a plausible excuse for why they weren't there or why they didn't get the big hammer when the Mandate came round with its correctional toolbelt on. Sometimes they just go easy on someone for no reason other than to foster this atmosphere of uncertainty and mistrust. Or sometimes your closest friends really are passing your name to the authorities. You can never know.

And so we fight. We, the men of science, go at it like schoolkids. I am no shrinking flower myself, and I was on the run, living like a criminal, for a year, even though my body has been dried out and rehydrated in the interim. And even before that, when subcommittee business got rough, I'd thrown punches and got into scraps. Parrides' fist only glances off my temple, and mine socks into his shoulder without moving him much. Then we start grappling, slinging ourselves back and forth as the rest of the Labour jeer and cheer. He tries to ram a knee right into my academic credentials and I try to yank a fistful of that wiry beard out. There are tears in his eyes. His yellow-and-brown teeth are bared. He tips me at last, throwing me into a table. The edge of the slab is like catching a truncheon across the kidneys, just like when they took me back on Earth. I come back swinging but by then three of the guards have rushed in. The crowd melts back to the fringes of the dorm and the thing that slams into my other kidney really is a truncheon. I'll be checking my piss for blood for the next day or so, is my best guess. They lamp Okostor too, slapping the pair of us about, and then push over some short man who's had nothing whatsoever to do with any of it. Having wrung out the maximum amount of amusement from the situation, they finally leave. In their place stands a hard-faced woman in prisoner overalls, her hair shaved close to her scalp.

"Parrides," she says. "Fucking back off." The expletive comes clipped and neat from her lips as though she learned it from a textbook. Parrides Okostor scowls at her and me and the world in general, but does as he's bid. Her bright bird eyes next turn on me.

"Daghdev," she says—"Dag-Dev," the same error of pronunciation Keev had made, someone who's only seen my name written down. She's not hostile, just short with me. I look into her bony face, the cheekbones protuberant as thumbs, the chin like a knuckle. Her bolt says 2019 CROAN. "Helena Croan," she confirms. "From the Misler Research Institute."

I fight down the ridiculous academic snobbery that, in another life, would have had me sneering, "Oh, *that* place," and passing some comment like, "I suppose *someone* needs to hold the test tubes and run the statistical analysis." Because that's a life I've not inhabited for a while, since the purge and going on the run and all that. I just nod. I don't bother with declaring my own schooling and it's a wonder she does, honestly. Some habits are hard to break and some become the teddy bear of normalcy people cling to, I suppose.

"I run Dig Support here," Croan tells me, prodding me in

the chest with a finger that feels like a sharp stick. She's weirdly, almost skeletally thin. I learn later that some people never really take to the reclaimed diet here. Every meal is a daring flirtation with yakking her guts out, apparently. Because when you're Labour, nobody cares about your intolerances or even your allergies much. Acceptable Wastage. But Croan has survived despite this, clinging on with her brittle nails and becoming head of my new department. Dig Support. Such an inspiring name.

It shows in my expression and she smirks. "Such a long face."

"Latrine duty isn't how I want to die," I say. "I liked the sound of Excursions."

"We help the research team with their work. The ruins, the ecosystem. You'll get dissection subjects and data processing and all the decontamination you can eat."

1611 Keev has hung about like a vulture, in case I fall into his remit after all. Now he gives my shoulder a push. Not an assault, not bullying, more like a man testing the structural stability of a wall and finding it wanting. "Fuck about," he tells me, "and we'll get you on Excursions soon enough." Then he strides off. And that's how I discover I don't want to be on Excursions after all.

"Our mission here is—" Croan starts. In that moment she's every moderator struggling to retain control of the panel.

"Don't fuck this up for us. We've got a good thing going on. That's our mission," says Okostor, butting in to jab me right in the metal bolt and sending a jolt of agony through me. "They fucking hate us, all of them." There's no indication if he means the prisoners, the guards, the Mandate, the vanished local architects. "We get to *study*, though. They don't waste good scholars in this place. So you study and you hand in the right results."

I stand my ground. As Okostor muscles in again, I do my best to muscle back from a definite position of weakness. Croan isn't having any of it. She kicks him behind the knee and shoves me in the chest. She's smaller than both of us but she has bony elbows and knows how to use them.

"What my learned colleague is trying to say," she tells me, "is I don't care whatever-the-fuck heterodoxy had you sent here. Whatever theory you had they didn't care for, or which-ever way you wanted to stretch the bounds of human knowledge, that's over now. It's not like you'll get the chance to publish. We give Terolan what he wants or we give him enough that he doesn't consign us to Excursions, you get me?"

"What does he want?" I ask. Then certain things fall into place and I say, "He's not a *Philanthropist*, is he?" They nod. My heart sinks. Just when I thought things had stopped getting worse, fate has one last turd to drop in my begging bowl. That one particular gem of Mandate scientific doctrine that we ripped the piss out of, back when we weren't prisoners or fugitives. It is, I suppose, as fitting a capstone —gravestone—to my academic career as any.

5.

If we'd held sweepstakes for who would end up on the fragmentation barges, you'd have bet on Ilmus Itrin. And, as it turned out, you'd have been right. Ilmus, the nonconformist. You have to understand that a big part of the Mandate was based on the absolute nature of knowledge. You can't dictate properly unless you have a list of things that are right and lawful against a list of things that aren't, and never the twain shall meet. The Mandate is very into polar binaries, it's in all their rhetoric. "What?" they'd say. "You don't want this unpleasant circumstance we're forcing on you? Then you're obviously in favour of this absurdly exaggerated opposite we've just invented." Or countless variants on that. "You don't want these laws? Then you must want rampant anarchy!" was the one you saw trotted out most often. And with a good enough speaker that kind of argument, shouted from the enshrined pulpit of Mandate-approved media, can sound very persuasive, mostly because there's never anyone there to argue back. The idea that there might be shades of possible in between any two opposites was anathema to Mandate thought, and this crept into their scientific orthodoxy too, which was where I most often struck sparks off it. Ilmus was someone who had rejected binaries all their life. Small wonder they were high on the list when the scholastic purges first came.

"'Scholastic purges?'" Ilmus echoes when I say it. Of course, they were on the barges before the name ever got coined.

"After they became widespread enough," I confirm. "After people outside the institutions got wind of what was going on, they needed a name for it. So they cast it as halting the corruption of young minds, think of the children... You know, the usual."

Ilmus, who has had more than their share of this in their life, nods. We're doing chores at the moment, just our allotment of the Labour Block work everyone has to do. Dropping plastic plates and blunt spoons into the reclaimer to be spat out anew for the next meal. Elbow to elbow. It's been long enough now. It's time for them to screw up their courage and accuse me outright.

Ilmus and I worked on exoplanet analysis together, constructing ecological webs and biochemical pathways from the decades-old data sent back to Earth. Focusing on the microbial worlds, and later Swelter and Tartrap, we looked at the differing ways the building blocks of carbon-based life could be assembled and still work. Ironically, we were always waiting for the Kiln info to come through. We were just desperate to get another data set. They kept this world thoroughly redacted, though, and now we both know why. Now we have our dream—to see it for ourselves. Be careful what you wish for.

"So I understand a certain flavour of academic orthodoxy preceded us here," I say heavily, given Ilmus is still clammed up, insofar as what I'm waiting for is concerned.

"It, yes, well, it's exactly as bad as it sounds," Ilmus agrees. "Ideologically. Commandant Terolan, he doesn't know much about science but he knows what he likes."

"Surely what they've found here knocks all that into a hat?"

"Not according to Terolan," they say. "We're, you know, right on the very cusp of finding something convergent, apparently. It's out there, in the jungles. The Wild Man of the Outer Worlds."

I make a disgusted noise which lingers like the last trump. Ilmus is staring at a handful of beige cutlery, crudely printed so that everything's slightly misaligned and twisted. *Like life,* I think, because when I was fifteen I wrote crappy maudlin poetry, too.

I realize they're not going to say it. I'm going to have to —the words that make you look guiltier than anything in the universe, but which have to be said.

"It wasn't me," I whisper. "They never took me in. I gave them no names. I mean, I'm *here*, damn it."

"If you think," Ilmus says brightly, "that nobody here is a snitch then, well, you won't last long. How was the commandant, by the way? Did you bond over dinner?"

"I don't even know what that was about. He's seen my writing apparently and wants me on-side for his pet science project."

Ilmus shrugs. "Oh well, don't polish your halo, mate. He had me up there too. Has Croan over every so often, along with the actual Science—I mean the team, you know. The non-Labouring academics. Our direct bosses."

"Wait, he had you in—" I say, peeved that I'd been getting the third degree for the same thing, but again entertainment is scarce in the camp.

"Our commandant, mate, is an *intellectual*. Proud of his credentials. Likes the company of educated souls. Even dissident convicts, don't you know, so long as they toe the line now. Which, well, which I did. Let him have his compliments and his choice of pronouns. But I know *I* didn't pass my name to the Mandate back home, and I know Croan is a time-server and a boot-licker but she was here long before I came. Then here's you in on the next boat, after eleven months of Earth I didn't get. How was it, old pal, old friend? How did all that freedom taste?"

"Fucking awful," I tell them flatly. "Living in squats and out of people's basements and attics. Always listening for the jackboots. Trying to skip jurisdictions to get to one of those mythical districts where the rules are lax and you can loosen your collar. Except I don't think they exist. They're just so the traffickers can charge you all your worldly goods to get into the back of a van and have your throat cut. Or else be dumped on Enforcement's doorstep with plastic ties around your wrists and ankles. Ilmus, please. I didn't. I wouldn't."

I see their face shift. Their desperate need to forgive is running up against all the places they've been hurt before and making headway despite the pain. Or maybe it's not even that. Maybe making the decision to trust me, and pretend they believe it wasn't me, is just easier than hating me. Because having me as an ally here is better, even if they'll never trust me all the way again. And I'll take that. It's better for me, too.

Then a hand slaps down on my shoulder. It's 1611 Keev from the jolly-sounding Excursions. He hasn't come to put his bucket and spade in the hungry mouth of the reclaimer, he's come to show me the business end of the machinery. Which sounds like a threat, now I say it. I reckon if a big deportee loomed over you and offered to show you how the reclaimers worked, you'd take it as a prelude to "His body was never found." But I see that Keev actually means it. The reclaimers are janky and they get jammed easily, so everyone needs to know how to sort that without adding some loose fingers to tomorrow's mix. Keev's hand stops on my shoulder longer than it needs to. It's not an intimacy thing; I'm more solid than he was expecting, for a poncy academy boy. His grip tenses thoughtfully before releasing, like a cattleman evaluating livestock.

So Ilmus won't spit in my face, and the dust-up with Parrides was barely worth the bruising. The storm hasn't broken over me yet but it's going to. I notice a number of the Labour gathering nearby, with a lot of eyes on me. I wait for the moment someone decides to knock me down and kick me again, to teach me about being Terolan's pet. I think through the commandant's gambit as Keev shows me how to retain my digits when the reclaimer's little cog teeth are chattering for them. The implicit promise Terolan made to me: be good and you'll get a treat again. Life under a life sentence can be better, or it can be worse. He showed me the first, and now I'm seeing the second. Or maybe *worse* is relative. I haven't seen Excursions yet.

As it turns out, I've got a fair amount of *worse* to go.

The reclaimer gubbins access is on a spur off from the big living space of the Labour Block. There's a corner of the structure that's machinery, and a narrow corridor alongside it where Keev has brought me. It's an awkward space, twisting around the buttresses and projecting process of the works, perfect for bruised elbows and banged heads. It's also mostly outside surveillance, I discover. So the ideal opportunity for my awaited comeuppance.

Another hand lands on my shoulder, and of a decidedly different quality. A pincer-grip that grinds bones together. I brace myself as it turns me effortlessly around, expecting a gang of big, unsympathetic men and women. And this is exactly what I get. A dozen of them, some scarred, most shaven almost bald. The man who's using my shoulder like a stress toy has a hand particularly suited to the purpose. It's prosthetic up to the elbow, his jumpsuit rolled and slit around it because it's bulkier than a real one. Garish red and orange plastic, like a child's toy. His face has all the sympathy of rough-poured concrete. No soft academic, no armchair revolutionary. The real kind. Thrown bombs and corpses. The sort of rough-handed thug that a genteel man like me would obviously have nothing in common with. Something he's about to make abundantly clear to all.

Keev stands there for precisely half a second and then takes a step back, ducking automatically under an overarching pipe. Making it Not His Problem, because it's not his problem.

I meet the eyes of the man who's got my shoulder and understand this is going to hurt and there's no way out of it. The pincer-grip drags me sideways a step until I'm in that narrow clip of the reclamation corridor that the Labour Block cameras can see.

"You like the taste of the commandant's arse then," he says.

I really don't know how this is going to go. Which, in a way, should tell you that more things are going on here than I've let on because it must look pretty damn obvious to *you*.

"I didn't ask for it," I say, loud enough for all. "I don't want trouble."

"You probably think we'd all like the taste of yours, now

you're the big man," my interlocutor tells me, for the benefit of the crowd.

"Not really." I brace, for all the good it'll do me.

He hits me with the real hand, which feels like cheating. It's still quite capable of driving the wind out of me. The plastic hand yanks me upright again when all I want to do is retch the commandant's fancy food out of me. He slams me against the lumpy side of the reclaimer. I feel the panel —the one Keev had opened to show me stuff—twist out from its brackets, and the Excursions man twitches forwards then. Me getting my ass handed to me isn't a motivation, but someone's going to have to *fix* that. Just a twitch, though. Keev's solid and tough as a strip of leather but he didn't last this long on Kiln by being anyone's hero.

I'm hoisted even higher by my collar. Luckily, the exquisite pain of having my collarbone bolt yanked about distracts me from the strangling. He leans in very close.

"Just so you know how it is," he growls in my ear. "No special treatment for fancy boys like you."

I make some inarticulate sound of confirmation and he drops me. The relief is blessed. I stay on my knees to demonstrate my penitence and because right then I honestly cannot stand up.

He crouches beside me, companionably, pinching the back of my neck to tilt my ear in his direction. He leans in close, his breath on my skin. The clatter of the reclaimer hides the soft-voiced threat the others must assume he's saying.

Instead he whispers, "Sound?" and I have to fight to make sure my pain and suffering are still on full display, because this is the message I've been waiting for. This is what all the fuss and fury were covering. The fact that he and I have a long history, that we're hiding from the rest, just like I hid it from you.

"Sound, Clem," I manage, eyes squinting sideways until I can meet his gaze halfway. He's not ever going to apologize for what he just put me through and I'm not going to ask it of him either. I understand it's how these things go. The rules of the playground, putting on a show. Now everyone will know I've been soundly chastised by the labourer body politic and paid my dues, or at least this instalment of them. This buys off the fancy dinner, or that's the idea. As much as if that plastic fist had "karma" moulded across the knuckles.

This is Clemmish Berudha. They packed him out on the boat before Ilmus's ride, two before mine. He's no academic, though. It's pure chance we've ended up in the same corner of extrasolar hell. His revolutionary cell collapsed, his subcommittee got infiltrated, and he was sold out. But not by me. He's had a chance to think it through and clearly decided I was never in a position to do the dirty on him. So he made sure it was him giving me a going over rather than anyone who'd have me pissing blood for a week. Because if Clem *did* think I'd sold him back then, this little interview would have gone very differently, and maybe I'd have made a donation to reclamations through that open panel. But we're square. We're sound.

We make a big show of me letting him help me up, knuckling under to his authority, accepting my place in the food chain. He's got me by one arm, and I recognize the woman on the other as another of my old confederates from back home. It's been two years on Kiln for the pair of them and I only see one other from that class. Their fellow insurrectionists were either sent elsewhere, executed, or have already been fed posthumously to the reclaimers.

Clem's fellows don't look like they think I'm sound, though. I'd like to think that my also being here, however much later, should stand me in good stead, but I remember what Ilmus said. The Labour Block has its share of Mandate informants, just like everywhere I've ever been. Like every academy class, every revolutionary subcommittee, every drinking den and dissident meeting or study group. There's always someone. They don't even need to buy you with a promise not to deport you on the barges. They can just promise you slightly less brutality at the other end. We're cheap. The Mandate makes us that way. It's fear of the whip, not greed, that turns us all into potential betrayers.

I realize there are guards outside, looking in. They've worked out something's up, though if Clem had wanted to stuff me into the reclaimer he's had ample chance. Through the Labour Block's one transparent wall they stare, and I almost want to wave at them. In the same faceless dark visors and plastic plate armour that hasn't changed much over the decades and light years. They have the mostly-not-lethal crowd guns, but the actually-quite-lethal pistols too, as well as chemical sprays and truncheons, all the symbols of a happy and well-adjusted state. Things I've seen used more than once. There are just a couple of them but their presence is more than enough to cow all of us. Even Clem looks away. I nod as if he's made some point I'm agreeing with, very "All friends here, Officer." I put a hand on Clem's arm, because I still remember how this is done.

The simple finger code, tap and clench and release. *Where*

are we? A necessarily vague question given the limits of the tactile language.

He removes my hand, showing every outward sign of distaste. His living fingers on mine say *Soon*. I feel a lurch, a thrill: horror, excitement, nausea. Though that last is probably just because he did actually hit me quite hard.

Back in the Labour living space, I'm shown how to upend the tables and turn them into bunks. Then I finally collapse into mine and count my bruises. There's a brief span of time between that and lights out, and Ilmus comes up asking how I am. I try to work out how much they're involved in it all —in Clem's side of the business, that is. I attempt to communicate the question without asking in words that a neighbour might overhear and pass up to the gantry level where the free people live.

"He's...Just stay on the right side of him," Ilmus says about Clem. "It's okay."

"He's sound," I say. A neutral word, of significance only to Clem's cell and their immediate confidants, such as yours truly. Ilmus was never a part of that life, I didn't want to put them in danger. Much good that did any of us.

"Sound," they agree, weighting the word precisely. We stare at each other, almost desperately, scrabbling at the silence. Ilmus was never revolutionary subcommittee material before, but I see that's clearly changed since they were shipped out here. Clem has been recruiting, and organizing, even under these conditions. *Soon*, he'd said.

I'm in a penal colony on another world, in another solar system. Seems hopeless? Except, contrary to the Mandate's fond imaginings, the universe isn't a place of binaries. Control is not either absolute or absent. It's a gradient, and here we are at the shallow end. The Mandate's writ here is finite and thin, a veneer of authority over an angry pulsing vein of resentment.

Full disclosure. Yes, I was deported for my crackpot heterodox thinking. That's enough to have you sent to the extrasolar labour camps in purge season. There was a whole extra rich seam of reasons, though. They only missed them because they already had enough on me and never dug deeper. I more than earned my place on the fragmentation barges.

Which will soon enough come back and bite me.

I'm given a crash course in the logistics of the Kiln labour camp from Ilmus. It's a lot to take in, and my head is still swimming with the names of the people I've just met and must absolutely keep straight and remember. The old faces who had beaten this path across the stars ahead of me. People I've heard of professionally but never met. New arrivals in my life who are still powerfully important because my life has shrunk to this one place now, and everyone here could be crucial. As I lie on my bunk, and they try to bury me with names, I clutch at the web of stations, relationships and labels, refusing to drown under them. And while I should be sleeping, I try to build mnemonics in my head to cover everyone around me. All the people who were as unlucky as I was in being shipped out here, but as lucky as I in that they survived to reach Kiln's surface and embark on a life of hard labour.

The names circle about like agitated birds in my brain. Dig Support: Helena Croan, Parrides Okostor, Ilmus Itrin. Revolutionary Subcommittee: Clem Berudha. Excursions:

1611 Keev, personal name unknown. The enemy: Commandant Terolan.

And beyond that are the basic sections within the labour force, divided and conquered as we are. Dig Support is the cushy number, and because of that everyone else will resent me. Excursions is the worst assignment. Despite Keev's longevity, turnover there is high and I'm going to find out why very soon, don't fret about that. Between these poles of privilege are the following intermediate stations on the road to hell.

Domestic, meaning going up top to do menial work for the Commandant, the guards and The Science, those real academics I'll be reporting to shortly. Domestic is also theoretically a cushy job, except the guards get frisky and are absolutely at liberty to treat prisoners however they want. A lucky Domestic can cadge a lot of favours. An unlucky one can find themselves dumped into reclamation because someone woke up cranky and wanted to start their day with an over-enthusiastic beating. You win some, you lose some.

Maintenance is a small but select group of prisoners who have some kind of hands-on mechanical skill. Tasked with keeping everything running under the eye of those same guards. This immediately seems a slipshod way of managing things, and I say so to Ilmus. They tell me every part of the labour camp system's robust with redundancies, and as long as we have reclamation, printers and decontamination it's all gravy. Maintenance is relatively cushy too, except when something actually does fail, when it's punishment detail all round.

Finally, General Labour, not to be confused with either Excursion or Dig Support. This is the actual hard labour detail, originally working on the ruin the camp was built around, and now being sent out into the great outdoors after Excursions have blazed a trail. There's a key difference in the way General and Excursions are treated, I understand —part economy and part punishment—but nobody out-and-out explains what. The majority of prisoners are General and it's seen as just one step up from Excursions in any event.

I'm used to the way things are done on Earth. Machines, surely. Big machines for the heavy work and small for the fine work. And yes, there are machines here, but they're limited, dumb and cheaply printed, absolutely requiring constant human operation and supervision, with a lot of the brute labour still being done by hand. This is me and Ilmus after lights out, by the way, talking it all over. Them huddling by my bed where they're out of sight of the window-wall and cameras. We're speaking in the lowest mutually audible murmur, but apparently this is standard Labour Block shenanigans. There are at least two other whispered conversations going on in the dark.

Ilmus explains the brutal economics of it all to me. Machines are expensive. Humans who've fallen foul of the Mandate's justice system, on the other hand, are in ready supply and can be shipped out relatively cheaply, if you freeze-dry them and don't have any intention of bringing them back. Plus Kiln has some delightful atmospheric factors that aren't kind to the delicate intakes of complex machines.

What about humans' delicate intakes? I ask. This, Ilmus says, is why General Labour is bad and Excursions is worse. Filter masks only go so far, apparently.

"Decontamination, then?" I note. Something of a belated

revelation. "But that means...what? Biological compatibility? Or extreme incompatibility?"

"It's...Well, it's complicated," they say. Then the denizen of the next bed along is kicking at us to shut up and Ilmus finally slinks back to their own bunk.

6.

The next day, Croan takes me to meet "The Science." That's how we refer to them. In the same way as law enforcement back home was "The Filth." It's an odd crop of researchers out here in the extrasolar camps, and it must be hard to keep the places staffed. Aside from a few mavericks who are just mad enough to want to see xenobiology in its native habitat, while still considered sound enough that they're not going to go native and hand over a spaceship to some kind of horrible alien spider monster, who can you find to take the trip? You have to source researchers simultaneously orthodox enough to wave a big old flag for the Mandate's preferred ideology, and low-status enough that an objective lifetime out of circulation isn't going to dent their career prospects much. The losers of the academic circuit, then, without either the spark to be rebels or the nous to get ahead in departmental politics. But, dull as they surely are, they have one big advantage over firebrands like me and Ilmus. They get to go home. It's a sentence, but with a full stop at the end, not just a trailing ellipsis that only closes with death. And when they arrive back, an entire generation will have ticked over on Earth. Perhaps they hope to return in a great triumph, publish and be lauded, found a new institution and have something named after them. Perhaps they'll fill dead men's shoes in their old alma mater, armed with their unique experiences. I don't know any of The Science from before, anyway. They're people who left Earth years before I did. And it's weird to think that when I began my own interstellar trip, they were still on their own ships—the expensive ones, good for more than a one-way trip. They were in transit even then. I have a dizzy moment thinking about these distances, these travel times. They don't fit in human minds.

Now I've arrived and they've been doing science to the place for years already, grappling with the world's quandaries, mounding up great reams of thought that I'm going to have to wade through if I'm to make any kind of contribution here.

I can't make it work in my head, and so instead the whole thing becomes like ancient times, when you sailed past the horizon and dropped off the edge of the world, and nobody heard from you again.

With Marquaine dead, I'm the only new addition to Dig Support from my particular ship of fools. Croan and Okostor take me to see the chief biologist of The Science, under whose auspices I'll be slaving, and whose triumphant return and future publication history will be built on my back, I'm sure. Not that I'm bitter, you understand.

Another name to add to my list, then: Doctor Nimell Primatt. A dark, fleshy woman around my age, walking stiffly with an artificial leg from mid-thigh. Her prosthesis is of a decidedly better vintage than Clem's hand, but she carries a cane too, swapping it from one hand to the other every so often. Her injury was a year ago, I learn, but she's still adjusting to the replacement.

She stares at me for an uncomfortable period of time, no

expression on her face. Its natural cast is one of narrow-eyed suspicion that makes her look profoundly disagreeable on first meeting her. And she is relatively disagreeable all round. Later on, after working alongside her, I come to realize she is very aware of the precise set of boxes I identified earlier, that she ticked to be given this particular, unenviable posting. And simultaneously she knows that she has immediate subordinates, not convict Croan of course but other members of The Science, who are ready to take her down a peg if they can. All the usual departmental fun and games, except now she's on a hostile alien world and privileges of rank include things like not being eaten while out collecting field data. She's already one limb down on the whole business, so a certain level of disagreeability is perhaps to be expected. Life hasn't exactly gone how she thought it would for Nimell Primatt.

"Arton Daghdev." She pronounces my name as though I'm some newly named species in a field she doesn't much respect, but at least she says it almost correctly. I have no idea from that if she knows me from the last two decades of publications —shipped out ahead of me and still in transit when I got on the ship. But no, I promised myself to stop thinking about it. Earth has been excised from my life and my future, and all thoughts of travel time and relativity and the rest can join it.

Helena Croan makes an abortive gesture. "We should…" she says, ushering, but not ushering anyone in particular, or towards any particular destination. Just trying to avoid something, I realize afterwards. Primatt pauses, teetering on some decisional fulcrum I'm not informed enough to understand. I think she's coming down on Croan's side of it when the rug gets pulled out from under her, because a couple of the camp guards turn up with their guns and truncheons, telling the pair of us that the commandant is having breakfast and would be delighted if we'd join him.

Croan has already magically put two metres of extra space between herself and us. Primatt waves her away, directing her to make sure Dig Support is...supporting the dig, I assume? Doing whatever it is we actually do. It's only Primatt and me who are invited.

On to Commandant Terolan, then. Twice in as many days. I really am the favoured child of the extrasolar forced-labour community.

The plates and cups at his breakfast are of a delicacy which confirms the printer he has access to up here is an order of magnitude better than the one in the Labour Block. We take tea, Terolan, Primatt and I. She's cagey, saying nothing unless directly questioned. Terolan's genial, his attention gliding off me as though I'm only there in effigy. As though Primatt brought an image of me or my personnel file.

"So you've seen your new recruit to Dig Support, Doctor Primatt," Terolan says, nibbling a rusk of printed bread.

It's not a question so she doesn't say anything. Then Terolan raises an eyebrow and, by the alchemy of expression, retroactively transmutes the words so that they were a question after all.

"It's always good to have additional help, Commandant," she confirms heavily. "What with turnover."

"Turnover, yes." Not quite in sync but treading on her words so that I know something like this conversation has played out before. "But I want to give you a warning. About *Professor* Daghdev, Doctor Primatt." I note the stress on my honorific, an un-stress on hers. Emphasizing that back home there would have been a very different power dynamic between the two of us. "After he left my quarters yesterday it suddenly struck me that perhaps you might assume it was just... the usual regrettable ill discipline of thought that led to his presence here." A mangled chain of weasel words masquerading as a justification for deporting someone off planet because they said something you didn't like.

Primatt doesn't even look at me. If I'm a personnel file, it's one she hasn't opened. She makes her face into standard-expression-when-confronted-with-authority number seventeen: willingness to be enlightened.

"According to his files, Professor Daghdev is something of an *organizer*, Doctor." Terolan tuts over the wickedness of the world. I go cold, waiting to see how far this is going to go. "His activities back home resulted in a number of otherwise blameless academics being drawn into his sphere of un-orthodoxy and subsequently being taken up. Some of them are in Dig Support even now, as a result of allowing them-selves to be swayed by his rhetoric. People who arrived *before* the professor here." A roll of the eyes and a shake of the head. Commandant Terolan is inviting Primatt to draw her own conclusions about why I might have remained free for a span while my poor acolytes were thrown to the wolves. I grind my teeth. But not too much. Because he's just displayed the limits of his knowledge where my past is concerned.

"So do make use of him," Terolan says, "but be careful to keep him on the straight and narrow, won't you?"

"I will—" Primatt starts but the eyebrow informs her that his words weren't a question after all.

"I think he should be shown the current example," Terolan says. Primatt goes still. He adds, "Don't you?" to indicate that this time she's to speak. All she does is nod, though.

"*Professor* Daghdev," she says, when we're out. There's that same stress on the title and I wonder how much professional envy is going to cost me. "Xenobiology, yes?"

"Xeno-bio and xeno-eco," I confirm warily.

"Then you'll appreciate this," she tells me. She stalks lopsidedly off, juggling her cane. Lurching down the gantry steps with perilous haste, always just managing to catch herself on the railing before a full fall. She leads me across the open centre of the compound, but not to those intriguing ruins. Instead we go to what I'd taken for a storage shed, perhaps. There's a sideshow to see in there, before anything else. A cautionary tale, catch it while you can.

We finally stop in front of the spectacle and look. For a long moment nothing is said. The ghost of the commandant hangs invisibly over us, until the words are drawn out of her.

"He was in Domestics," Primatt explains. I stare past the clear plastic of the container at what's on show within it and feel my stomach, heart and various other inner parts of me sink.

"I'm saying that just in case you think, 'Oh, Excursions, everyone knows how dangerous that is.' But no, Domestics," Primatt goes on. Honestly I *don't* actually know how dangerous Excursions is, although I'm getting a hell of a crash course in it via tangential reference.

"He was assigned to Science quarters. Cleaning duty," Primatt tells me. "But there he decided he would steal some of our samples. I don't have the first idea what he was going to do with them, whether it was for someone else or he just thought they were...I don't even know." There's the slightest fracture then in her voice. She's been making it very hard, cold and nasty, the ruthless department head who considers me no more than a walking piece of lab equipment to be used and expended. I hear the brittleness there too, though. At least some of it's an act for my benefit, so I put her right to the top of the list of people not to fuck with. Doctor Primatt is someone who has been fucked with in the past by a variety of superiors, peers and subordinates, I guess, and as well as gratifying the commandant, this sort of thing is her best chance at future fuckery pre-emption.

Or maybe there's more to it than that, because she goes on with, "There are always little mutinies brewing, Arton." She's a first-name kind of person, apparently, or she is with professors who are her new subordinates. "The samples were dangerous, a concentration of one of the outside agents we've isolated as most resistant to routine decontamination. And so the commandant decided he should be given the chance to contribute to the science." Still keeping her voice flat and businesslike, as though she's going over my work and pointing out errors in my maths. "Watch him."

"I've seen enough of him," I say and try to turn aside, but her fingers pincer the back of my head just above my neck—exactly where Clem had grabbed me, so I still have bruises there. Apparently this is the Kilnish equivalent of a handshake or something. She holds my gaze on the tank just so I absolutely and unequivocally understand what's going on.

Past the cheaply printed, scratched plastic is the Amazing Deteriorating Man.

He's ripped away most of his coveralls. The bolt that they were clipped to went with them. I can see the raw, puckered hole where it should be. His number, name and identity have gone with it. He no longer counts as human, to the Mandate's system here. Or perhaps at all. You'd think that terrible wound would hold my eye, but it's shouted down by the noise of the rest of him. His skin suppurates. Hives and blisters rise across it, which he scratches desperately. They burst and I see a faint haze of particulate matter released, fogging the air around him. The skin also ripples, the first translucent layers healing over the rifts and then beginning to swell again. His mouth is opening and closing, but his sounds are trapped inside the tank with him, until Doctor Primatt activates some microphone and I hear...liquid shouting. Nothing a human throat should be able to make. As though he's crammed full of the alien and it's demanding to be let out.

Woven through that appalling cacophony I catch the words "Where are you?" and "Speak to me!"

From somewhere on the gantry level a shrill, hooting reply issues out, echoing across the compound like the call of a lonely ape to its mate. Primatt shuts off the audio sharply. The call from above is repeated once, then no more. I stare at her, wide-eyed, because that was from inside the camp but it couldn't have been from anything human. Her own eyes are wide too, nakedly scared for just one moment before she collects herself and reminds herself who's in charge.

Kiln. Kiln is in charge. Any control we think we have is purely illusory. But she draws the illusion about herself like the emperor's new clothes and takes comfort from it nonetheless.

"What the fuck...?" I say hoarsely. There was supposed to be more to that sentence, something eloquent and befitting my professorship, but honestly there's just too much going on. I'm physically shaking. It's not even the horror of the sights, it's something in the quality of the sounds. The inextricable blend of the utterly alien with very human loneliness.

"Your first lesson in Kiln biology, Arton," Primatt says. She is being very pointedly brisk-schoolmarm, and pretending it's to put me in my place when I can tell it's far more about maintaining her own emotional equilibrium. "Why don't you give me your first impressions, as a scientist."

I blink. I don't want to be a scientist right then. I'm too busy being an empathetic human being. "It's...interaction going on inside him," I manage. "Not just reaction." Three out of ten, go to the back of the class, but it does at least encapsulate the major wrongness in what I'm seeing. Actually, no, the major wrongness is that there's a *man* in a *tank* being *tortured*, but from a scientific point of view the details of the torture are nagging at me. The perennial question we ask of the universe's stage magician: how is the trick done?

Primatt now turns her back on the tank, and rather than face her, and *it*, I do the same, side-eyeing her as she begins to lecture. Awkward but preferable.

"Life on Kiln uses a toolkit of molecules with about a two-thirds crossover with Earth life, because certain molecules form naturally, given the palette of elements commonly available to the universe via the exhalations of stars. You understand, Arton? 'The universe has a direction.'" This is one half of the motto of Scientific Philanthropy back home and I pointedly don't chime in with the standard rejoinder. Behind us, something thumps the clear plastic and I hunch my shoulders against it. Primatt ducks outside and starts limping across the compound, still pontificating, and I dog her heels gratefully. She's all business, all clinical, and I'm not fooled for a moment. I think it's been a while since she did this with a live subject in the tank and she's forgotten how distressing it is.

"Two-thirds shouldn't be enough," I say. I'm doing it too, the cool science act, because it papers over what I've just seen and heard with a veneer of professionalism. Walls it up like a madwoman in the attic. And what was that terrible call we heard answering the man? Primatt isn't going to tell me yet. Time enough for that later.

The rest of The Science and Dig Support are already hard at work when we return. It's only Primatt and me who've been skiving off on this horrifying jolly. On our way to the steps, through her laborious stop-start climbing of them, along the gantries, I'm presented with the essentials from Primatt. Basically it boils down to life on Kiln being very complicated. Life is, in general, complicated. A rule my colleagues and I have observed wherever organic life has been found is that it has a tendency to complicate itself, once you have the basic building blocks of evolution. Meaning competition for resources, and a sporadically fallible system by which characteristics can be inherited, or in some other way alter over time. We've found multiple mechanisms, and some without any commonality with Earth bio at all, but the *logic* is the same. And once you have that logic, life becomes complex over time, as new variations slot into new niches that then *create* the opportunity for further niches still. A continually expanding ideaspace of what life can do to make a living. But life on Kiln is *really* complicated.

"The hereditary encoding has considerable sideways transmission," Primatt explains as she leans on the stick and takes the steps one at a time. Having your chief researcher lose a leg apparently isn't reason enough to let her use the damn goods lift. What she's said can be decoded to mean that, firstly, the vehicle Kiln life uses to transmit information down generations isn't quite genetics the way we know it, though it serves the same purpose. And secondly, hereditable traits can be transplanted between the genome-equivalents of organisms, jumping from species to species rather than just being passed on within a single lineage. It happens on Earth, but only with bacteria and other very simple sorts. On Kiln it apparently occurs with large and complex organisms too, via some means of trait selection not yet properly understood. This gives rise to a kind of rapid-response evolution. Everything is adapting to everything else constantly.

"A lot of symbiosis," Primatt says, catching her breath at the top of the stairs. "Cut something open and there's something else inside it, wearing its skin."

That finally breaks my scientific reserve and she smirks at my expression, for a moment just as unprofessional. Oddly, I like her more for that. A bit of showmanship. A trait lacking in most academics under the Mandate.

"So what happened to him?" I ask her, because it's obviously what she's waiting for.

"The sample he stole was discovered gestating in an Excursionista who'd been too long between decontaminations," she explains. "It had bridged the gap." And abruptly all that humour's gone and there's nothing in her but the grim and serious.

"Gap?" I don't understand. Then I do and wish I hadn't. "How, exactly, if Kiln life doesn't have anything like compatible genetics?"

"Because it's not about genetics. It's about molecule shape." Still recovering from the climb, she half sits against the gantry railings, which groan a little. "It's the same as how a virus forces your cells to unlock, so it can do the dirty in you. How any part of your body does what it needs to. It's all to do with how your proteins curl up, keys and locks, all that elementary-school stuff. Well, molecules are molecules on whatever planet you go to. So some of the local spores or macro-germs, or whatever the bloody hell we're calling them, have a whole key-cutting shop as part of their toolkit. We are an utterly alien environment to them but they keep trying until they find a way to unlock us. They get into your gut and your lungs and start trying to find a niche. It's like that Immigration Mandate campaign, you remember? *Let one in, let them all in.*"

I recall the posters from my childhood, the great swarm of cartoonishly villainous undesirables designed to encourage people to shun strangers.

"Once one organism has found a place in you, it creates an opportunity for others," Primatt says. "They proliferate. Take over. As you see."

I do see.

"Madness," Primatt says. "If he was free, it'd be like rabies. He'd be running about desperate to infect everyone. Then it'd eat him from the inside. Just deconstruct him and turn his biomass into Kiln biology."

"When will they decontaminate him?" I ask. "I mean, if this was for my benefit, consider me duly chastened by this example. Now let the poor fucker out."

"It's for everyone's benefit," Primatt tells me. "He's past any hope. Once the raving's set in, that's the limit. The incinerator's the only cure. You can't save people. He's here for all of you, the Labour. I'm showing you this—"

"Because the commandant thinks I somehow need additional reminders of how this is a bad place and I have to behave," I finish for her sourly.

She's furious with me for just a moment, then humorous, swallowing down the temper. "I know you, Arton. Professor Daghdev." A good attempt this time, almost right. "I've read every paper. You were at the cutting edge of the discipline."

"You must be very disappointed in me now."

Her fingers—they look pudgy but she has a grip like a crab's—take my upper arm. "I *know* you. I could chart your fall from grace through each essay you published. No surprise you're here at last. Don't start thinking you can take liberties, though. They will break you."

"I had dinner with the commandant, and breakfast," I tell her.

"Maybe he'll come toast you with the good wine when you're in the tank," she tells me. "From now on, Arton, you are a champion of *Orthodoxy*. We are here to find out what happened to the *people* who built these ruins, do you understand?" That very deliberate emphasis. "This man, he's here for *me* too. For Science, as much as for Labour. To remind us what we need to find. Scientific Philanthropy, right? 'The universe has a direction.'" That trite little slogan again, the one we all used to take the piss out of, back when we were bold unorthodox free thinkers, confident the Mandate wouldn't care about us.

Except this time I've learned my object lesson and I just complete the close-minded couplet with, "And the direction is us." I'm confirming to her I've knuckled under. I'll be a good boy. No tanks for me, thanks.

But inside, I'm seething.

7.

For four days they have me doing stat analysis. I'm not even allowed to go into the lab areas. I certainly don't get to see the ruins again—and worry I never will because that's covered by a whole other arm of The Science, an Archaeology wing that Primatt has no say over and with whom she's constantly jockeying for resources.

Anyway, for now it's stats. I sit at a neutered little glorified calculator and run all the usual statistical tests on data that comes through to me shorn of any context. I learn precisely nothing. I feel like the worst parts of being someone's undergraduate assistant. And this, I understand, could easily be my entire life from here on in until the guards, the commandant or the planet kill me.

When the day's done, sometimes I'm asked to sweep up, too. At other times Domestics takes over that enviable role and I can slope down the gantry stairs with Ilmus, Okostor, Croan and the rest. Everyone's tired and nobody's willing to spontaneously start a series of lectures about what the hell Kiln's deal is. The little cautionary tale I picked up from Primatt and the man in the example tank are literally the most anybody's told me about what's going on.

At night, I'm mentally worn out by all the mathematical nonsense they have me doing but physically still jangling because my body is absolutely certain I'm in mortal peril and should be doing something about it. Sometimes I'm able to share a few words with Ilmus. At other times it's Clem Berudha sloping over to my bed under cover of darkness, or me creeping over to where he and his familiars are holding a huddled conference. The Extrasolar Revolutionary Subcommittee of Kiln. I sit at the edge and listen. I learn a little, but more about the dynamics of the camp than the world.

One night Clem elbows me, because I've been drifting. "You in?" he murmurs. "Or this place got you?" Because he knows me. He knows that every place I've ever ended up was because the science, the finding out, mattered the most to me. And Kiln is a great big abyss of finding out waiting to be plumbed. "If we turned this place over tonight," Clem puts to me, "and you could get on a ship and go home tomorrow, would you?"

Of course I would, and I tell him I would, and yet...my maddening ignorance is a hook in my head, and the line tied to it leads out beyond the wall and dome that separate *in here* from *out there*. I never thought I'd see another world, real alien life. I'd never have chosen to be deported, but I'm here now.

Except, for the first few days it seems I'm *not* going to see it even though it's there. But then finally one day Primatt hauls me from the stats work because they've got something new in and apparently it's time for me to get my hands dirty.

There's something in the lab. It's been thoroughly decontaminated but the brute dissection work apparently falls to Dig Support rather than The Science.

"You remember how to operate a scalpel rig, *Professor?*"

Primatt needles. She's lounging back on an uncomfortably narrow stool, using her stick as an extra prop.

"I remember wielding the knife myself," I say equably. "But yes, I did training for the new rigs." Thinking that they weren't even *new* when I left Earth, except to someone of my vintage. To Primatt they're familiar tech. To our peers back on the homeworld they're doubtless museum pieces by now. Weird little metal spiders of clamps, blades and saws, they're intended to be tireless and precise where human hands are fallible. In my experience they're a royal pain in the ass to actually get to do anything, but it looks like I'll have to dust off my skills.

Primatt was possibly baiting me for some *Do-you-know-who-I-am* outrage, but I'm far too keen to actually see a thing, even if it's not from any kind of elevated position. So we go into the lab and there it is, on the dissection table, under the poised limbs of the rig.

It's my first, first-hand look at an alien animal.

Basically it's a fat ochre sort of worm thing with big flaccid legs set too far back along its body. Maybe half a metre long, all told. No jaws, which aren't part of the evolutionary toolkit here, but the front end has a hinged arm with a spike on it, able to flick out and impale prey at a distance of perhaps half its body length. Liquefying and drinking your lunch is apparently de rigueur on Kiln. I take a probe and unfold the arm to full extension and then let it slip back into its resting position, which it does with an unpleasant suppleness. There's no rigor mortis equivalent here. Every joint of the thing has the flexibility and range of motion that it did in life. Except a lot of it doesn't even appear to have joints as I'd look for in an Earth beastie.

"That looks nasty." I tease the stabbing arm out again and let it slither back. The spike is around fifteen centimetres long, its distal half peppered with little holes it would use to slurp the lunch from whatever it got stuck into.

Primatt smirks at my expression. "Humans don't need to worry as much."

"They don't stab us?"

"Oh, they stab us." There's a moment when her eyes flick to the leg she wears, not her own. "Most of the digestive enzymes aren't geared for what's inside us, though. It just really, really hurts, leaving permanent nerve damage that feels like parts of your body are on fire. Until you beg for death." All this is said very politely and straight-faced, and I can't tell if I'm being hazed or if she's dead serious and on a constant cocktail of painkillers. I wait for the punchline but it remains unpunched. She nods at the dead thing on the table. "This is your audition, Professor. Why don't you show me you've not forgotten your student days."

It is, I confess, beginning to rankle. I open my mouth for a martyred speech about how I wasn't going to stand on pre-eminence, so could she kindly stop throwing my (now revoked anyway) title in my face at every opportunity. Before the words can clear my mouth I see the faintest twinkle in her expression which all the po-facedness can't quite hide. Yes, she is absolutely goading me, and having fun at my expense. But honestly I haven't seen anyone on Kiln having any fun so far. Even the commandant looked like he'd taken a mouthful of wasps right before he sat down with us to breakfast. Despite being the butt of her single joke, I warm to Doctor Nimell Primatt very slightly.

I turn my attention to the thing on the slab.

It has a couple of grapply arms near the front, in addition to the beak, which prevent the whole thing from becoming too phallic. Then there's an uncomfortable length of wrinkled body, and the leggy bit. Six tentacles, looking deflated and ineffectual in death. A very different structure to the raptorial stuff at the front. I prod them, trying to work up the enthusiasm. In death they are somewhere between cheaply printed uncooked sausage and rubber balloons full of watery jam. I feel my appetite slip out of the door, with no promise it will ever return in my lifetime. Some investigation reveals a compartmental structure, inflatable bits for liquids and gases. I discern this to be a paired hydrostatic and pneumatic system that would allow the creature to inflate separate bits of itself to rigidity, with various response speeds and potentials for the application of force. No joints, then. Or, rather, every part of it could be configured as a joint or a lever as needed.

The screen next to me lights up on a signal from Primatt which I'd missed because I am now entirely fascinated by this thing. The image there shows comparable structures, scanned and laid open and anatomized, to save me some time in getting up to speed.

"It's very light," she says, "for its size."

"How big do things get out there?" I think about the little glimpse of the great outdoors I'd had on arrival, still groggy from my forced revivification on the barge. Some of the tree-like structures had looked to be ten or fifteen metres tall at least.

"Very big and simultaneously very fast. Energetic critters," Primatt says. "Everything's a lot lighter than the same-sized thing on Earth. There are a couple of lineages, we think independently evolved at a best guess, which are...sail-beasts, we call them. The size of elephants or bigger, and they just spread themselves out and let the wind take them."

As she doesn't show me the relevant images or give me any other context, of course my mind's eye starts seeing enormous globular elephants—pink ones—just taking deep breaths to inflate themselves and then bobbling off like dirigibles. Doubtless the truth isn't half as charming. And maybe it's not true, Primatt's just hazing me again.

"I'm guessing they're not candidates for our vanished ruins builders," I remark.

"Vanished being the word," she says. "Vessikhan's tearing his hair out." The name, from context, must belong to her opposite number in Archaeology. "Or would be if he had any. Polishing his scalp in frustration, anyway. The builders left their buildings, but they cleaned out all their tools and possessions very neatly. So the commandant is relying on us to find them in the fauna."

I look at the dead thing. It's a long way from putting on a suit and completing Mandate citizenry paperwork. "I don't see anything in this that could have—".

This is what Primatt was waiting for. She jabs me under the ribs like a southpaw boxer. Hard enough that, if she'd been in the business of injecting liquefying enzymes, it probably wouldn't have hurt much more than it did.

"This isn't just an excuse for me to dodge the company of my underlings, *Professor*," she tells me, which had indeed been what I'd assumed, honestly. "You are getting a crash course in Kiln biology. Because you'll need it to be useful. You have your privileged place on Dig Support because your metrics suggest you have the capability to make a contribution. You're not here to publish papers, Arton." I am duly schooled that her first-name-terms thing is not meant to be friendly, but is just as much her putting me in my place as her emphasizing *Professor*. I probably look sullen and hurt for a moment, before I drag my face back into the realms of impassive. Primatt regards me, then sloughs off her stool and shunts me out of the way so she can instruct the scalpel rig.

"Anyway," she says, "that's not the thing. The Kiln thing. This is the thing. Look here."

She directs the arms of the rig to cutting and prying at the back end of the specimen until she's separated the legs from the torso, if that's even the word. The parting is surprisingly clean. There doesn't seem to be much in the way of plumbing connecting them until she gets to the dorsal surface, where a kind of barbed organ connecting to the legs digs into the main body's spineless spine. She then slouches back to her stool, inviting me to pick up with my investigations where she left off.

I stare at what she's reduced the specimen to. The flaccid, jelly-leg part is now divorced entirely from the grabby grub-like part, save for where the beak-looking element is firmly hooked in place. I re-evaluate what I'm seeing. Not "specimen." Specimens.

"Symbionts," Primatt agrees, at my conclusion. Gauging my reaction and finding me, I hope, agreeably interested. "We're not even done. Let's see your best knife-work. Make me an incision around where those holes are." Flagging up a scatter of pits in the hide of the leg-beast, I cut, setting my professorship aside to show how obedient I am. The substance of the creature, as reported second-hand by the haptic tell-tales of the rig, is rubbery and tough. Either a natural resilience or an artefact of preservation or post-mortem processes. Inside the thing's body I uncover a weird spongy maze of little sacs and connecting vessels and...

"Young?" I query. "It was gravid?" I've unearthed a nest of little things shaped like bullets, with flaps that were probably inflatable flippers when they were alive. They were possibly the young of the worm-like front half of this alien panto-mime horse, living in the back end of the symbiont for safe-keeping. Or hostages to good behaviour or...?

"A third species entirely," Primatt says. "Little macrobiotic mitochondria, we've discovered. They provide energy boosts for short-term high-speed chases. Leg batteries, basically. There's another critter you'll find *here*," highlighting a pouch set in the back of the arms at the front end, "that produces the digestive saliva for the beak to inject. But that's not the thing. That's not even the *thing*. So while these, and several other residents, are entirely dependent on the host, that doesn't mean the same thing here as it does on Earth. On Earth a parasite or symbiont is the ultimate specialist. The worm that infests the wasp, that breeds inside the fig, that strangles the tree, right? On Kiln, this sort of relationship is cross-species. The same organism can perform its specialist services for a range of different hosts. The whole biosphere is like that. Everything out there is forty per cent other crea-tures by weight, and by *design*, not just because they're all infested with parasites."

"By operation of evolution," I correct. It's the mildest of reprimands from her captive professor but she colours slightly.

"That's what I meant," she agrees, though we both know some strains of Mandate orthodoxy go very hard for that *design* part. "I'm showing you this so you understand just how difficult the work here is. It's like trying to think about animal microbiomes back on Earth—all the jungle of life that's a natural part of the gut biota—except here it's not just some bacteria and a fungus helping the digestion. A 'species' on Kiln is a whole community at the macrobiotic level, and each part of it can quit the team and apply for a better position elsewhere if it doesn't feel looked after. Honestly, living conditions on Swelter might be worse, but at least the biology is simpler."

"Except nobody's going to care about Swelter when they find out what you've got here," I finish for her, but that's a double-edged sword. Because it's the job of Primatt and this Vessikhan to present the findings on Kiln in a way that'll satisfy the establishment back home, and right now I don't see how that's going to happen without some great big stinking lies in the mix.

From shockingly close by I hear a weird, high gibbering, a human voice twisted into something utterly *other*. I jump and the scalpel rig spasms. I might have screamed a bit, honestly. Actual gibbering that makes me realize I've never really heard anything gibber before. It's the other voice, from before, that had replied to the poor bastard in the tank. That terrible, primal moment when you realize that the pair of you aren't alone, and you have no idea *what* the unwelcome third even *is*.

Primatt has gone very still, her mouth crunched to a flat line. The wailing and cackling goes on for far too long, horribly desolate, communicating a terrible unfulfilled yearning in its tone, and thronging with other things it simply cannot communicate to our poor human ears. Then it's cut off, very suddenly.

One of Primatt's subordinates pops his head round the door and says, "He's gone to poke the ape."

Primatt shoots him a look, obviously wanting the upsetting, inexplicable moment to just pass into history. I'm staring at her with my obvious, burning questions, though, and she looks away, saying, "The commandant. He goes to...look. At her. Opens the radio link sometimes, in case she...I don't know what he expects. That she's suddenly started saying...anything useful, but..."

"'She' who?" I demand, still profoundly rattled. It sounded like it was right next to the lab.

"Rasmussen," she says. "Ylse Rasmussen."

I stare at her, as well I might. Professor Rasmussen headed up the first science team to Kiln after the probe data had come back. Such excitement in the scientific community! The living-est world ever discovered! She'd set out before I was born and her first reports started arriving when I was a student. That would make her..."But she'd be over a century old by now, even if you subtract travel time."

Primatt's eyes have a frightened look, though the rest of her maintains her easy slouch. "It's the planet," she says. "It's in her. It won't let her die and neither will the commandant."

"Are you telling me," I ask levelly, "that Kiln *also* has the secret of eternal life?"

"If you can call it living." She laughs, hideously, inappropriately, covering her mouth in reflexive horror at herself. "Too much life, Arton. She's full to the brim with life and it's eating her but she won't die."

"I don't get it," Clemmish Berudha says later. It's him and me sitting up after lights out, tucked into the little corridor beside the reclamation plant access panels, where the cameras can't reach. He's directed the machines to spit out cups of lukewarm piss to keep our spirits up. That's what he calls it. I have a horrible idea it's the established name amongst the Labour for the one warmed-up drink our printers will vomit up.

The name anticipates the taste, frankly.

We speak in low murmurs. Not so much to avoid waking our bunkmates, whose ranks start practically within arm's reach, but because of the audio receptors that go with the cameras. Clem's people amongst the Domestics night shift claim that most of the guards don't actually keep an eye, or an ear, on what's going on, but who wants to take chances? Fuck around and find out what the inside of the example tank looks like.

"It's science, basically. Mandate science." I remember having a similar conversation with him, plus many echoes of it with others, after we first met. Him sounding out the cranky middle-aged boffin over why I'd risk my privileges for the revolution. Not quite believing it then, still not believing it now.

I told him back then you couldn't even start to understand the Mandate until you got your head around its relationship to science, but he didn't get it. Clem's a practical man. He sees social and political problems, then finds solutions from within the same brackets. The ideology that creates those problems never seems relevant to him. But to me it's the root of all the evil.

I try again.

"The Mandate is simultaneously deeply interested in science and utterly hates it," I tell him. "Science is what gives them their legitimacy. Their...mandate, actually. Their justification for doing everything they do is that they have a logical, rational piece of thinking, which means it's the best way to do things for the greatest number of people. So they love science, because it gives them permission to do all the shit they do. Right up to the point someone puts together an inconvenient but cogent argument that gets in the way of how they want the universe to be. They want very specific answers from science. Black and white answers to complex questions. Everything sorted into predetermined boxes."

Clem, the pragmatist, makes a rude noise, albeit quietly. "Guns give them the permission."

"I mean, *yes*. Obviously, yes. Or guns mean they don't need to ask about permission. But that's not how human nature works."

"This is your cognitive distance thing." He lifts the cup to his lips with his plastic hand.

"Cognitive dissonance, yes. It's not enough to be *able* to do a thing. People, human people, want to be able to believe it's *right* to do so. The first thing those in authority do, after they've used main force and brutality to take over, is paper over everything with reasons why they were *right* to do it. Both because it helps you keep people in line if you can get them to believe it, and because it makes it easier to enjoy the spoils of your brutality if you convince yourself you've earned it. Human history is full of social conventions designed to salve the consciences of the mighty and curb the ambitions of the small. There's something in the way humans are wired that means we want to be *right* by some external measure. So we invent philosophies to tell us *we were right to do what we did and we're allowed to do what we want.* You find a god, basically, who tells you you're okay. And maybe it's actual God, because that's an easy out. *God says.* Why? If you're asking that question then you haven't got faith and you're out of the God club."

"Watch it," Clem murmurs. He came from one of the God clubs, I suddenly remember. It isn't as though the resistance is free of it. You can have a divine backing for any angle of an argument, and it's not like religion just goes meekly away when persecuted. I get to my point hurriedly while Clem tops up the piss. From the machine, I should stress, not his personal supply.

"Anyway, you can have Science in place of God." It feels good to talk like this, even hushed and crammed into a corridor. I haven't had a chance to stretch these mental muscles for a while. "People've dressed up their justifications in a white lab coat since lab coats got white. Except science can also be powerfully inconvenient in that it's supposed to shift to follow what you've learned about the world, while doctrine is supposed to be iron. And the universe is inconveniently big and complex, you know? You keep moving out from your core need of 'we have to justify why we get to tell you what to do,' and the map keeps unrolling. There's always new territory you need to constrain to fit your social constructs. Until you've built an entire model of the universe with you at the centre of it. Whether God put you there or you're the inevitable product of evolution."

"And that's it, is it?"

"They call it Scientific Philanthropy," I say, naming the doctrinal elephant in the room, "which is nothing to do with giving to the needy and everything to do with being *given to* by creation. Orthodoxy says we're here to observe the universe, because the fine tuning of the universe is such that it's a perfect incubator for a human-style intellect. For humans in general. The laws of nature and the cosmos encourage conditions that give rise to life as we know it, and that life was always going to become *us*. Hence, we were *meant*. It's manifest destiny all the way down. A mandate from the dawn of time. Meaning that our Mandate is just the latest inheritor of a burning torch of meaning, the most perfect expression of the will of the universe. So long as you accept that the universe is specifically calibrated to bring *us* about." A pause. "They're very big on it, back home. It makes them feel very good about themselves." Another pause. "You can see how Primatt's got a job in front of her, though, because I don't see how anything like us could have come out of the mess I looked at today."

Clem drains his cup. His look at me suggests he's never heard such highfaluting bullshit in all his live-long days. "Well, sucks to be you," is what he selects from his stock of responses. "You go square that circle, I guess. I don't see how any of those words actually *help* the cause."

"How about: The Science is on a constant knife-edge of anxiety because Terolan wants pat answers that they can't really give him. It's all backbiting and rivalries, and Primatt looking over her shoulder because her subordinates all want her job. Which means they spend way too much time performatively writing memos and displaying for the administration, and not enough time checking their printer logs."

Clem goes still. "You kept me here drinking this piss and listening to your nonsense and all this time you had it?"

"Not just a pretty brain." Yes, I have the little filmy bag in my hands. Inside it are three tiny, complex parts. I don't

ADRIAN TCHAIKOVSKY

actually know what they're for—whatever device Clem and his people are building. I just know the Labour Block printer is shackled down so it only makes very specific items, and those poorly, whereas nobody keeps the same kind of eye on the printers up on the gantry level, where The Science does their work. Clem had told me what they needed and I'd bided my time until Primatt left me alone to finish the dissection and advance my education. Nobody, insofar as I am aware, suspected a thing.

With the exchange made, we creep back to our bunks. I lie there, thinking about my own knee-jerk mental patterns, which needn't be any more rational just because they always pull away from the Mandate's close-mindedness. Because *something* raised the ruins we saw. They were built, though we don't know how. They were designed with thought. There's art there, and something Vessikhan insists is script, though I think Primatt's not entirely convinced. For the commandant's purposes, though, we don't even need the alien builders to have writing. Probably we'd be happier if they'd become just advanced enough to leave their relics before collapsing into barbarism. Except over which hills did the barbarians retreat, exactly? Where are the hands whose ancestors raised those towers? Because I don't think phallic worm-spider monsters are giving us any clues.

8.

Over the next dozen days I learn how it's going to be. Myself and Ilmus, Croan and Okostor and the rest of Dig Support doing all the menial donkey work for Nimell Primatt and her handful of legitimate, i.e. non-carceral, assistants. We clean up and lay out, oversee the data entry and crunch statistics. We are somewhere between untrained menials and the sort of hardworking student assistants who aren't, under any circumstances, going to be credited in the end publication. I suspect we're all thinking about our careers back home and how we'd all had people to do this stuff for us, had taken them for granted, and hardly ever even spared them a thought. Humility is a humiliating thing to learn at my age.

Doctor Primatt herself is good enough about it, after our thorny start, meaning she doesn't rub it in and mostly ignores us. The three men who constitute her team aren't. They're all younger than I am, younger than most of Dig Support. I wouldn't have wiped my arse on any of them back home. Classic under-achievers and coat-tail hangers-on, which is presumably why they ended up here rather than in a comfortable common room back in one of Earth's respectable institutions. They are very aware of the shortcomings of their situation, not only having been sold an extrasolar lemon in place of a career, but not even being in charge of that

93

lemon. Within Dig Support we refer to them as Feep, Foop and Fop, after some spectacularly annoying cartoon characters from our collective childhoods.

Everyone else has already gone their three rounds with that triumvirate of academic failure. As the sole newcomer it's my turn to be shown my place. They recognize my name from the literature that's made its way out here. They know me as a rising star of the field, making waves, pushing the boundaries of orthodoxy. Feted for it, briefly, before the pendulum swung back and that sort of thing became unfashionable again. Now, watching my morning star reach a Luciferian end here on Kiln clearly pleases them. Mostly because, I decide, it validates their own mediocrity. They ride me hard when I'm on cleaning duty, pointing out invisible stains and marks I've missed, making me do everything three times until my fingers are raw with the bleach. I bring them coffee that's somehow never quite the way they want it and my statistics work is always sloppy and needs to be redone. Although honestly my stats work is pretty sloppy. I'm used to having assistants whom, I now consider uneasily, I probably didn't treat much better. We're none of us angels in academia.

One of our major exercises is taxonomy, which only highlights how utterly misplaced the Mandate's messaging is. Mandate biosciences love taxonomy, always have. That reassuring ladder of species, genus, family, all that; everything in its little box, the whole of creation anatomized in a spreadsheet. All those neat, branching depictions that coincidentally magnify branches of life, according to how close to the human they are, with humanity depicted as a kind of pinnacle, a fairy atop the tree of creation. And Linnean classification was always a bit uneasy from the start, because

Linnaeus himself was working in a period where deep time and the fossil record weren't much of a thing. His focus was on extant species in his present day. The same exercise applied to Kilnish life is flat-out insane.

Excursions bring us in more specimens, which Primatt ensures have been thoroughly decontaminated—unlike Excursions themselves, apparently. Dig Support then get to do the donkey work of physically describing each new instance of life, coding it and running the analyses to see where it plots out in relation to everything else we've found, in the hope that some sort of coherent tree will result. One that has a narrative and a direction and a useful gap where the ruins builders might be hiding.

Except that cataloguing any given specimen means identifying anywhere between three and thirty different entities, some of which might be familiar from other combined critters, while others are entirely novel. So what are we taxonomizing, exactly? What is the "creature"? Sometimes something comes in that's entirely novel, but it's been Frankensteined together by Kilnish evolution, out of parts that all exist already in our records. Simultaneously completely new and old news.

There I am, poking through some damn critter that's infested with worms, bugs and fungal-looking tendrils, not to mention the whole microbiome of tinier things which have mostly turned to slush under the decontamination. I use the scalpel rig to resect something that looks like the world's most suggestive carrot. Is it a new thing? I try to cross-reference it against the database. The best answer I can find is "maybe." On the other end of my worktable, Ilmus has the other end of the same specimen. This has turned out to be an entirely separate creature that's mostly visual sensors and whippy antennae, but with no guts or limbs whatsoever, just a lot of suckers it must have used to drain living fluids directly from other parts of the compound beast.

This brings to my mind an artistic mode called Exquisite Corpse that's absolutely banned by Mandate censors because it's basically sketchbook randomness and promotes indiscipline. You draw a thing, fold over the paper, then pass it on to the next person who takes up from the trailing lines you've left them. The results are a weird serial chimera of nonsense. Kilnish life sometimes seems to be the same thing moved into the field of biology.

Parrides Okostor, also here, throws up his hands. "We've *seen* this one. I spent two *hours* on this bastard creature and it's already on the system. It's just been given all the wrong tags." That's a problem too, of course. You see a thing in one context, which colours the way you describe it. Then the same commensal part can turn up doing something quite different, because of its current selection of partners, and you don't recognize it. Like meeting a workplace acquaintance at an underground meeting.

I look at his data, jostling elbows. After our initial pugilistic clash, we're working together well enough. Labour Block life doesn't leave us the energy for feuding in our personal time, and we're both pragmatists at heart.

"Is every damn thing just unique?" I ask. "I mean, you could go mad doing this."

A bad choice of words because, from close by, the unseen Ylse Rasmussen howls briefly, before her speaker is cut off. Everyone goes still, waiting to see if she'll repeat herself. She doesn't. A shiver runs from one to the next of us in sequence, as though we, too, are all parts of the same beast.

"There *are* species," Helena Croan insists. She usually takes on the mantle of Champion of Orthodoxy. "There are regular combinations of symbiotes that constitute a Kilnish 'species.' Or metaspecies. Macro-species. The same parts in the same configurations creating the same animal."

"With variations," Okostor growls. "And where do you draw the line exactly? I mean it's mad. One of these things snacks on its neighbour and twenty per cent of the exchange is cannibalism because of their common parts. They say this place made *people* who built *buildings*?"

"Parrides," Croan warns.

"It's more likely," Okostor goes on loudly, "that actual Earth humans used magic stone circle technology to come here and build ruins, than that anything like us could have come from this place."

"Enough," she tells him more urgently. Then Feep, or possibly Foop, is looking in through the door, as though he's scented sedition from his desk two rooms away. He squints suspiciously at the lot of us, then slinks away again.

"I keep having this dream," Ilmus says after he's gone.

"I don't want to hear it," Okostor decides.

"I meet the builders, and they're, you know, they're like humans," Ilmus goes on as they work on the programming of the scalpel rig. "Except when I get closer they're...just Kiln bits, Kiln creatures, squished together in a raw human shape."

"Thank you for that lovely image which won't at all come back to me after lights out tonight," Okostor growls. Meanwhile I palm one of the scalpel blades and slip it into the fold in my overalls, right next to the bolt in my collarbone where the detectors won't find it. Ilmus and Parrides cover for me, standing so that neither cameras nor Croan see me do it. Because Clem is an enthusiastic recruiter, and life on Kiln offers little enough hope that rising up against the Mandate looks like a good option.

The thing I'm working on collapses with a disgusting squishing noise, some part of its internal structure giving way. The decontamination process, targeting as it does a variety of organic structures, is not kind to specimens.

"Can we not get fresher meat?" I ask, then look up to face flat stares from most of the others.

"Unacceptable risk," Croan says.

"Nobody's going to be bringing lively biomatter under the dome," Okostor explains. "Even if we all suited up, something might get loose." As one, their eyes turn to a particular point, a wall that separates us from the perennial durance of Rasmussen, who I've still not seen. We wait for her contribution but mercifully there's nothing.

Our work is to biology what faking a set of books for the Taxation Mandate is to accountancy. There's the initial survey Primatt's team is compiling, and then there's the official record that goes to Commandant Terolan, written with words that are fewer, smaller and much more orthodox. And soon enough I'll be given a serious demonstration of just how ludicrous that can be.

One day we receive new pictures from one of the survey drones and Primatt shares them with Dig Support. As a treat, for all the hoops we've jumped through. There are satellites in orbit constantly scanning the surface, picking out interesting-looking sites according to some very humanocentric algorithms. Terolan has a technical team, which apparently boils down to one bored engineer named Mox Calwren, plus whoever he conscripts from Labour's Maintenance on an ad hoc basis. Calwren gets to look over the satellite imagery, dispatch drones to go take surface-level images and hope nothing tries to eat them. Where the drone imagery shows something is actually there, then Excursions is mobilized to go secure the site and clear it for further study. The satellite algorithm turns up a lot of false positives, apparently—the problem of asking a machine to see pictures in clouds. It probably throws up twice as many false negatives, except of course you never find out about them.

This time it's the real deal. A new ruin, the twenty-ninth to be located. Excursions are going to have a long trip in the near future. The drone footage is my first view of Kilnish architecture au naturel.

It's immediately evident why the satellite has had such trouble picking out the signal from the noise because you can barely see the structures under the greenery. Or the yellow-blackery, I suppose, given Kiln's colour palette. There's some kind of vine-growth all over it, popping out in funeral rosettes that look like flowers but perform a function more like leaves. Primatt prods me with her stick and asks if I notice anything odd.

I'm already thinking like an ecologist, thankfully. "The stuff around the structures is different to the vegetoid life in the surrounding forest. Endemic only to the buildings." I hunch forwards, staring at the buildings and wishing Mox Calwren had given me more useful angles. The forest biome around the place is more of the bulbous, ochre tubers, each wearing its crown of unfurled, photosynthetic petals like a rakish broad-brimmed hat. Tall lances poke between them, lifting little fists of sun-drinkers to the sky. Dark cords, like snakes with overgrown scales, climb up the sides of the larger life, leaching off them and maybe providing some benefit in return. There are the fantastical lacework structures of parasitic saprophytes, the pocked warts of galls induced by some motile species in need of a home. All of it is on a grand scale, according to the drone's reticules. The largest trees are fifteen metres high and half again across the hat brim. I call to mind what I've learned about their internal structure from my dissections and The Science's databases. Their interiors will be riddled with airways and tubes, a complex lab of gas exchanges and reaction chambers. Some of the intake holes are big enough for a human to crawl into, as Okostor proudly pointed out once. *And then die* seemed to hang around the words, so obvious that it didn't need to be said.

Then there's the ruin, detectable to my eye not because of the exposed work of hands, but because the life that cloaks it is distinct from everything nearby.

Primatt watches my reaction and then prods me painfully again. "Come look at something," she snaps, and poles off, shunting a peeved Feep out of the way. I scurry in her wake. Any excuse to get out of work, frankly. Most of the rooms The Science does its business in are inadequately lit and either frozen cold or stifling hot, as well as full of Feep, Foop and Fop.

She takes the steps down to the ground under the suspicious eyes of the guards, who don't like her much. We end up round the back of the Labour Block, as though we're about to light up some illicit smokes without the commandant seeing. This is where the central reclamation tank is. The thing everything goes into once it's been used up and broken down. The thing from which every new tool and toy derives. It's hard up against the boundary of the dome, at the one point not reinforced by an armoured fence. Instead, the outside of the dome here is crawling with exactly that breed of alien vines I saw on the ruins in the drone footage. And by "crawling" I mean that if I watch long enough, I can see hydrostatic elements pulse and shudder, so the whole network writhes slowly as its rosettes track the sun.

There's a big round plate connecting the reclamation system to the dome. The plants seem rooted to it on the outside, partnered to ducts on the inside. I see cables plunging into the earth and guess that they run underfoot to elsewhere in the compound. For a moment I expect to see them writhe lethargically too.

"What am I even looking at?" I glance at Primatt and meet her eyes because she's watching me.

"Power," she says. "The power of the ancient Kilnish."

"I thought it was geothermal? The bores beneath the ruins." There are glass-sided shafts descending deep into the ground below the structures. I've seen the geophysics scans.

"In part, though we think that's more to do with temperature regulation. This is what made the Kiln of yesteryear go. It's a hyper-efficient solar collector. The ruins here were covered in it when people first arrived. Most of them are when they're found. Except the Kilnish didn't bother with cables. They just encouraged the stuff to grow wherever they needed it. They were bioengineers par excellence, or else the way Kiln life works really lends itself to native intelligence relying on biotech solutions from a much earlier stage than human technology ever could. You're looking at the actual working engineering of the vanished Kilnies, Arton. Rasmussen figured it out in the early days, when things were far more hands-on and wild frontier around here. And even though that attitude's precisely why she's currently locked up in the attic, we still benefit from her discovery. Harnessed here and now for our use, providing the bulk of this whole camp's power needs, so that all the solar stuff you see up top is little more than a backup. We still don't understand a damn thing about whoever first pioneered this system. Makes you wonder what we could have had, if we hadn't burned the vines and everything else off the ruins here to maintain quarantine."

I make a thoughtful sound. It was about time I tested the boundaries of my intellectual cage. "You know the quarantine's balls, right?"

Primatt watches me.

"If you're not decontaminating Excursions every time they come back, which you're not, then they're bringing stuff in."

"It's not really a quarantine. It's just minimizing exposure," she agrees. "And they wash off Excursions about once every three days. Usually."

Which was just infrequently enough for accidents. When Excursions had come back last time, they'd been given a thorough gassing and one of them hadn't survived. The decontamination had killed off something inside of him that apparently he'd been using. Something alien that had eaten a crucial human part of him and then sat there. Until the deception had been revealed with extreme prejudice and suddenly there wasn't enough of him left to stay independently alive. I don't explicitly refer to the incident now but I reckon it's written on my face in big letters.

"It's a command decision," Primatt says flatly.

"That's what Fee— That's what your assistants told me,

when I mentioned it. They said I was welcome to join Excursions if I wanted to study the phenomenon first-hand."

"That sounds like their management style," Primatt says drily.

"They're not fond of me, I think."

"They're not fond of me, either."

I look at Primatt with surprise at her candidness. Her eyes are on the foliage clutching at the outside of the dome.

"Heading up the team here is the galaxy's smallest ever trophy cup," she says. "But they still jostle about who gets to piss longest in it." She leans on her stick, the lopsided pose giving her an unwarranted rakish air. I meet her gaze, wondering what she's about. The expected belittling hasn't come. Perhaps she's looking for an ally, though I can't see that I'm much use. Croan is a sycophant to her face, but I reckon that's only skin deep. The rest of Dig Support don't like her much either. Who else is there? Terolan is like a wolf at her heels, and I have no real idea how she gets on with Vessikhan, her opposite number in Archaeology. Do I *want* her as an ally? To Clem and the subcommittee she's the enemy. Almost everyone on the gantry level is.

The moment hangs too long. Whatever she was looking for, from me, hasn't come. She limps off, and I need to keep to her shadow or else the guards will decide I'm malingering. We go back to the airless hut to set down more records, and then construct the *other* records that we'll show Terolan. Feep, Foop and Fop eye me narrowly, as though plotting the demise of Primatt's new confidant.

9.

Commandant Terolan, then. What sort of a man is simultaneously consigned to and trusted with a venture like the Kiln labour camp? I meant what I said to Clem, about the science. Kiln is *important* to the Mandate, or at least certain sections of it. The universe is a pyramid: physics leading to chemistry, leading to biology; microbes leading to worms, leading to vertebrates, leading to apes, leading to us; then the broad mass of humanity leading to Mandate officials, leading to the fine minds of the Cientificos. Because why bother building a pyramid if it's not you on the very spindly tip of it? Yet none of those apex politicos would sideline their careers by being sent away, out of the loop, and out of the solar system to the far reaches of human experience here on Kiln.

They might have sent an obedient, unimaginative brute as I'd first imagined, but a brute wouldn't find them answers. They might have sent... well, someone like me, I suppose. An academic whose mind and mouth haven't always kept to the windy side of orthodoxy. But then the answers they got might not be the ones they wanted. Instead, some unimaginable selection process has given us Terolan, a man who is neither of those things, but can be brutal or intellectual as the situation requires. Or sometimes both at once.

Primatt had showed me the man in the example tank—

they took him out, shot him and fed him into the incinerator the day after that, in fact. As though the man's sentence had been extended for my personal benefit. And, knowing Terolan's attention to detail, maybe it was. The wretch's punishment, the very existence of the example tank, had been at Terolan's order. He is merciless, therefore. A brute.

And yet, though he's no career academic, he reads the journals. He's taught himself the science, biological and archaeological both. I believe he takes pleasure in it too. Not so much broadening his mind, because he's an orthodoxist through and through, but honing it. He reads over everything that we submit, and nothing is sent home without his seal of approval on it. Primatt confirms that her predecessor abruptly ceased to be head of The Science, and indeed ended up bottom of the Excursionistas, because he assumed he could slip some scientific sleight of hand past the command-ant. A little free thinking, messages to academics back home, perhaps just trying to tell the actual truth about the biolog-ical mess Kiln represents. "He thought Terolan too dull to read between the lines," Primatt says.

And it's not simply that Terolan's a time-server, a follower of orders. Ilmus and Okostor, with the benefit of their addi-tional year in the camp, reckon the man's genuinely invested in what we have here. An enquiring scientific mind and a rigid orthodox thinker, all crammed into that one head. Simultaneously driven to find out the answer, and absolutely sure he knows what that answer will be. Which means, to academics like us, he's a very dangerous man indeed.

Sometime after I've settled into my role as Dig Support's new wunderkind, we receive a dinner invitation. Commandant

Terolan wishes to entertain, and be entertained. The news knocks our work utterly askew, because that latter entertainment means he wants The Science to make a little presentation on the current state of our knowledge about Kiln. Some line managers might just call a meeting, but Terolan was obviously used to a certain level of decent society back home. Just as he'd had me over for a snack and menaces after I got off the barge, now he's having a whole formal dinner like the Mandate bigwigs still indulge in back home, though loved a whole lot more in his day. A faintly antiquated thing, in the same style as his wardrobe.

The invitation is not a blanket potluck for the whole department. We actually get little printed cards through, reproducing Terolan's own chop and signature, as though this is some optional event we might have difficulty fitting into our busy social calendars. It's a little twee, a little quaint. For a brief moment I both like Terolan more and feel a little sorry for him. Then I remember the example tank and all the other cautionary tales I've heard. Just because the tyrant dresses like a clown doesn't mean he's funny.

Obviously Primatt is going, along with Feep, or possibly it's Fop. I'm not just being mean; the three of them really do look quite similar: same hair, same lemon-sucking expression. Vessikhan from Archaeology is on the invite list too—aside from the baldness Primatt mentioned, I know very little about him. I'm not sure whether his job is easier or more difficult than ours. The hard-sciences snob in me suggests he's in a far better position to just make things up, but that is frankly uncharitable. Helena Croan, head of Dig Support, receives an invite too, and as the newest curiosity, so do I.

"He's digested the journals then," Croan says. It's her,

Okostor, Ilmus and me in the hot, close room with the data-crunching servers, going over the latest analyses so we can get our quota done before Croan and I have to dress up.

"Each time a barge turns up it uploads the latest literature," Ilmus explains for my benefit. "Oh, we don't, you know, get a sniff of it when it does, but it goes on the stack. The commandant's stack. He gets to everything eventually."

"He takes time over the long words," Okostor growls. He's less convinced of the commandant's erudition, or just sore over not receiving an invitation.

"And now he wants our opinions, probably," Croan adds.

"Are we allowed to read the journals ourselves?" I enquire hopefully.

"You'll get precisely what he decides to tell you about whatever topic's got his goat," Okostor tells me flatly. "And he'll make sure to report it to you in such a way that you'll come back with whatever opinion he wants you to have. It's like the Mandate in miniature."

"Enough," Croan says, because this sort of unorthodox talk makes her nervous. She's been head of Dig Support for some years now and apparently that's a trophy worth clinging onto.

We're all dressed to the nines when we arrive. Domestics —the Labour division who do the menial stuff up-gantry— have printed us out fresh clothes of Terolan's preferred vintage. Engineer Calwren is present as a helper, unzipping a screen for Primatt's presentation. While she's engaged in annoying him with specifications, Feep elbows me down the table so that he can take the seat next to her. I end up between

Croan and a lean, angular individual who I think is Terolan's guard lieutenant. They—I'm not sure of their gender although their personnel record certainly will be—have a black metal hand, foot, cheek and half their jaw, all polished up for the occasion. With Primatt's leg, Clem's hand and the other cases I've seen, that's a lot of replacement parts per capita in the camp. Clem's prosthesis is the result of a stint assisting Vessikhan's Archaeology team out in the field, his arm a recent donation to the planet's biomass. It's probably not even rotting, unless the biosphere has bootstrapped its way into metabolizing the proteins. Primatt's leg is the result of inadequate decontamination, or overachieving adaptation —meaning one dissection subject turned out to be considerably less dead than was previously advertised. The lieutenant's badges of honour occurred in earlier days, when the local biosphere was flexing its not-exactly-muscles against camp security. I don't want to think what the turnover on the Labour side was like back then. The local wildlife wasn't keen on being excluded and there were plenty of punchy species out there willing to engage in their own cross-biology research about what was and wasn't edible.

Once everyone's seated, we finally start eating—the good printed food, just like Terolan served me when I first arrived. It's a particular treat, and far better than The Science are normally given, only rolled out on special occasions. And that's daft, I know, because it's all printed and it's all molecules. Everyone could eat synthetic caviar every meal without it impacting on anybody's budget. But instead the food printers are heavily regulated and every stratum of inmate here on Kiln has a particular menu, for what we get in the Labour Block, what Science and Engineering (meaning

Calwren) are given, what the guards receive, and what Terolan enjoys—unwritten sumptuary laws enforcing an entirely artificial scarcity, because literally everything we have here is artificial. It's a command decision, just like rationing decontamination for the Excursion teams, and made for the same reason: carrots and sticks. The way men like Terolan maintain society and order.

Terolan makes the conversational running, as anticipated. He has indeed been reading the journals, and we're subjected to a succession of "I encountered a fascinating proposal recently..." and "I see that it's been suggested that..." Each nugget of wisdom comes shorn of its original authors as though the insights are Terolan's own. And Okostor was right: every topic turns up artisanally crafted so as to evince a very precise response, with we nodding dogs echoing whatever Terolan considers to be the correct thoughts on the subject. I look at the commandant and decide that he's not even doing it deliberately. He's going to walk away from the table convinced of his own penetrating intellect. All his clever dinner guests agree with him because he's so right and so bright, rather than because he puts us all in rhetorical armlocks and literally has the power of life or death over everyone in the room. The greatest privilege of power is being able to overlook that you're even wielding it.

Then the main course is over and, to go with the dessert, Primatt is set to perform the most ludicrous pantomime ever put on in the name of science, for her audience of one.

She talks through Kilnish biology—a skating summary and then a handful of new observations that post-date the last formal departmental luncheon. The words she uses aren't actually that small and Terolan nods along, if not an expert then an educated amateur up to date with the literature. Then she departs so violently from any semblance of rationality that I almost leap to my feet and flip the table. Well, obviously not. I'm no longer that young or that foolish. But Croan grips my wrist as though I am about to, which is obscurely flattering.

It's a man, the thing Primatt demonstrates to us. Well, I exaggerate. A man who might have arisen from the Kilnish creatures we've been studying. Two legs, boneless, hydrostatic, and yet somehow there's a midway crease that gives the illusion of a knee. Arms, terminating in a clutch of outgrowths—four rather than five because, remember, this is *alien*. And there's an opposable digit in there but, weirdly, that doesn't much offend me because something built these ruins and something needed to be able to manipulate the world. There are countless Earth examples of how to evolve one body part so that it works to press against some other bit of you. There are beetles, even, whose heads have become thumbs to pincer against the outgrowths of their thoraxes, making their bodies into a hand for the purpose of picking up and throwing away romantic rivals. The Kilnite thumb is just about the only part of the charade that isn't ridiculous to me.

She's given this mythical man some tentacular growths off its shoulders—perhaps some symbiotic vine organism like we saw covering the ruins. It has a head with big round eyes, featureless black because the photoreceptors of Kiln are derived from the same light-drinking structures that power their photosynthesis. They're positioned where human eyes would go, though, because Philanthropic orthodoxy states that's the perfect place for eyes, or else our eyes wouldn't be there. But it's the mouth she's had to really reach for, because Kilnish critters don't have one. No jaws here, because jaws are a modification of specific elements of fish anatomy that never arose on Kiln. So she's given the mockery a folding beak, like the worm-end of that first critter I was tasked to study. But the way it folds creates a kind of chin, and the line of a non-existent smile.

It's a hypothetical view of those who raised the ruins—a human of Kiln. The hidden people of the tuber woods who have kept just out of sight all this time but might be discovered any day. To her credit, Primatt isn't saying, *This is it*. But she's saying, *This is what we think* and *It'll be something like this*. As though maybe tomorrow this travesty will walk out of the woods but it'll have three or six digits on its hands rather than four, and the tentacles will be from its head not its shoulders, and Primatt will issue the appropriate correction and apology.

By this point I'm pissed enough (in the other sense too because there's wine) that I decide to step in and help her. I stand up, despite Croan's warning hand, and go over to the screen, then start pointing out bits of the Jenny Haniver creation Primatt's mocked up.

"Obviously," I say, in my best professorial tones, "the intestines pictured here are an independent symbiotic organism, such as we've seen in several of the larger mobile life forms here. Food is ingested…here—" a hand-wave at the tucked-away proboscis that Primatt's made look so much like a human jawline—"but the creature lacks the equipment to properly digest it, so relies on its little passenger." I trace the worm-like outlines of the guts which are now a thing of horror for all concerned. "Similarly these—" and if she's given the thing tendrils then why not tug on them?—"are a separate entity. Likely it uses its leafy extrusions to communicate, linked metabolically with its host. Possibly this squid-like assembly is actually the controlling partner in the relationship." Yes indeed, ho ho, steeple fingers, bright smile. Just like academia back home. I look around the table. Nobody's amused. Nobody wants their hypothetical Kilnish Wild Man to actually have Kilnish features. And right then, having quite forgotten where I am and what my actual status is, I keep crowbarring Kilnishness into the hypothetical Wild Man. Lampooning how what we've observed would *actually* have to be formulated to produce anything like this. How, if you want a Bigfoot, then you have to accept that its big feet are going to be two independent crablike claws that just happen to have attached themselves to the end of the legs.

"Obviously," I conclude merrily, "given that our builders have evolved from the biology currently being observed, they must partake of it, even as they inevitably converge on the human form. It's just a group effort, that's all. Anthropomorphism by committee." I've whipped the veils away and Primatt's hypothetical native is exposed to be as ludicrous as a surrealist's sketch of a face made out of fruit and flowers.

Terolan is stony-faced. He's scientist enough to understand the point I'm making, ideologue enough not to appreciate it.

"Sit down, Professor Daghdev," he says, and I do. I have more wine. It's bad, tart and sticky—printed wine is always horrible. I apply myself to it with academic rigour, though. I'm sufficiently unrepentant in the face of all their disapproval that it's evident to all I've been drinking far more than anyone realized, and possibly old Arton's actually a bit of a lightweight when it comes to putting away the booze. My outburst will be seen as something soluble in alcohol. I excuse myself afterwards, then bumble off to the high-class privies they have up on the gantry level. Get lost; wander around; blunder into where the on-call Domestics are waiting, a man and a woman attired like olde-worlde bellhops, awaiting Terolan's pleasure. A guard eventually finds me and redirects me to the table. I belch and chortle and present all that strain of muddle-headed boffinesque buffoonery.

As I'm led back in, Primatt is talking quickly under the withering regard of the commandant's lack of amusement, like someone trying to stitch a battlefield wound under fire. It's Vessikhan who saves the day, standing up with his own talk about the latest ruin expedition. He's been out at a new site, more complete than the one our dome was raised around. They burned and fumigated it to kill off the vegetation, as well as the myriad beasts and bugs that had made a home there, and now he pulls up plans of its interior organization: the underground spaces, the deep shafts, and plans of how heat exchanges through its spaces across the wide daily temperature gradient. There's virtually a constant temperature as air is heated deep below and then cooled as it passes across reconstructed vanes and fins. I sit there and want to say, *Termites, ants, wasps.* Social insects never wrote a symphony or built a telescope, but they evolved to generate this kind of instinctual engineering. I know this is where Okostor's thoughts are too, on the builders—that we're seeing intelligence in the instinctual workings of some nest of bugs or worms, or even something like the fruiting body of a fungus. Perhaps the whole business of the builders is even more of a will-o-the-wisp than I think. Listening to

Vessikhan talk about "design," I'm more and more of Okostor's mind. We always underestimate the complexities that can arise from simple systems. And there's so much mix-and-match going on in Kiln's ecosystem, is it any wonder this sort of thing might just *happen?*

Except then Vessikhan starts showing the latest reliefs and friezes. People had kept saying "art" but Okostor's grumbling convinced me it was all more faces-in-clouds pareidolia. I've never seen it, though. It wasn't ever relevant to the Bioscience workload. Yet here Vessikhan is showing images of the most recent examples. Art—not hung up or painted on but made a part of the structure as it was raised. He demonstrates that some parts of these structures are built up as mounds that are excavated, but the higher sections are fashioned not from regular bricks but from rods, folds and other components that must have been hoisted into place with mechanical aid, or by very large hands. Then it was all smoothed together to look seamless. This is beyond the mechanical abilities of termites, surely. And the art was clearly planned before the building because it's constructed in pieces. Geometrical art: circles and rays and angles. Mathematical proofs, Vessikhan thinks, though he can't actually demonstrate any.

And then there's the writing. Or he thinks it's writing. It was added afterwards, unlike the art. It flows in serpentine strips around borders and up shafts, little repeating symbols, a character set in the thousands, but definitely distinct. His list of the frequency of recurrence of related symbols suggests something other than random distribution. Not just life but thought. Vessikhan is no great speaker, stammering, correcting himself, bringing up the wrong images in the wrong order. Yet his message gets through in spite of his shortcomings. Everything that our biological sciences say *can't* be here on Kiln, his archaeology says *is* here. Or *was*. And if it *was*, then where did it go when it stopped raising these enigmatic structures? The Wild Man, returning to the woods. I am quiet, and remain so, my sarcasm failing me.

"Vessikhan charmed you," Primatt observes. "I could tell. You were like a man about to get into a fistfight until he started his circus."

It's now after the meal. Technically I should be back in the Labour Block, but I'm at Science's disposal and Primatt hasn't disposed of me. Croan's gone back down already. Vessikhan and Feep have returned to their own slightly more salubrious quarters too. I am still acting drunker than I am, quietly wondering what she wants of me.

"Writing," I say. "Except it can't be."

"Why?"

"Up shafts," I point out. "In holes. Behind pillars. Some of those places you couldn't ever get in to read it, without a periscope or an eyestalk. It can't have been carved in situ."

"Prayers, perhaps. Invocations stowed away for luck. For ritual purposes." She shrugs. "Listen to you: all scientific rigour when we try to make the locals *look* like humans but the moment there's a sniff of actual intelligence you're insisting they *think* like us. You want to see it?"

"What?"

"New writing. Recent."

She's playing some sort of joke but I can't see the punch-line and maybe I am actually drunker than I think. She leads me to where the dome's curve makes me lean dangerously out over the gantry rail. Until we're at a little windowless shed in the back of The Science's usual prefabs. I'd taken it for a guard tower, from below, or a storage shed, or a spare privy. We go in. It's not any of those things.

Inside there are two rooms, the one we're in and the one on the other side of the plastic-glass. And behind that plastic-glass is a ragged figure, sitting in a Labour Block jumpsuit which looks like she's been worrying at it with her teeth. It's Ylse Rasmussen. She's an old woman. Of course she is. She was one of the first on the ground here, the original owner of the shoes Primatt's currently filling. And yet the age that hangs on every line of her is just the shadow of what it *should* be. The years that should have seen her in the grave, even with far better treatment than she's very obviously had. Her wiry grey hair straggles past the loop of cord she's used to restrain it. She looks at us with a calm intelligence. There are some hatches and vents in her chamber but no exits or privacy.

On the walls, even on her side of the glass that stands between us, is writing. Not quite the crisp square characters Vessikhan showed us but something like them. An imitation or an evolution or a related alphabet. Symbols that are identifiably related to those in Vessikhan's presentation—not just a bad copy but pregnant with their own ineluctable meaning. A handful of characters, common enough to leap to the eye, that weren't in Vessikhan's presentation.

Rasmussen, lean, leathery, gaunt-cheeked, notes my interest. She reaches into a printed bowl and comes up with two caked fingers. She daubs on the glass. The receptacle is, I realize, for her biological necessities; her inks are self-generated. Blood, excrement, chewed-up food. If this was Earth her cell would swarm with flies, if any could get in.

Instead it's just her, cut off from Kiln and humanity, and the universe.

She puts her cheek to the smeared barrier, and speaks. I hear her, just: the sound conducted through the glass. She forms the words very deliberately, veiny eyes swivelling to fix on my gaze. "Join me," she says, the least attractive of offers, and then I think she adds, "A short path through a dry country." Carefully enunciated and yet devoid of meaning.

She throws her head back and gapes wide. I hear the same hooting call from before as she bellows at full volume in there. It's strikingly loud, even through the glass. There's modulation in that call, information as maddeningly occluded as the alien writing she's aping. I feel perilously close to a cliff edge of knowledge and, for the first time in my academic career, I shy away from revelation. Give me my ignorance. Keep me from the understanding that will turn me into the thing I see before me.

We step away, falling over ourselves to get out of that place. I feel the scratchy, barbed gaze of Rasmussen scrabbling at my back as we leave.

"She went outside," Primatt explains, once we've left the building. "A lot." The air under the dome is muggy and still but it tastes like liberty after where we've just been. "She was the first to study the life here," Primatt goes on. "Before they set up proper decontamination procedures. Accounts vary. It was before I arrived. They're always on the point of fumigating her, but Terolan won't let them. He thinks she understands something and comes to stare and listen to her most days. It's creepy as fuck."

By then we've made it to her quarters, pushing through

The Science's common room to reach the little sovereign territory she can lay claim to, as head of Bioscience. As we pass, I catch looks from Feep, Foop and/or Fop, who are all rolling eyes and curled lips. I assume I'm doing the gentlemanly thing by taking her to her doorstep, but when she has it open she just hauls me inside.

She drops heavily onto her bed and takes her leg off, uncoupling it from its socket and then spraying the area where the flesh meets the plastic. "Fucking thing," she says vaguely, and then looks up at me. "You know, you came very close to being taken out and shot tonight."

I do my how-drunk-I-am act. I don't know how much I'm fooling her, honestly.

"Yes. Well." She shrugs, setting the leg to charge—the drawback when you have something fancier than Clem's crude claw. She sits back on the bed. Stares at me. I realize the charade of her leg was at least partly so I could slip out if I wanted to.

"I'm not pulling rank, Arton. You go back to your bunk whenever you want. But I'd like company." Refreshingly frank, devoid of vulnerability, a business proposition as much as anything.

I find I want company too, and join her on the bed.

It's late when I head back down and I have to explain to about seventeen different guards how I was helping The Science with some out-of-hours research. I suspect they nearly all know exactly what I was researching. A lot of it probably goes on here.

Clem somehow knows to be awake when I come back in. He's blagged the bunk next to mine and waits until I'm settled before speaking. Someone else has hung something over the audio snoop to muffle it, and we're both fluent in murmur.

"Did you manage to?" he asks. I pass him the little thumbnail-sized datasquare I palmed when I was blundering about with the Domestics and pretending to be drunk. The man convicted of stealing, who they executed through exposure in the example tank, had hidden it there before they caught him. The filched samples were a diversion that spectacularly backfired. They never knew about the real prize, but Clem couldn't get to the goods either. Recorded on that little square sliver are guard rotas, as well as passwords and system backdoors that should be good until Calwren updates the system. Clem and his subcommittee have a plan. The cause is alive and well on Kiln and I am thoroughly back in the game.

10.

One day the camp has a deeply unwelcome visitor. There's a rumour, afterwards, that it was something brought in for the dissection table which was insufficiently dead. Such things have, apparently, been known to happen, and it was another reason why Dig Support was given the privilege of operating the scalpel rig rather than The Science themselves. Amongst the least educated and most credulous of the Labour Block there was also a rumour it was something that had hit the laboratory slab entirely dead but then we boffins—or rather the boffins, and we, their hunchbacked assistants—had brought it back to life. Ludicrous! Except when you consider that the life–death boundary isn't actually so clearly defined on Kiln, the doubts start creeping in. But it's all nonsense, I swear. Nobody ever does find out for sure where the damn thing came from or how it got in. All I know is that Maintenance and Mox Calwren are both raked over the coals for leaving some hole open in the perimeter, even though no hole is actually found.

Maybe it drifted in with Excursions like a spore, then found an isolated corner and just grew into the macroscopic horror we all see, by eating…I don't want to think what it was eating, honestly. The only certainty is that, one day, suddenly it's here and it's our problem. A thing from Kiln is inside the compound.

It sets up on the gantry level. No dallying with the hoi polloi down on the ground. It must have socially mobile pretensions, for a monster. It's presumably an arboreal-analogue monster on its home turf. Either that or it's adapted to living on scaffolding in record time, which is also not entirely impossible for Kiln. Basically it looks like ...Well, on Earth we have delightful critters named sea spiders, which are mostly leg, to the extent that actual vital organs end up squeezed into those legs because the body's so small. And the legs are very long, with lots of hooks and things at the end. They exist to punish arachnophobes who thought that diving into the deep ocean would keep them safe from regular spiders, and look like the nightmare distillation of all the things people hate about them. But at least they do only live in the deep sea and, being there, they don't skitter about like monkeys in the throes of a *grand mal* seizure. Oh, and sea spiders have the decency to be bilaterally symmetrical and relatively flat. This thing is very big on being in the third dimension. It has a body that's all long spines like a sea urchin, with a lot of legs projecting off from this at all angles, studded with thorns and hooks. There's no front or back, or visible sense organs. Or probably all of it hosts the little independent units that gather sensory info. It isn't interested in being stealthy, either. Just about the entire camp becomes aware of it at once due to the appalling mad rattle and thrash of its progress across the underside of the gantry. Every limb just bashes against the metal until it finds purchase, and then yanks the thing bodily in that direction. From that it should just go randomly round in little circles, but somehow this utterly directionless flailing results in the thing moving very swiftly along what certainly seems an intentional route. As though it's looking for something.

Everyone scatters. Those below, for whom this chaos-monkey-spider thing is right overhead, dive for the dubious safety of the Labour Block. They should only be grateful the thing doesn't follow them in there because, if it had, the only pertinent feature of the Block's architecture is the big front window, through which the guards could chortle at the Labour being diced by all those hooks and spikes. Live human flesh is not what it's looking for, however.

The guards are mobilizing by now, but that's not as dynamic as it sounds. Just like The Filth back home, they're all so terribly, terribly brave and good at standing up to actual danger. And so they all have to go armour themselves up, tell themselves how tough and strong they are, then work themselves into a proper mindset, maybe having a few cups of coffee and a sit-down before they feel up to the task. Anyway, Security basically just vanishes into the armoury, and for a good ten minutes this appalling thing is smashing about like an explosive sea mine possessed by lycanthropy and Saint Vitus's Dance. We of The Science and Dig Support cower in abject terror inside the tissue-thin walls of our prefab as it migrates from underfoot to the actual walkways themselves. For a moment it's just running riot, and I have a second to hope it'll pay a visit to the commandant to register some personal grievances on behalf of the planet, but of course his quarters are rather more solidly constructed. Then it's on our roof.

We have camera images of it, by then, captured from Security footage. Those great meat-hook terminations on its limbs are doubtless powerful enough to peel back the thin metal of our hiding place like foil, to reveal the trembling snacks within. It pounds about like thunder up there, prompting Croan to get out the ear defenders. Then it stops. For the first time its headlong progress becomes utter stillness, and we know it must be about to carve its way in and eat us. It's finally found what it was looking for, and that is the best scientific brains of Earth, boxed up and ready to serve.

It crouches above us—there are no cameras now, so we only have the treacherous little eyes of the mind with which to appreciate the full horror of it. We hear its hooks scrape as it shifts position slightly. I'm wishing it didn't have so many echinodermoid traits to its visual make-up, because starfish and their friends can do some spectacularly disgusting things to their prey, by everting their stomachs and all that fun stuff. Now I'm imagining the ceiling splitting open and the innards of this monster just oozing in through the hole to digest us all before swallowing, rather than doing it the civilized way round.

Instead, there's another noise. In the almost-silence I don't immediately place it. I'm not primed for it, though I've heard it many times before. And thanks to Primatt I was recently introduced to the source. It's the muted hooting of Ylse Rasmussen in her shed out back.

We hear the thing pick its way curiously over the roof—suddenly all that mad frenzy has gone out of it, but the deliberate tap-tap-tap is almost worse.

Rasmussen howls again—her mic's off so it sounds like she's up in the hills, far distant, the lone wolf of the Kilnish mountains crying for the company of the moon. And the thing answers.

I don't know how it makes the sound for sure—certainly not by using the human vocal folds that Rasmussen uses —but somehow it mimics her, maybe using the vibrating of its chitinous scales to eerily approximate her voice. Save that, of course, she was just making a nonsense hooting and so it's making nonsense back. We all flinch as the thing jumps. A sudden scrabbling sounds above us and then a boom as it lands on Rasmussen's roof instead. Then Security are finally there. The lieutenant and a bunch of her people, all fully armed and armoured up, having told themselves the requisite sagas of their courage. And what they do is march into our lab, grab me and Parrides Okostor, and haul us out.

Oh yes, the usual. We complain, protest, demand to know what's going on. In return we're given the gun butts to the shoulders and head, that persuasive answer Security uses to so many questions. But it becomes obvious what we're for. We were the closest expendables, what with everyone else sensibly hiding under the tables in the Labour Block. And Security, despite every technological advantage, want the thing to have some bait to focus on before they'll dare take it on.

And naturally we continue to dispute. We are not the expendables, we cry. We are fine scholastic minds filled with valuable insights. With the rather uncreditable implication that, look just a little further afield, there are more expendable minds out there for the discerning alien diner. Except we're up *here* and everyone more expendable than us, in the commandant's plan, is down *there*, and the guards can't be arsed to make the trip down the stairs.

So we go out, and there the thing is. I finally see it with

my actual human eyes. The appalling, crouching legginess of it, bristling, eclipsing the prefab prison cell it crouches on. Its limbs crook, high-kneed, around it. I have no sense of how far its reach might extend if it lashed them out straight. And inside, Rasmussen sings to it while it sways up there and sings back, matching her tone for tone. The horror is right there in me, but so is the science. I don't even protest any more when they shove me forwards, though Parrides does enough for both of us. We surely end up well within range of those ghastly legs, and the way it shifts its footing shows it's just as aware of that fact as we are. I'm only surprised the lieutenant isn't banging two pans together to call the thing to dinner.

They can't get a good shot at it, up on the roof, I understand. Or not good enough. The higher wall of The Science's block is in the way. They need the beastie to come down past the edge and down the wall, and then they can let fly at the son of a bitch.

I demand that they stand down.

I mean, they don't, obviously, but the sheer temerity of it actually gives the lieutenant pause. And into that pause I crowbar a great tirade of incensed-man-of-science-talking-to-brute-with-gun. Because we are witnessing something here. We are seeing a human and a thing from Kiln communicate. Maybe. If it isn't just some weird parroting adaptation that Rasmussen has unwittingly triggered in the thing. We are observing a unique interaction, never before witnessed. This is *science*! Expanding the boundaries of human knowledge and the raw bleeding edge of discovery!

My words are cut short when Parrides grabs me and bundles me to the ground, ending up with his considerable weight on top of me. Whether Security's plan would have worked in its original state is unknown, but with the added bonus of me shouting at the top of my voice, we've most definitely got the monster's attention. Its wave of hook-studded arms thrash the air just about where I was before Parrides grabbed me. And then the guns go off.

I'm absolutely sure they're going to shoot us through sheer wild enthusiasm, but it's not just a mass machine-gunning. Security make it hard for themselves. They go in at a weird angle and start taking potshots, carefully aimed, into the thing's body. It turns out that body is quite vulnerable to targeted force and on the ninth or tenth hit it cracks open, with most of the legs falling off. These thrash and writhe about, and Security move in to club them to death individually. It's at about this point I realize that the whole monstrous composite, when it was intact, was only about the size of a monkey or mid-range dog. In my mind it had been huge, even looking right at it. The hideous spindliness of it had fooled me into making it vast, sky-spanning, while it was in fact far smaller than I was. Whatever mysteries it brought now die with it, and Rasmussen's next expectant hoot goes unanswered.

I realize, as we lie there, that the weird care Security had taken when picking the thing off must have been because they didn't want, under any circumstances, a bullet hole going through the wall and making a channel between her and the outside world. The hermetic nature of Ylse Rasmussen's confinement must remain inviolate.

Once the killing is over, they decontaminate the upper gantries with a furious will, of course. Everyone still in the Science block ends up trapped there for two days while it's done. Parrides and I have a similar visitation on a personal level, with the usual bowel-disrupting side effects. We don't talk much during it. It's not exactly a congenial environment for a chat. I thank him, though. Sometimes you need someone to pull you out of the science of things before it kills you.

The other reason we don't talk is that, of course, there would be people listening. And at that moment both of our heads are full of some upcoming festivities we're looking forward to. Something intended to really shake up the way things are done around here. We've both just been deployed as live bait without a second thought, after all. It's just the sort of thing we need, to remind ourselves why we're about to do what we will.

It's hard to hold a proper revolutionary subcommittee meeting under surveillance. Yes, back home we worked out a range of subterfuge for passing on messages, but that limits the cut and thrust of enthusiastic debate which the movement was always built on. You need speeches and plans, complex things communicated eloquently. You can't do that with a handful of code words, touches and gestures. Plus, as the contents of the Labour Block arrived in shifts sometimes years apart, different classes of dissidents know different secret signs.

Clem hasn't let this dispirit him, though. He'd been a leading light in the fight back home, trying to prise the Mandate's fingers from the throat of the people, as he called it. In practical terms it meant that his brand of revolution was there to catch the others when they fell, give them their final marching orders when all other, less overt, ways of opposing the regime had failed.

The fight back home was always decentralized. There were legal types trying to loosen the bolts of the laws which held everything in. There were also scholarly fellows like yours truly pushing at the acceptable bounds of human knowledge where they so clearly conflicted with observed data. These genteel flags were waved languidly by the relatively privileged, who nonetheless got slapped down hard for it—as Ilmus, Parrides and I had all found. For an institution keen on its laws, the Mandate is not at all averse to destroying the law-abiding when they dissent. The next level down was the protest, the walk-out, the petition, the go-slow. Borderline illegality, often hard to prove; moments of group resistance relying on the size of the herd to protect them from the predatory police. And these, too, cracked and spilled their share of prisoners into the cells, as well as fugitives onto the streets. After all these were the hardline fighters, people like Clem.

Ilmus only ever got as far as stage one before they fell foul of the fragmentation barges. Parrides was definitely at stage two, low-level organizing and activism on the knife-edge of the permissible. By the time he was caught I had already been playing more dangerous games. I was Clem's man on the inside for years, sneaking him information and sympathizers, listening to the speakers he smuggled into the underground meets. Understanding that I had been placed in a position where I could either just play the Mandate's game, take my wage and close my eyes to the rest of it, or I could fight.

It might seem odd, that a mild-mannered academic like me was also an active worker against the Mandate. But you've got to care about truth, haven't you? I won't say that the speeches didn't move me, but it was the intellectual dishonesty of the whole orthodox thing that galled me into action. Science, as a creed, should care about truth. It shouldn't be bent for political aims. You shouldn't say there's a Wild Man of Kiln when there's clearly nothing of humanity about the place. And on such hills I die. That doubtless sounds stupid, to you who tell yourself you will take up arms when they starve your children, when they rob you of your goods, when they come for that demographic which includes you. But it's deviation from truth that lets them do these things. It's the lies, at all levels, which mean when they come for you and yours, the others won't lift a finger, because they've believed the lies spread about you. It is the lies that starve your children because you believe the stories about general shortages, even though the grandees of the Mandate feast off gold plates every day of the year. And it is lies about science which cut most deeply, telling you that this or that group of people are naturally inferior, or another group has an innate ability to lead. That there is sufficient genetic distinction to make the call, when in actuality we share the vast bulk of our inheritance with mushrooms. Or else that, because of this kinship with mushrooms, our leaders are justified in keeping us in the dark and feeding us shit.

So I went to war for the truth and joined those seeking to bring down the Mandate, and look where it got me. Top of the world.

In the end it's Clem's key people meeting in that crappy little space alongside the reclamation plant, crammed in shoulder to shoulder and speaking in impassioned whispers. Someone has monkeyed with the audio sensors out in the main space, in case anyone ended up making a speech loud enough to actually hear. For the benefit of the video, and direct eyes through the transparent wall, we've mounded stuff up under blankets to make it look like we're still abed. High-tech chicanery it is not.

Clem's immediate second is a lean, small-framed woman named Armiette Graisle, another of my resistance contacts from back before, shipped out on the same barge as Clem. Ilmus Itrin and Parrides Okostor are both present, eyes flicking between me and Clem. High-value recruits, because Dig Support has privileged access to areas of the camp off limits to most. Croan is absent, a careful time-server who's never going to put her head over the battlements. A life on Kiln isn't much, but she's clawed out her little space as head of Dig Support and she's not going to jeopardize that for anybody. She's made it very clear that, as a scientist, she wishes to remain as ignorant as possible about everything going on. Also absent is my earliest Labour acquaintance, 1611 Keev of Excursions. I look for him. He seemed like a capable sort of man and everyone gives him a senior survivor's modicum of respect. He's been approached, I'm told, and rebuffed the recruiters in no uncertain terms. Kiln itself is quite enough for 1611 Keev without sparing brain-space for revolution.

Along with Parrides, Ilmus and Armiette, there are a handful of other organizers from the Labour, names skipped through in a blur. Then one real surprise, and Clem's secret weapon. I see a short, saggy man with a bald patch who I last saw playing tech monkey for Primatt at the dinner. He's immediately marked out by his uniform—no collar-bolted overalls for him. He's staff. He's Engineering, the one-man tech support who keeps The Science running. And he's one of ours, apparently. I'm told by Clem later that Mox Calwren's overworked role means he spends way more time down on the ground than up on the gantries. He's seen a lot of bad stuff, so he's sympathetic. I also reckon he's snubbed by most of the other staff and doesn't get invited to anybody's departmental lunches. Perhaps it's that which pushed him over the edge.

And me. There are a lot of suspicious eyes, then. I'm new, and suddenly I'm at Clem's plastic right hand. He gives a low introduction to my history as a dissident scholar and revolutionary activist. He expresses his faith in me. I hope I'm worthy of it. But he's right to. I never broke. If it was me who'd sold him, when the police finally kicked his door in and hauled him from his squat, it wouldn't just have been the barges. They sentenced him as a menial of the subcommittees, never knowing they'd caught one of the leaders. Although the impact on the revolution's efforts was about the same.

Clem's oratory wins over the strangers, but I sense a few cracks still, between me and my actual old friends. We've been cheek by jowl in the lab, getting on. But that just means certain topics are omitted from the conversation for politeness' sake. Parrides' eyes bore into me, and he's made it plain he hasn't ruled out my complicity in his arrest. Ilmus doesn't stare, because they don't do well with direct eye contact, but there are trailing threads of doubt from our earlier conversation that neither of us have been able to tie off. And though I know the authorities never broke me, I also know it was because they hadn't bent me that much and everyone I was involved with had already been behind bars. I can't claim to be a paragon beyond the possibility of doubt when there was just nobody left for me to name by the time I couldn't run any more.

Clem and his people have been working on a plan for a while, long before I came onto the scene. That's what I cling to. I turn up and slot in, providing them with extra hands up on the gantries right when they need it. While the subcommittee's nominal heads of department speak to us, I have to piece it all together from out-of-order snippets and veiled references, running to catch up because they're all ahead of me.

The plan, as I reconstruct it, is a good one. Calwren heads up the technical element. He's going to set some timed sabotage that will jam the door circuits when the bulk of the guards are in their dorm, putting them out of the fight for more than long enough so that everyone else can do their part and secure the compound. The Manpower element, most of Clem's hands-on supporters, will storm the gantries at three separate points under the direction of a solid, broken-nosed woman named Alaxi. Storm them with what, I wonder? With the guns they've put together over months by clandestine use of the various printers. It's a masterstroke of careful logistics. Each printer has limits on what it can turn out and none of them is going to quietly produce a lethal weapon without tripping a hundred telltales. A gun is just a series of mechanical components, though, each unobtrusive on its own. A weird artificial echo of the way life works on Kiln.

So yes, even before I arrived on the scene, the revolution had guns. Primitive weapons that will shake themselves to pieces after a few shots, but every guard they can take down will arm the revolution with something better.

Armiette was always a communications specialist, running messages for Clem from cell to cell. As Manpower fight for the gantries, her team is set to make a beeline for the orbital link to make sure the commandant doesn't sabotage it himself or send a message locking the ship up above. The vessel currently in orbit is uncrewed, patiently awaiting the day when Terolan and his fortunate fellows are allowed to go home. The codes to activate its systems are in the data I just smuggled to Clem, pirated by a brave Domestic who ended up in the example tank. He hadn't cracked, or they hadn't asked the right questions, and so he'd become a martyr, while here we are with the codes. If Armiette can get to the terminal.

Her task is to talk the ship's systems into sending down shuttles. I'm introduced to another couple of Clem's long-time allies who have the relevant aerospace skills to guide the ship to Earth, or at least our home solar system in general. I'm assured they can operate the suspension facilities aboard. The lap of luxury compared to the fragmentation barges. As many people as the ship can fit would be able to go home right then. I wonder if I'll be amongst them. I know Clem won't be. His work here won't be done.

The intention is for Clem to stay on with an armed crew, ready to take the next prize. For another ship will turn up from Earth with the next shift of guards and staff. So he'll take that, too, and send another shipment of desperados back towards Earth. But what will this succession of pirated transports do when they've reached their destinations? Clem is already outlining solar colonies where there might be revolutionary sympathizers, places to go that aren't just delivering people back into the hands of the authorities. Although by the time anybody arrives that kind of thinking will be decades out of date. We just have to hope there will be a safe port somewhere for a ship full of people returning from the extrasolar camps.

That's Clem's big rhetorical moment. I think he's using it to cover the utterly fucked maths of the situation. The return of convicts condemned to the camps will shake the Mandate, he says. Being sent to the exoplanets to slave out your days on an alien world is a threat that looms large in the heads of every sane dissident. Nobody returns from the camps. But when we come back, word will spread across the Mandate like wildfire. To Clem, the whole complex exercise is not an end in itself but the prelude to a greater revolution.

And yes, the maths. It is utterly borked. Not the engineering or comms side, or anything to do with taking over the camp, but the people logistics. The actual number of people coming in on the fragmentation barges vs our capacity to get people back out. We'll never empty the camp unless the Mandate falls and they stop sending people out here. And even then, we'll probably never manage it. There just won't ever be capacity in the ships and most of us will die out here, just like the Mandate planned. But it is resistance. It is fighting. It isn't just knuckling under until we die.

Clem fields questions, waterproofing the joints of the plan. It's good. Minimum exposure, playing on the ingrained routines of the camp. We know where the guards will be because they're creatures of habit. We have weapons and equipment. Everyone with appropriate skills has a role that makes use of them, plus an understudy if anything happens to them. Mox Calwren, Armiette and Alaxi, head of the Manpower team, all reel off their duties, the timings, the subordinates. I have sat in these meetings before. I've seen a fair number of attempts at revolutionary action, from graffiti to hacking, protest marches to full-on armed insurrection. This is good. It's precise and well thought through.

It all goes about the way you'd expect.

11.

On the chosen night we're all ready. Or at least, those of us in Clem's circle are, which comes to about a third of the Labour Block. And, because of the way things are, what with the panopticon of this space, we're ready in bed ardently feigning sleep. Those who aren't in on it, like Helena Croan, are presumably actually sleeping. If the guards do pay their screens more than a passing glance, they'll hopefully see no difference between these two vitally distinct traits. And maybe some of us fierce revolutionaries do actually end up falling asleep waiting for the off. Maybe, in fact, yours truly needs a kick from Parrides Okostor to remember what he's doing and where he is. It's very hard to lie in bed after dark in a prolonged state of acute readiness.

I am playing it for laughs, yes I am. I am laughing because otherwise I'd weep.

Clem has a little hand-built communicator—audio and a couple of telltale lights, no screen. Like the guns, it's been constructed out of innocuous pieces the Labour Block printer might be expected to spit out for routine maintenance tasks, plus a few components half-inched from the gantry level. Under the covers, like a naughty child playing games after curfew, he waits for Calwren's signal. We, those of us who haven't dropped off, wait for Clem's.

Clemmish Berudha, the revolution's truest son, the ablest man who ever helmed a subcommittee. I remember how he'd been back on Earth, that angry combination of impassioned rhetoric and practical action. They caught him, like they caught everyone, but they didn't break him before his deportation date came about. If they had done, then I'd have been on a far earlier barge than I was. I had another year safe in my professorship before the big academic crackdown came. The one that snatched up Ilmus and Parrides and sent me scurrying into the cracks and gutters until my own come-uppance caught up with me almost one further year later. Good old Clem.

Clem gets his signal. It tells him that, one, Calwren has control of the doors up on the gantry level and, two, the surveillance feeds from the Labour Block are looping old footage. Not something that would fool serious scrutiny, but Clem's people in Domestics assure us the guards are complacent and don't care.

He jumps dynamically out of bed, puts on his overalls and strikes a heroic pose. Or I imagine he does, in retrospect, after Okostor's wake-up call. The guns are unpacked and handed out. I'm not given one, but then I don't want one and wouldn't know what to do with it. It's not like firearms experience is common outside the security forces or particularly hard-line subcommittee veterans. Clem raises a plastic gun in his plastic fist. He has everyone's eyes.

There's no shout before we vault the barricades. No sizzling rhetoric. Just a hard flat injunction to follow your section heads and follow the plan. Don't fuck up, basically.

We separate into our various elements. Okostor and I are with Armiette, heading to take control of the comms and send our stolen codes to the ship above. Ilmus is with Manpower, looking to secure control of the gantries and make sure everyone stays locked down up there. Ilmus doesn't have a gun either. They look wan and frail and I'm desperately worried for them. They never had that eleven months of tough education on the run like I did. They're not a rugged revolutionary, and were never a physical presence. I want to be fighting alongside them, my oldest friend here but Clem isn't going to rejig his plan for my preferences. All I can do is catch Ilmus's eye and try to communicate some amount of luck and resolve to them, through that unspoken moment of connection.

There are plenty of people awake now who aren't part of the plan. Some of them want to join in, others just want to be told what's going on. The sharper ones spot the guns and clam up, and maybe just pretend to have been asleep all along.

Clem springs the Labour Block door. Once we're out then the line will have been crossed. Because we can fool all the cameras we want but there are plenty of actual windows looking out into the open space of the compound's centre, and the only cover on the way to the stairs is the sanitized and over-studied ruin at its heart. The clock that will run until we're spotted will have swift-moving hands and a loud alarm.

Armiette is last out and she locks the Labour Block down after her. We don't want people who aren't *our* people wandering around, causing trouble or tipping off any un-tipped authorities, either deliberately or accidentally. Best they all just keep to their beds and awaken to a glorious new tomorrow, with a change of regime and an injection of hope.

Hope! That's what Clem has taken from extrasolar deportation. It seems as insane as Kilnish biology. Hope, drawn from the necessity that the Mandate can only have a limited presence here. There are no instant reinforcements coming from the next star system over, after all. If we take the camp at Kiln, we can hold it for ever. Or until a barge full of troops turns up from Earth in half a century's time, and would the Mandate even devote the resources? Clem was sent to an alien world that chews up people without ever having evolved jaws or teeth, and somehow found a positive.

We spread out across the compound, flowing either side of the ruins, to which everyone gives a wide berth. Superstition? It's not like there's some cryptic alien that's somehow hidden in that ceramic-like tomb and evaded a decade of study. We are on a desperate course of action, though. I don't know if anyone amongst us believes in horse-shoes, four-leafed clovers or black cats, but even I, the arch-rationalist, have no wish to tempt fate. We head for the ladders first, and the big Manpower squad that's going to keep order goes to take control of the cargo lift. This is loud and so we want people up top before we activate it. Armiette's team, and Clem's, and one other take a ladder each and begin scaling.

Up above, Calwren has done his work, or at least he's told Clem he has. Which means the doors to the guards' quarters —their linked bunks, armoury and surveillance suite—should be sealed. Doubtless they'll be able to force their way out eventually, but eventually is a long time in revolutionary politics once the people are on the streets. For a given value of people and a given value of streets. The commandant is sealed in, too—in his bed or else working late at his desk. I choose to imagine the latter and, as it turns out, I'm exactly right.

All's quiet above and we hit the communications suite even

as Clem and the others move to get eyes and guns every-where. There's one man there, one of the guards, and he is the unluckiest son of a bitch out of the Kiln labour camp staff. I still think of him, honestly. I don't know who he was or whose wife he slept with, but he was absolutely not expecting any of this. We caught him with his hand down his waistband as he was watching some pirated porn someone had smuggled into the last data freight. Not just porn but an eyebrow-raisingly specific kink that makes me wonder whether he ended up on an alien world for entirely personal reasons. Subduing him therefore turns out to be easier than expected, and Armiette starts on the comms. We hear the first shouts outside, and we take it for Clem and his people clashing with the handful of idling sentries who got the graveyard shift on tonight's rota. It's not, in fact. What we're hearing is the first sign of everything going south, but we don't realize. Our Security man in the comms booth may have been caught with his pants down, but he's the only one.

One of Armiette's people reports that Manpower, Ilmus included, is in the lift and on their way up, now the alarm's been raised. One of the teams has control of the lifthead. Everything's going smoothly. That's a lie, but told in good faith. The mouse has its rodent incisors in the cheese, basi-cally, and is just wondering what this moving metal plate is under its feet.

Snap.

Suddenly there are guards coming in, even then. At first it looks like just a few, and probably most of us think they've been displaced by Clem—maybe they're coming to hole up in Comms, or maybe they even think they can call for help from here. The first couple, eager sods as they are, run into

Armiette's guns and back out hurriedly. There's perhaps 0.4 of a second when we're congratulating ourselves at being so good at revolutionizing. Then they storm in, mob-handed and leading with bulletproof riot shields, and we're fucked.

The guns go off. At least one of Armiette's people is holed by the ricochet, because whoever made those shields wasn't pissing about and the guns aren't exactly military grade. Then Armiette's gun manages a couple of seconds of sustained fire that puts them to the real test. It's as much of a hazard for everyone else as it is for the guards, but then the sheer kinetic force knocks one man off his feet and the bullets go straight into the unshielded man behind him, and it looks like we're in business. Armiette takes a riot round to the face, though, breaking her jaw, knocking her out, and our business enters a rapid closing-down sale. Parrides roars and launches himself forwards right into someone's reinforced knuckles. He goes down so fast it's almost funny, and they just step over him like he's a drunk on the street. Security moves in with truncheons first, boots as a follow-up. We're kettled in. I do my best and rush at the shields, grabbing the top of one, then just drop with all my weight, yanking the thing down. If I'd had a couple of hard lads at my back then they could have crowbarred the opening into something useful, but nobody's in place to follow up. The man whose shield I grabbed ends up lying on me, the shield between us, and me pressed into a splayed position like a cartoon bug who's been hit by a book. That's my contribution to the fight.

I'll hear snippets of the rest later, about what goes on outside. Ilmus will tell me that Alaxi's group, the big Manpower detachment, end up halfway to the gantry in the lift before the power is cut. Some of them try to climb but most of them are stranded. Clem and the others up top try to fight, but the guards were waiting, armed, ready and in force. More of them come in from *outside*, replete with their expensive protective gear that's so much better and less necessary than the crap they print for Excursions. And, from his desk, working late, the commandant watches it all.

Calwren did indeed secure the barracks, except the bulk of the guards hadn't been in bed. They'd been out and hiding, armed and armoured, with gas grenades and clubs and theoretically non-lethal guns.

Because someone told. They knew exactly what the plan was. Any actual success on our part, transient as it was, came because we were too eager and ended up in places—Comms, for example—ahead of schedule.

We had the numbers, even so. Even with the action limited to those selected people of Clem's. There were more of us than there were guards, but they went for anyone with a gun first and after that we had nothing. It wasn't as if the guns were any good anyway. At least one of them blew itself apart, I'm told, killing the woman using it and the person next to them too.

Knowing where we were going to be, they got in between us, and divided us. Yet we could still have won. I, Arton Daghdev, armchair general, really believe so. If we'd had battlefield discipline and better fallback plans and more cohesion. And if Clem, or someone, could have looked down on the camp from above, paused time like in one of those strategy games, then given instruction from that godlike position about how to react to these new circumstances. If, moreover, we'd all had the same iron drive as Clem, to throw ourselves into the teeth of the guards until our numbers overwhelmed them. The truly revolutionary unity of purpose that everyone speaks about in subcommittee meetings but nobody has on the streets. While the guards are welded together by the Mandate's single purpose to control, we are all individuals seeking individually to resist. And so we break under their hammer. We splinter into ever-smaller groups or else get crushed together in too small a space. They contain us and they break us. All Clem's planning is undone. Someone snitched, because someone always does. The Mandate knows a hundred ways to turn a person, a great arsenal of methods made up of equal parts carrot and stick. And to someone in the labour camps, deprived of everything, under threat from everything, the runtiest root vegetable or the feeblest twig will suffice.

Dawn comes to Kiln, that flat lemon-pale light. Even filtered through the dome it speaks eloquently of all the light years between us and home. An inimical sun, for all that it's a close cousin of our own as such things are reckoned. It finds us kneeling around the compound with wrists plastic-tied behind us, and a blow to the head for anyone who dares look up from the ground. I've taken two blows to ensure that Ilmus is there, and whole. Parrides too, with a crooked nose and a beauty of a bruise flowering about his eye. Armiette is in agony, her jaw untended. Clem they have separated, because of course they know who our leader is. They've taken his hand away, leaving him with his cut-down overalls and the puckered skin of his stump.

They'll come with sentences soon enough. Because this is the Mandate, they can't just waltz out and dispense casual brutality. All brutality must be judicially assigned in proper sessions. No less brutal but it comes at a bureaucratic remove that somehow lessens you as a person. On Kiln we're all half number anyway. So says 2275 Daghdev.

But I don't see this. Because, while it's not all about me, some small part of it nonetheless is. Apparently I've managed to get under the commandant's skin just enough. And so, before the mass handing-out of fates, the guards come and pick me up, then haul me off for something more bespoke.

12.

And so, on that same flat yellow morning, I am the guest of the commandant again. In less congenial circumstances. I'm not offered tea. I don't even get to sit down, though my standing up is as much due to the support of the guards flanking me as to my own efforts. I have a livid bruise on my temple and a splitting headache from my skull being caught between the riot shield and the hard plastic floor of the comms hut. I can't quite claim I properly went down fighting, but there had been fighting and I had gone down in its general vicinity. I have swung a punch in my time and suffered the sore knuckles to prove it. The year I spent on the run back home was not a punch-free experience. But while it's not the first scrap I've gotten myself into, it also isn't the first time someone has handed me my ass. Hence I'm not sure my hard-won brawling experience has been a particularly worthwhile acquisition.

Terolan settles himself behind his desk, pins me with his reptilian regard, then checks off some items of footling bureaucratic book-keeping on his screen. Before him, dispro-portionately hideous by association, is Clem's plastic hand and forearm. Eventually he notes me staring at it and looks up at me brightly. All very brisk, even acting a little surprised to see me still there. *Yes, Professor? Is there something I can do for you? Extra pillows for your bunk maybe? A better reading lamp over your prison bed?*

He smiles thinly. I never saw so thin a smile. You could open your wrists with it. "I gave you a chance," he says.

I stare at him. I admit to no chances given. He rolls his eyes and stands languorously. Striding up, he looks me over with his dead little eyes. Within arm's reach, if my arms weren't secured behind me. Possibly I could headbutt him, if I'd been really committed to the overthrow of the Mandate. But with the way my head feels, I don't quite have the zeal for it.

"Why do you think I asked you to dinner with the others?" Terolan purrs. "I knew you'd have been made part of whatever nonsense was going on by then. I'd left you enough time. That was your golden opportunity to pipe up, Professor Daghdev. To slip me a note over dessert. To tell me that something was going to happen, and thereby confirm your loyalty and preserve your privileges. You do understand that you have been very privileged here. The lofty position you secured, amongst your fellows, by virtue of your erudition." He really does sound a little hurt by my ingratitude.

"You mean Dig Support?" I get out.

"I mean Dig Support," he confirms. I must look incredulous. As though I want a dictionary right there and then so I can show him the definition of "lofty," and indeed "privilege," and how neither of them mention acting as a skivvy for a team of glorified undergraduates at this point in my academic career. He lets the point go. He knows he's right. I know he's right. I was handed a genuinely cushy position and I could have held onto it by doing nothing more than keeping my nose clean. Holding Primatt's test tubes while watching men like Keev and Clem go out into the alien world and sometimes come back. But what sort of a man would *I* be, if I did that?

I'd be one up on whoever the hell shopped us to the commandant, is what I would be. There are always lower depths.

"Doctor Croan failed, too. She said nothing," Terolan notes. "But then she was also not rounded up with you and the others. She was still in the Labour Block. Locked in, in fact." He waits, letting the pause roll out like a tongue to see if I'll step onto it. I know Croan wasn't in on it, which is why she didn't have anything to say at dinner. But if I mention that, then I'm maybe flagging her up as someone the dangerous revolutionary Arton Daghdev wants to protect, ergo damning her. Or else I'm confirming she's irrelevant, hence saving her. I don't know which, and Terolan's face is giving no clues.

Then the silence has stretched too long and the tongue is retracted. I don't know whether I've done the right thing by doing nothing.

"You're lucky," Terolan says. He sees the shift in expression I can't keep down and chuckles softly. "Oh, not because of your doctorates and diplomas. We're not so short on qualifications here that I *need* the searing heights of your insight. But you're new. Your part in this business can only have been limited. You're hardly a ringleader. You are merely a bookish man who couldn't keep to the straight path of academia, and who has allowed his resentment at his correction to boil over into foolish acts of rebellion here on Kiln. But it vexes me, Professor Daghdev. Because yesterday you were someone who had the chance to contribute to expanding the frontiers of human knowledge, and now you are just a waste of potential. So you will not be sentenced to death, as will some of those more instrumental to this uprising. But nor will I simply consign you to your fate with the bulk of your fellows. I feel your betrayal, Professor. I feel it personally."

And he does seem to. This isn't some sarcastic rhetoric from a cold and detached man. Terolan cares about the science within the narrow parameters that doctrine permits. I was, for a brief moment, within arm's reach of him. An assistant, an asset, a collaborator in the mockery that the Mandate calls "science." Or so he hoped. And now I have put the knife in by becoming a part of what Clem cooked up. I want to tell him that I was on the subcommittees long before I was on the fragmentation barges. I should throw down the gauntlet, demand to be put against the wall with my fellows. Say something dramatic and pithy that will ring in the confined spaces of his head for all eternity. Except my own head hurts and I feel sick with fear and failure, and we've lost. I just stare not quite at him, as if even directly meeting his gaze will set fire to my aching skull again. Terolan reads my mulish impotence correctly.

"You will be assigned to Excursions," he tells me. "But before that, I am going to give you an opportunity to study Kiln first-hand." I twitch, quite violently, in the grip of the guards —the man in the example tank appears before me. But that's not what Terolan means. It's something arguably worse.

"Do give my regards to Professor Rasmussen," he says sweetly. "I'm sure you and she will have much to talk about."

They march me out and along the gantry. Below, the compound is mostly clear. Sentences have been handed out and people hauled off to whatever fate the judicial discretion of the administration feels they've earned. And I am about to get what I, in my personal offending of the commandant, have earned.

In short order I find myself in with Rasmussen. Right there, in the shed up on the gantry level, with the madwoman and her daubs. I don't even have the publicity of the example tank but am hidden away. If I bang on the wall they'll hear me over in The Science. But my former comrades will hunch their shoulders and turn away, just as they would if it were Rasmussen herself hooting and ululating her mindless creed. They might not even guess that the venerable academic's prison has become a love nest for two.

I look up and see I have her interest. There's a mesh barrier between us and she prowls back and forth on the far side of it like a tiger. Then she clings to it, fingers hooking at the fine screen. It seems flimsy enough that she could just tear it down if she wanted to. She's a wasted old woman, gaunt and filthy in torn overalls. Labour Block chic, but flapping loose at the collar because she has no bolt to secure it to. A prisoner now, but of course she used to be staff. She was the original. If she had one of those steel pegs in her it would say 1 RASMUSSEN.

She puts her lips to the mesh and breathes through it. It's fine, but not fine enough to keep her out. Nothing to blunt the smell, or the contaminants. And though my nose is all about the smell, my cognitive centres are very much on the other things coming through.

I retreat in my head, because I cannot retreat in the room. I argue with the patent biological fact of her, insisting that it can't end this way. This is an alien world. It can't *infect* us.

Except Primatt already laid it out for me, the inexorable logic of it. The adaptability of Kilnish life, attacking all the lock-and-key systems of Earth biochemistry like a burglar with a set of picks. Twisting molecules into shape after shape, until something fits. The minuscule pioneers of Kiln remain alien —different structure, different heredity, the product of an evolutionary journey wholly *other*. All they need is that one tiny sliver of overlap in the circles of our mutual Venn diagram, though. That's all the leverage required to start interacting in malign ways with our cells, with our bodies, with our poor vulnerable human brains.

Is this the lesson of life across the universe? That it'll always find a way to get you? Telling myself that Kiln is a special case is a weird kind of balm, even though Kiln is where I am confined. I build the theories in my head to blot out the sounds Rasmussen is making. The biology of Kiln is so *obliging*. We thought we knew about organisms hitching a ride, back on Earth. Parasites have been a major driver of evolution and diversity, as hosts do their best to promote a hostile environment, and the infesters adapt in turn. On Earth, anything that's going to live off the fat of another critter slims down, becomes the bare minimum there is to be. They carve themselves a very specific niche and live their best, least life. One host species, or a cycle of very specific hosts—one worm to one fish, to one bird, to one mammal, which may in fact be us. And the wrong parasite ending up in the wrong host can be fatal for both, as the host still sickens but the little passenger can't get itself passed on. That was our understanding of the lifestyle—less the sweet-to-do-nothing flaneur and more the laser-focused knife-edge desperado with one marketable skill.

On Kiln, however, they voted against living with demarcation. The things which lived off others became *more* complex here—added hooks and limbs and faculties. They don't sneak in through the windows of hosts like burglars. They knock brightly on the door, like hyper-persuasive salespeople with a suitcase of toys and gimmicks. *Let me in and I'll offer you all these handy-dandy biological processes!* And if they can't form a semi-mutual relationship with this species then there'll be another one along in a second. It's madness all the way down. Even with the microscopic life, a fistful of molecular processes bound in a tiny articulated sheath, there are hosts which are really good at getting energy out of the system and turning into something usable, and then there are the beasties that attach to and leach off them, lending them senses, motor functions, defences and all the rest.

That's the biological multitool I'm up against here. That's what I'm breathing in, from Rasmussen's lungs to mine, no matter how much of this tiny box I put between us as my shoulder blades try to dig through the wall. Those bolt-on life companions act as a series of middlemen between the alien horror of Kiln and the safe home counties of Earth. A sequence of ever more convincing hats and false noses until what comes knocking at the doors of my cell membranes could almost pass for my cousin. Until it takes its face off to reveal the eldritch hideousness beneath.

So yes, I'm trying to use science to deal with the situation and stop myself spiralling into a hysterical panic, but I don't think it's working.

Rasmussen is in my body now. She crawls invisibly on my skin. She seethes in my lungs, the Kiln of her seeping through the boundaries of my alveoli. She rides the rush of my blood from lungs to heart, from heart through my body, as though she's an invading army using the local transport networks to get where it needs to. Just tiny quantities of her for now, skirmishing with my immune system and setting up its own revolutionary subcommittees in backwater parts of my body. Cordoning off ghettos where things are done differently. Burrowing down into the slums of my physiology and setting up seditious little schools to teach the naive young Earth-born cells different ways to live. And I, in this scenario, am the Mandate. I am the authoritarian state trying to impose my rigid will on the chaotic whole. *This is how it must be!* I know there are other ways, just like the Mandate knows there are other ways. And just as those other ways of governance would result in something that wasn't the Mandate any more, so these new metabolic pathways would result in something that wasn't *me*. Even as the haunted husk on the far side of the mesh is no longer Ylse Rasmussen in any real sense. The parasitic choir has sung seductive songs to her and swayed all her Earth-made parts from her control.

I watch Ylse Rasmussen as she decays. Her skin seethes with rashes, her mouth with words. She scrabbles at the mesh and hoots and shrills inhuman sounds, as though what's in her throat bears no relation to what's in mine. Over and over, insistent, varying as though she's trying to find the precise combination of nonsense sounds that will unlock my ears to her meaning. Until I eventually break and shriek back at her to stop, to stem the tide of her gibbering insanity, because I can feel it eroding my mind like the sea devouring a crumbling coast.

Then, "You hear me, Doctor? You understand?" Actual

words, Mandate standard, rise up inside her. Disinterred from the grave of her humanity, clad in rags and paraded out before me. "Cure yourself, Doctor, cure! I'm so alone!" And more. Desperate pleas for me to take up permanent residence as her maniac-in-chief. Impassioned demands that I hoot and holler and howl with her because *how happy we'd be!* I think of the case with the Earth parasite trapped in the wrong host, killing the creature it inhabits but unable to fulfil its function, a dead end that helps nobody. Poor lethal germ. If only the tick that carried it had bitten a rat rather than this huge useless human, then the microbe would be able to pass itself on properly and you wouldn't be dying of Lyme disease.

I try not to listen to her. I turn my face away so as not to breathe her in either. But every inch of me itches and I don't know if it's in my mind or if her parasites are on my skin, trying to unlock me.

I retreat inside my head to conjure the humanoid Kilnite that Primatt had trotted out for Terolan. I can solve the problem, I tell myself. Even with the hooting, noxious monster that is Rasmussen, I can find a way to square the biological circle. Then they'll have to let me out. Terolan will decontaminate me and reinstate me, all forgiven. I'll have what he needs and be the scientific hero of the extra-solar camps. And *is* the whole thing as stupid as I made it out to be? What, after all, does a sentient ruin-building alien look like? Strip it down to its essentials, based on our best understanding of how biology works. If I reject Primatt's faux-conclusions, what can I build in their place? A creature that has eyes, as we have eyes. Kilnish life has complex photoreceptive organs not all that different from the camera eyes that Earth vertebrates evolved, or that Earth cephalopods evolved entirely independently. And the *light* that falls on Kiln is fundamentally the same light that falls on Earth.

And they must have had hands, or at least some means of manipulating their environment, capable of both heavy lifting and fine detail and control. Tentacles, pincers, inflatable pseudopods. I've seen a lot of Kilnish creatures with grasping limbs, which are often an entirely independent symbiont that's latched on where it can be most useful. Creatures need to manipulate their environment, pull things, push things, grab things. So, fine. They must have some way of getting around, too, so maybe a molluscoid foot or else a serpentine writhing, or legs? All of these are to be found on Kiln. So why *not* two legs? Why not two arms. It's an Occam's Razor solution, after all. One leg is silly and one arm lacks anything to lever against. Three legs and arms requires additional resources. So obviously two of each is the most efficient solution, just like the Scientific Philanthropists say. I skate clean over all the examples where evolution doesn't home in on the most efficient way of doing things, just settles for *good enough* and builds on that. In the face of Rasmussen's intolerable closeness I become an absolute convert to scientific orthodoxy. Yes, obviously two arms, two legs. And why not a head at the top, where those eyes can get the best vantage point, then stick the mouth right underneath so it can see what it's eating. Well, a thousand reasons why not, but at the same time, *why not*? Crouching as far from Rasmussen as I can get, I try to picture a Kilnie in all scientific rigour and my abused imagination gives me Primatt's image and nothing else.

PART 2
ÉGALITÉ

13.

I'm practically ready to sign off on the Mandate's Wider Scientific Remit Consultation Paper by the time they pull me out of there. It's been not quite two days. If they'd left me for one more, I'd have been painting the walls with my own by-products, too. A community art project, and shouldn't I be honoured to work with someone as eminent in her field as Ylse Rasmussen? Because, by the close of my confinement, she's starting to make sense. Not her words, or her abhorrent scrawlings, but *her*. The language of her, that leaks out at every joint and from the inflamed skin around her eyes. She moves and it speaks to me, entirely distinct from her wordless caterwauling or the occasional coherent sentences that come, clipped into orphanhood, from her lips. The *It*-ness of her, that creeps in to become the *I*-ness of me. I'm pathetically grateful when they haul me out, not because it was intolerable in there but because it was becoming *tolerable*. There was a part of me that had acclimatized, or had *been* acclimatized. Had accreted little additional friends, in my brain or my gut or my lungs, that had begun their invasive work. I had become infected by her.

She'd actually quietened over the final few hours of our shared sojourn. My company seemed to soothe her. Now she is distraught again as I'm taken away.

I'm given the most thorough decontamination of my life. Or, no: the second-most thorough. The guards who come for me are in thick rubbery protective gear from head to foot, almost comedy caricatures of Mandate stormtroopers. They strip me naked and throw me in the airlock, then gas the crap out of me. Literally. I suffer explosive disembowelment via the rectum as just about my entire gut contents expire, Earth-type and alien both. I vomit and retch. They jet me with caustic, searing sprays until my skin is raw. And this, I understand even as I'm tortured by it, is mercy. I have not been condemned to die a lingering death. I have been rapped over the knuckles to a precise, judicial degree and now my sentence is commuted to hard labour, here in the labour camp. There's something fitting in that, after all.

The Kiln-ness is stripped from me before it can take root. Before I can sprout, run mad and die. Or else before I can run mad and *live*, boiling over with that fecund life as Rasmussen does.

Then they give me clean overalls—the *luxury*, I could weep —and march me out into the sight of the entire complement of the camp.

Oh, it's not some special privilege just for me, I am by no means the main event. I'm just jostled into the main bulk of the crowd. But I am *marked* now.

I understand, now, the double game the commandant is playing. Yes, he wanted to give me a proper little gut punch for his personal feelings of betrayal, but he's an efficient man. He can multitask. I've not been on public show, after all, in my durance up with Rasmussen. It was a private hell for two, voyeurs not invited. So nobody knows what I've been through. To them it all looks like special treatment. Again.

And we were most certainly sold out. Someone in that crowd of sullen malcontents is, as the vernacular runs, the narc what done it. So all those suspicious eyes instantly turn to me, the commandant's pet, brought onto the team by Clem just in time to learn all the details and then spill them. I try to find Ilmus in the mess but it's hard to scan so many faces who are looking daggers at you. You can go blind like that.

We're here, I see, for one more formal exercise of power. Because the commandant's had his fun with me but for some it's worse.

They've given Clem the full exposure treatment. He's been in the example tank these two days, invasively infected with a shot of Kilnish microbiota and left to stew. Something very different to the mere passive diffusion I was trying to hold my breath against. You shoot someone up with a cylinder of even random Earth microbes and it's not going to go well. With Kiln germs it's like Earth microbes with a doctorate in invasive fuckery, and the concoction has gone to work with a will. There's stuff growing on him, out the edges of his eyes and from under the fingernails of his one hand. I see his stump sprouting too. He hoots, hollers and roars, but this is muffled because his mouth is full of plate-like growths. From above, Rasmussen's faint voice keens back at him, a terrible and meaningless dialogue. Clem's eyes roll and he finds me in the crowd. His mouth twists like rubber, quite unlike a human thing, as he tries to push out some message. I try to communicate back to him that it wasn't me. I didn't sell him out. That's *my* priority, though. He has other things on his mind. In his mind.

The guards set up a filmy plastic corridor from the example

tank to an opaque chamber set into the struts at the foot of the gantry. I can see ducts leading up from it to a couple of points above, and I know there must be buried conduits connecting it to the Labour Block's reclamation plant. We don't waste much Earth-stock molecular mass here on Kiln, but what we can't reuse we have a very definitive fate for. Clem is hauled out by guards wearing the same heavy-duty gear as my earlier escort, clubbed unconscious before us and then dragged into that plastic-walled box. Then the guards come out and, in the fullness of time, so will Clem. But he'll appear as a fist-sized dense block, because that little chamber is the camp's incinerator and it's only a mercy they clubbed him into oblivion before they threw him into it. It's only a mercy the walls of the hut are opaque too, or else we'd have seen the alchemical transmutation of human flesh into ash, to be compacted into a brick and then buried.

So runneth the funeral rites of Kiln. Another reason for the name, I suppose.

Armiette and a handful of others are just shot, old-style, before the bodies are fed back into reclamation. They die clean, after all. Clean and Earthly, fit to return to the communal circle of life. *Communal*, my bastard mind says. Not *communicable*. I want to weep but the decontamination wrecked my tear ducts.

And my mind, off the leash and desperate to haul me away from the horrors I'm seeing, wants to know why they don't *all* get the infectious treatment? Slam them all in the tank, shoot each one up with a different cocktail and watch them cross-infect each other. For science! Of all the damn things in this grotesque world, my mind hooks onto *that* as the crack in the logic of the Mandate's argument. The shooting is a form of mercy. If Terolan wants to make a point to dissuade further attempts at insurrection, he has a powerful tool available. Ancient empires lined the roads with their crucifixions, after all. It wasn't just the one. But Terolan has rationed himself, as though the Mandate gave him a cruelty quota and they'll dock his wages if he exceeds it. One body at a time in the tank. One, plus Rasmussen in her high castle, calling each to each. The bizarre leniency of it sticks in my mind like a burr, like something the decontamination couldn't remove.

After the last echo of the shots has died away, they give over the disposal of the remains to us, the co-conspirators. I am put to hauling Armiette's corpse, taking her arms even as Parrides Okostor takes her legs. He stares at me past his broken nose, as though he's trying to accomplish by spontaneous combustion what the incinerator did to Clem. Any spontaneous denials on my part would have the inappropriate feel of theatricality, the pantomime of *he's behind you!* And maybe it was him, anyway. It was *someone*. It always is. Anybody could have given us away. Clem's rebellion went the way of absolutely every other uprising I've ever read about, or been a peripheral part of. Someone talks, and then the crunch comes and everyone scatters in their own distinct direction. And we lose. The Mandate wants us to believe we can't fight its authority and, though I don't believe that, I admit it has all the material evidence on its side.

They glare at me, my comrades, all of them. They accuse me silently. I elide each stare but mark each face, knowing that one of them, more than one perhaps, protests too much. My mind works like a fever and I try to pick out who did it. A hopeless task, though. The only people I can cross off the list are being loaded into reclamation or spat out of the incinerator right now. And even then, it's not beyond the Mandate to muddy the waters by executing their own informant.

Calwren, I think. Mox Calwren, Clem's own man on the inside, the engineer. I don't see him here. He's not been busted down to Labour. But probably he *is* too valuable just to kick into the teeth of the planet. Not that it even has teeth. The raptorial arms, then; the syphoning proboscis. And it almost seems too obvious that it would be Calwren. Surely Clem was certain of this dubious man before trusting him with any weight. Was the turncoat a turncoat all along? Clem must have had better judgement than that.

After everything—the incineration, the shootings and the bodies going back to the mulch—it's me, and it's them, the air reeking of our mutual suspicions. The guards are watching, and right then that's probably the only thing stopping me from being lynched on general probabilities. I want to tell them about the two days at Chez Rasmussen but who's going to listen and who'd believe? People start to move away, aimless at first but a few shouts from the gantry apply the spur. It's a labour camp, not a loiter camp. And I realize I don't actually know where I fit now. I'm off Dig Support, I can reasonably assume. The commandant mentioned Excursions, but while everyone was being given their new marching orders, I ended up having shit flung at me by a madwoman.

A heavy hand lands on my shoulder that's still tender from the beating I got. One of them, anyway. Either from being pressed like an olive beneath the riot shield, or when they manhandled me to the commandant, or from him to Rasmussen, or when they yanked me out of there in their heavy gear, or finally dragged me from decontamination. I got a punch, or a slap, or a kick at every stage, the punctuation to my custodial sentence. The bruises clasp together to form their own composite organism of aches and pains. I turn, flinching, to see who it's going to be.

It's Keev, from Excursions. He looks on me without love, and I try to say that it wasn't me, I'm not the traitor, but the words jumble in my mouth until they're just froth. Behind him the reclaimer chunters happily to itself as it deconstitutes Armiette Graisle and the rest.

But Keev wasn't on the subcommittees and has nothing to do with the revolution. Fighting for better futures isn't his style; he's all about the present. Keev is a man who intends to survive Kiln even though nobody survives Kiln, and most particularly not anyone assigned to Excursions. I realize the utter lack of love in Keev's face is nothing to do with any high political ideology, loyalties, betrayals. It's because I'm a troublemaker sent to make his life more difficult. One of several such troublemakers, in fact.

They couldn't exactly send every insurgent to Excursions. They just don't need that many Excursionistas. As Keev assembles his work crew, and his peers do likewise, I work out that some kind of sorting has gone on, possibly just randomly. A bunch of us have been shunted onto Excursions while the rest ended up at the bottom of the heap in General Labour. The split seems arbitrary. Ilmus is here with me on Keev's team, though I know they were the most peripheral of revolutionaries. Parrides Okostor is on another Excursion detail, but Alaxi, who led Manpower halfway up the cargo lift and no further, is just cleaning privies in the camp. There is, I suppose, a limit to the amount of time even a man like Terolan will spend on making the punishment fit the crime. Only I merited a special touch, and that because I was his new golden boy fresh off the fragmentation barges and theoretically untouched by the grime of insurrection, so my betrayal was so much the keener.

So all of the Excursion crews have received an influx of post-insurrection new recruits. Enough, in fact, that a quantity of Excursionista veterans have been moved *off* the camp's least wanted assignment to something safer to balance the numbers. We actually did some good for someone, in an elliptical sort of way. Hooray for the revolution. If I had a little flag, I'd wave it in Keev's sour face, and then he'd rightly shove it up my ass.

There's little attempt at introduction. Those people I don't already know, I'll have to find labels for on the job, or sneak a look at the little stamped characters on their bolts. Some of them I'm familiar with already, of course. My comrades in arms from our doomed uprising stare at me with that same open hostility—*Was it you?*—and already more than half are convinced of the answer. Croan isn't amongst us. I spot her heading up the ladder, and see my silence apparently helped her more than my actual help would have done. She's still head of Dig Support, though her team has been slashed to ribbons. I'm wretchedly glad I didn't manage to screw things up for her.

Keev looks us over. His regulars, the people he's been left with, cluster behind him, staring at we failed revolutionaries with utter loathing. I think I understand it, then. Keev is sent out to dangerous places to do difficult jobs. He had a team of people he'd whipped into shape to give him the best chance of coming back with most of them intact. Now that team's been gutted and we clueless bumble-bodies have been dumped on him. We're inevitably going to make mistakes and, out in the wilds of Kiln, mistakes get you killed. That's what I read into his look, and I'm absolutely right in all respects, but I'm also wrong. I've not fully factored in the commandant's malignity, and there's one whole extra reason why Keev and his people have cause to hate us. I'll find out very shortly.

"Get inside," Keev says shortly. "I'm not shouting." As though even straining his voice might be the final straw that comes back to screw him over out there. He turns without another word, stomping into the Labour Block. His people shamble after him and then the fresh meat is shuffling in their footprints, cowed and beaten, bruised and grieving. I suddenly can't bear it any more, the utter isolation. I feel so cut off and lonely I could start howling like Rasmussen did when they took me away from her, desperate for connection.

I snag Ilmus's arm. I think they're going to slap me, but I hold on. Pinning them there, even though the guards might stride over to add another dose of brutality to the heavy regimen I've been on since that night.

"I didn't sell Clem," I manage to say. Scanning their face for any sign of what they might believe.

Ilmus Itrin's face is blank, as though they've retreated so deep inside themself that nothing they think can raise a ripple on the surface. Their arm, under my fingers, feels cold and limp. Stringy with bad nutrition, unresisting, unwelcoming. Dead.

"I wouldn't. But someone did. They segregated me to

scapegoat me. Ilmus, please." Words peter out against their stony facade. I become aware of movement. It's just us two left behind and the guards have noted it. I'm always causing more trouble for other people.

A twitch runs through Ilmus, like an electric charge. Their face jerks, spasming out of their control. For a moment I think I'm forgiven, or else they've made up their mind I'm guilty and we're just going to have it out right here like a divorcing couple, or a pair of ineffectual pugilists. But then they pull away, twisting from my grip and ducking into the Labour Block. They look back, though. There's still some thread of connection left, from all our long association back home. And so I have no closure, neither good nor bad. The guards put me in their shadow, so I hurry after Ilmus before they can punctuate me any more.

Keev stares at me flatly as I arrive. "Honoured you could join us, Professor," he says. In being last in, I've given myself one more reason to be singled out, but right then who's counting? I just hunch and look down, correctly judging that now is not the moment for some scintillating academic repartee. Keev squares his shoulders like a man before the firing squad, opens his mouth, and then the guards come in.

It's quite the rollercoaster of emotions for me just then. Abject fear, because they were supposed to just shoo me in at the door, but here they are and surely they've come to hit me again. Either of their own notion or because Doctor Commandant Terolan has prescribed three beatings daily until morale improves. And then hope springs. Yes, actual hope. Because there, flanked by that escort, is Nimell Primatt, joint head of The Science. I understand, in a sudden blessed flash of euphoria. I am forgiven. I am reinstated on Dig

Support. My unique scientific insights are in high demand. It was all a cruel hazing on the part of the commandant. They weren't ever just going to throw me away like trash.

The guards march Primatt in and deposit her amongst us. Then they turn on their heels and march out. Yes, she and I are on a more equal footing once again, but it's not that I'm raised up. It's just I've managed to drag someone else down with me.

14.

Nobody knows what to do with her at first. And I'm being a slow student right then. I don't clock why she's there, even though it should be spectacularly obvious to me. Nimell Primatt, left there by the guards as though she's driftwood and they were the tide. Standing lopsided, not looking at anyone, one hand clutching at the elbow of the opposite arm, the other gnarled around the head of her stick. Keev just waits, expecting instructions, some special turd of a project from The Science deposited on his poor Excursions crew. But Primatt continues to stand there. The silence lengthens like a piece of stretched plastic film, deforming and thinning until, inevitably, it parts. It finally becomes clear to Keev, and all of us, that the commandant has breached that inalienable class boundary, here on this alien world. He's plucked Primatt from her post up above on the gantry and hurled her down in flames to the dirt below.

Keev's eyes flick, from Primatt here with us, then through the transparent wall to the departing guards, to the upper reaches of the gantry, where the commandant has his lair. He moistens his lips. I half expect him to tug his forelock, produce a cap from somewhere so he can doff it, or wring it in his hands. The working man confronted by the mill owner's daughter.

"Right, then," he says.

By now this corner of the Labour Block has separated out into three groups. Keev is backed by ten people—those in his team luckless enough not to have been reassigned to less murderous duties after the influx of failed revolutionaries. They stare at us like gorgons, hating us to a degree that seems entirely out of proportion to the additional catching up they're going to have to help us through. Because, as I've noted, that's not the real problem, as Keev will shortly explain.

I am one of a quintet of failed revolutionaries sentenced to Excurse with the Excursionistas of Keev's crew. Similar reassignees will be going through the same rough induction elsewhere—one group at the far end of the Labour Block even now, in fact, where I glimpse Parrides amongst them —but it's we five who are Keev's problem. And there's also Primatt, of course, who's beyond all the pale there is, utterly friendless and alone.

Keev slams a palm down on the nearest table, cleared of the breakfast I never had, repurposed from being the bed I didn't get to sleep on. The modular and pragmatic life of the Labour Block.

"You all listen up," says Keev. 1611 Vertegio Keev, grey, broad and with what humour he ever possessed pressed and steamed out of him by years of surviving. Back at the start when he accosted me here, I read him as a senior factory foreman type, the sort who gets the job done but mostly thinks about retirement, save that Keev won't ever be given the chance to retire. The only thing years of good service will bring him is closer to death, his ability to roll with the planet's blows eroded day by day. His personal name, which sounds as though it should belong to an ageing pimp or theatrical impresario, is something I only find out later. It made me wonder what his story was, because he had to have done *something* to be sent out here, after all. But in the camp he isn't any kind of dissident, theoretical or practical, and I realize I'm not sure just what precise brand of wrongdoing suffices to get you assigned to the barges. I try to reappraise Keev now, consign him to some particular bin of criminality. Was he violent, fraudulent, larcenous, arsonous?

It doesn't matter, of course. What he is now is my new boss, and he's having none of any nonsense we're peddling. With his regular crew at his back he faces us down, we revolutionaries who hadn't turned enough of a full revolution to end up facing the firing squad. We shuffle, jostle and scowl right back at him. In that moment, despite whatever suspicions they might have, I'm right there with Ilmus and the others, dragged into them by the gravitational pull of Keev's disdain.

"You don't realize," Keev tells us all, "how you've fucked us over. Us and all the other Excursion crews."

I am absolutely keeping my mouth shut. Nobody wants to hear the wit and wisdom of Arton Daghdev right then. One of my compatriots hasn't read the room, though, a man called Booth, and I vaguely recall him from the Subcommittee. One of Clem's technical team, and maybe it's that illusion of being valuable and skilled that gives him the confidence to speak now.

"I'd have thought you'd be glad of us," he spits in Keev's face. "Misery loves company, right? So we're dragged down to your level, so much the worse for us. How's it any worse for you?"

Keev nods philosophically, actually smiles a little, a man conceding a good and valuable contribution to the discussion. He hits Booth in the face midway through the nod-and-smile, jarring as a song starting on the off-beat. Then they're all on us, lamping anyone who stands still for it. Five of us, eleven of them. Booth gets by far the worst of it, a solid and sustained kicking. The two of my fellows whose knee-jerk reaction is to go to his assistance cop most of the rest, knocked down or rammed face-first into the flat of a table. I'm given a solid sock in the ribs that, through some unerring desire for appreciative company, manages to locate a whole set of bruises from my last beating. I just defend myself after that, taking it on the shoulders, the forearms, shielding my face, gut and groin as best I can. Going on the run and then getting caught gains you plenty of experience in what to do when you're in no position to fight back. Valuable skills. If I'm ever reinstated, I'll teach a class in them.

Keev's people aren't interested in actually bludgeoning us down, just in slapping some frustration out of their systems. Then suddenly Primatt's on the ground with a high, shocked cry. She'd been standing against the wall of the Labour Block, staring into space like she'd gone catatonic, the odour of gantry-level inviolability still just about clinging to her. Except someone took a run up a bit enthusiastically and clipped her, and she went straight over. Ending up on her hands and one knee, a leg stuck out at a painful-looking angle. The false leg, of course, except the strained bit with the angle is a real stump. I twitch, wanting to go and help her up, but I don't. I am already standing under a great big arrow with "collaborator" on it in lit-up letters. I consciously decide not to add to it. It's not a moment I'm proud of, as

I watch Primatt awkwardly haul herself upwards. I also notice Keev assessing the leg and fully realizing he's been saddled with one more complication to screw him over when his team is in the field.

The interruption has served to end the impromptu beating, anyway. We separate out into our groups again. Keev's crew, we newcomers, Primatt. The guards who'd paused to spectate and kibitz through the transparent wall lose interest and move on.

"You *fuckers*," Keev shouts at us. "They *reset* our gas chamber clock." He glares. We look collectively blank, because we haven't been on Excursions before and don't know the knife-edge economy they operate on. "To punish *you*," Keev explains, more controlled now. "You've maybe killed some of us, you fucking *Jonahs*. So any one of you who so much as opens your mouth about the Glorious Necessity of Resistance, or the Cause, or any such fucking thing, is going to get left behind in the outback."

It's that phrase which lets me place and date him. *Glorious Necessity of Resistance*. I re-evaluate Vertegio Keev all over again. When I was a kid and my stepdad brought me to my first subcommittee meeting, that was the buzzword phrase du jour. I realize that Keev must have been at least peripherally of the Cause himself, once, and that that *once* was a long time ago. I wonder what he'd done, where they'd had him before they shipped him out here. What struggles and defeats have fallen into the spaces behind that hard, flat face. A disillusioned revolutionary is a dangerous thing. Like a cache of yesteryear's explosives that might never go off or could explode all on its own.

I don't quite understand what he means. Gas chambers,

clocks, this specific way we have crapped on his life from a height. It's obviously an Excursion thing, meaning it'll be our problem soon enough. But right then, nobody on their side is explaining and nobody on our side wants to risk a punch in the face by posing the question.

Something goes out of Keev as he stands here. It's his anger. If he'd been a man to hold it in, nurse grudges from embers to open flames, then he'd have been dead long before. The rage fills him up and then leaks out at the seams until it's just a weathered, sour man standing there, determined above all things to survive. From the point of view of the intellectual revolutionary in me, surely that's not enough. He's been sent somewhere that always kills you eventually, so what sort of victory is surviving just one more day at a time? Except I, the intellectual, have also been sent here and I, too, want to live. Yesterday I wanted to overthrow the commandant, and liberate the people, and get on a ship to go home. Today I'll settle for living until tomorrow, and tomorrow can look after itself. I find myself converting very rapidly to Vertegio Keev's philosophy.

"Right, then," Keev says. "Get them suited up. We're breaking ground on a new site."

There's not even a groan from his people. It's just the usual for them. Except they have to teach it to us.

Attached to the compound, through some big sliding doors, is the flier dock. This is actually where the guards came in from when they broke apart our insurrection. The guards who were supposed to have been locked in their barracks. It also houses the fliers that Excursions uses, because the vanished Kilnies didn't set up all their ruins within convenient walking distance of where the labour camp was going to be.

We are given our suits that will stand between us and the hostile territory of Kiln for the duration of our field trip. They are to protective gear what the fragmentation barges are to spaceships. Paper outers. Cheaply printed hoods fitted with masks and filters. Keev's people grudgingly show us how to put them on and engage the headgear systems. Then they tell us not to do it yet because the gear has a definite lifespan and we'll need it on the ground when we're actually being exposed. Exposed to what? To everything that is Kiln. That fantastically opportunistic biosphere that says, "Give me your tired, your poor, your huddled masses yearning to breathe free, and I shall find a way to infiltrate their biology and make them my own."

The flier, at least, is intended to make multiple journeys, but it's still made up of slipshod printed parts, a ship replaced piece by piece until even Theseus wouldn't recognize it. I can spot the points where this design, or perhaps this individual craft, is running into trouble. The ill-fitting components with seams, mould lines and sprue stubs discoloured and standing proud of their sockets. None of it gives me any confidence in the engineering. I want the whole thing sent back to the factory and the designer shot. But I'm standing in the factory, and the designer doubtless had a nice comfy office back on Earth until they retired some decades ago, safe in the knowledge they'd never have to travel in one of their godawful creations.

The machine has a rotary skirt covered with mesh screens that look like they're aching to be caught in it. On top is a depression like a covered bucket seat, and there's a long tail for what might laughably be called stability. The whole thing looks like a cross between a dragonfly and an upside-down helicopter.

Once we're up in the air it makes a sound like screaming children and our suits have no ear protection worth speaking of, or rather worth shouting over. The precise pitch of the shrieking tells us more about density gradients in Kilnish aerial plankton than any number of statistical analyses, as thousands of tiny lives are sucked into the rotors and chopped apart.

Keev, piloting, has the sole seat moulded into the frame. The rest of us go in the bucket, jumbled together with our gear. If we crash, or even hit serious turbulence, we're going to leave a trail of displaced Excursionistas all the way back to the labour camp. I sit crammed between Booth and Primatt. Booth is feeling at loose teeth, one eye already swollen half-shut My own handful of new bruises are no more than garnish on the rest of me. Primatt, by comparison, is fine, unblemished. Except she's not. She escaped being beaten on but she's a hell of a long way from fine. She hasn't said a word or acknowledged another human being since the guards brought her in, obviously still in shock at how mightily she's fallen.

Keev's people haven't exactly been forthcoming with the introductions and it's socially awkward to peer intently at the tiny letters on someone's collarbone bolt. I take stock of the people I *do* know, my collaborators, and who might therefore be classified as potential allies. Even though every one of them started the day suspicious as hell about my involvement in the failed coup, Keev's beat-down served to put us all on the same side. My square peg got well and truly rammed into the round hole we're all stuck in. So we have the punchy, and now punched, Booth, and we have Ilmus Itrin, formerly of Dig Support. There's a heavy man with a scarred face named Shoer and a small-framed woman called Frith, both from General Labour and both of Clem's revolutionary subcommittee. Then of course there's Primatt, former aristocrat and not in any way affiliated with the subcommittee or its doomed activities. I tell myself I don't know why she's here. But I do. I'm just refusing to acknowledge it because I've got quite enough burdening me right now. Clem's death, and Armiette's and the others', are still a raw wound in my head. The shadow the commandant has contrived to cast over my good name, such as it ever was. The fact that I'm now on this deathtrap of a flying machine heading out of the camp's dubious safety and into the very definite danger of Kiln's hinterland. In the scheme of things, Primatt's presence and my responsibility for it is something I am just not able to acknowledge right now.

And in any event, the horrible torment-sound of the rotor below us makes saying anything to anyone a trying endeavour. Primatt doesn't seem ready to talk anyway. She won't even look at me. Instead, Ilmus shunts their way in between me and Booth, and even that makes the flier wobble alarmingly. Ilmus had taken a fist to the gut and went down very quickly when things kicked off between us and Keev's people. If you can call such a one-sided kicking "kicking off." Going down straight away is, in my experience, a risky stratagem. If it's only a bit of high spirits, then you've shown them your belly and maybe they'll leave you alone. If it's a fracas or, lord help us, a real fight, then you get trampled. Ilmus had made the right call, though. Keev and his

Excursionistas had just wanted us to know how far down the pile we stood.

Ilmus shoves their mouth right into my ear, breath hot on the side of my face like they're auditioning to be my next lover, now things have soured between me and Primatt. Not that my brief encounter with her could ever really be classed as romantic. Their hand is abruptly clenched tight around the collar of my overalls, a grip carefully positioned to be hidden to just about everyone else. The flier jolts as Keev alters course and for a moment the sky outside is shadowed by a kind of whirling brown smog. The flier's hood is far from hermetic. Just filmy plastic over a couple of struts. Supposed to be secured about the edges, but the fastenings have already gone in three places. We're all breathing Kiln air. I could bore you about the airborne microfauna and the things that eat them. Keev has a satellite map showing the densest swarms and his job is mostly circumnavigating them to avoid the thick concentrations that would clog the rotors and bring us right down. He's keeping to the higher air, because there's a whole band closer to the ground where it's like soup. I now have a good look at those thronging regions below, because we're flying at a tilt and Ilmus has me right up against the edge, all friendly looking to the outside eye but I can feel their muscles bunched in preparation. They're going to try and throw me out, and give me a high-speed introduction to those busy lower air strata. Kiln kills everyone eventually, but it kills you a lot quicker if you impact into it at terminal velocity.

"It wasn't," I hiss. They can't hear me so I try to print the words on my face, but a lifetime of guarded expressions works against me.

"Tell me," they hiss in my ear. "You sold us, sold us out." They'd been here a year longer than me. More than enough time to become fully attached to all the people the commandant had executed today—not just the horror of their deaths to deal with but the absence of their lives. I'm a tourist by comparison. I wanted this conversation before but I don't now, over the noise of the rotors. I glower at them, dare them, ready myself to grab them right back if any hoisting is imminent. They don't quite have the courage of their convictions in the end. I want to tell them to go quiz Croan when we get back, ask about the dinner and my lack of out-selling despite that ideal opportunity. I also want to say that whoever was keeping Terolan informed must have been deeper in Clem's confidence than I ever was, part of the plan for far longer than I'd had the chance to be. Ilmus bares teeth at me in a vicious snarl, fighting themself more than me. The tears in their eyes could be anything. I just stare. I have no words I am willing to bellow over the noise, no secret wink or handshake to establish my innocence. I just have this face, that Ilmus knew for years before being sent out here ahead of me. I absolutely might have sold them out then. I might have sold everyone out now. But I didn't.

I see them tilt and balance their position about what they can live with, even as Keev does the same with the flier to get it back on the level. I know Ilmus. They never liked navigating shades of closeness. They were your friend or they weren't, no hearty backslapping and then bitching behind your back. So they have a choice to make, concerning me, with no right answer. I watch their face fight itself over me, knowing that if I'm a treacherous son of a bitch, then trusting me will just leave them open for the next gut punch.

I clasp their hand where it clenches on my overalls, and watch them crumble. Watch them visibly shake their suspicions free and decide they're my friend still. Unless it's all a masterful act. Unless it was actually Ilmus all along. I don't want to think like that but my mind's like a corkscrew sometimes and has room for all manner of clashing suppositions within it.

Soon after that, we start descending.

15.

We fall in juddering stages through the air, breaking through those denser strata in the lower atmosphere. Bands of micro-organisms drift in the exhalations of the forest like horizontal blankets of faint black smoke, along with the creatures that eat them and quarter the busy air like gnats with sieves and blankets. Or else they wallow through the aerial soup, vast as whales made from plastic bags and cellophane. If the flier hits one of *those* then, as they say, we'll have a technical problem. The Kilnie airwhale will have a problem too, because it might be a collective of cooperating parts but it won't enjoy being shredded through our rotor skirt. Neither will the skirt. "Losses all round" is probably the motto of humanity's contact with extrasolar life. And more than likely the motto of my life going forwards.

This is going to be gruelling, uncomfortable and dangerous. I may well not survive. And yet there is a thread of excitement in me, old as I am. These aren't exactly the circumstances I'd have chosen in which to stand out in the alien wilds and actually *see* the objects of my study in their natural environment, but it's the best offer I'm going to get. I'll take it. Except I glance at Primatt then, who presumably also did this at some point before, and who donated a limb to the cause. She does not seem consumed with scientific excitement, unless it looks a hell of a lot like misery.

Keev's veteran Excursionistas are hooding up, fitting their filter masks and checking each other's work. We newbies follow suit, as it were, fumbling at the fastenings. Booth, beside me, manages to tear his paper suit as he tries to seal it all up, and weeps with frustration as the shoddily printed material just parts along invisible seams. I do my best to help him but likely only make matters worse. The veterans watch us impassively. Someone probably just won a sweepstake.

I've done the maths, by the way. The camps have been in operation around seventy years on Kiln. I am 2275 Daghdev and there are around three hundred of us in the Labour Block. So seventy years and two thousand dead. That's three-quarters of a dead labourer a week. And I think to myself, that feels like a finely calibrated number. It's enough death to serve as a rod to keep people down. But it's not so much death that people lose all hope, shading into that dangerous territory where they might as well charge the guns because they've got nothing to lose. And while some deaths are internal and disciplinary, you can absolutely bet the majority of them are from Excursions. In fact, the weeks when no deaths occurred are likely when the crews weren't out breaking ground on new sites. And you can bet those that have occurred didn't just tick steadily along like a clock, but went from spans of silence to the machine-gun staccato of a Geiger counter suddenly discovering uranium. Because when Kiln wants to get its teeth in, it has a real wide mouth.

But right now it's Booth's problem. We use sealant and patches to repair his torn suit. A woman called Greely, who seems to be Keev's lieutenant, steps in at last to show us how. Her expression doesn't suggest she has confidence in the repair measures, though, or in us. And surely, you're thinking, we should turn around and go home. His suit's already compromised no matter how much duct tape and sticking plasters are applied. Except these suits just plain aren't that kind of hermetic, as I hope I've made clear. It's not about maintaining the unbroken sanctity of our human bodies; it's about acceptable levels of contact, slowing the assault just about enough. Acceptable Wastage.

Keev jockeys the flier about as we go through this rigmarole, then ends up holding us steady-ish in the air.

"Greely," he spits over his shoulder. "Pick a team for the throwers. Clear us some space."

Greely makes an internal calculation—how much efficiency does she want to lose now by including the newbies, in the hope that we toughen up and prove useful later? She looks at Booth, but he's still blubbering, convinced he's going to drop dead the moment he steps out. She prods me in the chest instead, and then does the same to Primatt beside me, after which she calls out three of her regulars so at least not all of us will need our hands held.

"What are we throwing?" I ask, to show I've been paying attention.

"Flame," she says flatly.

"You're kidding." We are about to step out into a priceless alien ecosystem, untouched by human hands or feet. An opportunity for study never to be found again. "Ha ha, no really."

She unclips something from a locker and shoves it into my hands. A bag, a hose and a long plastic rod so that the bad burny stuff theoretically comes out at a safe distance from the mook who has to use it. This flamethrower is as cheaply printed as everything else, even down to the fuel. I want to remind you that the only thing between us and big lungfuls of Kilnish microbiome is basically paper.

Greely hands out similar portable deathtraps to the other chosen. Me and two others also receive long plastic poles ending in hooks. They look…singed. I recognize the look of printed material that's structured to be flame-retardant, only not very well. It's always a temporary measure, but then that's what cheap printing is all about. The whitish plastic has gone piss-yellow towards the end and full brown around the hook, its surface tacky and honeycombed.

"What the hell is all of this?" I demand.

"Time to move," Greely tells me.

I point out that it can't be time to move because we're still in the air. She just looks at me. Down below, the canopy of enormous black rosettes is unbroken. They're not robust enough for us to touch down on, and there's no clearing. I realize that's what the flamethrowers are for: a volatile prybar to make enough space on the ground for the flier to land.

Abruptly the whole flier is tilting, slewing in the air until everything in the bucket ends up at our lower end, or else —if you're a veteran and knew this was coming—is left clinging onto the straps and handles. Not being a veteran, I assume the whole thing's going to crash, but this is actually ace pilot Vertegio Keev being considerate to his about-to-disembark passengers. We're meant to go out over the lower rail, and this lets us drop down without the inconvenience of passing through the rotary belt and coming out as hamburger. The truly terrifying part of this whole plan is that it's obviously something Excursions worked out in the field on its own. The actual design of the flier does not mesh with the environment it's been sent into or the job its crew need to do.

Greely clips plastic lines to the rail and we abseil down in twos, a new and unpleasant experience for both myself and my partner-in-descent, Primatt. The pair of us punch heavily through the edge of one of the huge sail-leaves in a spray of dark fluid, and then plummet into the void below. I land on my feet, just about. She lands on her foot and her artificial substitute skids out, causing her to wrench her hip badly. Her shockingly loud cry echoes from the bulbous tubers that pass for tree trunks on Kiln, and things listen. Irrational, I know, but I feel I can *hear* them hearing us, paying attention, deciding whether we're interesting enough to find out what we taste like. All those exotic Earth proteins, like sugar sprinkles which might or might not be bad for their teeth.

She shoves me away when I try to help her. She's groping through the paper of the protective gear and the cloth of her overalls, trying to feel out the leg's little calibration controls, because it's skewed in its socket, the knee pointing inwards. I can hear her breath, amplified by the filter mask, ragged and frustrated. I want to say something but she doesn't want to hear me. Unlike, it seems, the whole of Kiln. We stand in a tattered patch of sunlight from where we broke through the photosynthetic rosettes. That's our allotment of sky and everything else is shade. The other two couples are nearby, each in their own sunbeam. And at our back...

It's the ruin. Possibly it's the one that Primatt was showing me drone pictures of not so long ago, before Clem's uprising. From this angle, it's hard to tell. And, despite everything, that little worm of excitement moves in me again. I want to stand there and look, listen and feel. I want to smell, though that's not exactly health-and-safety recommended under the circumstances. And I want everyone to be quiet so the natural soundscape of Kiln can creep back in. I am a scientist, after all, not just an anarchist. *Discovery!* Even if my name won't be on the research paper when it reaches Earth in however many decades' time.

Except all I hear is the screaming-children sound of the rotors and Greely shouting at me to snap out of it and get to work. Greely, now that I see her on the ground and not just as a face squished into the crowd in the flier's bucket, is a sad, slope-shouldered woman to whom everything in life seems to have been a grand disappointment. Most especially me.

Greely picks a tree and positions the pair of us at the end of an arm of people facing it.

"Pull the lever when I say. Then run." That is the sum total of her instructions.

"What do I do with this?" I'm juggling the hooked pole with my flamethrower, which means I'm constantly in danger of depressing the incinerate-things lever with a knee or elbow by mistake. I see belatedly that everyone else has just chucked their poles aside. Apparently the hooking comes later.

She gives the word. We pull the trigger, aiming our flames over the outer rind of the swollen barrel trunk. Parts of it crisp into blackness and we see seams blister and split. It doesn't feel like we're getting anywhere, though. Primatt and I also forget the "run" part of the plan, so it's just the two of us left after the rest have legged it. Then we see the great round boil of a plant bloating outwards as something inside it undergoes catastrophic heat expansion. *Then* we understand why the running is important, except Primatt can't run well enough. I see her limp and realize it's going to be the death of her, so I grab her, bundling her along as best I can, and then just hurl the pair of us down. A half-second later the singed tree explodes. Fragments of rind scythe overhead like shrapnel. Some of them actually end up embedded in other trees. For a moment I wait for the chain reaction that'll clear the entire forest and leave only the ruin for future study, but Kiln life is more resilient than that. The exploding tree has cleared just sufficient space for Keev to bring the flier down, and there's more than enough wild left to oppose the human presence that has at this moment dared to intrude here.

I roll off Primatt, who groans. Greely is standing over us. "I said run," she tells us, which is one hundred per cent the entirety of the concern she's going to show. Then she and the other regulars are off to help Keev unload. Our near miss has apparently won us a few moments of idleness. I put out a hand for Primatt, who's not too proud to take it. Her look to me starts off furious and accusatory, and I brace for words of a similar nature when she opens her mouth. Whatever she tries to say gets tangled up in there, though, and there are tears of pain and shame in her eyes. I finally allow myself to understand. I mean, it's not even the rudimentary rocket science of the fragmentation barges, but I've been intentionally avoiding the implications of her being here.

"Because of me," I say. "That's why you're here. Because of us."

"You knew what was going on," she said. "When we... you knew." Like revolution is an STD and I got it all over her when we slept together. Which I guess I did. I didn't think, at the time, that the liaison would figure into anyone's calculations. That I was making her ideologically unsound by association. And if I had thought about it, maybe I'd have seen it from the other side, from a position of hope, because of course we were supposed to *win*. Maybe her link to me would have become a lifeline, rather than a lead weight tied to her ankle.

"They thought I was part of it," she says tiredly. "Whatever stupid games you were playing. They thought I was smuggling the data, the parts out. All the shit you did behind my back. Didn't want to think the Labour could have managed it on their own. And so it all came down on me. They called me a *ringleader* for fuck's sake. Because of you."

I should apologize, but I'm not quite there yet. And she should explode like the tree, attack me with a hooked pole, just generally curse me out in front of everything, but I can see she's already past that. Husbanding her strength for living.

"Your suit's torn," she observes, and she's right. There's a parted seam at the armpit on mine, and on hers there's a little rip at the hip. Our hoods and filters are intact and that's probably the important thing. But it's not a delight to discover your future health and wellbeing hang on a word like "probably."

Keev hollers at us to stop slacking. I catch Ilmus's eye as they disembark from the flier, burdened with kit. They've been partnered with one of the regulars; hopefully that means they're insulated from the worst cack-handed rookie errors Primatt and I will doubtless make.

The job is a raw, animal piece of work, not science. Human presence getting tooth and claw into the resident alien and tearing it apart until we get to what we're after. The ruin is in there somewhere. Like a sculptor chipping off every part of the stone block that doesn't look like the elephant, we burn, cut and hook away the rampant growth of plant analogues that disguise the ruin, treating it as no more than a growth of the forest. It's amazing the drone algorithm ever picked it up, except, from above, the ruin leaves that telltale signature in the composition of the canopy. Keev and one of his regulars go at the more flame-retardant bits with chainsaws mounted on spindly exo-arms that are constantly coming apart at the elbows. The gold we're mining for is the distinct species of vegetation that Primatt says grows only on ruins. Or not "species"—the specific combination of symbionts that make up this particular visual signature, which all exist independently elsewhere with other partners, as though the entire biosphere is one big polyamorous love-in. If it'd been *them* coming to *us* they'd have been appalled at how repressed, one-note and boring all us Earth types are.

Anyway, being repressed and boring Earth types, we spend the day hacking at it all, carving and scorching away the living part of the ruins so we can get to the dead beneath. We're only interested in the dead. The dead can speak to us in a way the living can't. A safe and controllable way that won't lead to anyone being hastily shoved in the incinerator to control rampant infection. "Dead" is the default way we learn from things. Ask any scientist. There's a limit to what you can learn just by watching the rat frolic around the maze. Eventually you have to cut the sucker open and section its tissues.

If a lion could speak, as the saying goes, we couldn't understand it, but we could sure as hell anatomize its larynx.

There is a lot of kit to unload from the flier: tools and even some automata. There's a thing like a weed strimmer that you throw, grenade style, and then it scythes down everything within ten feet of it with little monofilament whips. Which means only Keev and Greely are trusted with them, because that "everything" definitely includes human ankles. There are little acid charges calibrated to Kilnish tissues, which eat through the more robust stalks and branches. Mostly it's human sweat and toil, though. This sort of thing is hard to properly automate, while humans are good at adjusting and adapting on the job. That's part of it. More than that, though, it's *expensive* to automate, and would require a highly trained crew of valuable technicians and operators running your fleet of shiny machines. Because once you invest in automation, you have to take care of your junk. With labourer-class people, not so much. It's cheaper to have a half-assed crew of expendables that you know you're never going to have to return in good condition or risk losing your deposit. Earth has a lot of surplus people and the Mandate can afford to run its transportation policy with extreme prejudice.

As we continue to hack away, my mind goes back to our dinner with Terolan, and Vessikhan's presentation. His determination to crack through to the mind behind those enigmatic, alien scrawls. And at last we expose the not-quite-ceramic of the walls, and there it is. The writing. Or the pictograms, the pictures, the abstract art. Looking at it there, I can't say which it is. None of us can, save that it says *intelligence* to the human eye. Encoded intelligence, the past speaking to the present, even if it's in a language we'll never understand.

16.

We don't even know how the lost Kilnies did it. There are no tool marks. The attachment points where the vine-like, plant-like living sheath clings on seem to avoid it. They dig their fibrous claws in everywhere else but do not efface the cryptic histories written there. I instantly discern distinct characters, and I know that The Science has catalogued countless individual symbols. Each ruin has a particular set that overlaps partially with others, a language with localized and generalized elements. Perhaps. Or else these pictures represent physical things, and aren't an alphabet or character set at all. Pictorial renditions in a stylized tradition that means nothing to human eyes but was blindingly obvious to its lost makers. Or it isn't a visual tradition at all, and alien fingers felt through the meanings of these raised markings to understand them. *Raised*, not incised. It's easy to overlook that, and the implications didn't occur to me back in the camp, in The Science's labs. The alien scribes cut away everything but the meaning, somehow. Or else...

I stare at the abstract squiggles and blocks, imagine them growing there, pushed out by carefully cultivated fungal hyphae painted onto the surface of the ruins. Which themselves are mysterious in construction: too few bricks and separate pieces. The foundations are constructed grain by grain, and again I think about termites, wondering if the whole implication of intelligence isn't a hoax. Or it's grown whole from some bizarre cross-disciplinary alchemy disowned by both biology and geology. Huge rounded pot-buildings in imitation of the tree boles. And tall fronded spires like nothing on Kiln, but recalling Earth seaweed reaching towards the sunlit surface from benthic anchors. Some of it is breaking apart now, with the stony substrate having fractured long ago but still held together by the obscuring cloak of the vines. Until we came along. We vandals, destroying what we seek to study in our greed for answers.

Except we are not The Science, incentivized to trot out pat explanations cut from an intellectual cloth to suit the commandant's doctrinal purse. We are Excursions. Our goal isn't to find answers but to survive until evening so we can return to the luxurious safety of the Labour Block.

Whenever the work ebbs, because some stage is done or a technical problem requires emergency on-site maintenance, the forest encroaches. Kilnish life has no dedicated ears, but a kind of lateral-line system of sound receptors. The exploding tree, the descent of the flier, the chainsaws: these things left a hushed vacuum. In the gaps between our noise-making, the forest finds its voice again, from a murmur to a gabble, to a kind of omnipresent rush of sound. Like a crowd of people in an echoing place. It's not at shout-out-loud volumes; Kiln is quiet by Earth standards. Instead there's an insidious, constant conversation, over us and through us. Whispers and mutters, buzzing and rumbling, a dozen ways of making sound. Little winged things flit past us, making a weird hopping progression through the air with sounds like the static of a dead radio channel. Something out in the forest is crying out *Hah...hah...haaaaaah* like it's finally seen the joke on the way home from the comedy show. Lithe, multi-stranded things, like intertwined and inflated rubber gloves with too-long fingers, fumble over each other underfoot. They whisper as they extend and contract to ooze over the ground. It's a disturbingly irregular motion unlike any Earth thing. After a while we Earth people start talking over the whispering, because otherwise the sounds are just close enough to speech to put the fear in you. Even the trees seem to talk. The great rounded vases of them rumble softly, as some part of their composite being makes itself known to the world.

We finally break to eat the plastic-sealed leathery bread they printed us for packed lunches. Ilmus drifts over to me, eyeing Primatt warily. No need to make introductions, obviously; we all shared a lab back before things went south. The former Science head just sags, not onto the blackened ground like most of us but onto a chunk of tree she can use as a wobbling stool, so she knows she'll be able to actually get back up to her feet again. She looks grey and worn out, every part of our physically demanding job being that much more of a travail for her. Around us, people talk. Around them, the forest complains bitterly about our presence.

"Kiln is *loud*," Ilmus says. And though it isn't really, compared to the engines and industrial processes and Mandate policy announcements of Earth, it sure as hell doesn't shut up.

"You've noticed," Primatt starts, then tails off, watching to see if Ilmus is just going to turn away and snub her. By then we're all sufficiently comrades in adversity, though, so she's bold enough to go on. "You notice too that it's not just metabolic function? They shut up when we arrived, and now they're used to us, they're talking again."

"'Talking,'" Ilmus notes. "Not...Well, not very *scientific*, Doctor."

Primatt shrugs, in that moment freer than she's been in years, because the requirement to walk the commandant's ideological tightrope has been taken from her. "It's speech. Or they're communicating something. Trees talk on Earth, but they do it biochemically, through the root matrix. Here they actually talk, audibly. They have various motile parts they employ—literally 'employ,' like hiring-and-firing employ—to perform non-vegetative roles for them. On Earth, some plants produce food for insects, even form hospitable dwelling structures for them to live in, so the insects will defend the plant from more damaging herbivores. Here that's magnified a thousandfold. Every living thing has a whole job market going, a suite of functions it prefers to outsource rather than deal with in-house."

As I chew over the rubbery rations, I watch the forest. Beyond what my ears pick up, there's other speech going on that we're even less equipped to detect and analyse. The air is misty with chemical signals. Little creatures raise photosynthetic sails that flash briefly with metallic colours as they adjust their structures to refract the light. Strange vibrations pass through and under us, surely the long-distance telegrams of unknown beasts or plants, or some hybrid thing that makes a mockery of the distinction. The bush telegraph of the Wild Man of Kiln.

Primatt has used tape to seal her paper suit at mid-thigh, and co-opted one of the smaller cutting tools to slit both paper and overall to expose her artificial leg. She picks at her knee with the point, finding it fouled with dirt and the airborne drift of particulate life. Which shows how much good our protection is actually doing, I suppose.

"What did you do?" Ilmus challenges her. "You throw the, you know, the commandant out of bed or something?"

Primatt's eyes flick to me. I am tactfully silent, and Ilmus doesn't pick up on what seems like glaringly obvious subtext. They were never the sharpest about that kind of social small print.

"Some of Keev's people think you're here to tattle on them," Ilmus goes on. Not quite confrontational, but not conversational either. "I said nobody sends the Bioscience chief to play informant. But I didn't see you at our meetings either, and Berudha never mentioned you, not like—" They stop before they say "Calwren," our one man on the inside, in case the extent of his involvement in our councils hasn't been fully understood by the authorities.

Primatt flexes her leg joint by joint, a weirdly uncanny-valley sequence of movements. She's obviously preparing an answer and I wonder how much it'll drop me in the shit, and what Ilmus will think about my going off to earn extra credit with teacher. Except it's not all about me, of course.

"This idiocy of yours provided an excuse. I was caught just close enough to accuse, and be incriminated. One of my underlings made a play for my position." Primatt's tone is flat and angry but the anger isn't just for me. "It was coming for a while. Terolan was getting sick of me trying to walk the line. It happens to every Science chief sooner or later." She looks up at the pair of us at last, with something of her prior prickly temper. "You know the old saying: 'Your work is both scientific and orthodox, but...'"

" 'The parts that are scientific aren't orthodox and the parts that are orthodox aren't scientific,' " I finish for her. "Who's taken over, then? Feep, Fop or Foop?"

She stares at me, and I remember those aren't actually their *names*, just what we called them in Dig Support. Then she clicks, and I get at least 0.35 of a laugh out of her. It sounds strange, a laugh out here. Wild, unexpected. Partaking more of the Kiln chorus than human interaction.

We fly home in the evening. That's about the best thing you can say about how our work is structured. I wouldn't have put it past them to keep us out there until the site was cleared. On the flier, on the way back, I actually mention this to Keev, as Greely is piloting for the return flight.

He gives me exactly the look of a teacher whose slow student has unexpectedly asked a fast question.

"Well, they used to," he says. "Before my time. Only it was 'inefficient.' "

Inefficient meaning, I work out later, that attrition amongst the Excursionistas was so high that the work wasn't being done.

So this is going to be our life for the next few days. We'll go out into that stretch of unplumbed alien wilderness, the hotbed of undiscovered and vibrant life awaiting study, and we'll burn and hack the fuck out of it until nothing's left but the bones of the ruin. All in preparation for Vessikhan's people to arrive and take discreet rubbings of the inscriptions. When you can't see the woods for the trees, then you just clear back the trees to an appropriate distance, so you have a properly sterile arena to do science in, right? And be careful because those trees explode when you set them on fire.

When we get back to the camp after that first day, I find out just what other shoe there is to drop, because the deal's even worse than I'd thought. There's the little matter of why Keev and company were so pissed at us from the start.

Excursions kills you. Or at least kills you more readily than just generally having an address on the Labour Block. There are things out in the wilds that will kill you so they can experiment with just how indigestible Earth biomass is, but honestly that's a marginal cause of death. On that first day virtually nothing tried to eat me at *all*. I felt almost rejected. But on Kiln you need to sweat the little things, the microscopic elements. Once Kiln gets into you... well, we've all seen the example tank.

I'd noted to Primatt, before, that you weren't keeping the camp clean if you didn't scrub Excursions down every time. And then, not being on Excursions right then, promptly forgot all about it. And now I'm the newest Excursionista and about to get the final object lesson in my current crash course in the Use of Carrots and Sticks in the Extrasolar Carceral Programme.

On returning, I expect us to be stopped at the gate but they just let us in. There's no airlock, no gas chamber, as the Excursionistas refer to decontamination. We just... walk straight in. I actually then expect a firing squad because this seems the only plausible alternative, and even that's unhygienic. Gas us, then shoot us, surely. Except we go into the Labour Block and get right on with dismantling the tables and turning them into our bunks. Our bunks which are now all down one end of the Block, with everyone else keeping their distance.

I discover that I, subcommittee man as I am, have missed a whole underground conspiracy that's been going on behind my back. Sure, I'd noted before that Keev and the Excursions crew all bunked together. But then they all worked together. I'd guessed it was by choice. And sure, I'd been given a quick spritz with the decontaminator every week or so, even though I'd never been near a piece of Kiln biology that hadn't been thoroughly prepared for the scalpel rig, but that seemed just good practice on a world like Kiln. It *was* good practice. But here we were in Excursions, having come back from a day out in the woods wearing paper suits, and nobody has sprayed us down.

I timorously raise this with Keev and he looks like he wants to thump me.

"You get decontaminated after the third day," he tells me. "Full heavy gassing. You'll love it. Not the light mist of piss everyone else gets."

"That's mad," I protest.

"Costs saving, they say," Keev explains. I pick up on his tone and expression, the whole thousand-yard stare of him. He is, after all, a man who has been on Excursions for years, measured out in those three-day instalments whenever his crew are out clearing a new site. Three-day periods when he must register every twitch, flush and fever of his body, every errant thought and mood swing, and wonder if it's *him* or if it's something external pulling his heartstrings.

It's not a costs saving. Or, if it is, it's so minuscule a bean as not to be worth counting. It's a threat. Not even to us, because we're already neck deep in it, but to Dig Support, Domestics and the rest of the Labour—even to the actual staff in Science and Security. It tells everyone, *There are worse things. There's always Excursions.* And it's mad, inefficient and dangerous. It makes a mockery of the actual dome and quarantine and everything else, because here we are tracking Kiln about on our boots, breathing it out of our lungs and crapping it out of our guts. Our native microbiome and the intrepid Kilnish explorers are combining and recombining, until they find a configuration of molecular locks and keys that can bridge the gap between *us* and *them.* So they can eat us. So they can use us. So they can *be* us.

I stand there before Keev's withering stare and shrink at the thought. I want to reach into my own body, claw open my innards, and tear out everything that looks mouldy. I imagine things growing already in my body cavity. Three days of this. I don't know how I'll manage. I'll go mad. Except there's Keev in front of me, and he's survived it all. A man of leather, bone and spite, and here I am just flab and book learning in comparison.

"We did two days," Keev says quietly, "before you political sons of bitches got dumped on us. Then you reset our clocks. This is day one *again* for us."

I goggle at him. For a moment the enormity of it is beyond my ability to understand. Then I think of the commandant's nasty little abacus of a mind and the maths works out. If we insurgents are to be punished by getting assigned to Excursions, then it must be a punishment from day one. We have to understand the full horror of it, which the rationed decontamination is part. And so when we joined, it was a new calendar, Day Zero, for Excursions. But the knock-on effect is that this time it's a whole five-day stretch before any of the veterans can have Kiln cleansed from them. Meaning maybe that's too long and even Keev's hard-won equilibrium will be tipped.

I stew over this as we eat—all crammed in at the end of the Labour Block furthest from the reclamation plant, because nobody wants more of us going back into circulation than is strictly necessary. We're already one down by then, on the crew. Booth has actually been hauled away and decontaminated, because he was vomiting on and off, and his day with torn filters earned him extra privileges. The word comes that he's slacking over in isolation and won't be on the crew tomorrow, so we're a hand down, along with everything else. While we sweat, Booth is given a day in bed. We turn the thought over enviously. Maybe—I'm thinking it so probably most of us newbies are—we should follow his lead and tear our own filters tomorrow, if that's all it takes. I could live with a mouthful of vomit if it gets me out of Excursions. Be careful what you wish for.

17.

The different Excursionista teams don't mix, as a rule. No grand camaraderie in adversity. And I wonder if it's just personality clashes, or whether they also don't want to mix the stuff we've brought back from the great outdoors. Bad enough that each of us carries a novel microbiome from our particular region of interest. Probably best not to see what happens when you combine it with the germs from another site entirely.

A handful of people are bold enough to cross the biological picket lines, though. For Ilmus and me it's Parrides Okostor.

"How bad was yours?" he asks in a hushed voice. His day seems to have been easier, working on a ruin already half scoured of life.

I'm about to tell him exactly how bad it was when Ilmus, beside me, says, "The actual work, it wasn't so bad."

I cock an eyebrow. "Seriously? We laid waste to an alien ecosystem. We just...we did anti-science."

Ilmus looks at me, unrepentant. "Sometimes," they say, "you just need to burn something to feel better." There's a weight of untold personal history there that neither Parrides nor I feel we can break into. The unspoken Ilmus, who has always been meek and neat and controlled because, when you don't fit into the precise boxes the Mandate orthodoxy prefers, you try not to have too many protruding spikes and edges to your persona, in case they catch on something. In the end it was their intellectual edges that tore the veil and had them swept up in the purge, but now I wonder just how many other heresies and idiosyncrasies Ilmus burned inside themself before then. Sacrifices on the Mandate's altar, just so they could keep on living.

We've made too many sacrifices, all of us. And it doesn't stop. I look over at Keev and his people, joylessly chewing like it's their last meal, and decide I have to do something.

After we've eaten, I contrive to attract the attention of the guards. They come in with truncheons and gas grenades at the ready, in case I'm already back on the insurrection game, but instead I tell them I want to speak to the commandant. I'm well aware everyone can hear me, and for those who think I shopped Clem and the uprising to the authorities, this is surely just more ammunition. But right then I am fired up with righteousness and I don't care.

The guards almost seem to have been expecting this. They escort me out and up to the gantry, where I shuffle my feet out in the open for a while before I'm eventually ushered into the great man's office. Terolan is there as always, save that he is pointedly wearing a filter mask—something fancy and durable and not made of paper.

"Ah, Professor Daghdev," he greets me pleasantly. I am not offered a chair, there is no tea, but the cordial tone of voice remains, like the emaciated corpse of his former hospitality. "Am I to understand that you have some manner of complaint? Perhaps you feel you are being treated unfairly." As always, that cordiality has a core of cheesewire to it, cutting to the bone. He clearly still feels that, in turning against the Mandate, I also betrayed him.

I take a deep breath of his fully filtered and uncontaminated air and do my best to look him in the eye. "No," I say.

He lifts an eyebrow. "Something of a volte-face for you, Professor?"

"I appreciate that within your own doctrine you acted justly." It comes out between gritted teeth.

"Here I was thinking you would turn up with a petition," he remarks. That old tool of civic dissent so many people resort to, knowing that it achieves nothing but also that it lets them feel they've achieved something. And they can at least believe it's not serious enough to see the enforcers at their door, though that's not always true. The commandant is probably trying to bait me into a show of defiance that will justify a beating. Not that he actually needs the justification, but he'd prefer it, certainly.

Under other circumstances doubtless I'd be dumb enough to oblige him, but I'm not here for me. "By that same justice, though," I say, "I am asking that you allow the Excursion teams to decontaminate."

Whatever specifics he was expecting, this isn't it. Perhaps he thought I really would come crying to him for special treatment, the soft academic showing his blistered hands after a day of hard work. I can see him begin to make some quip about how noble I'm being, but it doesn't emerge. Instead, he considers me for a long while, toying with the virtual display on his desk, shifting budgetary blocks and resource allocations back and forth.

"But that would cause logistical inconsistencies, Professor," he says, using my title like an enforcer with a bludgeon. "If we allowed decontamination today, after you and your fellows had only served a single day on the crew, that would be showing you preferable treatment rather than the punishment your assignment there is supposed to evidence. And if we decontaminated the original team and not you, that would be messy. You'd be out of sync and we'd end up having to run more decontamination sessions overall. A waste of resources." He looks up at me, the skin about his eyes crinkling to indicate the pleasant smile hidden from me. "No, I can't see any way around it. Ah, well."

He is, of course, enjoying himself, but I bite back my rage and say, "Justice. It's not just to bring this down on their shoulders. I accept my punishment, I bow my head to it, Commandant. But you're endangering the most experienced of your labour force for no reason."

"I wasn't under the impression that setting fire to a few trees required a great deal of experience. I'm sure you got the hang of it even today," Terolan says lightly, and then leans forwards on his desk, abruptly engaged, the casual smirkery of him gone. "However, I appreciate your communal feeling. Perhaps you now wish you'd been working towards the greater good of the Mandate's mission here. I will, therefore, consider your request. A deviation from standard practice is not impossible. Here." He takes out a tablet and slides it to the very teetering edge of the desk. I pick it up, seeing a list of names on the screen. It looks to be the whole of the current Labour Block contingent. In fact, I see Clem and his people there, picked out in red, ghosts awaiting a final deletion.

"If you would be so kind, Professor," Terolan says, "I'd like you to identify the full complement of conspirators involved in your uprising. I'm sure you were marking faces at the meeting."

I blink slowly. "What?"

"You are asking me for a favour." His voice is suddenly very hard. "You, a prisoner, are asking me, the commandant of this facility, for a *favour*. Officially, of course, such things are not done. Unofficially, it has been known. If the individual in your shoes has something to offer. So with what will you buy this favour, Professor? The one thing you have to offer is information. I wish to ensure that everyone involved in your act of civil disobedience receives that *justice* you were talking about. I'm sure we've missed a few. Just check off all the names, if you would, and I'll take your request into consideration."

I look down the list. Obviously everyone already assigned to Excursions might as well be pre-checked, but there are some who are still in their old jobs. I think of Alaxi, who was with us but missed the sideways promotion I received. A lead figure in the revolt and barely a slap on the wrist, and she's not even someone I knew back home. And there're more, plenty more. At least a dozen names come to mind —would that buy a turn in the gas for Keev's people?

I suspect it would. I think Terolan considers himself a fair man. So long as he can also feel that he has the upper hand and has outwitted me, made me knuckle under to him intellectually. He'd let me buy Keev a chance to scrub clean, if I become exactly what half the Labour Block think I am anyway. A fifth columnist, turning over the names of my fellows. For the very best of reasons.

And, horribly, I feel my footing shift, like a mountaineer just before the landslide. I would *never*, and yet here and now

I am *almost*. Are all the things I thought were iron about my principles actually just as cheaply printed as everything else around here?

"You have everyone," I tell Terolan, my voice dry. I check off every name I safely can, my own included. All of us who've already had our punishment, one way or another. The rest are probably known to the authorities anyway, but I can't know for sure who might have squeaked past their notice. And so I find myself standing with my hand on the lever and the trolley rumbling down the track towards the points. "You got us all already. What am I supposed to say?"

"Well then," Terolan purrs, "I suppose you have nothing to offer, in exchange for this favour of yours." He even gives me a moment to reconsider, tidying up his accounts with little satisfied noises. When he looks up again, it's with one of his little burlesques of surprise at finding me still there. He sighs.

"Well then," he repeats, and signals for the guards to escort me out. Glancing back, I see one of his people with gloved hands dropping the soiled tablet into a reclaiming bin. Unfit for human contact since I touched it with my foul, contaminated touch.

When we come back from the next day's jaunt, I hear that Booth is dead. The decontamination treatment didn't do enough, someone says. Or else he badmouthed one of the guards and their instinctive beat-down went too far, so they're writing it off as another death-by-planet because it's tidier that way. Another Excursionista darkly hints that Kiln had already eaten too much of him—*after just one day!*—and he couldn't survive once it was gassed dead inside him. And still no decontamination for the rest of us.

That night, registering every gurgle and tic of my body as though it is the harbinger of some dreadful fungal end, as it might be, I listen to Rasmussen's wordless crying, muted by her glass prison but still sounding across the camp. I imagine the forest calling back to her, the blend of alien sounds neither more nor less comprehensible.

On the third day, there's a nasty incident when an elephant attacks the flier.

I mean, not an elephant, but I swear to you that's what I see when the thing comes shouldering between the trees like some gentrified local, demanding you move your food truck out of their nice clean neighbourhood. It has a trunk, and at first glance I think it has upward-curving tusks below, which all says "elephant" to an Earth-adapted eye. Admittedly no elephant has eyes on stalks like that. Plus the fact that it lollops along on three extending and contracting pillar legs is a bit of a giveaway that what's come to remonstrate with us isn't your average pachyderm. Oh, and it has a pair of flame-coloured metallic plumes jutting from its back that I'm sure are some other creature entirely. Its long whip tail has a fan of bright scales on the end that semaphores wildly at us. The main body of the thing is a pale mouldy green, and it makes weeping sounds, as though it's devoured a clutch of unhappy kittens.

We're mostly clearing away the last of the ruin-specific vines from that structure, hooking the strands away cleanly where we can, while sanding off the stubs where they've got a more tenacious hold. The entrance of the elephant isn't loud, because those inflatable feet walk softly. Its meeping and yowling blends into the background susurrus too. Keev had a couple of people on rotation at the flier, though, and it's their shouting which alerts us. An intact flier is the one thing between us going home to sleep on beds, breathing filtered air, and dying out here in the wilds, so they go head to head with the creature.

One of them has a big staple gun, not a million miles from the weapons Clem's subcommittee had printed. The projectiles tear into the elephant, which mews angrily at them, lashing its trunk in the air. What I'd interpreted as tusks turn out to be semi-retracted arms ending in barbed spears, like the business end of a mantis shrimp. Even as we're registering the problem, they flick out and one of Keev's people is practically exploded by them. Not even pierced through so much as the sheer kinetic energy of the blow turning them to paste. The other sentry very sensibly runs away, turning to send more staples into the thing, gashing its hide open with great slashing wounds. Inside, I see what should be intestines, except instead of slithering out through the holes, they sprout their own stubby spurs and limbs, clutching at the edges of the tears and pulling them closed. Suturing their host from the inside like good little symbionts. By then we of the ruins-clearing crew are performing a peculiar manoeuvre, which can best be characterized as running over to help while simultaneously not wanting to get very close. But if this creature trashes the flier we're all very highly screwed indeed. Someone's shouting to get the flamethrowers but of course we've used up the stingy ration of fuel they gave us in doing the thing the flamethrowers were meant for. Nobody budgeted extra napalm for anti-elephant purposes.

Keev has a pistol, a real chemical propellant gun of superior printed manufacture. He unloads at the thing and the thunderous sound seems to cause it more distress than the projectiles, which just leave puckered marks like love bites. The elephant rears up onto its single hind leg and makes such a sound as I... For a moment I kid myself that I feel its alien confusion, anger and hurt, translating those mewling cries into human sentiment, just as we'll surely never translate the alien ideograms into comprehensible meaning. Being shot is the universal language, maybe, and all those fictional alien invaders are just trying to say hello.

In the wake of the firearm's speaking there's a moment when the monster is quite still. As though all the sound and fury, the shots and the spectacular evisceration of a human being was just the Kilnie equivalent of a polite introduction, and an Earth-style nod of the head in reply. Now we can get down to talking business.

With a weirdly fastidious motion, its trunk slicks off the ruin of Keev's man from its folding tusks, sloughing a mess of suit and skin and redness onto the alien ground.

Ilmus doubles over and vomits, mostly inside their hood but some of it jetting out of a poorly secured seam. Their continued retching is the only sound. The whole forest has gone quiet again, all of alien creation holding its breath. Ilmus's Earth fluids spatter onto the fibrous soil-analogue of Kiln and interact with it. There are close encounters of the fourth, fifth and sixth kinds all happening at once. The dead Excursionista's torn-apart corpse, Ilmus's stomach contents, the chemical propellant of Keev's firearm—this is a major meet-and-greet of planetary chemistries. I hold my breath too, waiting for some revelation. For the elephant to suddenly start speaking urbane human language, having picked it up from the spatterings of us which our immediate surroundings are painted with. It's of spurious significance, of course. Kiln has killed plenty of Earth biology before now, then fitfully part-digested it as it tried to unlock the unexpected proteins and organic combinations. Fumbling for meaning at the organic level, even as we do at the intellectual.

The elephant just leaves, almost placidly. As though it's tacked up its cease-and-desist notice and is going to inform the local Mandate offices. Greely helps Ilmus as best as she can, cleaning out their hood and unclogging the filters. The dead man stays dead.

The forest still holds its breath. I know, rationally, that it's just a response to the unexpected sound of the gun, but anthropomorphically I can read all sorts of speculative intent into the silence.

It's late in the day. Though we'd normally have another solid hour or so of toil, Keev makes an executive decision. He tells Greely to fetch the recording gear out of the flier —it's the first I've heard that we even have such a thing, but on Kiln you learn something new every day. Usually something you wish you'd never found out, in my expanding experience.

"Record it," Keev says. He means the dead man, the state of Ilmus, maybe even the shallow impressions of the elephant's podgy feet. An explanation to show our taskmasters back at the camp. *Please sir, we couldn't finish our homework because we were attacked by an elephant.*

The recording gear craps out halfway through, because that's our life these days. The only positive out of the whole incident is that we newbies are very much part of the team by now, even Primatt. Nothing like seeing a random monster come out of the woodwork to murder one of your number without reason, and then just fuck off back to the outback without having the decency to be killed. It's a bonding experience. I'm sure that if someone could contact the ghost of the dead man and explain it to him, he'd absolutely agree that his appallingly violent death was more than justified by this outcome.

In the absence of any further ability to immortalize our situation for future generations, Keev gives the nod. We climb into the flier and go home. They're going to finally cleanse us of Kiln this time round and right then I'm more than ready for it.

18.

We spend another two days on that first ruin. The work started as a rugged explorer's job, a brazen fanfare as we carved our human signature into the blank canvas of the wilds. It finishes with a damp raspberry, glorified cleaners swabbing away the last fibres and stains so that Vessikhan's people will have a nice pristine ruin to come and take pictures of like tourists. We actually complete our work ahead of time, with half a day to spare. I expect us to hightail it back to camp then, but instead we gather in the bucket of the flier and Keev breaks out a plastic bottle of spirits someone snuck out of the printer. A commodity we are not supposed to have access to but, as always within the Mandate's iron fist, people find a way of squeezing things between the fingers. It's not quite a celebration, or at least not of the concluded job. We don't have pride in the work because the work is brutal and for suckers to boot. I earn myself an extra half-point of popularity when, emboldened by drink, I say that Vessikhan will learn precisely nothing from all of this. Oh, he'll add another three dozen symbols to his expanding Kilnish alphabet, none of which will mean anything. He will painstakingly map the interior of each structure, the internal ridges and whorls that seem neither structural nor decorative. He'll never know, though. Because I'm a biosciences man, and to me the interesting bit is what we just evicted with extreme prejudice. The communities of life that had colonized the ruins after their abandonment. That weird vine with its yellow starburst florets that never grows anywhere else. *That's* something we could learn about. Not learn what Terolan and his ideologues back on Earth want to learn, maybe, but *something*. I think I've gone too far by then, because I am somewhat implying that everything we risked and lost, including two lives, was basically for nothing. But they all know it's for nothing already, and most of them weren't ever interested in the academia of it anyway. I'm just giving a professional seal of approval to their privately held belief that it was all rubbish, and somehow that makes me more one of them than I had been.

What about my poor biosciences, then? I ask. Keev says that people used to go on bring-'em-back-alive missions once, only that turned out to be too dangerous and Terolan's predecessor discontinued it. A lot of Kiln life can be hard to contain, or even classify as dead or alive, especially as each apparent individual can turn out to be a lot of Kiln life. Excursions still gets sent out to trawl the outback sporadically, though. They have a variety of trapping, netting, gassing and shooting strategies, basically wide-scale killing of everything that can't move fast enough to get out of the way. Then they record the corpses like they're immortalizing a war crime. And back home, Primatt, or not Primatt any more, of course, but whichever of the triumvirate now has the top spot, would put a request out for whatever looks promising, as though Keev's provided them with a take-out menu.

Which means... well, I despair. It means that ecologically

you're learning nothing. You can't just cherry-pick the animals that interest you like you're some old-timey gentleman collector. Ecology is all about context. And yes, on Kiln each creature is its own ecological context. But those little co-operatives—little subcommittees, I tell myself—all exist because they work as parts of a wider ecosystem. The only reason any particular assortment of critters came together to make a macro-species is because of the pressures caused by other macro-species around them. Basically, Kiln has an additional layer of mechanics when it comes to adaptation, compared to Earth. Which makes the biology here an order of magnitude more complicated, something that should be studied for its own merits. Not just some wild goose chase for Wild Men. And certainly not just as detritus to be scoured away so some bald place-server can come and tack "for ritual purposes" on the dead parts that remain.

I complain about it all angrily to Primatt in the flier. She still hasn't become "one of us." Even Ilmus is standoffish around her, and Keev's regulars won't give her the time of day. Primatt, who was the one ordering off that take-out menu until very recently, scowls at me.

"It's all biology," she says. Her focus was biochem and biomechanics, after all. She doesn't much care what comes out of the woods, because it's always going to have something for her to look at. I go off on a bit more of a rant about how you can't learn anything about an animal if you separate it from its environment and eventually she just laughs at me.

"We can't ever know. I've seen the notes. I've seen *Rasmussen's* notes. She thought the same as you. It drove her mad."

"Kiln drove her mad," I say. "Literally. It's growing in her brain." *And hasn't killed her somehow*, I add, a sudden uneasy revelation I somehow overlooked before. They threw Booth into the incinerator quickly enough, after all.

"Before then," Primatt says—we're practically shouting in each other's ear over the shrieking of the rotors—"she despaired. How can you learn the ecology when everything can switch partners the moment the dance changes tempo? She wrote…" Her voice is going and she rolls her eyes, making "later" gestures. Except, when we get back, she's hauled straight off by the guards to explain some part of her former work that her subordinates haven't been able to puzzle out. I suspect Primatt left intentionally bad notes because she could feel her usurpers creeping up on her. Idiosyncratic codes, personal references, gaps. Like an old alchemist eliding some memorized but vital part of their formulae so it couldn't be stolen and replicated. Most likely in a way that would blow up in the faces of the thieves too. Feep, Fop and Foop may have a merry old time of it with the commandant when they try to present any kind of coherent findings based on Primatt's records.

What Rasmussen wrote, I find out later, was a weird rambling screed about the way ecological shift and evolution work on Kiln. She claimed to have seen it in action, changing as the ecosphere reacted to human intrusion. Different combinations of mutualistic organisms, a whole shift-change of ecology in areas that had seen human tread. And life—the wider net of life—is reactive on Earth too, but on Earth it's mostly reactive over generations and centuries. There's a limit to the speed with which most species can change their ways in response to shifting conditions. And most certainly a limit to how far they can change their actual *being*. Evolution takes tens of thousands of years for even small changes to gain a foothold, millions of years for anything major. Yes, fish repurposed their swim bladders into lungs, and that gave them an advantage when the dry times came. On Kiln, though, if things suddenly dried up, you'd have the biological equivalent of a door-to-door lung salesman doing big business as it sold its services to everything that was finding it hard to breathe. Everything is an opportunist here, but the opportunity in question isn't the chance to eat something or out-compete something. Macro-species become extinct all the time, I guess, but the pieces that comprise them go on to form new partnerships, like directors of bankrupt companies setting up under a new name.

Primatt will tell me something else about Rasmussen, too, when they bring her back. Or she won't *say* it, but she'll stop short of saying it in such an obvious way that I practically hear the words in her voice anyway. Rasmussen was getting desperate towards the end of her tenure as head of The Science. Not just because the then-commandant was increasingly impatient with her hedging, but because she was understanding the true extent of her lack of understanding. Primatt thinks Rasmussen infected herself with Kiln. Not just that she got careless, but actually deliberately introduced the biology of this world into her own body, encouraging them to shake hands and play nicely together. I don't believe it, but I can't account for her continued longevity either.

After that revelation, I dream, of course. I wake three times overnight, kicking and screaming and falling off the hard slab of my bunk. I see Rasmussen enter the Labour Block, crawling, dragging herself, save that the underside of her body undulates like a slug's foot, extending in a ripple of fleshy pseudopods to haul her along. Her stick-thin arms are thrust out ahead of her, waving blindly in the darkness like feelers, spidery fingers splayed. Her eyes are closed, or maybe whatever's behind those withered lids aren't eyes any more. Her puckered lips mouth my name. Like the commandant, she pronounces it correctly, without an enunciated "g." She crawls down the aisle between the bunks, gasping and wheezing, and I know she's desperate to impart her great revelation. Her understanding of Kilnish ecology that came to her, after irremediable contamination precluded her from retaining her position. After they took her away to become the sole permanent exhibit in the labour camp's sideshow. I wake each time as one of her hands hooks the edge of my bunk. As I'm yelling at the top of my voice that I don't want to know, I wake everyone else as well and I am very unpopular by the next morning.

Primatt still has a bed up in Science. A twisted, awkward arrangement. Sleeping in the same block with her former colleagues. As Vessikhan the archaeologist. As Feep, Fop and Foop, one of whom had taken years of stalled progress and added the secret ingredient—a liaison with known dissident Arton Daghdev—to paint her as a long-time saboteur of the Mandate's work on Kiln. She sleeps up there with the gods at night, and then picks up her role as the lowliest sinner on the devil's own chain gang during the day. Watching her limp down the steps each time we're set to go out, I half think the chief reason she has her old bed is just so they can put her through this. Which sounds petty, even for Mandate bureaucrats, except they still won't let her use the lift.

Alternatively, they segregate her up there because, given our fumbling liaison, they don't want her fraternizing. As if that's something on either of our minds right now.

On the next tour out, I do my best to bridge the gap between her and the rest of Keev's crew. Even between her and Ilmus, over whom I surely should have some emotional leverage. All I manage to do is strain my own bonds, though, until Ilmus flat out tells me that my advocating for one of *The Science* isn't helping my case. Primatt is still an ideological traitor as far as Ilmus is concerned, and just a flat-out *one of them* to everyone else. I keep trying, though. I ask Ilmus what she's supposed to do, what she could have done differently. Primatt couldn't even have been core academic orthodoxy back home or they'd never have sent her out here. Even as Staff rather than Labour, it's not exactly a mark of favour. Change a handful of things back on Earth, either of us could have been in her shoes. Shoe. But Ilmus won't have it and, the more I argue it, the more they side-eye me as though maybe I am the snitch after all.

Despite my every effort, I still ask myself the same about them sometimes. Who says being assigned to Excursions is any guarantee that we're neither of us traitors? Just about the only one it *can't* be, out of our batch of novice Excursionistas, is Primatt herself.

This is what sinks revolutions. The heavy hand of the state, squeezing everyone. The surveillance and informants, and neighbour watching neighbour, until you end up doubting everyone except yourself. You even end up doubting yourself. Was there something I said or did, in the commandant's presence or at any other time, which gave us away? Was there some loose word back home that brought the jackboots to Ilmus's door? I said a lot of things. I got very complacent, believing we academics had a licence for a bit of unorthodoxy. Thought experiments and speculation and what-iffery. Until they had their crackdown and half my friends weren't there any more. I want to apologize to Ilmus, just in case it *was* me, except that will only sever the last ties between us, because there's no room for forgiveness in a culture of constant suspicion. And what if it *was* Ilmus who sold out Clem and the rest of us? How stupid would my apologies sound then?

This is how they get you. This is why we lose.

We have three weeks of this, by the rigorous Earth calendar we use, even though the actual dawn-to-dusk days are longer here. By then I'm fully apprised as to where I fit in. It's not just losing my bunk at the good end of the Labour Block. When Excursions aren't actually out risking our hides for the sake of the watered-down gruel passing for science here on Kiln, we're given the crap jobs back home. A disproportionate share of cleaning dunnies, or unclogging the sewerage units and the like. Someone once said, probably, that exploring an alien planet was terribly intrepid, bold and glamorous, and that someone can sod off, frankly. Because, once you have a full-on space industry and alien planets you can physically go to, you find it's actually quite inconvenient to do so. The business of physically exploring them becomes devolved to your society's equivalent of the unpaid office intern. Someone who won't be missed, and whose sudden demise won't much impede the mission. Or it devolves to a machine. Or finally to convict labour, if you find that machines are simultaneously not good enough at the job and also a bit high-maintenance for your budgetary oversight committee.

Even though we in the Labour Block are *all* convict labour sent here to die on this murderous world, Excursions are there to be looked down on by everyone else. It's explicitly engineered that way by the system. The miserly rationing of decontamination makes sure that nobody else wants us around them. And within Excursions, we newcomers and troublemakers are set up to be the butt everyone kicks. Just so we can properly appreciate that our reassignment is a punishment, as if that wasn't already obvious. We were crowbarred onto the team in a manner that specifically made everyone else's lives worse, just to encourage them to hate us. Because that's how the commandant and his staff maintain control. Divisions within divisions, every one of us turned against our siblings. And this was Clem's cardinal sin. Not that he dared to raise a hand against his betters, but that he brought people together to do it. His uprising didn't work, though, and here we are, the lowest even of the low. Because there's nothing more embarrassing than a failed revolutionary.

When we have a chance to conspire, Ilmus and I bandy names about. After three weeks on the same chain gang, we've reached an uneasy equilibrium. I've kidded myself Ilmus would never sell me. Said it in my head enough times that cognitive dissonance makes me halfway believe it. They swear they have a similar confidence in me, and I can only hope that's the case. Or at least that they're squashing each suspicion the moment it lifts its head, just as I am. We've both worked out, in any event, that the best way of quashing our mutual suspicions is to be suspicious of other people. Hence we agree to the polite fiction that obviously it wasn't either of us and speculate as to who *did* sell us. Or what combination of people, coming together unwittingly to form a compound traitor. Plenty of suspects, then. Enough that it's almost easier to imagine they were all in on it, all those people still working Maintenance or Domestics or Dig Support. We look at the other Excursion teams, at Parrides in his new post. Doesn't he always seem to have it easier than us? Clearer sites, more manageable monsters? Is that meagre difference a reward for betrayal? Or we look over to the far end of the Labour Block dorm and see our former colleagues who retained their privileges. People like Alaxi, who still casts a guilty there-but-for-the-grace-of-God look our way. People like Croan, who have decided they don't know us any more, for the fair reason that we're unhealthy people to know.

We pass those names back and forth, Ilmus and I. But we can't know, and will most likely not be around long enough for it to matter, given the attrition in Excursions. We couldn't do anything about it if we did, either. The knowledge would just lodge inside us like the things of Kiln, slowly eating away at its host.

It was probably Calwren, the engineer. He's still doing staff work, after all, when the relatively blameless Primatt got booted to Excursions. Calwren, now sporting a shiny tracking peg driven into his collarbone, but now we suspect him, that seems like an ostentation. Traitor chic, a feeble gesture to deflect suspicion. Sometimes you find out that what hamstrung you was just Occam's Razor all along. Calwren, the establishment man, was actually working for the establishment all along. Shock revelation! My internal compass is dragged away from *Surely Clem wasn't such a fool?* to *Clem was a fool to bring him in.*

Then there's the other train of thought. The one I don't share with Ilmus but turn over in my head every night before I sleep. Because I could make it all go away. Actually, I don't really know this is true, but most of the time I convince myself of it. That, if I asked, the guards would take me back up to Terolan, and he'd have a fresh tablet waiting for me with those names. I could just check them off, all the lucky bastards who were in on the plan but didn't find themselves sent to Excursions. Why should I suffer when they don't? And if I did that, I'd probably even catch the traitor too. I dream of myself doing it, when it's not Rasmussen clawing at my bed. I check off the names. I don't see the actual characters on the tablet, but I know exactly who I'm shopping. I tap on Alaxi, damning her to the slow death of this planet. Sometimes I tap on Croan too, even though she wasn't in on it, because I resent her standoffishness. And sometimes I damn people who aren't even here on Kiln, colleagues left far behind and long ago on Earth. I don't wake screaming from these dreams, but they're worse. The guilt of them seeps into my waking mind and I go about furtively, flinching, as if I've become the traitor half of them think I am. Most likely the commandant doesn't spare me a thought and any window for my collaboration has closed anyway, but in my dreams he's still deeply interested in turning me. The loyalties of Arton Daghdev are more important than locating the mythical Wild Man and solving the mystery of the ruins.

Then one day the guards come for me anyway and I feel such a conflicted agony of response that I just stand there and let them bundle me off. I know the terror of the prisoner singled out, who has no power to protect himself and could be subjected to anything. But at the same time, I know an ugly traitor spike of hope. *Am I saved?* Will that tablet be put in front of me, and will I break this time?

They tell me the commandant has a treat for me. An old friend to have tea with. I think of Vessikhan. I wonder if Feep and co have been so lamentable that Primatt's been reinstated. But instead they take me to the shed beside Science. To Rasmussen. She sees me and splays herself against the plastic like a lizard on a wall. Half her face is pressed flat, the eye, the actual naked eyeball, deformed where she's shoving it, open, against the barrier. I see her lips move, even pushed out of shape as they are. One of the guards opens the mic and her howls fill the room and go gibbering out across the camp.

"She was asking for you," one of the guards tells me heartily. "Unfinished business, we reckon."

And I understand. The commandant has indeed been waiting for me to come to him with my list of names. He's given me three weeks, and now his patience has run out. I'm going back in with Rasmussen and this time, maybe, they won't let me out. I try to fight them then, and almost slip out of their grip because I'm punchier than they expect. There are three of them, and they end up pushing me against the plastic, eye to hideous eye with Rasmussen. Her voice comes to me, buzzing through the barrier that separates us and booming from the speakers. Hoots, cackles and simian whoops and, fighting their way clear like the tatters of an army in retreat, actual words. "Give him to me!" and "Let us join!" and "The bridge!" I scream, fight and weep, pissing myself with fear, not just that I'll die but that I'll worse-than-die. That Rasmussen's filthy and festering being will push inside me and I'll never be myself again.

Then the guards have released me, letting me scrabble away across the limited space this half of the shed allows, putting all that meagre distance between me and the horribly flattened figure of Rasmussen. And they're laughing. One of them turns off the mic and the jangling cacophony of their amusement replaces her wailing. Apparently it's all been a bit of a joke. The commandant hasn't spared me a thought, but someone snuck them word of my nightmare and they thought they'd put the wind up me. Just a joke, no hard feelings, Professor. Ho ho ho. I'm marched back down to the more mundane brutalities of the Labour Block. All eyes are upon me, but this time they heard me screaming and so at least it's not an extra burden of suspicion.

The next ruin we're sent to turns out not to be one. The drone algorithm burped and, after clearing away a lot of innocent flora and fauna (or rather a lot of indeterminate things in various combinations, some motile and some sedentary), it turns out to be just an actual rock. We're permitted to go home on the second day and even earn ourselves an early decontamination. It's like all your religious and non-denominational celebrations come early, all at once.

And then, a few days of banal drudgery later, there's a new assignment and it's Keev's crew on the rota again. This is when it all goes spectacularly wrong.

19.

This time it is a real ruin. When we've exploded a couple of trees to get boots on the ground, we can see it. Furred over with vines and some luminous phallic things like dry-land sea squirts that I haven't encountered before.

The forest's strange here, even by Kiln's standards. We've gone in a different direction away from the camp and there's a distinct shift of biome. The ground is lower and damper, and new balances of species interaction have prevailed. The pot-bellied trees are lower, their outsides less rigid, so that they quiver like water-filled balloons when you touch them. When we explode them, it isn't the hard-rind shrapnel I'm used to but a burst of wet skin and a vomitous gouting of colourful innards formerly held under pressure. It's like blowing up paint-filled balloons. They're not pressed as closely together as in the more forest-y regions, either, though not so far spaced that we could get the flier down unaided. Or else Keev just wanted to explode a few trees to work through his ongoing frustrations. Between the trees—always remember that they're not actually trees, or even plants really —are tall stalks studded with translucent windsocks and topped with a helix of sun-drinking teardrops, the Kilnish equivalent of water-meadow wildflowers. The sunlight catches them and strikes rainbows from their edges, and even the rainbows aren't quite like those on Earth. Light's the same the universe over, but Kiln's atmosphere, its blue-yellow-black sky with the drifting veils of aerial plankton, filters it differently. I don't think anything else brings home just how far I am from Earth more than those alien rainbows. That and the fact that these wildflowers are hungrily carnivorous. They make a constant sound, like heavy human breathing, as the windsock parts of them suck up the miasma of drifting spores and particulate life. The air immediately over the mushy ground is thick with it.

As Keev passes round the hooks and flamethrowers, I take mental ecology notes—or that particularly Kilnish discipline which partakes both of ecology and anatomy. The stalks give the windsocks support, and most likely the windsocks pay rent in the form of a percentage of the catch. And they move. Slowly and occasionally, but at the foot of each stalk is something like a stone on a mass of tube feet piloting the whole assembly around, jostling over the best momentary real estate. The tallest of them barely reach my waist but they are a world in miniature.

And then there are the ruins. The vines that cling to them are a different breed, the dark wells of their photosynthetic blooms interspersed with bright orange thorns. These quiver and track us as we move around and prepare to incinerate them. And I anthropomorphize; you always do. I feel the pinprick points of them all the time, the poised eagerness of the whole composite thing to do me harm. I sense, deep in my human soul, that it understands we're here as imperialistic invaders, come to steal its archaeology and murder its life in the name of science and progress. I know it hates us, even though I also know that hate is an Earth thing, a human thing, and this barely sensate conglomeration of foliage can't even understand what we are.

Yet it gets me, gets all of us more than once. As we hack and burn it off the near face of the ruin, those little stinger bastards lunge at us like a fencing team, even shooting off the vine to jab at us in spectacular suicidal leaps. Needless to say, they go through the flimsy stuff of our protective gear like it's not there, and they inject something when they dig in. The mindless vegetable fury of it actually drives us back to the flier for the first time, and Greely hauls out the rudimentary medical kit with shaking hands. She shoots us full of anti-inflammatories and allergen suppressants and we wait to see if we'll get sick. If whatever Kilnish toxin the thorns are full of can reach over the light years to poison Earth biology. But in the end it's just mechanical pain, and a nasty earwax smell that creeps in even through the filters.

Later, too late really, I put my ecologist hat on and speculate that the smell—faint to us but maybe trumpet-loud to the Kilnish equivalent of nostrils—may be a signal. A general alarm to another assemblage of life that has a stake in the vine's survival somehow. Part of some ridiculously complex dance of life cycles, all trading off partners and going in little circles. Because before we've cleared too much more, the Elephant's Dad arrives.

That's where my head goes, when it stomps through the trees. The thing that went for our flier on the first ruin job was the Elephant, and this seems like something akin to it. Only there's more of it and it's considerably angrier from the get-go. Another tripod thing on broad rubber feet, half stepping, half rolling. Its upper reaches are armoured, an accretion of minerals from its diet secreted out onto its skin in rippling plates that glisten as though they're still drying. And the arms. Three arched, articulated limbs held high to the elbow and then hooked down, folded into its body. Some empty space within it, or maybe some vocal and semi-dependent passenger, makes a hollow knocking sound. It's exactly like the big door-knocker of a creepy old house in some horror media. A death knell, though we don't quite understand it, because although it's big, it's slow. In retrospect I understand it's charging furiously at us, but it's very slow on its podgy little legs. Hard for anything living at a human timescale to characterize as angry, rather than merely languorous. Except those booming percussions are a battle cry, I come to realize. We've triggered a response to our intrusions at last, and here comes the cavalry, responding to ancient alliances of shared biology.

It squeezes its body between two of the jelly-fleshed trees before coming to a juddering halt. They wobble. It wobbles. Its armoured pieces and those crooked limbs seem like the only hard things in this whole ridiculous world. We stare. And I feel...

Something.

It has a lot of eyes, some scattered like acne across the flabby parts of its anatomy, others positioned like little security cameras atop its elbows, the highest parts of it. But there's no contact there. Not like you'd get with a human, a dog, a mantis. A fish, even. I just look on clusters of fist-sized orbs that are windows onto receptive linings, evolved from the photosynthetic surfaces that Kilnish life does so well. And those eyes are most likely their own thing. Semi-independent symbionts holding up signs that say, "Will provide superior vision for food," and then taking root in their new host's original eye sockets.

There's a thing on Earth, a marine isopod, that eats the tongues of fish and then replaces them so it can keep on stealing the fish's food. But to do so, it has to be a fish tongue as its second job. It's good enough at it that the fish goes on living, and maybe, because the new independent tongue has a load of little scrabbly arms, it's actually better than the old one. I mean, are fish tongues particularly good? I can't remember, and I left my notes several light years away on Earth. There's another thing too, I think it's a mite or some other minuscule arthropod, which hitches rides with army ants, attaching to their feet. But because ants need their feet, often for quite complex things like attaching to other ants to form bridges and similar instinctual architecture, the mite has to actually do ant-foot things, and it does. It holds on when it needs to, lets go when the ant wants to let go. Like the mite has become a tiny waldo which the ant might use to handle hazardous objects. And that's just on Earth. As we keep observing all around us, here on Kiln evolution has leant into that idea hard, and every damn thing is like that.

The Elephant's Dad stares at me with something else's eyes.

It is four metres tall at the elbows and looks like it should weigh two tons at least. It makes its empty sound again. Knock knock. Who's there? Kiln. Kiln who? Just Kiln. Kil'n. Killing. That's what's about to go down. Because we are the invading forces of Earth and we are here with fire and the sword, always humanity's most enthusiastic exports.

One of my fellow ex-revolutionaries—Shoer, his name is —has a flamethrower to hand, and he lets fly with it. I can't even tell if Keev gave the nod. He doesn't blaze away in a crazy frenzy, though I realize that's how it sounds. Like we're the desperate cornered soldiers in some drama, confronting the monster. It's no more than an admonitory puff of flame to warn the thing off. The incendiary equivalent of a rolled-up newspaper across the nose.

It's enough to serve as a declaration of hostilities.

The Elephant's Dad staggers back on its ballooning legs as though someone just punched a sports team mascot. Then shit gets real. The big armoured limbs snap down to become new and better legs, lifting the thing's sagging body up over human head height. Suddenly it's scuttling towards us, stilt-legged and spider-swift. Like the driving privileges just got usurped by a completely different beast, an angry alter ego that happens to be sharing the same composite body.

One of those legs strikes Shoer and flicks him aside. He hits one of the blubbery trees, only it goes hard as stone for the moment of impact, like one of those liquids which becomes a solid if you slap it. Bones break and he's screaming.

Keev has his gun and empties it, blowing chips off its armoured surfaces and useless, momentary holes in its underside. In response, the three saggy columns it had been walking on distend and turn towards us. And damn me, but where the soles of its flat feet should have been it's got *mouths*. Gaping, circular orifices lined with grinding radulae, so it can browse on the go. One of them snaps out, a convulsive three-metre lunge, and it has Shoer. Half of him's in its gullet before we even register the move.

We don't try to save him. Not one of us, not even a gesture towards it. He's patently a lost cause, and surely it'll take a moment to devour and digest him before coming after the rest of us. Except the part of it busily seeing whether it can metabolize Shoer isn't the part of it that's interested in killing us. I have a moment when I *know* it understands the significance of the flier. Anthropomorphic nonsense of course, but our ride is definitely a big piece of alien metal and plastic that doesn't belong here, and so it is worthy of the monster's ire.

It jumps. Two tons at least and it jumps like a fucking *flea*. Its elbow-knees must be spring-loaded. We just get a sense of it overhead and then it comes down on the flier so hard the whole thing is instant scrap and broken pieces. More thoroughly destroyed than if a bomb had gone off in the fuel tank. The Elephant's Dad wheels and dances on the wreckage, tilting its body to wave its mouths at us obscenely. Shoer's boots are just disappearing into one of them.

We have a frozen moment of utter Oh-God-what-now?

We run for the ruins. It's like a comedy, if you only added the jaunty soundtrack. The Elephant's Dad doesn't jump this time; it just scuttles after us at an almost sedate pace, like we're the mischievous urchins and it's the fat man whose lunch we just stole. Our flames and hooks had got as far as clearing an opening into the nearest gourd-building, and now we use it as our entrance. No time to worry about what might already be inside it. There's a man called Pellamy right behind me who's just about to shove himself inside when the vines catch him. Those thorns clutch like a hand and they've got him trapped. They weren't barbed before, but they certainly are now. Some new shareholder in their personal limited company has turned up and added backwards-pointing prongs to their tips. He's snagged in six or seven places and, though it's not going to kill him, he really can't get free.

The Elephant's Dad is what's going to kill him, of course. The vines are just upholding their part of the social contract by pinning him in place until it can saunter over. I try to haul him off them and he screams as the barbs rip through his flesh. But I can't get him free and he's thrashing so much that I'm not even sure he wants me to. It's not clear what the lesser of the two evils is. Then we're in the shadow of the monster, which wants to make clear it is very much the greater of however many evils we might be facing right now. It tilts back, one jagged leg held high to rest against the ruin's wall. A sandpaper mouth blubbers down and clears everything away: vines, Pellamy, thorns, all of it. Just scours it all away as though showing us, *This is how you clear a ruin, lads!* I'm left with the man's arm, the flesh at the wet end twisted into a weird spiral against a polished nub of bone.

I make it inside. We all do. It's only been three minutes since the Elephant's Dad turned up. That's how Kiln gets us. That's how it happens.

It's not as though we didn't know being sent to Kiln as labour was a death sentence. The principle of Acceptable Wastage makes that plain enough. The only variety is in how they kill you and how fast. Kiln is a cushy vacation compared to some, but it's still death. Sooner or later, even for a man as doggedly tenacious of life as Vertegio Keev. Only, once you're in the camp and you have a routine, a bunk and meals, you forget. You overlook the fact that your future has just been truncated. That there are a range of possible ways this could go, but none of them involve dying of old age surrounded by doting friends and family. You look at the death they sentenced you to, and squint until you can pretend it's living.

There, inside the ruin, we know that it's killed us at last. And yet, because we're human, we don't give up. We don't open our throats and spill our Earth blood onto the mat of interlaced tendrils and mulch that is native Kiln soil. It's my fourth excursion with Excursions. We were decontaminated recently, and so we can at least believe that the planet hasn't started eating us from the inside and colonizing our brains. We newbies have settled down and proved we can pull our weight, even me, even Primatt. We are a team, and we have the immortal Keev as our leader. We were going to live. Yet now we're going to die.

Someone has a torch. It's a meagre, flickering beam of light, cranked by hand and dying out again the moment they stop. They make themselves a nuisance by shining it in everyone's faces to blind them. Only after the fact do I work out it's Greely and she's counting us off. Excursion Team Three, or at least what's left of it. Our leader, the redoubtable Vertegio Keev, whose stretched-out luck has just run down his trouser leg and away forever. The light picks out face after face: nine of us frightened Excursionistas. Ilmus, Primatt. Four others of Keev's regulars beyond himself and Greely. Frith, the other survivor of Clem's crew. Then it's my turn to be flash-blind as the torch turns on me. Shoer and Pellamy are gone, sacrifices to the Elephant's Dad. And here are the rest of us, *inside* a ruin that we absolutely have not cleared, in a biome nobody knows much about. Not that we actually have a useful handle on *any* part of Kiln, despite all the hard work put in by Rasmussen, Primatt and yours truly.

The cramped entryway we all squeezed through, abrading away our protective suits as we did so, was made for mice. Now we're in a big open space fit for mammoths. The torch clicks out, but there's still just enough light to see our own shapes against the darkness. I look up and see the stars.

Well, no. It's daytime. But I see pinpoints of day in irregular patterns across the curved upper surface of what must be a ridiculously tall chamber. Definite patterns, and there's no way I can talk myself out of seeing it as anything other than a map. A star map. A recreation of the night sky that at some point in time was significant to the Kilnies who raised this place with their incomprehensible methods. Nobody's ever seen this before. If anything similar was found in past ruins, Vessikhan has never said. It seems such a human thing I'm sure he'd have laid it before the commandant in anticipation of a pat on the head. The ancient cultures of Earth have imbued the stars with significance since prehistory. Why wouldn't you? They're your calendar and your clock, the universe's own way of measuring the year for you. I stand there in the dark, and for a moment I can forget the dire peril we're in because a wave of wonder washes over me. The thought that maybe *this* is a constant of intelligence, anywhere you can see the sky and have eyes to do it with. Does all life of sufficient complexity look up after sunset and wonder at the lights and what they mean?

Anthropomorphizing, surely. The elusive Wild Man of Kiln. Except here we are and above us are the pinprick constellations of a Kilnish night, baked into the very structure of the building. With some computer-modelling tools and a view of the sky, I might be able to calculate a range of moments that this display could be commemorating. Given precession and tilt, I could perhaps work out when the building was created, date it to within days maybe. It's not a priority, given what we've just gone through, but the thought makes me weak at the knees nonetheless.

Outside, the Elephant's Dad lets out its knocking call, as

though it's politely asking if it can come in. I imagine it licking the blood of Shoer and Pellamy off its vicious legs, the spiky armoured ones it used to move so quickly. Or perhaps the beast that licks is distinct from the beast that has the legs. Fucking Kiln biology. And inside it, our fractious Earth proteins might cause it a little discomfort. Probably our former comrades will be shat out, mostly undigested, before some tenant of the Elephant's Dad can work out how to pick the locks of our cells by working through its big ring of molecular keys. It's not about feeding, between Kiln and us. It's just about death.

Someone else has a better light now. A dim hemisphere of chemical illumination that lends the whole interior of the chamber a sepulchral glow. In it, Keev is glowering at me. I don't see, though, how this particular misfortune can be my fault in any way. I will freely admit to my share of guilts, but not this.

After a while, Greely starts talking, her voice shaking only slightly. She wants to go out and salvage things from the flier. She wants to set up a line of communication with the camp. Maybe they'll send a fresh team to come and get us. We are a resource, after all. Someone else suggests they'll send drones out after us when we don't return. And maybe they will send drones out, but the mood is that it won't be *after us*. I'm naive enough to suggest that the tracking pins they saw fit to embed in our collarbones will tell them where we are, and I find out I'm the very last person to realize they're only good for tracking our movements within the camp. They are one hundred per cent an anti-insurrection security measure and precisely zero per cent useful if you get lost in the wilds.

It all comes down to the inalienable maths of the situation. We're not a priority. They have plenty of warm bodies they can replace us with, and the next shipment of fragmentation barges is already in transit from Earth, and the next few after that, spread out between one world and another like a dotted vector of misery and damnation. If the worst comes to the worst for them, given it already has for us, then The Science can chew over old data until the next consignment of convicts comes in. You don't really understand what worthless is until they put you on Excursions.

20.

We spend the night in the star chamber. If I had expected to look up and see a perfect conjunction between the holes in the ceiling and the night sky then I am disappointed. Sporadically, the hollow cannon-shot knock of the Elephant's Dad sounds, but it's further away, as though it's lost interest. Aside from that, the curved walls of our new home mute a lot of the disturbing, wordy chatter of the forest.

The things that live in here with us are quieter, if no less creepy. There are long stringy centipede critters that scatter into individual skittering segments if you startle them. There are squat purple slugs the size and shape of a shoe, their dorsal surfaces a lacework of slightly phosphorescent threads that are a separate creature. I guess they're probably metabolizing whatever the main body eats and turning out something nutritious as a by-product, or else something toxic that makes the whole living sandwich taste like shit.

The walls of the chamber have been colonized by fans of something like skeletal bracket fungus. By the light of a torch, I can see they put out slender tendrils that reach all the way to the outside, metres and metres long. They terminate in disturbingly hand-shaped clusters at each external port and window, photosynthetic black and ready to wave at the dawn. The whole compound assemblage is patrolled by little wasps that are actually more like three-pronged seashells with a fan-dance of thrashing feathery vanes, part wing, part filter-feeder. We think of them as wasps because the little bastards sting, which we find out fast enough. They don't want our alien proteins anywhere near their weird stretched-out fungus. The stings don't actually hurt much—any venom doesn't get any purchase on our biology—but nobody wants more Kiln in them than absolutely necessary.

Greely shows us how to cannibalize parts of our tattered suits to augment our filters. We try to sleep half-smothered in fraying scarves of the stuff, waking at every twitch and moan of the others, or when something outside gives out an extra-loud belch or mutter. The nocturnal life of Kiln is less well studied than its daytime equivalent, and that's because no fucker wants to go out into the pitch dark with a butterfly net and trust their luck.

And I dream. Or I'm not sure if it even qualifies as dreaming. I'm back and forth across the sleep boundary so much I probably don't get into proper restorative sleep. I have a sequence of quite unpleasant visions, though. I lie there and feel myself drifting, and soon enough, without rational transition, I'm out in the dark. Kiln murmurs restlessly around me through all its many spiracles, mouths and drum-like membranes, and all the other biomechanical ways sound can be made. I hear my name there, not spoken by a voice but as a composite, made up of a dozen different sounds that, struck together in the right tempo and sequence, make up the syllables "Arton Daghdev." The planet can even say it properly, like the Rasmussen of the dream before.

I must be fully dreaming by then. I see a fire out there

between the bloated jelly trees. There are dancing figures around it, some kind of alien bacchanalia whooping it up within sight of our ruin. I have no sense of the actual physical struggle to get there; my point of view just glides over. There are people dancing around the fire and they want me to join them, and I want to as well. I know them. I see Armiette Graisle there, and Booth and Clem, and the man Primatt showed me in the example tank. There's Shoer and Pellamy, all better now after being eaten by the Elephant's Dad. They're having a fine old time. Clem waves the arm he doesn't have. It's not a plastic prosthesis now. He shows it to me and it's like a bunch of flowers that open as I watch, only the flowers have eyes and teeth, and keep opening, and opening, like a dreadful fractal sequence, everything peeling onto a new horror that itself contains multitudes. I understand, as they caper around me, that the abstract concept of "a human who is dead" is somehow just one more brick that Kiln can incorporate into its construction-block biology. A metaphysical symbiont helping to complete the whole.

I mean, it makes sense while I'm dreaming it. But eventually that hideous bouquet arm of Clem's opens onto something that's too much even for the deviations of my sleeping mind and I wake shouting and thrashing. Everyone else wakes too, but it's not exactly for the first time, just my turn to be the annoyance. I'm given a few slaps and harsh words, then we all settle down again. I am so groggy I find one of the purple slugs under my head and, for a bleary few seconds, decide that it's kindly decided to be a symbiotic pillow for me, and that's absolutely okay. Then I come to my senses and yeet the thing the hell away from me. Because it's disgusting and alien, even though this is its home and

I'm the intruder on so many levels. I try to sleep again but the floor of the star chamber is hard and I can't get comfortable. I feel like I lie awake all night, except then dawn is needling down from the holes above and time has passed swiftly.

When I wake up, Keev, Greely and a couple of their regulars are gone. My entirely reasonable conclusion is that they've abandoned us for good, because the rest of us are simultaneously Jonahs and dead weight. They come back into the chamber, though, dragging a plastic sheet piled with miscellaneous parts of the flier. While the rest of us slept in, they've actually been remarkably industrious, salvaging pieces that might conceivably develop into a radio in some highly optimistic future. They have what they could find of the medical kit too, not that it was up to much in the first place, as well as other supplies that weren't crushed or burned up when the Elephant's Dad landed on the flier. These include a roll of tools and unclassifiable bits that might just have been loaded onto the sheet in haste, or maybe looked useful in the good light but now, in our straitened circumstances, are clearly just junk.

We find another chamber of the ruins that has a wider skylight. Keev asks who's good with machines. Greely is already heading up the Reinventing The Radio Subcommittee, so we should apply to her. Primatt applies, which garners a lot of suspicious looks, because pretty much everyone assumed her competencies were mostly just "good with paperwork." Ilmus advances themselves as mechanically minded too, as does Frith. I do not put myself forward. I can do more heavy lifting than you'd expect for a scholar of my years, and I can do heavy thinking, but the gap in between those poles where practical mechanics falls is not my forte.

"We'll get a signal to the camp," Keev tells us. "If we can. To tell them we're here. I know what I said before but still, they might come and get us." Presumably this is Greely talking him round on their trip to the wreck.

"Surely they'll come and get us," I say. The walls around make my words echo hollowly.

While the tech team are working on Project Radio, the rest of us have a variety of jobs. We use sealant to repair our hoods, and there are some spare filters amongst the salvage. We're all down to overalls now. Any intact part of our protective suits has been repurposed as headgear, but then it wasn't as though they were particularly protective to start with. And Earth-made human skin is a wonder at keeping out stuff you don't want inside you. Kilnishness bounces off it just like pathogens back home. We use more sealant on any open wounds and exhaust the last of the antihistamines and booster shots. I imagine the Kilnish inhabitants of the ruin interior are regarding us with contempt.

We organize our rations. There's considerably more than I'd expected, given we were only supposed to be out on a day trip.

"You planned for this," I accuse Keev. For a mad moment I think the whole thing has somehow been staged and the Elephant's Dad was in on it. Is there some hidden camp out in the wilds? Are the two thousand expired Labour Block numbers actually living it up as children of alien nature, having escaped the commandant's scrutiny under cover of being dead? Is the incinerator just the platform of an underground railroad and Keev in fact the greatest revolutionary liberator of the extrasolar camps? The answer to all of these things is, of course, a big fat *No*. But Keev is a cautious son of a bitch, and he knows, more than most, that things go wrong. And so, even though I know there's no damn way we can actually survive out here for long, he'd secreted long-life rations away in every flier so that nobody starves to death while waiting to find out how they're going to die. The little tins the things come in even turn out to be mostly elephant-proof. They might be the most durable human-made things on the entire planet, honestly.

Halfway through the day Greely and the tech team actually get a signal. After discovering about the rations, it seems utterly unthinkable that any more good news would come along, but Greely, Ilmus and Frith between them turn out to be at least two-thirds of an engineer, because they've managed to rig up a transmitter and receiver out of the salvage. Primatt is sitting back, looking sour and upset, because she wasn't the tech whizz she had apparently thought herself to be, and nobody had any paperwork they needed completing. Once more she's failed to win herself any points with the surviving members of the crew.

I don't recognize the faint, scratchy voice, intermittently drowned by waves of static.

The attempted conversation that follows requires more reconstruction than the actual makeshift radio they've cobbled together, but Keev eventually manages to make clear that we are indeed a stranded Excursions team and not some Kilnish life form that's got hold of a crystal and a couple of wires. He confirms we're still alive at the ruin we were sent to clear. He even names the people who are, in fact, still alive. He gets my name wrong, but he makes sure he says it, and Primatt's and Ilmus's as well, in case our academic credentials will help. The faint voice on the other end confirms receipt of the transmission and tells us to hold our position. It's not as though we have much choice in the matter. After the end of the fitful conversation, the Elephant's Dad knocks distantly again, like the punchline to a long and rambling joke. As though Keev and Greely snuck out during its morning constitutional but it's back in place now and can come stomp us at our convenience.

While we wait for word from base camp, we sit around the star chamber, chewing at the meagre ration of rations that Keev allows us. Looking back, that frugality shows he knew how things were going to go. Nobody's fool, Vertegio Keev.

"What happens if they don't?" Ilmus is the one to actually ask the question, although I know we're all thinking it.

Keev weighs up his words before answering, as though they, too, need to be rationed. "Well, then we'll walk."

We look at him like he's mad.

"We stay here, surely," Primatt states. "Where the wreckage is. Where they know we are." In the wan lamplight she's ashen and drawn, all her defeats written in lines on her face. The horror of what we've been through, how far she's fallen. I know one thing the flier medkit didn't have is all the stuff she normally takes for her leg, the tissue regenerators and pain-control drugs. Her stump must be getting steadily more inflamed. So she's hurting and, simultaneously, she's the last person on the team whom anyone has any time or sympathy for. I *do* have some sympathy, but I can do precisely jack to help her, except spend my own limited energy to take some of the burden off her share of the work. And, because she still thinks of herself as someone with extra privileges, she isn't shy at throwing her opinion out there.

"They'll send drones," she insists. "They'll send another team to finish clearing the ruin. It's on the schedule."

"And that never changes, right?" Greely needles her. "Like, every time there's a ruin where the locals don't want us."

"But Vessikhan, his studies," Primatt insists.

"Because ruins are such a scarce commodity on Kiln?" Greely pushes. "Your man Vessikhan, he needs *this* place right now, within the little window we can hold out in? He needs it so bad that they'll send the cavalry, fight off the animals, risk more workers and maybe some actual valuable lives? Or he can go to that nice easy ruin that C-team have already cleared and they write us off?"

This is all news to Ilmus and me, at least, but Keev and Greely have been in this job long enough to know it's standard policy. You get a ruin site where the local fauna has too many teeth and a bad attitude, it goes to the back of the queue and they just send Excursions somewhere easier. They'll get round to the problem places later, and maybe by then they'll be less problematic. This wetlands site has just been punted down the list as far as it can possibly go, after the loss of a flier and two deaths. And us stuck in a bottle under the artificial stars.

But Primatt isn't buying it. "They won't just hang us all out to dry," she insists, and in that "us" there is, I suspect, a lot of "me." She is Staff, after all, former head of The Science, with a bunk still kept warm for her on the gantry level. "They'll print out a new flier, a big one that can carry us and a rescue team. You don't just *walk*."

"Scotter," says Keev It's just a noise. As though Kiln's already got into him enough to speak through him, like it does through Rasmussen back at camp. An idiot alien glossolalia. Except it's a name. One I've never heard, for the decent enough reason that Scotter was long dead before either I or Ilmus arrived.

"It won't be like Scotter," Primatt says. "Not again. We had words, after. In Science. I went before the commandant, even."

"Someone tell me who the fuck is Scotter," I demand.

"You 'went before the commandant,'" Keev parrots to Primatt, ignoring me. "Before your good friend the commandant, over a nice glass of something. Before he pissed you out here with the rest of us."

"Lay off," I tell him. He looks at me like he only just remembered I exist and isn't happy about the reminder. I square my shoulders, because this is going to be him establishing dominance, fists first. He's tougher. He's also older. Maybe I'll get a good lick in before he can throw me down. He sizes me up, working out how he can take me without risking injury, then weighs up what it's worth to have Primatt as a punching bag against having me as an enemy.

"Scotter," he says, like he's rewound time back to my previous question, "and his team got themselves into just this mess. Oh, they crashed rather than a goddamn dinosaur coming out to trash their ride, but the result was pretty much the same. Camp knew where they went down. Sent drones, even. Saw plenty of sign they were still alive. Only there was no rescue party. There wasn't anything worth rescuing. Only people. Three other Excursion teams are at work. They clear places faster than your fancy bastard can study them. This one catches fire, they don't need to piss on it. That's how it goes."

"That won't be how it goes," Primatt insists. This time it's her words that just ghost by, ignored by everyone.

Greely gets back on the radio, trying to raise the camp. After almost an hour, and two changes of our limited stock of batteries, she gets that same scratchy voice telling us to keep holding our position.

We eat another meal, and by now we all understand Keev's stingy hand on the supply bag is a grim prediction of what he knows is going to happen.

"We can't do it," Greely tells him. "Nobody's ever done it." Although she flat out loathes Primatt, the two of them are absolutely of the same mind on the walking issue. Keev stares into the lamp as though it's a crystal ball and he sees a better future there. Or maybe just a different future. Maybe he wants to die doing something active, outside these confining walls. Die as a free human being and not just another kind of prisoner.

"I reckon three days," he says. "If we make good time. We have the supplies." The murderous logic of his own fore-thought. "We can make it."

"Keev," Frith says, "these filters aren't worth shit."

"They'll hold," Keev insists. He's almost messianic—not with a raving religious certainty but just a weird calmness that goes right to the core of him. The filters will somehow keep doing their job because what other choice do we have? "We'll tear up the overalls for extra layers. Three days' walk, and then we're home."

Home, butt naked and with Kiln growing out of every orifice, I think. We all think it, but nobody says it. Keev's calm radiates out like heat from a fire.

"Tomorrow, dawn," says Keev. "If we haven't heard, then they're not coming."

"They'll come for us," Primatt insists, but she's like the

whispering voice beyond the firelight and once more nobody answers her.

Late that night the radio speaks to us again. It's a bit of a shock as I don't think anyone realized it was still on. For a moment the distant human words are the voice of the planet, finally pushing its tendrils through the language barrier so it can taunt us with its indefatigable vitality. But it's not. It's not even the regular comms operator. It's Mox Calwren, possibly disgraced engineer.

"Keev, you there? Keev, man…"

"Here," Keev answers, voice hushed, although it's not as though they'll overhear him in the guard barracks back at the camp.

"You need to know," Calwren says, surfing in and out on the wash of the static tides, "they're not coming. Terolan said no to a rescue."

"I see," Keev says.

"They weren't even going to tell you, man," Calwren says. "I'm sorry. They've written off the whole site. I'm sorry."

There's real emotion in his voice, let through for just a moment by the fluctuating connection. The parting strands of some old friendship between Excursionista and engineer.

That's all we get from him, and Keev sits back and stares at the intestinal mess of wires and pieces that is our radio. He doesn't need to say what happens next, what comes with the dawn. We're going to walk.

21.

From amongst all the things I find within myself at that moment, the most shameful is the exceptionalism. I am Arton Daghdev, the *professor*, from *Earth*, maybe you've heard of me? The commandant certainly has. He had me to dinner, the moment I got off the barge. And yes, I was assigned to Excursions later, over the little matter of an armed insurrection, but still, *dinner*. Then he personally singled me out for torment via the odious presence of Ylse Rasmussen. Did that mean *nothing*? Is he going to ghost me like this? Where's my rescue mission? Why isn't the commandant combing the jungle for me just so he can bring me home and personally victimize me some more? Did all that time we spent together mean *nothing*? The knee-jerk reaction of my heart is that of a jilted lover. I hate myself for it. I clam up, not because of the appalling horror of our situation and the utter impossibility of what Keev is proposing, but because I can't let anyone glimpse the true *me* that this news has exposed.

The next morning, Greely has already snuck out to the wreck again and brought back the makings of a portable heater salvaged from engine components. She shows how she'll be able to flash-boil water and condense it, because water is water, once you've freed it of the organic detritus that silts it.

"So, as I said, we have rations for everyone for three days," Keev announces. He's even laid everything out on the ground so we can see he isn't stinting us. Meagre little meals, two per person per day. There are two left over, which he doesn't mention, though. Maybe they're going to be prizes for good behaviour or something.

"We can't do it in three days," Frith says flatly.

"Four days," Keev suggests. "And we arrive hungry." Nobody says, but everyone must surely think, that we'd arrive hungry even in three, looking at the miser's portions he's allocated.

Someone else, a lean woman named Hakira, suggests, "How about we do *that* with some of the locals?" Pointing at the water boiler that Greely's got working, and showing her lamentable lack of basic science skills.

"Just be glad," Ilmus tells her, "that there's enough… enough *distance* between Kiln life and Earth life so that's not possible."

"Biomass printer at the camp can do it," Hakira says mulishly.

"They don't, though," Greely puts in, disassembling the boiler for ease of transport. "They recycle the Earth mass as much as possible. Even though the reclaimer breaks everything down to loose molecule soup. Just in case."

"If we could eat them, then they could eat us," Ilmus presses.

Hakira stands up and fronts them, fists clenched, scowling. If we knew then what we find out later about her, maybe Ilmus wouldn't have stood their ground. But the science is just about the only thing they, Primatt or I have to bring to our predicament right now.

"They already fucking eat us," Hakira grates.

"They really don't, not easily. They have to *work* at it. These filters?" Ilmus plucks at the rags about Hakira's neck, which aren't really filters any more. "You think they're doing much, doing much of a job any more? If you were territory that Kiln life could colonize easily, you'd be all-over mushrooms right now. You'd be...be *sprouting* at every orifice." They actually push Hakira a bit, and the image they've raised is sufficiently nasty that the woman doesn't shove back. "Kiln life has to *work* to get a foothold on us. Has to fumble with its keyring a whole lot before it finds something that fits." They nod to me as it was my metaphor first. Then they turn to Keev. "But it will. Four days of constant exposure. Five. More. That's what we're not talking about, isn't it, Vertegio?"

All eyes are on Keev, then. Yes, it's theoretically possible for us to get from here to the camp using nothing more technologically sophisticated than our feet, but what then? Will they let us in?

"We've all seen the example tank," Ilmus goes on. An image of Clem comes to me, Kiln growing on the stump of his arm. "More, we've seen what happens to people after a few days in the tank." The ever-hungry incinerators, for when Earth biomass is so irretrievably contaminated that you can't even risk recycling it.

Keev faces up to them, to all of us, levelly. "I don't hear you suggesting an alternative," he says. "You want to sit here and die with rested legs, you be my guest."

In the lamp's wan light, under the artificial Kilnie stars of the ruin we're in, I catch a glint of tears in Ilmus's eyes. I hadn't realized they were so close to breaking down.

"Vertegio. Keev," Ilmus says, and there's a weird moment when one precise intonation within those words connects like a circuit in my head. Somehow I can read into it that Ilmus and Keev have been an item, at least once, somehow. Just as Primatt and I have. I've no idea when they would have found the opportunity, what illicit fumbling and exploration, what personal excursion for the two of them alone, but I am immediately convinced of it, beyond all evidence or reason.

Keev draws a heavy breath. "Listen," he says. "It's not Kiln that kills you. It's protocols." He gathers the rations, then distributes them. Everyone carries their own and if you decide to binge now and starve later, that's a gift you can give to your future self. Greely is passing the other kit around, too: the medicine, the boiler, tools that might double as weapons. We haven't heard the Elephant Dad since yesterday but that doesn't mean it's split into its component pieces and gone to pursue more peaceable ecological niches.

"The incinerators are for when you go crazy with it," Keev says. "That's the point of no return. You all know Rasmussen." I'm not sure if he's offering the woman's continued existence as a sign of hope but, if so, it's a severely fucked-up debating gambit. We all know Rasmussen and we do not want to end up like her.

Greely dumps something heavy into my arms, barely contained in a fraying sling she's improvised. It's about half the radio.

"When Kiln gets into you," Keev tells us, "some stuff it makes poisons your head. Starts you hooting, frothing and hollering like she does. That's when you've gone too far. It's the sign the damage is done and, by then, there's probably a whole chain of stuff living off you. They give you the real hard decontamination then. The fire. Kills Kiln and Earth both. So here's the deal. Any of us start raving and foaming, we leave them. Better, we knock them on the head, take their rations, keep going. You leave *me* if that happens to me." And now we see the working behind his neat sums with the rations. Because it's not really three days to camp. It's not even four, or five. We're so far out, out here in the marsh. But the rations could stretch if we don't all make it.

"Jesus, Keev," Greely says quietly.

"They won't let anyone in who's turned like that," Keev says. "So no point in bringing them along. But if the filters hold, we can stave it off just long enough. And if we can stave it off, we're fine. We're safe. They'll put us in quarantine, see if we'll turn, but we'll be fine. We can make it. We're fine." Solid, sensible, no-nonsense words.

I am about to say, "Remember Booth?" He just flat-out died after a day with slightly torn filters, and here we are wearing our entire surviving protective suits like neckerchiefs. Except I wonder, then, if Booth had died under regular decontamination like everyone said. Maybe he started with the froth and the babble after they isolated him, and they threw him in the fire. So I say nothing. Because, against all logic—against Rasmussen raving in her solitary confinement, against Clem in the example tank—I want Keev to be right.

Ilmus just gives out a scornful, despairing laugh. They don't think we're fine. They're a diligent scientist and know far too much about just how many discrete microbial organisms can pour joyously into your lungs with every single breath, like tourists rushing into an amusement park full of new rides to try out. They know how quickly our crappy filters would clog and degrade even if they were still intact. Kiln is already with us, the call coming from inside the house.

But they don't say anything more because, like Keev says, they don't have a better plan, or even a worse but different plan. Keev has leveraged his position as leader and veteran to propose something utterly impossible. The thing nobody's ever done.

The last wrangle before we leave the ruin is over the radio, because it's a big, dead weight dragging at my shoulder and I don't fancy it. I want to leave the damn thing because we've already established beyond reasonable doubt that we'll get nothing useful from it. Frith, who's carrying the other half, heartily concurs. But Keev and Greely think that, if we were to make it within a day of the camp and then end up too injured to continue, or in some other dire straits, they might reconsider the rescue. If we were literally just on the horizon, almost at the gates. It seems a weird Zeno's Paradox of a proposal to me, the idea that the closer we get—ergo the less in need of rescue we are—the more likely they are to rescue us. Especially if you place the base probability of rescue at zero per cent, which it most certainly is. So, if we get halfway to camp, the chance of rescue may well be double what it is now, but that's still a big fat zero, because maths doesn't give a shit about your indomitable human spirit. Then Greely points out that the camp has a nav beacon and the radio can pick that up. So this great weight of scrap plastic and metal Frith and I are lugging between us is a high-tech, space-age substitute for a little compass that would weigh only twenty grams and fit in a pocket. But which we don't have, because that would be terribly nineteenth-century of us. Hooray for progress.

There is no sign of the Elephant's Dad as we emerge. Obviously Keev and Greely have been scavenging the wreck without any obvious incidents of being trampled or eaten, so *that* part of the plan was always decently likely. We're able to see the open air and the bright sky again, but it doesn't enthuse us as you'd think. The sky remains that yellow-black-blue colour like nothing ever seen on Earth, which still jangles at my eyes with its essential wrongness. The dome of the camp filters it out so it's only when you're actually excursing that you're exposed to it. And it's sufficiently unearthly—literally—that you never get used to it.

Below that confounding sky are the wetlands—the jelly trees, the windsock stalks and the marshy ground. Keev has already taken a reading from the radio, pointing at landmarks to make for. We can't even cut a straight course without going knee-deep in sludge, and of course that sludge is festering with organisms large and small. We can see it quiver and churn with life even from here. Nobody's keen to go paddling. Wheezing through our patched-together masks and scarves, bent beneath our burdens, we pick our way over the higher ground, the drier ground, trying to curve back towards each of Keev's waypoints.

Things that aren't insects keen past us, darting up in sudden excesses of activity and then dropping down, wings open like parachutes as they harvest the floating bounty of the air. That same bounty we're desperately trying to avoid inhaling. Even then, at the outset, Primatt starts falling behind. I keep going back to help her, and that means I'm also falling behind and running out of strength. Strength that won't really be replenished much by the crumbs of rations I can permit myself.

I wonder ghoulishly if anyone is going to play the odds: scoff their meals all together, keep themselves strong and then wait like a vulture for the first of us to fall. That would be the smart game. Someone'll think of it. It won't be Keev, because he really does intend to save his entire team. His self-image as a survivor is inextricably entangled with that of himself as our leader. It won't be Ilmus, either, because they were always a rules-follower at heart. But someone will work out that their own personal survival can be better safeguarded if they bet against the rest of us like that. Not even actively sabotaging anyone, just working the numbers on the basis that *someone* will end up in the Rasmussen way soon enough, and then they can refill their supplies.

Once I've thought of all that, of course it becomes very tempting to *be* that person. To tell myself that, given one or more of my fellows have doubtless already made that choice, I'd be a fool to keep following the rules. I'd be playing into their hands. I ought to prioritize keeping my own strength up.

I think of this particularly on the first day when we come to the river. Nobody had thought of the river, needless to say. The flier didn't care about it, but alas the gravitational pull of Kiln is within tolerances of Earth's, only a little under. We cannot do great big moon-leaps to vault across that murky, brackish flow.

At least this gives Primatt and me the chance to catch up. I see a few hard looks from the others. Predatory looks. *Aren't you decently frothing and mad yet?* looks.

The river stretches ahead of us. It's not actually that far. A little prodding with an extendable rod Greely has salvaged shows it's not even that *deep* either. Probably over your head in the centre, so deep enough, but barely a stream, honestly. It's full of life, of course. There's plenty of stuff anchored to the bottom and coursing with the current like waterweed, as well as other stuff eeling between it, or frogging, or jelly-fishing. All the many ways that different bits of Kiln get around, which they rent out to other organisms for a share of the communal take.

"Is there a ford?" I ask. I receive a range of odd looks. Some people who want to communicate, *How the fuck are we supposed to know?* and others who haven't even come across the word "ford" before, because it's not exactly in daily circulation in our modern age.

Keev is staring at the water like it was put there to personally spite him. It's Primatt, of all damn people, who has the thought. She goes to the nearest jelly tree, which is podging there by the waterside, dangling finger-like growths into the flow. She whacks it with her stick. Its soggy rind goes rigid under the stroke. She prods it: soft. She whacks it again: hard. I see her square her shoulders, brace her artificial leg.

She goes ape on it, basically. Battering at the exterior of the tree like it gave the commandant the idea to demote her. Venting all of her frustrations on it. She lets out strangled, brutal grunts as she flails at it, until I think she'll shatter her stick, and then what will she do? Until everyone assumes that she has indeed given into Kiln-madness and we can strip her of her rations, and throw her in the river once she's exhausted herself. Which would be, I think horribly, a great waste of the large investment of Earth proteins that Nimell Primatt represents.

She stops eventually, gasping for breath through her swaddled mask. She prods at the tree's side. It's solid now. She's bruised it into a hard mass of shiny carapace, no more jelly left in it. It's learned, basically, that staying rigid is more efficient than shifting back and forth. Or something like that. Some biological lesson Primatt picked up in her time as tenured department head, now put to practical use in the field.

"Cut it," she gasps out to Greely. "Cut it open before it sends any signals to unclench." In the face of our massed blank looks, she adds, "Fucking *boat*, you ignorant fuckers."

The boats are good enough on the water at first that we speculate about just punting all the way home, until Greely puts a hole below the waterline by pointing out that this river doesn't actually go in the right direction, not even slightly. Also, by the time we reach the far shore, our conveyances are getting decidedly soggy and unresponsive to further belabouring. Still, our entire band make it across the river on the first day and nobody's going mad even a little bit.

When we sit down to eat, as the darkness in the sky overtakes the yellow, I think about my earlier considerations. The metagame of rationing your rations, short-selling the expedition against the idea that the more responsible of us, in stinting themselves, will grow weak and fall soonest—like Primatt, say. Would anyone else have thought to beat jelly into a boat? Because that sounds like some weird thing out of a folk tale, until you see it done. I speculate about there being a band of lean, mean and selfish survivors, half our number or less, but all strong because they've been holding back from everyone else. And then there's another river or similar obstacle, and not enough of us to work together to cross it. That kind of game-theory thinking only works if you treat the people around you as resources and dead weight. If you assume the natural unit of survival is one individual, and not the group.

I ponder on that, and on Kiln's life strategies.

After the river, towards the end of the day, and still within the curtilage of the wetlands, we hear the Elephant's Dad again. Not close, but not far enough. Or else another Elephant's Dad, the same community of parts making the same macro-species, or perhaps a community of different elements coming together for the same general effect. Generating the same hollow sound that throws our hearts into our throats and freezes us to immobility as we wait for the monster to waddle, or scuttle, into sight. But the jelly trees which press all around us are undisturbed by its bulk, and when it sounds again it's further off. Still, after that, it's always with us, in my head. Tracking us, feeling out every inch of Kiln we've contaminated, tasting us with the mouths it has in its feet, then passing that information to its internal Subcommittee In Charge of Punishing Aliens. Ilmus speculates that it had eggs or something laid in the ruin, some external life-cycle stage of elements in its inner community. I just know it's really, really angry with us.

Then it starts growing dark, and Keev needs to pick somewhere to spend the night. Now's our chance to ham-fist the logistics of camping out in the wilds of an alien world. The ground is firmer by now. We're coming to the edge of the wetlands, following a new waterway girded with the violent yellow spears of reed-like organisms. They rustle and move like the quills of a porcupine, and beyond them the stream is unquiet with life. Globular trees resume the forest a few metres from the water. As the darkness deepens, the many voices of Kiln talk to us like a hundred multilingual news channels all broadcasting at once, all with only bad news. We're never going to make it.

PART 3
FRATERNITÉ

22.

Their faces when we make it back. Even through the gas masks. To see us stomping out of the forest, without precedent, without warning, then almost at the gate of the camp before they've worked out what's going on. Keev's lost work party of Excursionistas, back from the almost-dead.

I'm jumping ahead now, I know. But there are more tales of the march to come, don't worry. Days of it, until the most erudite of any potential audience will be thoroughly sick of my surmises about Kilnish ecobiology and will wish that the Elephant Dad had eaten us all. But first I want to show how it was to them, in the camp.

There are guards at the gate as we reach it, some still dragging their protective gear into place. The good gear, the rubbery fetishwear stuff, not the paper outers they gave us. They've got guns. It's not as though the trek thus far was exactly free of life-threatening peril, but we come very close to being shot right then and there. Shot and buried in a shallow grave decently far from the camp, never to be mentioned in Terolan's reports. As we knew it would be. The journey of seven days and nights in a wilderness starts with a single step, and it can end with one too. So we'd had to time things carefully, to give ourselves the best chance.

Even I knew a lot of the camp's work routines by then,

and to Keev they were second nature. Being assigned to them was practically high holiday for him, because if he was on them, it meant he wasn't out in the wilds being eaten by nature. And one thing that the camp had to deal with regularly was cleaning the outside of the dome. Kilnish air is inconveniently full of life, and a lot of that life is looking for real estate where it can set up minuscule home, then invite some like-minded friends over to join the newly founded commune. So every day a General Labour team was kitted up in paper suits and sent out with hoses and scrubbers to debarnacle the dome exterior. Because they won't hose down Excursions but God forbid the Commandant's precious view is ruined. Based on Keev's foreknowledge of this, and a synchronization of watches, we make sure we turn up just as one cleaning shift troops back in for decontamination and another is coming out. By the time we're standing before the guns of the guards, the word's run round the camp seven times already. *Keev's back. Vertegio Keev has done the impossible. He's brought them home.* I imagine the commandant's androgynous cyborg lieutenant reporting to him in breathless tones, asking what's to be done. I imagine him, Terolan, the complex man of sophistication, weighing the scales and trying to guess what the current going rate for a drachm of Hope is.

Hope is what it's about. That most human of qualities. People may rise up if you deny them food and water. They may take up the torch and the club if you suppress their religious beliefs, or separate them from their children, or a variety of other liberties that authoritarian regimes have dabbled with. But hope's the tricky one. A people without hope, what will they do? One of two things: nothing, or *everything*. And the commandant couldn't risk either of those extremes. Neither the nihilistic uprising where everyone knew they were doomed, and so why fear one death over another, nor the sitting-on-your-hands of utter despair. Because it was a *labour* camp and was therefore dependent on the actual labourers putting a bit of effort into it. And what's hope on Kiln? It's if you find yourself cut off in the wilds and manage, by insane luck, grit and savvy, to find your way back, and they don't just shoot you dead in your disintegrating shoes because you might be a contamination risk.

Might is doing a lot of work in that sentence. We do not look pretty, we returnee Excursionistas. We've done our best to scrub up but it's past the spit-and-elbow-grease stage if I'm brutally honest. We're all a little shaggy with pieces of Kiln that have become fond of us. Become, as it were, attached. We stand there, and the guards stand there, and everyone waits to see what order the commandant will give.

He might try to have his cake and eat it: have us taken somewhere nicely out of sight before making our last act of labour the digging of our own graves. Have us gassed, only it turns out—oh no!—they were too far gone to save. But nobody would believe it. There aren't enough fifth column-ists on all of Kiln to swing opinion that far back towards the party line. Or he might have us shot and just gamble on the collective hope of the rest of the camp not taking too much of a hit. I try to put myself in his shoes, and know that he's just a work boss, at the end of the day. All the scholarly pretensions and fancy uniforms in the Mandate don't change that. He has a job to do and is expected to turn in results. He is, like all of them, dependent on his workers, whether convicts or employees. And that last is the final sore point, because we have brought Primatt back. Primatt, who was sent out with Excursions but was never technically a convict. So can he be quite so cavalier with her as he might be if it was just we merry band of ragamuffin prisoners? I mean, yes, he obviously intended her to die, and be forgotten, but that's a world away from ordering her shot in the head.

None of us are frothing or gibbering, not even a little bit. We stand there, as neat and orderly as anyone could be in the circumstances. Not a touch of Rasmussen to us, nor Clem in the example tank, none of that. So we wait to be let in, and the guards wait for the order that will restore vital function to their little trigger fingers, and then to the bigger phallic substitutes they're clutching in their sweaty, rubber-gloved hands. Everyone in the camp holds their breath.

They put us through decontamination forwards and back-wards, needless to say. *This* is the big one, the most extreme hosing-down I've ever had. They scrub us until our skin's raw. Some of it they have to scrape off, even cut out. The stuff that's grown in, set down hyphae and roots, anchors and hooked claws in our skins. Damn me but it hurts, coming back to civilization. I feel ten kilograms lighter, denuded of everything they scour from me. I see the heap, before they burn it. The pile of Kilnie biomass they've flensed from our outsides, not even including the stuff we shat out, that died inside us under punitive decontamination. Necessary sacrifices, we all understand. Sometimes just wiping your feet on the mat isn't enough. Nobody suggests that we need to go for another few work days out in the wilds before we're given our chemical shower and deworming tablets. Excursions catches a break, this once. We huddle together in silence under the blistering bleach of it, choking on the fumes, eyes screwed shut and lips clamped. Taking solace from the company, because we came *back*. All of us. We did what nobody does. We found a way.

The airlock they keep us in has clear walls, like so much of the downstairs portion of the camp. Naked together, backs braced against the searing spray, we feel the eyes of the world on us. The wonder of the Labour, the discomfort of the guards. They don't know what we are.

And they're still not taking any chances. Fair enough. I can't blame them for a little caution. Extraordinary claims require extraordinary proof. Unless they're claims made in accordance with Mandate doctrine, of course, in which case they're just handwaved through, in my experience. By the time we've been thoroughly decontaminated, they've printed and assembled a pen for us, like in a zoo. A big box with transparent plastic sides, just in case any of us thought that there might be renewed privacy in our near future. They connect it to the airlock, so we've walked from the outside to the chemical showers, to the quarantine pen, without ever sharing a breath of air with any other human being in the camp. There we are, in our big transparent box, the new monkeys in Terolan's Mediocre Menagerie. They want to see if we'll start screaming and hopping about. Throwing shit like Rasmussen. The one mod con we've been allowed is a two-way link and that's strictly for their convenience. It's kept switched off, unless the lieutenant is there to quiz us about just what the hell actually *happened* to lead to the inconvenient fact of us coming back from the presumed-dead.

Keev is our spokesman, of course. He tells them over and over what happened. Not even a long story, because he's not a natural raconteur and doesn't bother with the trivial details, like what tried to eat us and the witty topics of our repartee on the road. He tells them that we walked, basically. The impossible thing, just walked. He demonstrates, clownish, miming, one foot in front of the other, when the lieutenant appears unable to even understand what the word means any more. We survived Kiln. That's the jagged peg that won't fit into their hole of a mind. We made our filters last, used the rags of our suits, tore up the artificial fibres of our overalls. And, finally, we just about held our breath until we got here. We eked out our rations, boiled water, stretched the inadequate bounty of a day's supplies to cover a week's hard trek through the monstrous wilderness of an alien world. We're heroes. They treat us like monkeys but we're heroes.

Primatt sits against one of the transparent sides, adjusting the new prosthetic they've printed for her to replace the useless, crusted stick she left behind on the trail. She's down another half-inch of leg, but they'd calibrated the replacement using the original dimensions of her stump so she's now screwing it out longer at the knee. They'd had to cut hard where the old scars of her stump were an open door to Kiln, and maybe then they cut some more because she symbolizes their frustration with the entire inexplicable situation. The surgery, carried out through clumsy waldo arms, and without much in the way of anaesthetic, means she's in considerable pain. But she's lived with that forever anyway. The thing taking up tenancy in the pain centres of her brain isn't new, just the old leaseholder with a few guests having a loud party. We do what we can: a hand to the shoulder, a word, an understanding. Spreading the burden until each of us carries a needle of it and Primatt can rest.

We sit there, naked in the glass box. Staring, silent, at those who come to stare at us. We do not go mad. None of us leaps up to scream and caper and beat at the walls or scrawl cryptic sigils in excess biology. We are the work crew of Vertegio Keev, and we are reporting for duty after an unauthorized absence. Very sorry; mitigating circumstances.

In the end they have to let us out, because as a permanent exhibit we'd cause more disruption. Kiln did not drive us mad. It just drove us together.

Primatt and I are given the red-carpet treatment of inquisitions. Former head of The Science; former professor back on Earth. We are, just peripherally and by our fingernails, of a sufficient social class to be hauled before Terolan himself. It is not for dinner, and we don't dress up. Primatt is still unsteady on the adjusted leg, so I make myself a part of her walking rhythm, a hand to her elbow at the swing of each step. She abandons her balance, over and over, because I'm there to catch and correct her. We make a three-and-a-half-legged walking machine between us.

They make us don paper filter suits to cross from the monkey house up onto the gantry. The commandant doesn't want us trekking either another world or another social class onto his nice clean management floors, and he's hardly going to want us there like Adam and Eve. The Wild Man and Woman of Kiln. Even then, we end up in a private primate enclosure set up in his office so the great man doesn't have to share our air. He also has friends in to enjoy our apery and japery. Helena Croan and Parrides Okostor are there as our former colleagues from Dig Support too, doubtless to judge whether there's anything about us that's less *us* than it should be. And I could tell them. I could explain how we're both one hundred per cent *us*, one hundred and ten per cent, never been *us*-ier in our lives. Even if, separated by the glass and in that shabby paper formal-wear, there's more than the whiff of *them* as well. But then the Mandate was all about those neat boxes, those false binaries. Orthodox and unorthodox; his and hers; us and them.

Also present, on behalf of The Science, is Vessikhan for Archaeology, looking a bit blank at what precisely he's supposed to contribute. And true, he and Primatt worked cheek by jowl for a long time, but his areas of study are usually safely dead for centuries before anyone asks him to draw a conclusion, so he's a bit out of his depth. By his side, looking actually frightened by our very presence, is Foop, representing the very biological sciences he's currently shrinking from. His real name is Iudas Esteveril, Primatt has told me. I am not even kidding that he's called Iudas.

Terolan regards us with reptilian patience while the others quiz us. Vessikhan is quiet and reasoned, asking us practical questions he's prepared in advance. "Tell us again how you survived certain death?" We take it in turns to speak. I wanted to try finishing each other's sentences to freak them the fuck out, but Primatt vetoed the idea because it would probably get us fed into the incinerator. No student practical jokes on the commandant right now. Instead, we praise Keev's steady leadership. We give them a selection of the hardships we endured, and how we overcame each. When I falter, Primatt has my back. When she stutters, or her leg stabs at her, I'm ready for it. I'd prefer the moral support of the others, the full dramatic troupe of survivors re-enacting our epic journey, with offstage sound effects and some iambic pentameter, but this is enough for now.

Croan takes over. Her questions veer into the specialist, chasing our revealed challenges down scientific alleys. It's less an inquisition and more defending our thesis before a panel. I hadn't realized just how committed she is to the curriculum, in her quiet way. A convict, yes, but a researcher first and foremost. The flame of scientific enquiry leaps high in her.

Terolan cuts her off and she shuts down. She's only Labour after all. Parrides Okostor tries to take up the slack but he's quite overcome: starting, stopping, eyeing the commandant. "How...?" is as far as he makes it into the outback of our trek. A plaintive demand, and I remember him going down in the wretched squib of Clem's uprising. I can only guess at his inner monologue, but surely *It could have been me out there* must loom large in it. Him stuck in this box too, or out in the monkey house. Or never coming back at all, like Shoer and Pellamy. His dry voice creaks to a halt.

Foop, desperate to justify a promotion the paint's still wet on, accuses us of...what? He wants to throw something at us but he can hardly have us executed just for maliciously refusing to die.

"They've been fully decontaminated," Croan says tonelessly. Before she can be shut down again, Vessikhan backs her up, eyes on Primatt. "We've all seen the logs," he states. "And we've seen the test results. None of them is showing the mental distress we're all...familiar with." He gives a twitch of a glance in the direction of Rasmussen's solitary confinement. "And we're short-handed until the next barge arrives, what with the..." There's another twitch, in the non-spatial direction of dead Clemmish Berudha and his lieutenants. "I need a wider data set of glyphs. They're Excursions. Veterans." None more so.

Terolan stares at him as though suddenly reconsidering which side of the glass Vessikhan is supposed to be on. "You have claimed to be on the point of a breakthrough for years, Doctor Vessikhan."

The bald man holds his gaze. "There is nothing more important in the world, Commandant, than decoding the Kilnish writings. *Writings*, sir. An alien civilization has set down its thoughts here. And, as that civilization has now vanished, and Bioscience has found no trace of anything that might have created it, those writings are all we have. I need the experienced manpower to clear new ruins and record more of the script." It isn't script and he'll never decode it using the usual Earth-based means at his disposal, but his dedication to the idea is touching. The academic in me appreciates him.

"So," Terolan says, the judge with a black cap halfway to his head. "They survived." He shrugs, a weirdly normal human gesture for the big man in the big chair. He looks at the two of us, behind glass like exhibits. "Don't think this moves you out of Excursions."

There is nowhere we'd rather be. We're counting on it.

They send us back down to the monkey house, and they'll burn the paper suits after we doff them. Still no contact. I don't get to brush past Vessikhan on the way out, which is just as well. The weird euphoria that's gripped me means I wouldn't be able to stop myself whispering, "I know what they mean," in passing. Leaving him gaping like a fish.

Rasmussen is screaming to herself as we go down the gantry stairs, and I want to tell her, "Soon, soon."

We don newly printed overalls, then file out. They're watching us, listening to us. There will be cameras and mics on us, and quislings hovering nearby to catch some suggestion of omission in Keev's story. They'll haul each of us in, over the next few days, rough us up, shake us down, demand to know what *really* happened. Hope to squeeze us individually for the pips we didn't give up as a group. But we hold out on them, we few, we happy few, we band of siblings. Of somethings. So it is that we're eventually allowed to return to the Labour Block.

Back in the Labour Block we eat our meals, use the facilities, perform our chores. We touch the surfaces and breathe the air. I feel as though an armoured gauntlet within me, that has been clenched tight, is now loosening one finger joint at a time. The near end of a bridge that leads all the way to the ruins builders of Kiln.

23.

The march: day one

So, going back a few, or many, steps, it's our first night on the march. Nobody has much experience with the nocturnal scene on Kiln. Personally, I'd expect a whole shift change of chimeras, with the incomers bearing adaptations—meaning whole new onboard organisms—for the cold and the dark. In the end, I find I'm not familiar enough with the day shift to be entirely sure. I also realize I'm showing my Earth assumptions, because it's not technically necessary here. Maybe every Kilnish creature carries some independent elements which sleep out the day and then wake to provide specialist services after dark. Perhaps something evolved to be a midnight automatic pilot, taking over the thinking while the main brain goes to sleep. Or each composite species has day and night variants with a different selection of passengers. We just don't know. Even with the libraries of findings by people like Croan and Primatt, all the way back to Rasmussen herself, we still know so very little.

There's an attempt to make a regular fire, caveman style. A couple of us have lighters, but everything we try them on fails to burn properly. Some parts of the ecosphere just crisp black. Others sweat themselves so damp on the application of heat that you couldn't have set fire to them in the camp incinerator. Still more things, seemingly entirely vegetative, take violent offence to being set alight. Frith is viciously bitten by kindling. So we give up on singsongs and spooky stories around the campfire.

Greely boils some water with her heater. The dried scum left behind after evaporation turns my stomach, like one of those particularly whole-food herbal teas I remember from some subculture or other I hid out in. We take meagre bites of our rations. Keev is forcing himself to be optimistic, radiating positivity so that we can practically warm ourselves by him in lieu of the fire. The ferocious, aggressive, uncompromising positivity of the team leader who tells you it's going to be in on deadline, even though the deadline was yesterday. A maniacal, frightening confidence that holds your gaze and dares you to challenge it. I see what he's doing. He's no fool. He just knows that the moment we lose heart—hope, that ephemeral but absolutely necessary rung on the hierarchy-of-needs ladder—we're lost.

It's not like we can't do the maths. Or maybe some of us can't. There could be people who believe the five-day march, or even the three-day march. I myself don't know. I was never that good with distances. Or maybe there are those who believe that our vanishingly small stock of comestibles will last three days. Surely nobody believes five. Or the longer-than-five our march will surely take. But however you slice the time, you'd have to be as crazily positive as this act Keev is putting on to believe we're going to make it. I see the same thoughts in every face.

Then suddenly the "rock" half of us are sitting on moves, upsetting Greely's water boiler as it levers itself out of the damp ground. It's a thing like a boulder except it's also a crab the colour of bruises. Eyes weave out from under its stone shell, where a multitool of pliable limbs glisten against one another like intestines.

Keev's gun is out, except he has no more bullets. Ilmus has the flamethrower, which contains just about enough salvaged fuel for one more fruitless attempt to kindle a campfire. Everyone else scatters, yours truly included, and it's a wonder some of us don't become lost to the darkness and the planet.

The boulder crab regards us and makes an *ugugugugug* sound, thoughtful and contemplative. The eyes are in constant motion, making me wonder how it can focus on, or process, anything. Except maybe each eye is an individual thing that somehow pretties up its data before sending it on to the central visual component of the creature. I try to imagine the thing getting together with its rock-crab pals to build ruins and inscribe language. Have we discovered the elusive Wild Man of Kiln hiding under this shell? It seems unlikely. Humans and alien crab monster regard one another thoughtfully. Those of us who'd fled further out creep back as the chance of another Elephant's Dad scenario recedes.

The boulder crab's shell tilts ponderously round until it has turned its armoured back on us. It settles again, canted at a steep angle. I have the distinct impression we are being shunned by the fashionable neighbours.

After a while we start using it as a windbreak.

We're leaving ourselves open. It might get up again and use its horrible selection of limbs to eviscerate us, or eat us, or inject its eggs into our fragile human bodies. Although, biologically, only the first of those things wouldn't require some serious on-the-fly adaptation. But we're tired, and being scared takes energy we don't have. Our stash of rations is sufficiently small that perhaps the creature's in more danger of being eaten by us. Although we, too, lack the ability to cross that chasm of differing biologies to digest much on Kiln. Possibly somewhere, something puts out a nectar-analogue that is just a very simple carbon-hydrogen-oxygen molecule requiring absolutely minimal effort to crack open for energy. Because that might actually be glucose, and therefore just the sort of sugar the commandant could serve along with the tea, and we could eat it for a quick fix of sustenance. An alien biochemistry, but using the same elements, because we're all in the same universe. We are all star stuff, as the man said. Even on worlds circling around other stars, the stuff of those stars is the same.

But if anything on Kiln is giving out free candy, we don't know about it. It's not something that Primatt ever discovered. So I sit there, hungry and in the dark, dog tired but unable to get my thoughts to stop racing around the backyard of my mind. Sometime past midnight, I conjecture the hypothesis that nothing on Kiln will be giving out sugary treats to enlist the cooperation of some other life form. Not because of divergent biochemistries, but because the whole flowers-and-bees co-evolution business—one of the great heights of co-specific dependence on Earth—is just baby steps for Kiln. Here they went past that kind of ham-fisted bribery millions of years ago. You don't need to advertise for help like flowers do. There are species with long résumés already pre-adapted to fulfil all your symbiosis needs.

Most of us have thrashing dreams at one point or another, and people are constantly being woken up to take their turn on watch. Keev's low murmuring snaps me alert every time he bends over someone to tell them it's their shift. When it's his own turn to get his head down, I find I can't sleep at all anyway. He's across the far side of our little huddle of bodies—big-spooning for Ilmus actually—but I feel like he's standing over me. I'm weirdly *aware* of him, in a way I've only ever been when, as a much younger man, I was at a party with someone I was achingly in love with. I will tell you up front, I am not in any way in love with Vertegio Keev. But still, I'm so keenly alive to him being there, awake, brooding. His years, weariness and disappointment. With life, with everything. Bitter, bitter Keev. I know he was a fighter, once. He doesn't talk about himself but, after my initial suspicions, I'd had the lowdown from Greely.

He'd fought the Mandate over workers' rights, at the factory he was foreman for. And somehow that transferred over, after they transported him. A need to do the best for those he's responsible for. What had him sent out here is what's trying to get us home. No big causes for Keev any more. Getting his handful back to camp, though, is something just small enough to fit into his shrivelled heart. And I lie about staying awake; I am drifting by then. Even my interrogative mind is worn down by its exercise, until every part of me collapses inwards towards sleep. I fall into a pit of Keev's bile and Primatt's pain. Where Greely's shoe has rubbed her foot raw. Ilmus shivering, spooned against Keev for warmth, because their circulation has always been bad. The boulder crab's deep, slow philosophy. The Elephant's Dad, still out there, and the ruins we left, and, far off, mad Rasmussen crying out, all swirling and recombining in my hypnagogic mind.

We hold together and we open up, that's what we do. On the next day's march, when we pause to savour the crumbs Keev prescribes, we start talking. About the *us* we never spoke of before. That old prison adage: do your own time. The time of others is emotional labour that adds to the physical. Opening your door to someone else means there's no longer a door between you and them, if they've got a shiv. Except that's what we do—the opening, not the shiv-ving. We start to talk about the "before." Because we're human, and we're a social species, though not quite to the extent the locals are. We don't go mad. Not a froth, not a gibber. In forming comprehensible words, organized into real sentences, and passing these gems of human creativity around the circle, we reassure each other that our wits remain intact. That we still have each other.

I think of Rasmussen. I suspect we all do, because it's all very there-but-for-the-grace-of. Our journey has two destinations. One is the camp, the other is to that hell Rasmussen has been consigned to. The peculiar Kilnish take on the madness of crowds that you can exemplify all on your own. Ylse Rasmussen, pioneering scientist and the only victim of Kiln-madness they didn't send straight to the incinerator. The thought which surprises me is that her sporadic human utter-ances are no more than the truth. That she is lonely. Even we, condemned death-marchers, have one another. She, in the heart of the labour camp, is completely alone.

Thoughts run to nostalgia. After all, there's not much else to talk about. The act of walking is mechanically simple and gives rise to little of interest. It's not as though we can spec-ulate enthusiastically about what we'll do when we get home. And so we revert to the past—distant both in space and time.

Do you remember Earth? We all do, of course. Like yesterday. Even Keev. We assemble a communal Venn diagram of the Earths we recall, fitting our experiences together and finding the areas of overlap. A busy planet, light years away, and yet we're not even the strangers we think we are. I was in the same room as Keev once. I was very young; he was just younger than now. A firebrand giving a speech about safety standards and industrial action, after they'd found out half the retirees that year had radiation poisoning. That had been his thing. Not regime change, not violent systemic overthrow, just "Please let us work in a way that doesn't kill us quite so much." Did it do any good? Was it worth watering down the fire so much just to try and achieve some sort of result? Keev's presence here on Kiln suggests not. But, now we've happened on that shared moment, I remember. My parents had taken me there. They'd wanted me to reach adulthood with open eyes. We'd managed to get out before the security enforcers arrived to break it up. There's always someone who tells, after all.

Greely talks about a bank-robbery job that some of us vaguely recall from the news channels. She's not political and never was, at least until now. Being incarcerated by an oppressive regime makes you political by default. We find out the public reporting of the job was almost entirely fiction, designed to vilify the perpetrators. There was none of the guns, safes and smash-and-grab business, just Find The Lady with a string of zeros and ones that briefly made her ridiculously rich. But one of her gang turned out to be undercover and that was that. She talks philosophically about that turncoat. How they were integral to the planning. And how, without them, nothing on the same scale would have happened. Not the first time the security services have knocked something over just so they could get a pat on the head for clearing up the mess. She's sure they squirrelled a decent chunk of the take away in unmarked accounts before they turned everyone in.

Ilmus Itrin has a confession. It hovers and twitches about their face while Greely talks, until they can hold it in no longer. They sold me, once. They were the rat, though if so then it was one already in the maze and presented with a single way out. They start crying as they confess it, and I think of every damn conversation we had, when *they* were accusing *me*. I wait for the tide of anger to lift me to violence or denunciation. I'm owed it. For once I actually get to rant and rage and be *right*. Hear me roar! They don't even put distance between us. They present their glass jaw for my avenging fist, because surely that's the first step of any apology.

The chasm that opened in me, ready to receive all that righteous rage, it stays empty. Where the courage of my convictions should have been, I find just the sad under-standing that I'm a hypocrite, and I would rather have Ilmus here as my friend than salve my pride. I feel the threads of history and association that connect us pull taut, and I do not want to sever even one of them.

They seem to understand where I've gone to, without my needing to articulate it. I am giving them the space to tell the story, and they do. When Security had them in the chair, deploying sleep deprivation, sensory overload and the wrenched fingernails, there was a point when they broke and gave me up. Named me for The Filth and piled such incredible fictions of revolutionary zeal on me that the

Mandate should have had conscripts searching all the kingdoms of Earth door to door to track me down. Except by then Ilmus had gone through so much they could only mumble, and the interrogators didn't catch what they were saying, or that it was a name, so therefore didn't go after me. Otherwise I'd have been here on the same barge as them, with them all the while knowing it was their fault. I understand, and perhaps I always knew deep down. I don't need to say anything. The words that have been knotting Ilmus up inside for so long are out now, and they know they're absolved. I feel the release of a tension between us that I'd registered but misinterpreted as their suspicion of me.

Frith was in a cult, her personal unorthodoxy. Secretary to a Great Mandate Man but secretly religious, all her life seeking something *More* than the mundane universe around her. A desperate hunt for meaning, like pouring the water of herself out onto parched earth. And it found its way downwards through the usual channels, because people who organize cults tend to be quite same-y. It's amazing how many different religious start-points quickly find the same old stress fractures which allow the cult leader to sleep with a lot of young women and take a lot of drugs, while everyone else is permitted to earn sanctity through adulation and slavish obedience. Then one of her fellows had an existential crisis, was deprogrammed and passed over their hidden sanctum to the Mandate. Frith goes over it all without vitriol. Between the words, I understand that, here on Kiln, she's finally finding what she was looking for, but which was never there on Earth. In a way, I teeter on the brink of my own revelation, but being a man of reason, I shrink back from it.

Yeremy, another of Keev's people, was a data analyst and

never did anything at all, certainly not the thing they accused him of. A blameless cog in the Mandate's machine, until a bureaucratic error pointed the wrong finger at him. So here we have someone who was never on a subcommittee, or robbed a bank, or even fiddled his taxes, but the algorithm looked into his data footprint and electronic pareidolia did the rest. If you program your computers to expect wrong-doing, then they'll most certainly find it.

Another of Keev's folk, Hakira, exemplifies the other end of the spectrum. She cut the throats of three people. She did it because they were Mandate infiltrators, and it was that or let them betray the cause. Except now, as she talks over the events, the truth leaks out between her words. We know she didn't know, or wasn't sure. Made a terrible judgement call. And, in the moment of moving the razor, knew such joy it frightened her. I look to Ilmus and can see they won't be facing off with her again anytime soon.

The second day passes into the third. That's a whole Excursion tour before decontamination is finally permitted. Or two whole tours because, of course, we're pulling double shifts. Normally we're not roughing it out under the stars at night, after all. Kiln is starting to learn us, all that insensate micro-biology, with its alien combinations of familiar atoms. A strange language of molecular shapes that our body strains to understand too. And, in straining, finds itself catching at first the odd word, then phrases, sentences. It's not even that our bodies change, at first. We are all the Mandate, in make-up: no interest in new ways of doing things or seeing the world. So the language changes. Long-chain polymers click-click-click into experimental configurations as the Kilnish life tries to decode the hieroglyphs of these new strange temples, our bodies, it has crept into. Countless minuscule beings die in the hostile alien terrain that is us, but they persist. We breathe them and we swallow them, and they slip through the pores of our skin and the tear ducts of our eyes. We are the ruins they look around and wonder at. Our molecular biology is the curious script that they puzzle over. And, eventually, they start to decode it. They don't happen upon a protein sequence which we have on Earth, necessarily. All they need is something where the electromagnetic valences of its component atoms twist it into the right shape for us. Our own dumb Earth biochemistry can't tell the difference. Until we've made the handshake and then looked up the arm to find an alien face leering back at us. That's what's happening right now inside us, by day three of the march. We all know it. But it's Primatt, Ilmus and I who know it best, because we have the right education. It's no blessing, all that book learning. In my head, the pages of my brain blotch and swell, left out in a fungal rain. Kiln is a weight in our guts, a fur on our throats, a rattle in our lungs. And we keep waiting for one of us to go the Rasmussen way, for the insidious alien locksmith to click with something in our brain chemistry, unlocking the froth and the babble. Despite Keev's instructions, we don't really know what we will do when that happens.

The rations are dwindling too, and each of us stares down at our meagre handful. The optimistic Keev who'd said we'd be home in three days was the pathfinder, the pioneer, The Man Kiln Couldn't Kill. Except right now he looks a lot like the tired old man Kiln just hasn't killed yet.

I sit, gnawing the least corner of a tasteless food bar. It

isn't Kiln that will kill us, I decide. Not this thriving biomass-rich environment which looms on all sides, and is just a shadow of what it must have been, back in the warmer, wetter climate when the builders thrived. No, it's our own Earthly limitations that will be the end of us. God, there's a picture that blooms in my mind then. A really old picture I saw once, that I'm visualizing now in hallucinatory detail. It's of a world of monsters, animal-plant-machine chimeras, and they're devouring and tormenting people with absolute glee. It's a kind of hell, except it was called *The Garden of Earthly Delights*. The joke, I take it, being that it's a delight humanity is excluded from. Everything else in the picture's having a grand time, living it up at our expense. Being on Kiln feels like that to me. I can almost hear the pop and fizz of the planet's biosphere having its riotous party in the next room, and here's us gumming our dwindling foodstocks because we can't eat what's around us, and it can't eat us. It can't eat us *yet*. But it's trying. It's learning how.

Frith is weeping. Or at least her eyes are wet. She turns away from us, and strangely that makes me hear the sound of it, the sobs she isn't actually making. Just the turn of her back creates the auditory echo of it. And she's thinking, *Is it me? Will I be the first to go?* So am I.

24.

Back in the camp

It might be some vengeful motivation from those in charge which has us turned around so fast. But I suppose we've had seven days in the monkey house to match our seven days in the wilderness. If you're a Mandate bureaucrat looking at the camp records, all you'd see would be some Excursions crew that had an unprecedented fortnight's holiday. Not a chore done, not a ruin cleared! How lenient is that rascally Commandant Terolan, exactly? So maybe it's only this consideration which has us sent straight back out into the wilds again the moment we're rota-ready.

They break us up. They'd have sent each one of us to a different crew if they could, because the commandant doesn't know much about what's brewing on Kiln right now but he knows what he doesn't like. There are only four active Excursion teams, though, including the one that was thrown together after they gave us up for dead. Which was the moment Greely called in to tell them we were still alive.

Keev, Hakira and I are put in as bottom-rankers with the new team. The team who have every reason to despise us because, before we got lost, most of them hadn't even been on Excursions. Aside from a couple of veterans who were shunted sideways, they were just promoted downwards to fill the sudden vacancies. We're under the command of a heavyset woman named Okritch, who eyes Keev nervously, as though he'll open his mouth and it'll be mutinies all round. They don't actually despise us, though. They fear us a bit, because of where we've gone and where we've come back from. Mostly they hold us in awe, like we're back from the actual dead with monstrous warnings. Prophets emerged from the desert carrying the words of God. Gods. God.

I almost expect our first excursion to be the same wetlands ruin we left off. The one that was our sanctuary and prison when the Elephant's Dad came calling. That would be narratively satisfying. But the Mandate is so seldom narratively satisfying. Picture grim and repetitive state-mandated propaganda stamping on a human face for ever. It's another ruin we go to, a whole other biome in fact. Here the land is undercut and crumbling, dry as bone yet laced through with countless rivulets of water which all the life dabbles long thirsty fingers into. The hydrography is impossible to make out by mere physical principles. The Earth model of runnels to streams, to rivers to seas, isn't some local peculiarity but the basic behaviour of liquids and gravity. Here the water never gathers, but then the soil isn't soil. We walk on semi-permeable mats of interlaced lichenous fronds, and the water tunnels through them, forever following a gradient that the biology ensures never actually goes anywhere, like the constantly descending staircases of a surrealistic sketch. The dry country has led to the evolution of self-irrigating foliage. Kiln's symbiosis shares the water around, like our rations on the march.

The presence of this unclassifiable hotch-potch beneath

our feet seems to preclude the big trees, and in fact there's no big static form displaying the dark photosynthetic surfaces we're conditioned to expect. Some property of this crawling weed—and we can *see* it crawl, albeit slowly—prevents anything rooting. Instead, there is a constant flurry of little motile forms that creep through the mossy ground and then hop and flutter through the air, spreading broad sails that are simultaneously wings and leaves. And there is the fault, the rift, the *something*. The ground falls away some ten metres, exposing the honeycombed strata of the lichen-weed, and the ruin we're here for stands at the very boundary of it, clogged by the customary vine but this time all the way down, with the root of it exposed as though it's a precarious tooth.

Keev and I exchange looks. He goes, places a hand on the stone, feeling through the coat of vines that flexes aside from his touch. Not a flinch, just shifting over like someone making room on a bench. Okritch sees it. She is thoroughly, appropriately, freaked out. I see her hands tighten on the flamethrower.

Keev can feel the ridges and bumps of the writing, the lower reaches of it that lay buried here until the land shifted. And which lies concealed under every ruin, if Vessikhan only knew, where none but the blind things of the soil can trace its outlines. Keev's face is impassive but he's smiling. We're renewing an acquaintance the airlock hosing-down distanced us from.

"We…" Okritch says. "We've got…got to burn it." And then adds, after a bizarre pause, knights in the church faced with a recalcitrant priest, "It's the job." There are reams of horror written between the words of her speech. Or that's how I interpret her, what I parse, from the way the words come forth. I can't know though. Her filters are all intact. Hardly degraded at all, yet.

Keev, Hakira and I spent the flight over here covertly ripping at our own. Pulling ragged gaps where they won't show: armpit, back of knee, under the sag of the filter mask. By the end of the day everyone will sport the same ragamuffin chic, and our little acts of sabotage won't even show.

"Of course we do," Keev agrees and holds his hands out for the flamethrower. For Okritch's flamethrower. She's caught, in that moment. Snapped in the very trap she opened for him, looking from his reaching fingers to the weapon-tool in her grasp.

I think I hear her sob as she hands it over.

We go at it with a will, flames and machetes. By hometime the exposed face of the ruin is mostly clear, never a more efficient job done. We look at the pillars of smoke. Hakira has an almost religious feel to her, as though it's a sacrifice, the fatted calf offered up for a good harvest.

The characters which are exposed speak to me, the implications filtering back with everything else I've opened myself to. Slotting neatly into the grooves that were painstakingly chiselled into lung and gut on our march. Scoured bare by the decontamination, sure, but the hosing and gassing is just removing the pegs. It won't change the shape of the holes. If you don't change the molecular locks, then don't be surprised when you find the old squatters taking up residence again.

But enough of that. Plenty of time for that later. For everyone. Right now, as Okritch's pilot warms up the flier, I look over the exposed wall of text. The histories of the people of Kiln, written here for when they would forget them. Who they were, what they did. Everything Vessikhan so desperately wants to find out from his posting here. He won't want for data on our watch, and perhaps one day soon he'll understand these carefully formed characters too. Understand that they are not the figures of an alphabet, nor characters signifying a sound or word or concept, nor hieroglyphs or representative drawings. And they are not mere inscriptions of some king or law, commandment or treaty. They are each one of them a living document, a library waiting to be added to.

I trace where the ceramic-feeling exterior is clear, the outlines of what must come next. This new chapter in Kiln's story. But I am not the scribe for it.

And the vine will grow back.

We're not decontaminated on our return. Okritch and her people complain bitterly, but they've been set back to day one. Just like Keev's crew was when we troublemakers came to join him. I can taste the echo of his exasperated weariness now. But, knowing what we do, it's not so bad. Okritch is frightened and angry, yes. And she'll go to some guard, or to The Science, and tell wild stories about us. But I don't think she will be believed. Nothing she has to say fits the orthodoxy, after all.

We sleep on our pallets in the Labour Block, close-pitched bunk after bunk. We touch the surfaces and breathe the air.

Another seven days are counted off, this time from when they put us back to work. The ruin in what we're calling the Spongelands is cleared in record time, and without incident. We hear the hollow knocking just once. I imagine the

Elephant's Dad soft-footing it over the rubbery mat of the ground, its foot-mouths sampling the fronds as it goes. Despite the lack of cover we don't see it, there's just the sound. Perhaps it's burrowing. Keev and I exchange glances.

Vessikhan has been sent the first images of the place and he's jumped it to the top of his list. The Archaeology team are heading out even as we finish off. I imagine him standing there, scratching at his scalp through the good protective gear that The Science are given, staring at those formerly subterranean records. Realizing now that he's only ever seen half the story, and not realizing he's not even seen that. I won't know what he thinks about it until later. I'm not exactly in his discussion group any more.

Primatt still is, though, at the edges. They talk late at night, after she's limped her way back up to the gantry under the stony and unhelping scrutiny of the guards. She says Vessikhan is at the very point of unorthodoxy. The shape of Kiln has grown spiny and encrusted in his mind, until he can't shove it into any of the set moulds that Mandate academia requires. One day soon he'll say something to the commandant that just comes down on the side of science and reason, against the prescriptive and polarized party line. Maybe he'll end up down here with us after that.

We return after the last day at that particular ruin. It's time for decontamination, but by then things have moved on. Okritch understands. She's come to terms with how things are, as have her crew. And as have the other three Excursion teams, who've been host to Frith and Ilmus and the other survivors of the march. The regular three-day hosing-down they give us is nowhere near as thorough as the one we had before the monkey house. And we've been tracking Kiln into the camp on our boots for several days anyway.

When they'd put us through that most extreme of scourings, after finally letting us in and deciding they couldn't just shoot us dead, it was as though someone had put their thumbs in my eyes, spikes in my ears, and cauterized parts of my brain that have only grown back now. The pissant little attempt at cleansing we're given this time, after three days on-site, feels more like a brief ducking underwater. A momentary dulling of sound, with closed eyes, but then you're up again and it all comes flooding back into you.

Keev and I meet several gazes as we come back into camp. People from the march, other Excursionistas. People who've slept alongside us in the Labour Block. Our kind of people. Those who understand what we went through. The innocence we lost and all the things we gained. Or maybe "picked up" would be the better phrase. But what doesn't destroy you, right? Kiln didn't destroy us, but that's because destroying things isn't what Kiln's about.

In the Labour Block a new subcommittee accretes around Keev. Keev, who was a firebrand in his youth and has been a dull ember ever since. But he's the one people listen to now, not some mouthy professor from an ivory tower. The old Kiln-hand, the man who'd led more Excursions than any three other people and who always returns. His myth is cemented by our march. They think he defeated a whole planet to get us safely back. Anyone who goes out on Excursions wants to be with Keev. He'll get you home, they say. We others just share in his reflected glory. But he shares it with us. His glory is ours. The precise linguistics of how it all works are still going through the relevant subcommittee in the space between us. Typical, really. Every revolutionary group I ever knew spent far longer clutching for how to describe what they were than talking about what they were going to do.

We don't need to now, though, not quite. I know Keev, and he knows Ilmus, and our knowledge is moving through the camp, spreading out like ink dropped into water.

People come round to our way of thinking soon enough. Primatt's still awkward on her printed leg, but she's growing into it. It won't be too short much longer.

Between Excursion missions, Ilmus and I are pumped for information by The Science. We play dumb for Vessikhan, as he fumbles and creeps about the edge of things, maddeningly close to revelation, save that the madness hasn't quite got purchase on him yet. I can see it twitching at the corners of his eyes, a solid academic who wants to know the truth so badly, but he can't quite find the right questions to ask, and it's not our job to volunteer the information. These things need to come to you organically. They do, they really do.

The ruin the camp is built around is like a flensed skull. Vessikhan and his team have studied it with such absorption, like scholars turning their back on the wreck of Troy to reconstruct the ancient world from a single potsherd. To find a list of dead kings and imagining it represents all that can be said about the wealth of life there once was.

The new lords of the bioscience brigade won't talk to us directly but they deputize Croan. The three of us spend long hours in an enclosed space, which is of course ideal for our purposes. We talk over the march and what we saw, describing new species and relationships, and hitherto unexamined biomes we tromped through on our way back to the camp. We're helping to expand the frontiers of human knowledge. Croan understands.

I look up sometimes and try to catch a glimpse of Commandant Terolan, a sense of him. He's in his office, behind his filters and his seals, as though the whole camp is merely a prison, designed to keep this one man isolated. I can't know what he's thinking or whether any of his many suspicions are homing in on the truth. The Domestics who go near him wear gloves, paper suits and filter masks, at his order. He wants nothing to do with us—the return of the marching band clearly gave him a bad scare. He's practically living the life of a hypochondriac, Primatt says. Feep, Fop and Foop are the same, and the guards keep their rubber hoods on at all times. They want to make sure a hard line is drawn between the privileged few and the chained masses, and that suits us just fine. I mention once that they're paranoid but Ilmus corrects me, pedantic to a fault. Paranoia, they note, is a term reserved for irrational fears.

Another Excursion comes around, but this holds no terrors for us. Everyone knows by now that we live charmed lives, we marchers. I'm assigned with Frith this time. We end up in deep jungle, where we have to firebomb an opening because we can't even find space to abseil down with the flamethrowers. Instead of the gourd trees, the sessile life here is a network of interlinked jointed stalks, festooned with hooks and barbs, like a three-dimensional chainlink fence built of barbed wire. Its upper sections are overlapping scales of photosynthetic black, the back of a sun-drinking dragon. The stalks are reactive. Pre-wound tension in their joints means that damage to their structure causes them to lash out wildly towards wherever the damage came from. There's plenty of torn suits and minor injuries. Frith and I mastermind the first aid, using not too much antiseptic. And by the second day, the language that is inside us has reached this new biome. As we learn, we teach. We grow wise together, the world and us. The story of this new ruin, this node in the mind of the world, unrolls inside us. First Frith and me, but by the time we've conducted our inflammatory vandalism, the whole team knows. It's on the air like smoke and we take it home with us too. Everyone returns with the understanding that you don't beat Kiln. That's not what Kiln is about.

This all sounds bad, I know, but it's not what you think. The gift is not a muddying of the mind with alien influences, but a clarity. An understanding of those around us. Finding that they were always our friends, but we never appreciated each other until now. From those who participated in Clem's uprising and survived, to those who were too scared to act because they didn't know who to trust or what to believe. Slowly we come to know them and they us.

I see now that Helena Croan of Dig Support is full of regrets about chances she never clutched at and stands she didn't take, only to be arrested and transported despite it all. Sometimes you go through your whole life not rocking the boat and they throw you over the side anyway. Any oppressive system needs an element of arbitrary punishment just to keep people properly on their toes. I understand how Croan never put a foot wrong, but enough of her colleagues did to make her tainted by association. Simply not informing sufficiently on her peers became a sin worthy of being cast out of Heaven for. She eyes Ilmus and me as she debriefs us, knowing that the fears which dogged her all her years aren't a concern any more. She knows where she is with us. And that opens the door to many more fears, because she has a scientist's enquiring mind, but we can face those fears together.

Then there's Mox Calwren, the overworked and unhappy engineer. The gantry-level man who spends most of his time fixing things down on the ground. The man who ended up with a bolt and a severance of privileges after the uprising. He was never a secret political, never a traitor to the cause. Just someone who grew to really, really hate Commandant Terolan's patronizing leadership. Someone who loathed his job from early on, and hated his colleagues. Despised the way that, as engineer, he was simultaneously the hardest worked, the most essential and the least regarded of all the staff. Because he got his hands dirty, he became Labour by association and a stirring streak of sour yellow negativity began to run through him, like someone had pissed in his coffee. And so he fell in with Clem, and fell for him. Who'd have thought love could flower in Mox Calwren's withered little walnut of a heart? Yet Clem's words set a fire in parts of him he thought had atrophied entirely. This all goes into the mix, into what we're brewing. And sometimes you need the taste of piss in your coffee to wake you up and remind you how the world treats you.

We still use words and discussion to form our intent. It's just that there's no ambiguity about what's being said. We survivors, we marchers, find places to meet to exchange a handful of efficient sentences. And when we go out on our diverse excursions again, we know it's the start of a new phase of the plan. We have another three days before they decontaminate us. The camp's cruelties against the lowest of the low will be turned back against those on high. When Primatt limps back in after the first day out there, her leg is heavier by half a kilogram than when she went out. Nobody notices, but we know. Behind the Labour Block, in those crannies where the cameras don't reach, there is street theatre. They hold me down and carve me open so it can all come out, then stitch me back together. And fuck, it hurts, but I have faith in the cause. I've orbited the need to bring down the Mandate all my life. I've gone on marches, listened to speeches, argued the science of it. I shielded Ilmus way back, taking the bruises on my own back when the jackboots came to stamp on someone who didn't fit. I joined cells, sat on subcommittees, passed stolen information, made plans. I was betrayed, narrowly escaped, lied my way out of trouble, and in the end, not even that. And yet I never truly committed.

I understand what it is now to be part of something body and soul. And I understand what must be done to preserve that thing. The clarity cuts deep, exposing things you don't want to know but need to.

There is a task that needs doing, and soon, before we're all betrayed again. Croan slips me a plastic dig tool held back from the reclaimers. Where I can't be seen, I hone it, shaving it down until it cuts like a razor.

25.

The march: day three

On the third day of the march, we pass around the shore of a lake. Vast discs of photosynthetic film, like soft plastic, form Venn diagrams on the water, connecting to who knows what submerged roots or bodies beneath. Things like crabs on stilts pick their way between them, carrying mosquito-faced toads that serve as anchor-points for pairs of long-handled tongs that dabble in the water. Three visible creatures, unknown secret partners, the whole coalition approximating the shape and life habits of a spoonbill. I know, from my studies here, that I'd find these same symbiotic units in other combinations with other "species." Everything is a Bosch chimera until the very concept of taxonomy becomes inadequate to the task.

Let me tell you a fable. There's a thing like a scorpion, and it asks a thing like a frog to carry it across the river. The not-frog is concerned that, halfway across, the not-scorpion will sting it and they'll both die. But this is Kiln and it doesn't need to be worried, and soon enough there'll be some hideous bloody frog-scorpion thing terrorizing the waterways with its poisonous sting.

Keev says nothing but I know he's fretting. The lake isn't

on his mental map, just as the river hadn't been. But that's okay. I know we're on track, just the same way I know he's worried even though nothing about him shows it.

Night three. There's no conversation. Nobody wants to open their mouth in case the ghastly extraterrestrial glossolalia we're all waiting for comes out. Or in case they suddenly have a centipede-thing for a tongue, or their teeth sprout wings and fly in and out like bees. I feel Ilmus's dry throat, and the odd vibration every time Greely draws breath. I was about to say we're like condemned men, but we are literally condemned. Each of us feels the planet is holding out a fistful of straws to us, demanding we draw. One of us will pick the short one soon, and start stammering and twitching as the world takes hold of them at last. And we'll leave them behind. Because in them is Kiln's proof of concept of How To Hack Earth Biology, while the rest of us are still running the same terrestrial operating system and we don't want it in us. We don't. Even though it is already.

I curse Keev silently in my head. We all do. He knows it.

When the Elephant's Dad knocks hollowly it's almost a relief. An outside threat. We don't see it but the sound is unmistakable, haunting us. It's amongst the trees, under the lake, in the fog that the plant lookalikes around us exhale each morning, then suck back in at night. If I shouted out right now, "Everyone point to the Elephant's Dad!" we'd all end up indicating the exact same patch of jungle.

We go slower and slower when we really need to pick up our pace to make up lost time. None of us have any solid way of calculating how far we've gone and how far there is to go, but I feel it's not three, not five, not even seven days, but twenty, thirty, for ever. Primatt plods along at the back still, her leg audibly grinding. The minds of the others circle her like flies, wanting to blame her for our slow progress, but it's not even her and they know it. We've hit jungle that no amount of working human legs would suffice to run through. A webwork of bloated, warty-boled trees pressed close together. Where they touch, they merge into single, mutant masses of hollowed flesh. The warts intersect like kissing mouths or gape open, wide enough to thrust an arm in. Arm-sized things force their soft bodies in and out, like parcels of information travelling from one tree to another. It's a forest of body horror just quietly going about its business. I do not thrust my living human arm into those hungry spaces, but the horrifying thing is that part of me wants to.

The Elephant's Dad's call comes again, like a polite laugh from another room. There's no way so large a creature could make its way through this topographical nightmare realm, but somehow it's still out there. It's gained a taste for us, from its earlier victims. It's learned Earth people. It's learned they're delicious.

Or else—this is after we camp and my mind is screaming to itself at night, loud enough to keep us all awake—or else it's the others. The people the Elephant's Dad ate, their personalities and knowledge encysted in it, having become merely loaned-out parts of the Kilnish bazaar ecosystem.

We stop to camp because there's a clearing. We could have writhed on through the jungle for another hour maybe, but the open space halts us. Each of us thinks the same: we just can't go on. And there's an old friend to greet us. Another stone crab, clutching into the soft ground. Or perhaps it's the same one as before, having impossibly run ahead of us to prepare the way. Maybe this is why there's a clearing at all—the trees politely shifted aside when it came looking for a home. It eyes us with its eyes. They are dead orbs, alien things, any similarity with either our eyes or those of Earth crabs pure chance and convergence. Except when I meet its gaze, I feel a shock of contact. I half expect it to open perfect bright human peepers, then bat its eyelashes at us coyly. It watches us and I sense that it's been waiting for us. I try to shuck off the knowledge, like the filthy tatters of my paper suit, but it's sunk its roots into me. Beneath the stone crab a thousand plagues incubate, in the old religious sense. Flies and locusts, frogs and lice. Everything save for the Angel of Death, because Kiln doesn't do death like Earth does. Kiln does life.

Oh God, let this cup pass from me. Each of us is still unknowing enough by this stage that we're horrified by what we know. We can't put it into words. We can't bring ourselves to enunciate what we are learning, because to say it would make it truer. And I know that when we are able, we won't need to.

Day four

We march. Making accommodations to the terrain. Heading for home like climbers hauling ourselves arm over arm up a chain in which we are all links. The bridge. Rasmussen was right, if I'd only had ears to hear.

Then we come to a ruin. I'd say we just stumble onto it but I don't think that can be true any more. I have ceased to believe in randomness, because seeing random chance in the world is the result of insufficient data and we all know too much now. I can see how all the pieces go together, because I'm in the jigsaw. I experience a fractured moment from Ilmus's childhood, realizing just what an existential quandary jigsaw puzzles represent. What is the base unit, exactly? Is it the solitary piece which contains parts of multiple figures, or the individual figure within the image that overlaps the boundaries of multiple puzzle pieces?

This ruin isn't on Vessikhan's maps. It's pristine, being so heavily furred with growth, it had never been noted by the aerial surveys. We stand before it like penitents at a cathedral. Inside, a hundred interlocking life forms stir. I step forwards before I can stop myself, pushing my hands into the vines, and the worms, and the slick layer of decaying, dead matter that is still part of the system. I touch the pictographs, raised and rough beneath my fingertips, anxious to impart the dense coils of their information to me. These aren't histories or myths, the lost pasts that Vessikhan is so desperate to uncover. They're a succession of todays, a roll call, a class photo, a visitors' book. But, because they are sequential, yes, they make up a kind of history. A record of change, because every instant of the present is different, pages in the book of time. I touch my forehead to it, heedless of the filth that smears me.

I fugue.

In my mind I see the Kilnie. The Wild Man. It steps from the puzzle, and I stare at the gap it leaves but cannot tell if it's a piece or figure. It has Keev's face and my hands, Ilmus's narrow chest and Primatt's one leg. Even as I watch, it breaks apart, all those pieces creeping away on borrowed limbs, experimenting with semi-independence, finding new friends. I see clearly what our research had already told us, that there was a time on Kiln when the climate was wetter, as it had been before that, and as it shall be again. The forests of Kiln that we see now are only the ghosts of what flourished then. Shrinking in the drier climate as they cut the cloth of their biodiversity to suit the current climatic purse. Except on Kiln biodiversity is reactive in real time. No need to wait for slow old evolution to come up with something new. Let the fertile times come again and all the life forms will be out swapping body parts like trading cards once more.

We live in the echo of what was. And what *was*, at that point of peak richness, was the builders. The minds that built these ruins and set the records of themselves down in these sigils.

The others drag me off the ruin and throw me to the equally sticky ground, waiting to see if I've finally gone. If I'll be the first. But I blink at them, my reverie interrupted. I then stand up, quite calm, not sure what happened or where all this knowledge has come from. But I know. I had a dream of the builders and it's the only thing that makes sense of what we've seen here. Can I tell Vessikhan, if we get back? Can I say we've met the builders at last? For I saw their lost world through a glass darkly. The ruins provide a bridge between what they had then and what is left now in the dry times. The withered world, for all it still seems so alive.

I think the key is that Kilnish life doesn't centralize like ours does. Tissues spread throughout the body, with less reliance on discrete organs. Even the tissue that originates and sends out instructions to the rest of the organism—the brain in us—is diffuse.

I want to tell Vessikhan that he can relax. The builders of Kiln are absolutely out in the wilderness waiting to be found.

They have two feet and two hands and eyes properly oriented above their noses and mouths. They are the epitome of Mandate Orthodoxy, only in a way that absolutely nobody will want to hear. I laugh, and some people eye me worriedly, while others are in on the joke already too.

In the middle of the next night, Ilmus is the first. They begin to go mad. Clutching at Keev, grabbing painfully, burrowing their face into his neck and shoulder. He gets the hell away from them quickly, and we all watch them fitting on the ground, eyes rolling where the lamp falls across their face. Some of us want to abandon them then and there, past midnight. They've caught Kiln, gone Rasmussen, only the commandant doesn't need a matched pair of babbling freaks. They'll never be let back into camp now. It's not like we can stuff their mouth with leaves and carry them all the way home trussed up.

Ilmus gabbles at us, but hears nothing we say in return. They call out to the trees and the Elephant's Dad knocks back, once for yes, twice for no. When I go close with consoling words, speaking their name, trying to draw them back, they clutch my head. Grip it like they're trying to crack it open to speak directly into my naked brain.

The others force them away, putting distance between us again. As though there is any safe distance, and we're not all breathing the same air. Ilmus stumbles off and I feel a tug in my head which makes me trip. It stutters Ilmus to a halt, still at the periphery of us. I don't want to be mad, I don't want to be sick. Being with Keev and the others is safe, secure in our Earthness. Our little bastion of non-native biology holding out against the howling hordes of a place we had no business ever coming to. And yet Ilmus and I go way back and I'm torn between two gravitic pulls. Ilmus's mouth opens and sounds come out, an awful mewling. Terrifying in their alienness, appalling in their humanity.

Day five

On the march the following day, Ilmus is still able to walk with us and trails behind Primatt as we break from the jungle. They physically hold their jaw shut, except those dreadful sounds still leak from the edges. Feeling the pull of them, I fall back and watch the figures of Keev and Greely recede ahead. We are strung out now, a straggling trail of desperation winding our way in the vain belief that Keev still knows where he's headed. Except I know he does. And I know he knows he's right yet he doesn't understand how he's doing it.

I go back to Ilmus, and to Primatt. To my considerable surprise, I'm doing the right thing. When pause to eat I sit close by, watching over Ilmus, who doesn't know me by then but wants to. They explore my face with hands that can't quite grasp why they joint the way they do. They weep strangeness at me, caught between two worlds. In the end, I hold them, clasping them close as though trying to make some Kilnish symbiont. The others stare at us leerily, waiting for us to start exchanging mindless animal squawks. But I am still, my mind abrading away like the paper suits, and yet I am *me* still. My fingernails hook into the humanity of me and hold on.

Later Keev takes us uphill, where the forest is sparser, each fat tree holding its own court. The ground at their base seethes with an ecology of little courtiers, ambassadors from other polities bringing gifts. We wind between them as though that will help preserve the Earth in us, the purity of the clay God made us from. We step over little thoroughfares of exchange between each tree's domain. Nothing here is hermetic. But then life never is. We classify it and assign it two Latin names and a holotype, and forget it's all just twigs of the same tree.

That night Ilmus takes themselves off, away from the rest of us. Even out past Primatt, who'd basically dropped where she stood when everyone stopped, making her own camp of one. Ilmus's shoulders are hunched inwards, arms wrapped around themselves. They double over every so often, as if they're vomiting, but all that comes out is words. I am an expert now in Kiln's many sounds, and to me it seems that Ilmus's throat is being twisted into making them. Trying to render unto the jungle something it might understand. In return the jungle roars, buzzes and chirrs, and cackles and belches, but there remains a gap, the last struts of the bridge, preventing Ilmus's meaning from crossing.

I think they're going to die, just walk off like some old-timey explorer. *I may be some time*. Except I also know that's not it. They're not looking for extinction but connection, and they can no longer connect with their fellow humans.

I trail them past Primatt, whose face is a clutch of pain lines. She's pushed herself past all endurance, haggard and worn, her pain leaking out at every joint and the stump of her leg a raw ruin of agony. But being left behind is worse. I can't believe what she's endured. I experience a blast of it as I pass her, like a radio tuned briefly into a station of blaring, jagged music. Then I'm with Ilmus and the stone crab.

It's followed us. Except it can't have followed us. It's there like a big table, up on the intestinal inflations of its various legs. Ilmus has their hands on it like they're about to chair a board meeting. They open their mouth and stuttering, tongueless words fight their way out.

The stone crab mutters to itself, but I know it's not in response to Ilmus, just the tips of an alien internal monologue breaking the surface.

"I'm here," I tell them. I'm not really, not for them, but still, I'm there. When Ilmus lies down beside the stone crab, I lie beside them. In case they need me. And I feel Primatt close by too but obscured by the trees, as well as the others, an unravelling knot of mind, beyond that. If the Elephant's Dad happened on us we'd be like an all-you-can-trample buffet, but we've ceased to care. The march is all and the world can do what it wants to us.

That night I understand, with a dream's twisted clarity, that the stone crabs create a peculiar local ecology. They are hubs, wireless routers through the busy interactions of Kilnish life. Like priests, they demand sanctity around them, and Keev has somehow led us in a join-the-dots path from one to another, knowing instinctively where will be safe to rest. Except it can't be. Even in the dream, I know it must be nonsense. My Earth-science mind hammers out its own doctrine and I walk away from Keev and the stone crab, and the Elephant's Dad eats me for my hubris. I wake screaming, fighting. Some of the others, off lost on the far side of the fat, rumbling trees, shout at me. Ilmus sleeps on. My sounds mean nothing to anyone.

In the dream I have later, I reach over for Ilmus's shoulder and they come apart. I feel the pieces of them shift and disassociate within their ragged overalls, individual segments and joints creeping and scuttling to escape their cuffs. It's a hideously visceral sensation as the human shape of them just crumbles and tumbles away beneath my fingers. I wake and clutch for them for real and they're not there.

Day six

Day has arrived and I blink stupidly. There are voices nearby. I get up and see that Ilmus is sitting on the stone crab with Greely, the two of them exchanging low murmurs. Not wanting to wake me, I realize.

"Ilmus?" I croak, and they smile at me. They name me, wish me a very good morning. Human words. Not even a sliver of Rasmussianic raving.

"What?" I get out.

"I... Well, I got better," is all they say. They look a bit embarrassed, as if they'd been faking it to get out of sport.

I feel tears come to my eyes. I'm amazed everyone else isn't there having a goddamn party, in fact. Because it's not just that Ilmus is back with us, Ilmus got *better*. They'd had the Kiln-madness, which Rasmussen has been a victim of for decades, and which Clem died of. Except what Clem actually died of was being thrown into the incinerator for being mad. Just like Booth. And just like the man in the example tank whom Primatt showed me way back. The madness, and then the execution. Camp policy. But Ilmus got better. And Rasmussen never got better. Somehow, right then I can't work out what the salient difference in their cases is, though it seems blindingly obvious to me later.

We go back to the others, we three. Greely and Ilmus, almost shoulder to shoulder, me a little further off, somehow unable to be properly with them. Keev and the main body of us react—delight, surprise, and yet...somehow Ilmus doesn't reintegrate completely. Even in the midst of us, they're not quite with us. As though what they've gone through was a pupation and they carry vast invisible wings of a hundred unseeable colours. In the midst of us they walk with Greely, but not with us.

Keev sees it too: his second, Greely, is suddenly not his best friend. Does she still have his back? He doesn't know and neither does she. Frith has the twitches now too. I see her mouth twist and flap like a hooked fish. By mid-morning she's walking more with Ilmus and Greely, marching to the beat of that same different drummer, even though we're all walking together. There's a slow migration across that sightless but eminently permeable barrier over the course of the day. I remember staring at Keev, and him staring back at me, like we're the only ones left. As though everyone else is a doppelganger, a changeling. In the end he drops back, and I do too. We make it all about helping Primatt, because otherwise she'd just become completely lost and abandoned at the back. She's always been the outsider, but now Keev and I find ourselves just as *outside*, and Primatt is the only fit company we have left. And we do help her. She's wretchedly grateful by then, no strength left in her, her leg grinding and screeching as its abused joints degrade. I don't mention that nobody seems to need Keev to lead any more. It doesn't seem politic.

We eat the last of our husbanded rations. The high-energy compact foodstuffs that were never enough. We're not home.

The simple maths of it—distance, foodstock, rates of infection—none of it ever actually worked. It was all just Keev telling us what we needed to hear to get us moving. Can-do attitude can't always do, though.

Late morning, Primatt's prosthetic leg dies. The knee has seized and the motor's died. The constant drifting micro-life of Kiln has gotten into it and murdered it, leaving her a leg down. She's barely slept the last two nights, having no more painkillers and her inflamed stump searing at her all night.

Primatt sits on the ground, twisted to keep her balance. The leg is across her knee, panels open. Inside I see the mess of fungal growth that's sprouted so horribly fast, colonizing the plastic, feeling off the industrial polymers. I don't look at the stump itself, I don't have to. It's growing on her, too, as though Kiln has been exploring the liminal zone between mechanism and flesh. I know she's tried to scrape it away and felt a deep-rooted pain that goes all the way into her.

Before anyone else can say it, say what they're surely desperate to, she declares, "You're going to have to leave me."

"No," I say, and Keev shakes his head too, because Primatt and me, we're all he's got right now. I wait for the others to all chorus "yes," possibly in uncanny unison like the congregation of a cult. Something shifts between us all. I *feel* it, like an invisible creature hanging in the air, its trailing tendrils brushing my face.

"We'll…" says Keev. There aren't words, though.

I make a sound, just a sound, and see Keev and Primatt stare at me. I feel a hand on my shoulder and know it's Ilmus's. And I know it doesn't matter if it's Ilmus's hand or not. What I feel is not fear or harm. It's release. A man finally taking the plunge into a frozen pool, experiencing the shock and then the indescribable relief at having *done it* at last. A thousand little ticks and tells suddenly snap into sharp focus, and what was noise becomes information. My fragile clay was thrust into the Kiln, and I feared the burning, but now I see the shape of me as I'm drawn out. Fired and fit.

Keev's eyes are wide and terrified. He can't know how he knows, but he understands he's lost another ally. And of course he'll be the last. He's closed himself off for years, to survive here. Put up barriers in his mind to keep himself sane and hoping. But sometimes border walls are a prison.

"Nimell," I say to Primatt. "You can..." She can come home with us, I know she can. Because we're going to get home, all of us. Fed and sane and more than able to think through just how to approach the camp and the guards. All of us together. Primatt stares up at me. She has felt the sea-change too, the tide lapping at her very heel, though not quite taking her out yet. She and Keev, one closed off by pain, the other by indomitable will. But they're teetering at the brink, I feel it. We all do. And there's a fracture of hope in Primatt's face, because she can say "leave me behind" all she likes but she still desperately wants to get home.

At our backs the boulder crab chuckles and rasps.

Ah, Kiln. You hear "survival of the fittest" and imagine evolution like a boxing match, where the last champ left in the ring takes the belt. What makes you "fittest" isn't being bigger and stronger than everything else. It isn't even necessarily being better at any given thing than everything else. Because you *need* everything else. That's how biology works. Each cell needs the other cells, each organ needs the other organs, each organism needs the other organisms. The base unit of life is all life. But let me tell you about Kiln. It makes Earth look like a boxing match. How do you become the fittest on Kiln? It's not about how many enemy empires you can trample to dust with your sandalled feet. Surviving on Kiln is all about how much life you can interlock with. The services you can provide. On Kiln no species is an island. Nothing needs to be ruggedly self-sufficient, because there's always someone who can do the thing for you, better than you could, in exchange for what you've got. Evolution as a barter economy. Everything becoming better and better at finding ways to live with its neighbours. Daniel in the lions' den lets the lions eat his legs, because then they will carry him meekly about on their backs.

There are no lions on Kiln but the stone crab's back is broad and the forest moves for it.

26.

Back in the camp

Splitting us up, separating us, must have looked like a good idea. It should have been. It's the old playbook against the industrial organizers. But you don't contain a disease by dispersing it. You don't stop the spread of a message by spacing the transmitters further apart. And the message is tailored for the hearers now. It was given a chance to practise and adapt, with us. Not just the yowling babble of the lone Rasmussen but a persuasive text that dovetails neatly with the proteins and membranes of the human organism.

We go out embedded in the other Excursion teams like splinters. We come back amongst friends. After the third excursion, we return to a warm welcome. It's taken hold within the camp, this Kilnishness. Dig Support, Maintenance, Domestics, General Labour—colonized one by one. We pass through the camp, each pair of eyes a window, feeling the coming together of people, of plans. We exchange murmured words in hidden corners, or out in the wilds where there are no cameras or microphones.

In the camp, when we arrive back that time, I see Vessikhan come down from the gantry, looking at the bleached bones of the ruin they built the dome around, that has been studied

311

and restudied until it's barely a conversation piece any more. I see him now look at it with new eyes, lips moving like a slow learner. But not quite there yet.

And now there's a task that needs doing. Many tasks, but this one is mine. I volunteered for it. Some messages should come from an acquaintance, not a stranger. Tonight, when everything is due to happen, I sit up in my bunk in the Labour Block. Everyone's awake, feigning sleep. Those of us who will take the first and most irrevocable steps are stirring, but I know everyone else is waiting for us. I stand, eyes straying to the dull red light they never turn off. From within my overalls, I take the blade they all know I have, hidden less by artifice than by the consensus of the many. It slips into my hand, and around me I sense everyone's fingers move in sympathy.

I slip from my bunk and pad lightly across the dormitory. It must be now. Tomorrow will be too late.

The march: day six

After all that happened, we move faster. Because we have help and because we help each other. I don't recall so much of those final days. Perhaps it's because I'm undergoing a reorganization, at a microscopic scale. New tenants are setting up and changing all the plugs so they can get connectivity. I know we eat, even though our rations were exhausted, even with the privation measures Keev had mandated. But now we gorge, growing strong on it. Because it might be symbiosis heaven out there but it's a symbiosis red in tooth and claw. Or yellow, given Kiln's palette. Everything eats everything on Kiln. It's just that the Kilnish ecosphere works at an additional level of organization, combining and recombining, evolving universal adaptors so the planet's lives can trade parts and facilities. As though everything is just modular toys owned by inventive children.

A knocking sound is what finally brings me back from my reverie. We've not heard it for some time. The Elephant's Dad, pacing us. But I understand now. Not because it has some deviant taste for Earth flesh. Think of it rather as the first disciple, just as Primatt's boulder crab is the second. There is a special place for those who recognize the Messiah on the road and do them honour.

Keev is the very last to go. It should have been me, the one who's been on Kiln the least, still virgin territory that the planet hasn't been able to get its teeth into. Keev, though, has been chewed over for years, but he has such a tight hold on himself. A tough outer rind that lets nothing in, not people, not Kiln. Towards the end of our march he's broadcasting but not receiving. We receive chapter and verse on what it's like to be Vertegio Keev when all his crew have left him to follow a more persuasive piper. Paranoia, revulsion, looking at the faces of his comrades and fearing the thing that has come to wear them. Believing himself the only bastion of sanity. He considers fleeing into the wilderness, save that the voice of the Elephant's Dad sounds once more, and he fears it more than his own turning mind. I want to tell him it isn't what he thinks, because there is a narrative born of our humanity and its fears, and that's not what Kiln has done to us. I want to tell him, for that matter, that if it's insanity he fears, well, there's a thing out there that he sincerely believes in, with three mantis legs and three tardigrade stumps, and he's calling it the *Elephant's Dad*, and doesn't he think that's a little bit odd? Madness and sanity are judged by majority norms, after all, and if it's all of us on one side and just him on the other, who's mad exactly?

He cracks at last. Flees us, tearing at his ragged overalls as though seeking to rid himself of the final barriers between himself and everything else. He whoops and carves his feet on thorns and the sharp tongues of stones. Scrambling like a five-year-old through the close-packed swollen trunks of trees.

Keev comes face to no-face with the Elephant's Dad and he laughs at it. It cannot, under any circumstances, be a real creature. Nothing of Kiln can be. That is Keev's final, despairing defence. Not this interleaved and borderless mess of interspecific relations, like a vision plaguing a taxonomist as they wake from drug-fuelled delirium.

Except we rush after him and haul him away before the Elephant's Dad—which absolutely did kill two of our number —can add Keev to its tally. Even as we do, its sluggish mind goes *Huh*...as it registers what Keev is becoming. What he is becoming a part of.

He is still Vertegio Keev. I am still Arton Daghdev, the biologist, and the biology, of that name. Nothing's changed except the way we see the world around us and those who inhabit it. Ilmus's grief and Primatt's pain, my frustration, Keev's bitterness. What links us to the world links us to each other. What links us to each other is part of a chain that reaches far into the past. Kiln's complex and mutually reliant ecology has found the precise sequence of steps to build Rasmussen's bridge. From the macrobiotic assemblage that is Arton Daghdev to my own microbiome, to the microbiology of Kiln, to its own interdependent macro-forms like the Elephant's Dad. From me to Ilmus, and Ilmus to Keev.

Back channels of information passing into us and out of us through pores and nose, eyes and ears and the touch of fingers. We sit there at our camp and know one another. Our purposes and our preferences, our mutual determination to survive. But not survive apart. Join or die, the old rallying cry. If Kiln had a flag, that would be its motto.

And, in that revelation, I am not just a part of a band of humans, knowing one another and sharing our purpose. I am a part of the wider world of Kiln. Then, understanding that, I realize who the builders were and where they went. And that they have returned.

They were always going to return, in due course. Over a thousand years, as the world span and conditions changed. But we altered that, we specific humans. Keev's death-marchers. We've awoken the builders on our march, as surely as if they clawed their way up out of our footprints.

We march on. We reach the camp. When I falter, someone comes back for me. Empathy is a hole that lets the rain in. That's how they get us.

Back in the camp

I feel the stretched-sheet tension of it all. From my innards to the inhabitants of the Labour Block, to the world beyond. I walk down the rank of bunks. At the far end of the room, he's sitting up.

"Arton," he says.

I don't stop.

"Arton, no," he says. Because it's reached him, the connection. Infiltrated him as it has all of us. Letting us know him as we know each other.

"Wait," he says. "Listen to me. I'm not…" He chokes on the words because he knows they're a lie. And he can't lie to me any more. I stand at the foot of his bed, blade in hand, and know him. His mind shrinks from me, hiding its face in its hands so I might not see the guilt there, but I do see it. I know him, and he knows me.

We all know. It's a knowledge of the other that comes like self-knowledge. We discover all the hidden moments when each of us were weak. Ilmus sold me out, they already confessed as much. But they did it so quietly and confusingly nobody noticed. They broke under duress, because everyone does, and tried to give my name up, only nobody heard my name amidst the noise, and so it didn't even matter. We know, all of us, and we understand. Frith also broke when they had the electrodes on her, the sleep deprivation and the music that came and went, ear-gougingly loud at random intervals. Frith sold her surrogate family. We know that.

And I broke. I gave up Marquaine Ell, who never came back to life when our barge fragmented. After they'd taken me, after my year's sabbatical on the run, living in the gutter. They starved and beat me, stripped me and froze me, all methods so primitive I might have been part of a living-history display, and I broke. I told them where Marquaine Ell was hiding. I didn't have anyone else to sell, to redeem my poor pawned soul. I'm the reason she was taken, and I'm the reason she's dead. Or else they'd already taken her by then and my little betrayal was pointless as well as craven. But I still gave her up. Everyone breaks when they twist you hard enough. It's what the Mandate's good at. It's what's behind all Terolan's polite words and dinners.

But for some it was more than that.

"Please," says Parrides Okostor, the traitor. The man who sold Clem's rebellion to the Commandant. Who'd made his niche here in the camp, burrowing into the subcommittee like a parasite, earning himself back-handed privileges, treats, even just a dodged beating or two. Such small coins in payment for a betrayal. And doubtless, if I were his analyst, I could build a whole house of justifications for why it was him who ended up as the informant, not me or Ilmus or anyone else. It might have been any of us, but it was Parrides Okostor in the end.

"Helena," he says, appealing to Croan now, reaching out. The head of Dig Support sits on her bed and won't look at him. He didn't even betray her, because she wasn't part of anything that needed betrayal. A little part of him even did it to protect her and the rest of the team, fearing the disruption that a wider insurrection might cause. But Clem died, Armiette died, and others, because he passed every detail he could to Security and the commandant. He feared we'd fail, so he made sure we failed. And now he's inducted into this conspiracy, he'll do it again. Because of all the things our new pan-global revolutionary subcommittee is good at, secrecy is not one of them. We're all about open borders.

Although it's been all grass-roots activism so far, I know there's a slow-growing unease on the gantry level too. Because there's a slow-growing infiltration up there, Kiln gaining its foothold from all the material we've brought in. It's impossible for them to pin down, devoid of explicit clues, but Terolan and his Security forces are becoming twitchier and twitchier yet don't know why. Planning crackdowns against an explosion they can't see coming for once. Abusing the Domestics, who they insist wear gloves, masks and paper shoes. Ever since Keev's death-march, they've been tightening the procedures. Except it wasn't a death-march. It was the life and soul, and tonight we're bringing the party.

Parrides Okostor of Dig Support, like a rotting fruit. Eyes white and wide in the red light. The taint of Clem Berudha, sold to the commandant, leaks from his memories, sweating from his pores. *Parrides must live* is his sole goal. And looming like a grand shadow behind all these Kilnish transgressions is his history on Earth. Parrides Okostor, the academic, the revolutionary. We went to the same revolutionary cells, we sat on the same subcommittees, we shared a common room at the Panoptic Academy. And all the time he was on someone else's payroll. He was turned long before, feeding the hungry maw of the Mandate's secret police. Not broken, not twisted, just rotten.

It hadn't even saved him from transportation, in the end. Every time he'd turned someone in, a little of the unortho-doxy had stuck to his fingers, until he'd looked as dirty as the rest of us and they shipped him out. It didn't even keep him out of Excursions here either, just had him on the easy team rather than Keev's advanced course. It's amazing how little you can buy someone for, sometimes. Now he knows the plan, having seen it hanging in the space between us. We couldn't hide it from him, just as he couldn't hide his nature from us.

He understands, when I stab him. His mouth opens again, but there are no last words. No new protestations of inno-cence or diversions of blame. The old paranoid fire that sets everyone at everyone else's throats, until the only way to catch the traitor would be to burn the entire revolution to the ground and start again, is gone. All is transparency now.

Every traitor stands accused by their own self-knowledge. Okostor is my first murder in the name of revolution. I'd always just talked a good fight before.

He doesn't stop the improvised blade going in. He realizes that his death is necessary to prevent the betrayal that he would also find necessary. He is simultaneously a traitor and a martyr to the cause.

When I stand up from the deed, I don't need to say anything dramatic like "It's time," or "We have to act fast." Everybody already knows.

The eyes they placed in the Labour Block, their own extended sensorium, will have seen. Is there a living watcher intently manning the cameras every moment of each night? It's unlikely, but they will have algorithms and probably the final in-character act of Parrides' life will be to appear as a flag for concern on their system. Security will be coming shortly. It's time for us to move.

I am Arton Daghdev. We are the revolution.

27.

We swarm out of the Labour Block, and the coordination of our invincible hive mind means we effortlessly overpower Security. We're like ants: kill one of us, it doesn't matter. Only the colony counts, and hence the subcommittee survives by subsuming all its constituent parts. We become the ultimate commune, and the littered used-up husks of individual units are trampled underfoot for the greater good. Onwards to victory!

Except it doesn't work like that, of course. That's not what Kiln has given us. And honestly, it might be easier if it were the case. *Let this cup be taken from me*, I think, and isn't my *self*, the understanding of my individual separation from my fellows, that cup? Take it from me and I'd not fear hurt or privation, even torture at the hands of the commandant. I'd just be one little segment of the great driving centipede of revolutionary fervour. But as I said, that's not how it is. *I* am not actually the revolution. I am just Arton Daghdev. One amongst many, yes, but not many becoming one.

So, we'll release our alien mind-control spores, and they will rise up to the gantry level for the commandant and all his people to breathe in. Then they'll basically be our people, slaved to the greater Kiln-thing that we've all become. Or else maybe we'll tailor the spores to bring those cruel people into our omniversal vision of peace and love. The spores can get into their brain and turn them mad, but it's only madness if you're a devotee of the Mandate's fuckery. By any rational human standard, it's sanity. Everyone will smile and hug it out, and we'll run naked through the happy woods of Kiln like nature's children. And possibly, if we're to continue this ridiculous hypothetical, there'll be some hairy Kilnish Bigfoot shambling out of the trees in a bathrobe, come to teach us meditation and yogic flying or something. Yes, you can probably tell by the way I couldn't even make this one stick that this isn't how it works either. Because sometimes the only way to make the revolution happen is to fight. And nothing that's happening to us here on Kiln particularly changes who we *are*, which is why I had to knife Parrides Okostor. Even though he was plugged into our network enough for us to uncover his past treacheries, he wasn't suddenly going to become our best mate, raising a pint to the cause. The one change that Kiln had made was that he couldn't hide his opportunistic, weasel nature from us. He'd still betray everyone.

And so we…what? At first I thought we'd just follow Clem's plan, but better. That's what tends to happen when there's a plan in the air. It makes an invisible mould that people pour themselves into. Clem was a leader, a thinker, a doer. He was a good man. Which means, with the world and revolution being what they were, he'd done a lot of bad things, but he'd done them for people and against the system. That's why he was a convict who'd gotten himself transported to the extrasolar camps. If he'd done bad things for the system against people, he'd be the commandant.

We act, and the plan comes together between us, because that's another thing Kiln is good for: the free and frank exchange of views. A discussion that doesn't need words, quite. I must make clear it's not mind-reading. I can't look at Ilmus and know the thoughts that scud across their brain. But if Ilmus thinks a thing, it tugs at me. If they see something, I'm drawn to it. There's an interchange of information at a subconscious level because of the veritable haze of biological signal in the air around us.

We are connected, but it's not a superpower. We do not cast off the shackles of our human bodies or forget who each one of us is. But we know one another, deeply, and that counts for something.

Even the laxest security operative up on the gantry will have seen what's just happened in the Labour Block, but most likely they won't be characterizing it as the start of the revolution. I just stabbed Okostor, and a couple of other inveterate snitches got themselves brained or strangled. Security may or may not clock that the people who were murdered were their past informants. Even if they do, they're not going to go on high alert for a few dead tattletales. Instead, what we receive is half a dozen of them coming down from the gantry with guns and clubs to take the malefactors into custody. They tell us to stand away from the doors before they come in. They're not hyper-cautious but they're not making dumb mistakes, either. They have full protective gear on, masks included, and gas grenades in case they need to put down a general riot. But most of all, they spark fear. That's how they get you. How a small group of uniformed stormtroopers can always face down a turbulent crowd. Fear of their weapons, of their discipline, of the brutal force they can mete out. How many of us would it take to bring one of them down? How much better is the care their wounds would receive than any treatment we'd get afterwards? And, working in a labour camp, you come to understand how even small hurts drag at you, compounding over time because the work is hard, and you're not cut any slack for a twisted knee or a broken finger. They can be bold. We can only be craven. That's how it went on Earth and that's how it goes on Kiln. They stride in and demand the culprits surrender themselves on a count of five, or else the beatings will start.

They get what they want, as they always do, but don't get it quite the way they expect. They don't understand that we're *all* culprits now.

I remember a workers' rallying cry back in the day: *One out, all out*. Right before the Mandate sent in their blacklegs to do the work, and their troopers to shut down the strike. Clem was in the thick of that. He told me how it went, when the lines clashed. There's always a point, he said, when you don't know whether the man on your left or the woman on your right will still be there a moment later. You can't be sure that, if you rush the riot shields, people will be at your back, or just left behind. And nobody wants to be the one to charge The Filth on their own, to be beaten down and then stomped on as their line pushes forwards, then cuffed and hauled away behind that inviolable, advancing barrier. We've all seen it happen, someone too reckless or fearless or just plain dumb or drunk. You don't tend to see those people again, save in the casualty figures.

That's what Kiln has given us. We know and lean on one another. If I falter, then Ilmus's resolve is there to catch me.

If Greely or Keev flinch, then I'm there, and they can count on it. We're all in this together. *One in, all in.*

So we all go in. The whole Labour Block rolls forwards at the same time against half a dozen Security. There are shots. One of them picks a grenade off their belt and pulls the pin. The Block floods with pale irritant gas, but that's a trick plenty of us know. And if one of us knows it, we all do. We've got bandanas soaked in piss, sterile saline and a chemical by-product of the reclamation plant that someone knew worked to neutralize the stuff. It still stings like buggery, causing streaming eyes and nose, and the back of my throat's on fire. But what doesn't happen is the instant isolation those sensory assaults bring, locking you in your own head with the pain and disorientation. We all feel it, but we all know that we're not alone. The brute clay of us has been fired to something hard and determined by mutual intent and proximity. And there's someone from Maintenance who throws the extractor fans into overdrive to clear the air, but we don't wait for it. We don't give Security a chance to either overawe us with bludgeons or pull out. We jump in to fight, with our eyes red and weeping. We tear at their masks, twist the guns from their hands. I hear seven shots and feel two of my fellows die. Two more take agonizing wounds, but the pain is spread across us all. Blunted. Necessary. That's Kiln. Symbiosis and carnivory, an understanding that death is just a part of the deal.

In the aftermath, with the air clearing, we stand over the bodies of our victims. But we can't stop or regroup. There is only forwards. We've smashed the cameras, blinded our enemies, and there'll be full-on panic up top. They'll be waking the commandant. The Science will be blinking blearily at the sound of shouts and running feet. But what we inherited from Kiln, they have through training and discipline. I picture Terolan's formidable lieutenant already kicking awake the day shift, cursing them all into their armour and kit. So we rush out of the Labour Block, wedging the doors open even as our techs fight off their initial override codes. If we'd dithered, stayed behind walls, turtled down, they'd have gone on the offensive, kettling us in and beating us. Lessons learned back on Earth: there's nothing the enforcers like more than a target that's not fighting back. So we take the offensive, sally forth. There's a little shooting from above, but they're still reacting, and we have a few guns to return the favour with. Everyone in the Labour Block knows the angles of fire from the towers, anyway.

I see Security's night shift rushing to hold the stairheads and the lift, because they remember Clem's plan, too, to seize the comms hut and therefore gain access to the orbital ship. Onwards and upwards. Clem, for all his vision, thought like an Earthman. He had a plan that was entirely comprehensible to the commandant, because it involved essentially replacing the commandant. Seize the head of the snake. It's all about the higher functions, the brain of the camp.

We're not thinking like that any more. And it would be pat to say that's because Kiln doesn't think like that. It's not all about the Great Man theory of evolution over here, all those neat trees of life the Mandate produces, where human beings are the pinnacle of the uppermost branch, closest to God. The thing with a tree, though, the thing with a snake, the thing with a human... that branch, fanged mouth, or vaunted highly evolved brain are absolutely fucked without a trunk or a body.

So we don't rush the stairs into the teeth of their automatic weaponry. We go under the gantry, where they don't have a good line on us. The tools we were brandishing aren't planned to be repurposed as weapons. We use them the way they were intended, and start taking things apart.

They have an emergency generator on the gantry level, because the camp designers thought that much through. But the main power comes from the weird Kilnish bio-network of flowers, and that's down here with us. We cut them off, and that puts them on a clock. Yes, there are old solar collectors up there, but nobody's dusted them off for years because Kiln had such a reliable alternative.

The reclamation plant is also at ground level. The source of the rendered-down slurries which all the printers feed off. Inorganics and organics both, neatly sorted and held in big tanks ready to be drawn on to produce everything from clothes to tools to lunch. The tanks are down here too. They like their living space uncluttered up on the gantry. We cut them off as well. They'll have whatever's in the pipes, and whatever stocks of food and ammo were already fabricated, which'll last them a while, but again, it puts them on a clock.

We break the decontamination airlock, making absolutely sure they see us doing this. A couple of people are shot at, but mostly it's done from inside, where they can't draw a bead on us. That communicates a very particular game plan. And by now Commandant Terolan has, I'm sure, hauled Vessikhan, Feep, Fop and Foop into his office. We're finally confirming his suspicions of us, which took root and grew like a fungus up there ever since we came back off the march. We brought something back with us, despite the utter lack of gibber and froth. Despite the heaviest decontamination they could deploy.

It wasn't some super-resilient microbe, by then. What we brought back was our understanding of Kiln and how it worked. Our memories of how it had bound us together on the march. It was easy enough, the next time they sent us out on Excursion, to reconnect with our acquaintances and bring them back into camp. Spread the love, share the load, get to know our neighbours.

It does, I admit, sound profoundly sinister when I talk about it like this. But I mean it literally. *Know thyself* is the Earth adage, but here on Kiln it's *Know one another*.

They must have been worrying about what they missed. And then, of course, someone up above had the bright idea of using Primatt against us. Because despite it all, she'd kept her bunk up top. But they'll burst into her room and find her already gone, and in her bed a riotous explosion of festering life. I imagine them reeling back, choking, desperately fumbling for masks if they're not already wearing them. The horror! It isn't Primatt transmuted to a lump of hideous alien flesh, of course. She is already clear and on the run. It's the latest consignment she smuggled in, in her leg. Just a few fistfuls of Kilnish biomass, but the point is to guide the response of the commandant. Right now, he'll be sealing himself and his favourites inside his personal chambers up there, turning on the air scrubbers and taking every other precaution against contamination. Which suits us fine, because it means he's burning power and resources at twice the normal rate, and we really don't want him being a part of our collective, thank you very much.

We have some vital time in hand before they work out

what we're doing. They're probably not watching the technical side of their operation like hawks while they prepare to defend beachheads on the stairs. Especially as Calwren is one of ours. He's already gone over the side, gone rogue. Primatt can't exactly monkey down the scaffolding, but when she jumps we're ready to catch her. For the moment, at least, we retain the initiative and control the ground floor of the camp. We keep pulling wires and cutting pipes, killing cameras and staying out of the sweep of the tower guns.

That's when a hive mind, or alien mind-control spores, would have been really useful, frankly. Because there's only so much momentum we can spin before it becomes a waiting game. We've cut them off. The clock's ticking and they've worked out our game plan. Now it's on them to respond, and we're going to have to deal with that as best we can. They muster up above and pass round the guns, with their limited stock of ammunition. There's also the truncheons, which don't run out of bang but which we can match with what we've got down here. They know we have fabricators at our end, and we can start making crude piecework guns like Clem had, but we can also make sharps and blunts, and maybe cook up some nasty chemicals. Certainly we can make breakable containers full of violently inflammable liquid that can be stuffed with paper-cloth wicks. Sometimes insurgency needs to go back to its roots.

The clock runs down, but it's our clock too because they'll be coming any moment now, the stairs covered by the towers so we can't bottle them at the bottom.

The essential fragility of our plan is exposed, the fragility of the human body subjected to bullets and beatings. But we have a unity of purpose no revolution ever had before. We have confidence in our comrades, rooted in absolute certainty. And they have the guns.

28.

Guns count for a lot, I won't lie. Aside from a little pot-shotting, they're not immediately used to best effect, though. Security are still waiting for us to storm the stairs, working to Clem's top-down playbook that we've mostly abandoned. While we wait for them, the most technically savvy of us fight an entirely separate war over the printer in the Labour Block. Someone on the commandant's team was sharper than we anticipated and tried to junk it entirely. They remembered Clem's makeshift guns and thought we'd be turning out more of them post haste. Which indeed we would have been. We just manage to stop them turning the printer into an inert block of dead circuitry. And then we stop them filling the output trays with rapid-printed, quick-drying glue, which I have to say displays an inventiveness I did not expect from our enemies. Someone in Security is a profoundly frustrated prankster.

What we don't prevent them doing, while that battle is going on, is imposing a bunch of restrictions on the printing and then locking us out of higher privileges. Basically they make a list of everything offensive they can think of and tell the printer it isn't allowed to make them, including the individual gun components that Clem had snuck past all the regular telltales and restrictions. They also prevent us from printing Earth food, because they want to put us on that clock, too. They don't understand that we can forage now. There's life out there, Kiln life, and we can eat it, with a little impromptu treatment and cookery. It's not as efficient as snacking on a cheeseburger but it works. We'll not starve. The clock they put us on is broken from the start.

But we can't make guns unless we want to take the printer offline for a day, while it restores to factory settings, and even then the machine has some hardwired restrictions. These mean the crappy piecework stuff Clem had is all we could coax out of it. What we do have is matter, the camp's main supplies of it, so we use the printer to just make big dense slabs. We then put together a rat run of barricades that cover us from the towers, and we shift them around to counter wherever Security sets up to snipe at us from. We make it very plain we are hunkered down for the long term.

Up above, they muster. They throw smoke grenades down, and then they try actual poison gas, lethal crowd suppression measures. By then we've broken open the airlocks to let that good fresh alien air in, though, getting a nice throughflow going. You can actually see the faint haze of aerial plankton eddying through the camp. And that means everyone on the gantry level can only go out in full protective gear, of course, the masks, goggles and rubber suits, like a particular flavour of S&M convention is in full swing up there. Which stretches their resources, patience and personal comfort that bit further too, running their limited decontamination facilities full time to clean them off every time they cross from outside to inside. And the commandant is still sitting in his office at the heart of it all, probably not even having direct contact with his subordinates.

We see civilians from time to time, mostly briefly. But then they send Vessikhan down to talk.

The head of Archaeology wallows down the stairs in his best fetishwear. When he tries to speak to us at first, he doesn't have the mic on and we just hear a mumbled buzz from where we're crouching behind our barricades. Admittedly we play it up, after that. Even when Vessikhan fumbles the controls to broadcast his voice, the idea leaps from one to another of us that we should just gaslight him about whether we can understand him, and we do it. Nobody even needs to make the concrete decision—no votes on the subcommittee. We're all just in on the joke. And it is funny, because Vessikhan can't hear his own voice as it issues from his suit, so we just cup our ears and make faces. And he gets more and more frustrated, shouting at us. Then we hear him quite plainly shouting at the Security tech team listening in, telling them they've screwed it up.

He takes his mask off. Not something we were expecting, but his patience just snaps and he does. It'll be a full decontamination for Doctor Vessikhan later, or maybe they'll just chain him outside the huts up there, like a dog.

Presumably he still has an earpiece in, but it doesn't sound like he's particularly on message by that point. His face is red and sweaty—it's hot in those suits—and his eyes are wide and frightened. But he takes some breaths of the air and it doesn't kill him, and we're all there with just our bandanas about our necks. None of us is foaming at the mouth or sprouting mushrooms. Then he goes seriously off script. He looks from me to Primatt, then up to the gantry where the guns are trained maybe on, maybe near him.

"Let's talk," he says. "Nimell, Professor Daghdev." Actually getting it right, so he's been practising. "Doctor Croan. You know me. Let's talk." Another look at the gantry. They'll have him mic'd up, and probably Terolan's lieutenant is shouting in his ear about sticking to the plan, but Vessikhan is tired and angry—not even with us so much as his own side, if he has a side. "Let's just sit down and talk. That's what they want—" Then, to his listeners, "You sent *me* out here, so this is how I'm going to do it." And then, "I don't *care*." His expression is very much that of a man who doesn't care.

We move to a precisely calibrated distance out of sight of the gantry, and a crate is hauled up for Vessikhan to sit on. Primatt, Croan, Keev and I sit facing him but covered by our big slab barricades, arranged like a fancy screen as though we're about to get changed and prudishly don't want the guns to see our naked butts. Greely and Ilmus are out there keeping watch and tracking the snipers, who are trying to take advantage of this hiatus to pick off the leaders of the insurrection. We've made sure there isn't a good line on us, but also it wouldn't matter. Even Keev isn't really a leader any more.

"They want to know what your game plan even is," Vessikhan tells us. He looks to Primatt, then to Croan. The two he knows best. And perhaps what he's looking for is a sign that he no longer knows them. They must have a whirl of theories up top about what we brought in from outside.

We offer him water. It's actually proper distilled and uncontaminated water, but he doesn't drink it.

"You're stalling," Vessikhan points out. "We can hold, up there. We have the link to the ship. All you're doing is preventing the work going ahead. And eventually, the next barge will arrive and you won't even know, which means the next consignment of prisoners—of *you*—will all die on delivery. Because nobody'll be there to meet them. Then there will be a new shift of personnel, and how are you going to hold at that point?"

"Years," Keev noted. "You're suggesting you can hold out years."

"Well, either we hold out or Security storms your barricades down here. And they're all very well for hiding you from snipers but we're *above* you. When they come for you, they'll just drop down right over your barricades. You've just made some trench-warfare sim for yourself. Look, I'm not going to lie. There is no good exit for you. They're going to want their pound of flesh from people like you, the leaders. But if you roll over now, then they'll keep the rest alive, for the work. Because that's what this camp is for. If you push, though, then they'll just kill everyone and rebuild from scratch. That's more palatable to the commandant than any kind of compromise with you. I'm not even asking you what your demands are because it doesn't matter. Nimell, please. I can even convince him to spare *you*. You're not one of these people." He's nakedly appealing to her, even though the rest of us are right there. "Please let me salvage something from this."

Primatt hunches forwards on her own crate, one leg shifting and then the other, the knee flexing beneath her overalls in two distinct places, drawing Vessikhan's gaze.

"I'm one of them," she says softly, and very pointedly leaves the words without any stress or indicator to qualify how she means it. What wider *us* is she severing herself from? Vessikhan can only wonder.

His gaze flicks to Croan, to me, stopping short of Keev, because the man was never on Dig Support. "The work," says Vessikhan. As though that would motivate anyone to continue being slave labour. Except it might with Vessikhan, even. And it's just as well, because I reckon he'll be on the ground floor of Labour Camp 2.0 if the commandant has to start again, given his performance in these negotiations. But Vessikhan has a need to know. He's studied the fragmentary fingerprints of the lost Kilnie civilization for years and learned precisely nothing. The lack of closure is eating him up inside.

The fact that I know that about him, with absolute certainty, shows how he's been cutting a lot of corners. I smile.

"The work," I say. The others cede me the floor.

"Terolan," he says. "The commandant. You may not believe it, but it's important to him as well. He wants to know. It's his life's work to solve the mystery of this place. And you must want to find out too. You're a man of science. You're all scientists." Again, excluding Keev from the conversation, trying to split us even if he doesn't realize that's what he's doing. "Look, maybe we can come to some accommodation. Just... We're a tiny outpost of humanity on a hostile world. You have to have order. You have to have someone in command, making the decisions, or we're all dead. I don't believe you have a game plan. I don't think you ever thought about what happens next, now you've done this." Standing up, he becomes more and more agitated. "No, wait, listen to me. You've made your point, now make your demands." Even though it was absolutely clear a moment ago that no demands would be considered. "You want more regular decontamination? You want different shifts? You want—"

"We want," Keev says, "your surrender."

Then we're all on our feet, moving apart. The shot that would have taken Keev in the head strikes a scar off the slab he's just moved behind. Ilmus was spotting for snipers, and we knew it was coming. Without needing to be told, the urgency leapt to us. Vessikhan is left out in the open, the one viable target. I understand that his last desperate gabble wasn't really for us. He had them in his ear lining up the shot and was trying to stop what was about to happen by wringing some nonsense concession, some progress in the "negotiations" that he had thought were in good faith.

"The work," I tell him, from round the side of a slab. A couple more shots come from ground level and I hear one bullet strike sparks from the scaffolding. "It's done, Doctor Vessikhan."

"What do you mean?" he demands, even as the gantry shudders to the sudden movement of boots above.

"We know who the ruins builders were," I say. "We know it all. Lay down your guns and I'll let you and Terolan peer-review my paper on it. What do you say?" I feel the jab of Ilmus's amusement at my words. Just like old times, back before the academic purges. There's a sudden lance of nostalgia that we share, and that everyone else feels and vicariously understands.

Vessikhan is staring at me, naked hunger on his face. I can actually hear the tinny voice in his earpiece as Security scream at him to get out of there. "You know?" he demands. His own desperate desire to share in that knowledge is like ecto-plasmic fingers fumbling at my scalp.

"Tell Terolan he'll never work it out, not if he runs the

camp for a hundred years," I say, and then Security is coming for us and we're pushing back.

They have the guns. They have discipline, radio links, the genuine confidence and courage that a lifetime of bully's victories gives you. When you wear the boot you kick and don't hesitate. That's what they've got. They come down on us like an enforcer's special-issue hobnails through someone's door at two in the morning. Like most of us remember, from shortly before they took us.

We meet them. With our handful of guns and pockets of ammo, as well as our repurposed tools, cutlery and scaffolding bars. We throw incendiary cocktails like it's happy hour, to see just how hot we can make it in those protective suits. They don't like it but they take it. They continue to push forwards because they know how this goes. They are the hammer, and we break. That's the Mandate model. It worked back home, as everyone on both sides of this fight has ample cause to remember. Their unity, training and gear, but also just the simple natural order of things. The wolves to our sheep. And I have been at enough protests, at subcommittee meetings, when the boots came in. I have been in desperate running street battles and remember being a sheep, trying to stand up to the wolves. The confusion and the panic of it. The dreadful fear that everyone else will fold, and so it won't change anything if you, you alone, stand firm. Or rather, it'll change everything for *you* but make no difference to anything else in the world.

But this is a different world.

There is no hive mind, no alien over-mind, no indefatigable horde of fungal zombies. We're just fragile human beings under the boot. But as I push back against Security I know

I'm not alone. When I rush around the edge of the barriers with the knife that killed Parrides, Ilmus is at my back. Keev is. Greely is. We all are. There are no sheep on Kiln. I see Vessikhan drop, his hands covering his head, shrinking back from the violence. In all that savage scrum, he is the sole person who is alone, neither electronic nor biological contact to bolster him.

That would be the satisfying narrative conclusion, wouldn't it? They come for us with the guns and we, unified, indomitable, charge them. Perhaps everything slows down as we do. Stirring music. A fuzz of soft focus, the gunshots echoing into infinity. A list of actors and crew who brought you such sterling entertainment. Life's not like that, though, not even on Kiln.

The thing about solidarity, about being the crowd which acts with unity of purpose, is that you have to make the same calculations as the hive mind does, but with none of its impunity. You're not the chess master moving out your sacrificial pawns; you're the pawns, deciding together that sacrifices must be made. And you're thinking: Professor Daghdev, that's terrible. It must have been traumatizing for you to watch your friends die again. Was it more or less terrible this time, with such an intimate connection? Were you holding their hand, in their minds, or were they screaming in your ear? Did Ilmus give themself to the guns, or was it Keev? Did Primatt lurch forwards to beat them to death with her leg?

It's a chance thing, basically. It's down to whoever is there, who must plug the gap, hold the breach, act as a shield so someone else can live to strike the blow. Because the hardest thing about sacrifice is not knowing if it'll be worth it. What's the point in taking the bullet if the person behind you in the charge loses heart, dithers, runs away? You may as well have stayed at home. You only have one life after all. It can be very hard to know when to throw it away.

But right then, when they come to scour the camp of us, shooting, beating, stamping, we know. We are many minds, individuals, but with one mood between us. I throw myself at the guns and they shoot me three times. I fall at the very foot of the stairs, knowing pain, but knowing I've bought Ilmus and the others moments. Seeing the boots that had been advancing so ferociously now skidding backwards in my limited, ground-level sight. In my pain.

And it is close. We have the numbers, but the point of automatic weapons is that numbers don't actually matter. "Whatever happens we have got / the Maxim gun, and they have not," as the bard writes. But there is a moment, in such clashes—I am hypothesizing here because I was not in their heads—when something shifts. A moment when the iron discipline shows the rust beneath the paint, as we fail to break in the way they were trained to expect us to. When we just press them despite the guns, tearing the weapons from their hands, cutting open their protective suits. And after that fulcrum moment, the chaos and panic that they sought to export to us comes to roost in them. Each one of them is alone inside their rubber mask, their owlish goggles, their breath coarse in their ears.

So we drive them back, and I see the bodies left behind. Our bodies. They take their own fallen with them. Then I'm jolted up—it's such agony I cannot describe, making me black out, and then I'm immediately shocked back into consciousness by fresh pain. I see I have retained some sliver of my special status from when I first arrived on Kiln. Professor Arton Daghdev, noted academic and dissident. Because I find myself being hauled up the stairs alive, in their hands. The commandant has apparently noted me falling in the front ranks and he isn't done with me yet.

29.

It's a net positive. I don't necessarily feel that way immediately, but Security medics patch me up and so I'm not
dead yet. If we were the merciless alien hive mind then I'd
not care about being dead and would probably have a kill
switch in my brain, ready to just snuff the brief candle
before they could torture anything out of me. Or maybe
my body would bloat violently outwards with the pressure
of the killer death spores breeding in my necrotic flesh and
I'd go *bang!* They'd all fall over choking and clutching their
throats and...

Well, none of that's on the table. I'm on the table, though.
They stem the blood loss and pump me full of various things
that will stop my abused body from shutting down, though
decidedly light on the painkillers. They are absolutely not
averse to me being in any level of pain short of the death-
by-shock sort. And that latter spore-explosion scenario has
obviously occurred to them, because they go through all this
medical circus while in full protective gear. Even more than
their gunmen wore, due to the considerably more intimate
acquaintance they're making with my insides. I am conscious
on and off, as all this is going on. It would be arguably quite
interesting. They find a certain amount of stuff in me that
isn't in the Earth-based user manual, certainly. A furry coating

of Kilnishness. Maybe that helps to keep me together, too. I hear snippets of a debate over whether they need to just blast me with decontaminants until I'm restored to factory settings, but the dissenting voices suggest that might not leave enough of me to be viable. And it's something the camp medical records have a fair amount of data on, given past accidents and incidents.

And they need to keep me alive to pump me for information, which, objectively, is hilarious. Not that I'm laughing right then, as they stitch me up.

I'm healing, though, inside, because Kiln is good at that. The myriad little passengers living their busy lives within me are good tenants, ensuring the apartment is kept in good shape for the landlord.

I flex the new senses I have, feeling the inner hum of it all going about its business, replastering and applying a few coats of gloss. Not exactly good as new but healing.

But there's nothing else. No camaraderie, no sense of my fellows. Because when they've finished with their stitching and their drugs, they dump me in a sealed cell, right next to Rasmussen in fact. It's a bitter pill that they don't throw me in with her, like they did before. We'd have so much to talk about. The lack of company is the real torture. In my box I am alone with my thoughts, and all the little thoughts that aren't quite mine. But it's all just my own microcosm, the goldfish bowl and echo chamber of my private being. That's a terrible thing, when you're used to the broader connection Kiln has gifted us all with. Through the wall I hear the faint and muffled calls of Ylse Rasmussen, first ever human ambassador to the builders of Kiln, and finally I understand her dreadful anguish. Not driven mad by the festering contagion in her brain, only from being so very, very lonely. Deprived of the company of a whole world.

They're going to question me, I know. That's the only reason they saved me. They want to know our strengths, weaknesses, plans. But I don't really know those things any more. If they'd only let me out into the air, I'd find out, but they won't do that. The precise paranoia that keeps me locked up alone here denies them any chance of learning about the insurrection's next move.

I'm there for a day, blind to what's going on below. Sometimes I feel a shiver through the floor as some action happens. I imagine jackboots pounding down the stairs, snipers hustling along the rails to take a shot, ceramic incendiaries breaking across the riot shields. I'm going mad with not knowing already. Not feeling. Not being with my fellows, my friends. I husband my fading memories of what it was like when I was superhuman, part of something greater. Blowing on them like kindling, trying to hold onto the sense of it. But the dull human-ness of me is creeping back. The old Arton Daghdev who lived with fear and uncertainty, and never truly knew another person. Who doubted everyone, and because of that came to doubt himself. Who lived in a world where the vast mass of billions of people were crammed shoulder to shoulder and in each other's armpits and yet each one alone.

Eventually they come and get me. I am still in considerable pain—unable to rest, sleeping in fitful, hallucinogenic bursts as my subconscious struggles to recreate What It Was Like using only my poor human brain and the little community I carry with me. And then the guards in their heavy suits are there, caught in that weird Schrödinger's Thug situation, where they want to drag me about as painfully as they can while simultaneously not aggravating my condition to the extent it will lessen the impact of all the rest of the pain they have planned for me later. There is absolutely nothing I can do about the situation, certainly. I neither cooperate nor resist. I'm mostly irrelevant to the action.

I anticipate a slab and some drugs, and the high-tech equivalent of splints under the fingernails, but what I get is Commandant Terolan. It's the same deal as before, a plastic umbilical leading to a plastic box within his study. There's a speaker so we can communicate electronically, but not the slightest chance any biological material will pass from me to the man himself. Which is just how I want it.

Yet I'm curious. By now I'm far more familiar with the commandant's office than any prisoner should be, who isn't an active informer. And of all my many sins, I was never that.

"Professor Daghdev," comes his voice through the speaker inside my box.

"Commandant," I reply. A voice that doesn't sound like my own, washed-out and hoarse. Being shot will do that to you. I'm just about standing, mostly thanks to the drugs they gave me, but now I gingerly let myself down to the floor. This forces him to peer over his desktop at me because they didn't quite think through the sightlines.

"No doubt you've been expecting some manner of gallant rescue," he suggests, though I have the sense his heart isn't in it.

I'm about to answer when the door—the regular door, not the hatch to my umbilical—opens and they bring Vessikhan in. Not as a prisoner, though you wouldn't know it from his tight, uncomfortable posture. An unhappy man. I replay our last conversation as his eyes bore into me.

"You can tell me how it's gone down there, if you want," I say politely, "but it won't matter. I can't really rely on anything you tell me, or know if it's the truth." Once you've been in a position where you *know*, without doubt, when people are true or not, then anything else is just a hollow echo. There's nothing Terolan could swear to that would fill in for that subconscious certainty I shared in, however briefly.

Vessikhan starts to say something, then glances at the commandant and is shut down. Terolan stares at me.

"We will drive your fellows into the woods," he says.

I laugh at him.

It's not the response he expected. Being driven into the woods is a serious matter. He's never seen the woods himself, of course, but he's seen drone imagery and read a hundred reports of when Excursions went wrong. He knows that not everyone on Keev's team came home, even. Nobody wants to be driven into the woods, where the wild things are.

He tries a new tack. "Your fellows have abandoned you. They've made no attempt to recover you." The shifting ground of his arguments hints at an underlying desperation. What he's really telling me is *We have not been able to secure the ground.* He's trapped up on the gantry with dwindling resources, and it's no great victory that he's made me his cellmate.

As though divining my thoughts, he insists, "They can't hold out down there. We have recovered the drones now. We're outfitting them as hunter-killers."

I take a deep breath. It is...tedious and vexing to have this kind of conversation. And to a greater or lesser extent, all my past conversations with other people were like this.

Words dropped into a well, then attempting to read the ripples for the true meaning of what's being said. But Terolan is trying to do that subtle threat thing, which means he's dropping those words in sideways and out of order. Basically it's impossible to get any real information out of him at all. He's all noise.

"You're all noise," I say. I don't particularly mean to but, between the drugs and the pain, and my runaway inner monologue, it just slips out.

"I assure you I am very serious." He can't understand me, either. He can only hear the words I use and interpret them through the filter of his own nature. He can never *know*. The vagary of the conversation is maddening.

"Commandant Terolan," I say, breaking into whatever triviality he was saying next. "Why?" That should suffice, but of course it doesn't. I try to push myself far enough outside my head to be able to pick the right words to communicate my meaning. "You keep bringing me here. Talking to me. In your office. If we were back home, I'd be wearing my fancy trousers and some aftershave."

He recoils, meaning I lose him entirely past the lip of the desk. Not very metrosexual, is our Commandant Terolan. I hear a couple of murdered orders. I think he was about to demand his guards haul me to my feet, except they'd have to crawl in through the umbilical, and then what if I just hung there like a dead weight? The sheer logistics throttle his authoritarianism.

"What I'm saying is, why me, here, now?," I tell his desk and Vessikhan, who's still staring at me like a dog denied its dinner.

A pause. I picture Terolan smoothing down his composure,

pulling his clothes straight, though I can't *know*. He reappears past the desk and there's something in his face I'm not ready for, because I'm used to it being a closed book—the sort of book used only for recording Mandate doctrine and the results of interrogations. But now the pages are cracked open and I almost connect, being to being, with the man who masterminds the misery here on Kiln. There's a frankness, a vulnerability there I hadn't looked for before.

"I have only ever been a man of science," Terolan says, quietly enough that I have to put my ear to the speaker. "They sent me here because something wonderful occurred in this planet's past. Something my predecessors broke against. The Mandate must understand the builders of Kiln, Arton. Professor Daghdev. There is no greater mystery in all the known universe. A race of people who arose here, and vanished, leaving nothing of themselves except these hollow shells and this meaningless script. Who were they and where did they go? And you... You and a handful of other voices, who could think beyond the strictures placed upon you. It gave me hope that one day you would push too far, and be sent to me." He's come round the desk's edge now, standing right at the plastic of the box, his gaze devouring me. "Because I needed your thoughts. Everyone they sent me as staff was a dullard, too stupid to advance their career back home and yet too orthodox to push the boundaries of original thought." Vessikhan's right there, but Terolan doesn't much care for the self-esteem of his staff. He is a man alone, after all. An island. The feelings of others don't register with him.

"You think I've betrayed you," I say. Ludicrous, because I was never *his* for any action of mine to count as a betrayal, but he feels it nonetheless.

"This could have been your crowning achievement," he tells me. "To contribute to solving the mystery. Instead of which you make it all about *politics*." Thus sayeth the politician when the scientist ventures an opinion.

I could give him the grand lecture about the Mandate's scientific orthodoxy, which means everything is politics. About all the careers I've seen destroyed because my peers had inconvenient truths they wanted to advance. All that. But either he already knows it or he wouldn't listen, and breath is something I'm short of right now.

"He said..." Vessikhan stutters and stills. For a moment Terolan's going to ignore him entirely but then he makes a single, impatient gesture and Vessikhan continues.

"He said they know who the ruins builders were now."

"And from where is this revelation supposed to have come? During your seven days in the wilderness?" Terolan demands.

"Yes," I confirm.

"That's not science!" Terolan spits. "Science is what you can bring back and analyse. Test and reconfirm to within a statistically verifiable margin. If you discovered evidence out there, bring it to the camp. Let us examine it. For the furtherance of human understanding, Arton...Why are you *laughing*?"

Because I am. I wish I wasn't, because it hurts a great deal, but it's so very funny.

"We *have* been," I choke out. "We've been bringing our findings back to camp for some time now, Commandant. For the...'furtherance of human understanding.' Exactly! Come on, open my cage. I'll introduce you to our discoveries." Then it hurts too much and I'm fighting to breathe, feeling all three gunshot wounds pull and twist against my inopportune hilarity.

Terolan's face is a wax mask. Vessikhan's teeth are bared as though he's about to fight for his life. I see terrible things shadow past his eyes, but I can't *know* and it's maddening.

The Commandant rushes back behind the big desk, as though I might burst through the plastic and leap at him. "Don't die, Professor," he says flatly, which suggests I must look pretty bad right then. "I still need you." And, when Vessikhan twitches to speak again, he adds, "But not for your insights. That window has passed. Any contribution you might have to the science would be as contaminated as you are. But we still have *you*. The ringleader."

I've got myself under control by then. Enough to raise an interrogative eyebrow.

Terolan braves the near side of the desk again. His face is set hard, scowling. Is the man behind it of the same shape, or cowering? There's no way to know. "Your fellows are hiding behind their barriers right now, but perhaps they'll come out for you. *Professor* Daghdev."

"Is that," I ask, "how you think it works?"

He stares at me. He can't know what I mean.

"There are no queen ants," I say. I admit at this point I'm just being cryptic for the pure fuckery of it, but I would also need more words than I have the energy to speak to try and explain how wrong he is. If my fellows could rescue me, they would, but not because I'm a *leader*. Not because I'm highly placed on the revolutionary subcommittee that Terolan probably imagines we have, even though the real revolution we've been through has rendered subcommittees obsolete. And not even for what I know, because I don't really know anything in particular. I'm not the special prize that Terolan thinks I am. My absence impoverishes the whole, but not so much as all that. No more than anyone else's would.

He sees it in my face, I think. How little I rate that particular threat. In his face, he shows me disappointment, genuine regret, frustration. The man of science who finds me wanting in his determined drive to discover not the truth but the one specific lie that his orthodoxy demands. And in that one thing I can at least satisfy him.

"Know this, then," I say, "if it'll make you happy. You were right all along. The ruins builders are out there right now. The Wild Men. They're just like us. More like us even than Croan's mock-ups. They're so close, Commandant."

Seeing the hope, fear, despair, hunger and disdain, all of it readable from his features, I have no idea what's rising up from within him and what I'm just doodling there with my own assumptions. Then he has the guards clamber in and haul me off, because he's lost the initiative in this conversation, just as he has against the insurrection.

30.

I'm back in my shed again. Alone. I bang on the wall I have in common with Ylse Rasmussen and she bangs back. We could probably work out a code, get a dialogue going. Prisoners have done more in the past. But I can't. It would be like telling a professional athlete to run a marathon after you've cut off their legs. Mere dialogue would starve me, after having partaken of the polylogue, the omnilogue. And so I batter at the walls of my box and feel the howling building up inside. Keep me in here long and it'll be me and Rasmussen shrieking at one another, just to hear each other's voices. And even then it won't help because what is a voice? What meagre and unsatisfactory communion is contained in simple human words. Ylse, I *understand* her. But I cannot *know* her because they have put walls between us. My breath is not her breath. My extended biome is severed from hers, and everyone's. You can't imagine the torture of that silence. One that every human being is born into, but doesn't realize is there until they've had it filled with the comforting presence of others.

The commandant comes by to hear my desperate communicative percussion, and doubtless it gives him pleasure. It represents to him the reinstitution of the natural order. Arton Daghdev is infected and has gone mad. God's in his Heaven, all's right with the world. So I restrain myself. I sit on the floor of my barren little kingdom and hug my knees. These thoughts of mine, that were my stock in trade and livelihood, were always enough for me in the past. I was the great thinker, wasn't I? So why do I feel each individual idea rattle around the inside of my skull like dried peas, without anyone else to appreciate them? A late time in life to learn that I am indeed not an island. Not even a peninsula or an isthmus, but a landlocked little county utterly dependent on cross-border trade with all my neighbours.

A day goes by. I'm kept alive, if you can call it living. I try to imagine what's going on. I hear gunfire occasionally, the clatter of feet, the pop of grenades. I am assured that there's been no mass killing or capturing of my truant fellows for the sole reason that the commandant would absolutely let me know if that had happened. The rejected academic fanboy would want to show his fallen icon just how I'd chosen the wrong side.

A day turns into a night. There's no dramatic rescue attempt from below, but I have faith that's because it's the right thing not to do.

It's just how ants make decisions. Or how our brains do, on a deep neuron-to-neuron level. These are shunted up to the conscious levels of our minds to become attached to justifications and rationales. It's not a hive mind, in the popular conception, because that implies some top-down direction controlling all its component parts. Ants and neurons are democracies, that old political saw the Mandate works so hard to discredit. You have different groundswells of popular opinion gathering momentum, and picking up new adherents like a snowball, until one urge or impulse reaches a critical mass, after which the whole—the nest, the brain—adopts that tabled motion wholeheartedly. And here's where the hive aspect comes in, because those elements which were rooting for the alternatives give in with good grace and wave flags for the winner. There's no holdout of political grousers claiming someone else won the election. The whole institution acts in unison the moment that threshold is crossed. And that's us. No demagogues having to harangue the crowd, no self-interested cult leader talking everyone into servitude. Just a group acting together, for everyone's best benefit. Even mine. So, they've not made a desperate bid to rescue me. All to the good. More chance for me if they're not dead under the barrels of the guns.

Another day and night. The appalling solitude. There's less sound of fighting by now and I picture Security turtled up here, waiting for the grand assault that they *know* must be coming. That's how the revolution triumphs, by storming the fortress of authority. A last dog-end of outdated thought and the reason so many subcommittees-past foundered and fell. The idea that you can only fight the Mandate on its own terms, struggling for control of the structures that it has created. Become monsters in order to fight with monsters. Instead of which, here on Kiln, we can gaze into the abyss until the abyss turns its much-sought gaze back on us.

Halfway through that night I have a visitor.

There's the viewing area walled off with glass, which I've stood at the other end of before, peering in at Rasmussen. Now I'm in half of Rasmussen's old space so the commandant can come and watch me fling excrement and bellow my madness at him. But it's not Terolan who comes in this time.

It's Vessikhan the archaeologist, looking so furtively guilty I feel I should arrest him myself on general principles.

There's a long, doubting moment when he stares at me, waiting for me to go ape, but I just sit there, holding myself together. Just. Not Rasmussing too much, not yet.

With a nervous, jerky movement he activates the speaker. If I start howling now the whole camp will hear and Vessikhan's gaffe will be blown. But I sit, I watch, I wait for his offer. Because that's my best read of him. And, because all I have are expression and body language, and the other inadequate tells of Earth, he wrong-foots me out of the gate.

"They're going to kill you," he says. "Terolan's out of patience."

I digest this. It seems better than a long period of solitary confinement. I lack Rasmussen's stoic endurance. I nod.

"They're going to set up projectors," Vessikhan goes on, voice hushed, "and will broadcast your execution. To break morale."

"It won't," I say. He flinches, but I'm quiet and controlled, entirely urbane. Even though the howl is prowling about the inside of my head, demanding to be let out.

"They're going," Vessikhan repeats, with emphasis, "to kill you."

I nod and, because he obviously expects more, say, "I don't see that I can do anything about that."

"Aren't you going to ask me to help you?"

"Why would you do that?" It's almost as though something changes behind my eyes, a different set of lenses clicking into place so I can look at him differently. Vessikhan seldom leaves the camp, as a rule. He mostly studies images and broken potsherds brought back by other teams. Which means he doesn't go through decontamination at all. Nor does he go about in heavy protective gear within the camp. He bunks next to where Primatt slept, and associates with Dig Support a lot. It's not as though there's some helpful gauge hovering over his head to tell anyone just what percentage of him might be touched by the gifts of Kiln, but there's more of us in him than there is in the commandant or Security.

"You said you knew," he says. "I need you to tell me."

I nod.

"I've been studying this goddamned world for years. I have a mountain of data on what its inhabitants left behind. I've read everything that Nimell and her predecessors have written about the bioscience end. But I am no closer to an answer than I was when I stepped off the shuttle. You've found out, though."

"I have," I confirm. And something comes over in my voice that shakes him, actually staggers him, a weakness of the knees that almost has him joining me on the floor. An utter certainty, somehow communicated just by the pitiful inadequacy of mere words.

"Tell me," he insists.

"How are the others getting on?" I counter. "As you can see, I'm starved for information here." The understatement of the universe.

I'm not strictly making a deal here but Vessikhan takes it as one. He puts forward some goods on credit. "They're holding out," he says. "Security has barriers and fences up top now. We tried to shift them with chemicals, with bombs. We sent drones out and lost those too. I hear Terolan and Suiye arguing, about how much another assault down the steps would cost."

I nod. Suiye must be the lieutenant, head of Security, a little speck of new data that does me no good at all. The rest is useful though.

"You want to know about the builders," I tell Vessikhan. "Go out and ask the others. Ask Ilmus or Croan. Ask Keev. Ask anyone."

"But you're—"

"My professorship was revoked. The only tenure I have isn't the sort that comes with a stipend." I can't believe how very calm I am, given all the hollow howling inside. Here in my final moments, before they feed me to the incinerator, I am sanguine. It's because the others are well. I'm cut off from them, and the basal substance of me cries out at the severed ties, but I am a man still. I am a mind, and the greater good can be grasped by the solitary intellect as well as the community spirit. And a free turncoat, Vessikhan, is more of an asset than I am right now.

"Any one of them can tell you all you need to know," I say to him. "Go find them."

He makes a noise. A little of desperation, a little of laughing. "I wish you'd just beg," he says. Not meanly, not playing the demon king to his captive audience. "I wish you'd set some store by your own life. That way at least I'd know it was you."

"Harsh," I note.

"*You*, I mean. A human. Not…something else."

I am a human and I am something else. I don't say this, because I feel it would muddy whatever waters he's currently gazing into. Instead I say, "You ever think about the fundamental paradox of our society? How they build a tight-knit machine of a state by breaking everyone down into solitary units turned against each other? How you compel mass obedience out of the most individualistic drives of selfishness, greed and fear?"

"Arton," Vessikhan tells me flatly, "I do not care for that political shit. I just want to *know*."

Then he brings something out. For a moment I think it's a gun and he's actually going to threaten me, through the clear plastic. It's a tool, though. Something I've seen before but I can't immediately place. The shapeless bag thrust through his belt turns out to be a mask that he deforms over his head, then wrestles with until his eyes and the lenses are roughly in line.

And then he cuts. It's the same device they used to free us from our bags after we were spat out of the disintegrating barges. The tool carves through the plastic like a laser through butter, but the bitter scent on the air suggests it's some sort of chemical debonding exercise as well as heat. I just goggle at him until, halfway through the exercise, I understand that if he'd just opened the cage up the normal way, he'd have tripped all sorts of alarms. He's thought this through. And also, very obviously, this isn't just Vessikhan giving the condemned man the chance to stretch his legs and get some vital anthropology off his chest before the execution. This is a permanent rescue.

He cuts a hole just big enough for me to squeeze through. I'll still have to clamber, though, and the effort seems insuperable. Being shot will do that to you. I have to try, though. Just me, alone. Inside me, something is reaching desperately for connection, scrabbling at the wider walls, at the pores of Vessikhan's skin, but I'm still alone. I'm also weak and hurting. Vessikhan has an orderly mind, though. He's thought of that, and sometimes Earth ingenuity is a substitute for the fortitude I'm lacking. He beckons me to the hole and then shoots me up with a little metal cylinder of something that quickly has my heart going double time and the edges of my vision vibrating. The pain, which was clinging to me like a family of drowned children, is kicked off the lifeboat to splash around with the sharks for a bit. It must be something military grade, fit to lift a half-dead Mandate enforcer back on his feet, to continue brutalizing the enemies of orthodoxy.

"Just don't overdo it," Vessikhan warns. It's a good warning because I want to overdo it. I want to lift this entire shed over my head and drop it on the commandant. A wild, unfounded confidence that interacts badly with the Kilnishness in me. I also want to run naked through the camp, tearing people's heads off and shouting mad revelations down the stumps of their necks. Behaviour unbefitting even a defrocked professor. Instead I clamber through the hole and, though my body is insisting I can leap tall buildings with a single bound, that effort still takes most of the wherewithal out of me. The edges of the hole are cool but sting my skin with the residue of whatever process was involved in the cutting. Vessikhan backs off from me, breathing heavily through the mask.

"Tell me," he insists.

"Here? Now? Shall we invite Terolan along too? Maybe I could set up a screen, give a lecture?" I'm speaking too quickly, in a jerky rhythm I can't quite rein in. And weirdly, the sarcasm obviously helps him. Alien hive minds aren't bitchy.

"Okay, you're right." Vessikhan's in-detail planning doesn't seem to have gone much further than this point, but I assume his next move is getting us both past Security's defences and to ground level.

"Give me the cutter," I tell him.

"No."

"Well you come and do the work then."

"The wire?" he asks. There's a blank moment before I realize that's what Terolan's people have done: printed out bales of jagged spikes that they've festooned the gantry with like bunting. Everyone's always fighting the war before the last one.

"Not yet." And to test just how far he's gone, I wait to see if he can catch the other shoe I'm dropping.

"No," he says eventually, but it's the right no. From my mind to his, he knows what I'm considering.

"Yes. Non-negotiable."

"You're mad. She'd wake up the whole camp. We can't—"

"She'll be fine." I can't know that but I hope I'm right. She might be genuinely mad by now, considering how long they've had her in. But I can't leave her. She, the first of us to enter into that wider world. And they locked her up for it. They thought she was mad and infected, when in truth she was only one of those things.

Vessikhan is already bitterly regretting his life choices. He wants to run back to his bed and pretend none of this ever happened. A less studious man would do just that. But he *must* find out. It really is as simple as that. He is a man who's butted heads with a puzzle for so long that he is willing to become a traitor to the Mandate in return for the answer.

"I will tell you everything," I promise. "But I'll not leave her."

He drops the cutter, then kicks it over to me. He won't

get any closer but simultaneously is becoming closer. The mask is a fig leaf. It barely hides the nakedness of him.

The silence, when we move to Rasmussen's half of the shed, is deafening. Her muted howling tails to nothing and she watches. That tells me all I need to know about her mental state. That it's easier for her to shriek, gibber and act up, to try and cover for the aching absence in her mind where All The Rest Of Everything should be. But she knows when something's up. There's alertness in her old eyes. Vessikhan hangs back, and I cut open the prison that has held Ylse Rasmussen in for so long. I take a deep breath of the air that stinks of her sweat, excrement and incarceration, and I know her, and she me.

She stands. The madness of her flies at me and tears about us like an exorcized ghost. Trying to make me a part of its own idiolectic mind-space, eddying out into the wider world now that there are no barriers any more. It dissipates into the wider spaces of Kiln, until its concentration is so few parts per million against the backdrop of all that *life* that she is sane again. Ylse Rasmussen, the pioneer, the first.

We should probably clasp hands, *Doctor Livingstone, I presume.* Hug it out. Touch foreheads in deep spiritual communion. But Vessikhan is hopping from foot to foot and we need to get out of here.

Outside, it feels as though some harsh plastic version of the Kilnish biosphere has colonized the gantry. Every railing and edge bristles with spines and jagged protrusions. The fenestrae that Security have left to use as shooting ports look like spiracles. As though the whole structure is about to take a deep breath and come to thorny life. Rasmussen and I share the same moment of disconnection and mordant humour on seeing our enemies becoming just like the very thing they loathe and fear.

Vessikhan breaks for the nearest section of wire but falls back instantly when he sees a patrol coming. There are sentries, and the towers are still manned. We end up getting clear of the prisoner shack, making repeated and abortive sorties towards the edge of the gantry. The spiky defences are designed to repel boarders from below but we still need to cut through them if we're going to descend. Vessikhan has actually printed out a ladder, a segmented plastic thing we can climb down. I can't even think where he'd have found the pattern, so maybe he's an unsung programming genius. Certainly nobody's going down the stairs anytime soon, because there's a permanent Security presence at every potential beachhead, and it's not as though we can just show our day passes to nip over the border.

We actually make it to the wire on the ninth try, taking advantage of a gap between patrols at a point the cameras can't see. I sizzle away at the plastic for thirty seconds but then Vessikhan starts hurrying us back into cover again, almost sobbing with frustration. The guards are seething all around the edges of their elevated kingdom like—ironic thoughts—angry ants. My fellows below are keeping them on their toes, even if a full-on assault isn't practical. I feel the distant tug of their presence and resolve and take strength from it. They know I'm free now, and Rasmussen too. The terrible isolation has washed away in the current of the air. But we can't get to them. The gantry level has become an outpost encircled by hostile natives. And intellectually Terolan will tell himself that the people down there *aren't* natives; still, he's not wrong.

We make three more abortive attempts, each time moved on like deadbeats by the tramp of the patrols. Vessikhan keeps eyeing Rasmussen, powerfully unhappy that she's with us, waiting for her to explode in hooting and jabbering to bring the wrath of the camp down on us. But Rasmussen is calm. Almost preternaturally so. She is stick-thin, filthy, an angular scarecrow of a woman with hair that's more knot than lock, but since she's been out in the air, she stands tall and peaceful. There's something in her eyes that even I quail at. The places she went, before they caged her. All the steps she took down the path I am on. And those parts of her, the linking parts, have been starved of contact for so long, but now they're unfurling invisibly from her. Undergoing inner gestation and development like fruiting bodies. Reaching out into the air of the camp, and the background level of Kilnish biota we imported, like tunnel-digging prisoners sifting soil from our trousers. I can sense triggers within her, some late-stage life cycle of her Kilnish community, as though they've suffered through a decades-long drought and now the rain has come.

By now the alarm has been raised, and we hear shouts from the direction of our former residence. Vessikhan is hurried, twitchy, hustling us into a container, then closing and sealing the door. And abruptly it's all gone, all that wider world. Rasmussen opens her eyes and mouth as wide as they can go, the howl of protest rising in her. But she locks gazes with me, similarly deprived, and we connect. I am here. She is there. We are enough for each other for now. We hear boots pound outside, shouts. I wonder how long we can hide here. Cramped and airless, horribly cut off. But while part of me wants to run free in the night air, I understand. There is a bolt in my collarbone. While I am in or near the camp, they can locate me. The container Vessikhan selected is thick-walled, metal, a relic of the original landing perhaps. Enough to baffle the signal.

"We'll wait," he says. "They'll find where you cut the wire and think you got down." To my mind I didn't cut enough of the wire to make an exit, or we'd have exited, but Vessikhan is talking very fast, leaving no room to slide my doubts in. "We'll let things calm, let them assume we're long gone. Then we can get out."

I nod. And he's committed now. Even if he turned us in, there's no real way he could spin events that wouldn't bring the wrath of Terolan down on him. They busted Primatt down to Excursions for far, far less. He takes a long, shuddering breath.

Rasmussen taps at my locator.

"This." Her voice is like dust, just a rasp and a weird intonation. As though isolation for so long was a foreign country and she's come back with its accent. "This is after my time." But she understands what it's for, in part because I do. An idea passes between us. Not as some magic telepathy, but the infiltration of emotions and urges, a subconscious ballet of molecules translated into, and back out of, an alien script.

I close my eyes. I very much don't want this but she's right. And I'm not sure how much longer she can hold all that late-stage Kilnishness in.

I hand her the cutter.

Vessikhan watches, wide-eyed. He doesn't like that she now has it. In his mind, she's still the mad wife in the attic, dangerous and unpredictable. He doesn't understand that what we have is the greatest stabilizing influence a human mind ever encountered. Having someone else to lean on isn't a thing anyone should be ashamed of. I'd never be able to do this without her.

She unclips my overalls from the peg. We don't exchange looks because we don't need to. Something in her says *Ready?* and something in me confirms that I am. She activates the cutter and bends very precisely over my bared neck and chest. I stay absolutely still and the agony goes somewhere into that greater space. Oh, the injection helps, but that's wearing off by now, and Rasmussen can take up the slack. Under Vessikhan's horrified eyes, she carves the peg out of me as the inside of the container fills with the smell of roasting meat.

There's still a trample and a thunder of feet outside. We settle down in our box and wait. I wonder if we should have put an address on the outside. *To: The Revolutionaries, Ground Floor, the Labour Camp, Kiln*, in the hope they absent-mindedly deliver us.

And, because he's earned it, and what else is there, I nod at last to Vessikhan.

"I suppose you want to know," I say.

31.

"What you see out there, the life of Kiln, it's impoverished. A severe contraction of what we might have seen if we'd arrived a few thousand years ago." It's Rasmussen speaking, not me. She's been out of the loop, yes. Academically and more than that. But she knows what she knows. She blazed the original trail that The Science have been following ever since, and then she was the first of us to... She was the first of *us*.

"I know all that," Vessikhan says sharply. He's desperate for it. Terrified that he's taken this dreadful, irrevocable step to free us and we're going to short-change him. "Just tell me."

"You know all that because you read *my* notes," Rasmussen replies, and I suspect she never was someone to suffer fools gladly. Then we clam up because we hear them kick in the doors of the container. The metal had baffled the peg's signal enough to screw with their instruments, but they located it eventually and now they're staring at it, lying on the floor of that metal box in a welter of blood. I hope it gives them chills, picturing the operation in squirming detail, and they think of us as monstrous creatures, immune to pain. I hope the mental images it conjures drag at their feet when they continue their hunt.

Rasmussen hunches in on herself. We've picked our new

hiding place, having once more tried and failed to squeeze enough time with the wire to saw through it. And the cutter was running out of cut by then. So here we are, in hopefully the last place they'll search: tucked right up against the back of the commandant's own prefab office block, crammed into the shadow of his air vents, fans and cooling vanes, because there's enough ambient heat from all that gubbins to mask us if they're hunting for thermographic signatures, and because it's unobserved. Sovereign Mandate territory that surely no revolutionary would dare defile.

"The orbit that Kiln is on lends it an alternating sequence of warm, wet periods and colder, drier periods, adding into the diurnal variation we already see," Rasmussen continues. She's hunched with her back against hot vanes, as though she'll never get warm again, and I suddenly realize how haggard she is, how much she's just skin and bones. How dead she should be, honestly. Stuck in that box for decades, dabbling her fingers in her own filth, locked in her head in an intolerable loneliness. Now here she is talking science as though nothing ever happened. As though the Rasmussen-ness of her was just hibernating until social conditions swung back round to something she could survive in. And it stretches, like a skin over bubbling yeast, and still that patient voice speaks on. "We are currently past the nadir of the cold phase, and in a thousand years the planet will start to really bloom again." A cracked laugh. "That would be a sight to see, wouldn't it?"

Vessikhan's masked face nods several times, prompting, but she won't be hurried.

"They wouldn't believe it, when I first put forward my evidence. Because Kiln is thronging with life. Just look outside. Forests, jungles, marshes. There are deserts and badlands and all the rest too, sure, but our Earth eyes see riotous, fecund life. We have no idea what was, and what will be."

"And the builders—"

"Under normal circumstances, absent human interference, they'd be back for the rains." Her head's tilted back, eyes closed. A small smile comes to her face, like she's basking in the sun. What she's actually basking in is our company, Vessikhan's and mine. And we make a meagre sunbeam between us but it's more than she's had in a long, long time. Small wonder she wants to string the man along.

"So you're saying they're... what? Sleeping? Or is it eggs or... seeds, or..." Vessikhan's mind flails about like a loose end of rope in the silence she leaves him. "But that can't be the case because... I mean you're not telling me anything I haven't worked out. Whenever I can date anything —the little there is that I can date—then yes, each time Kiln goes through a wet period, more structures are thrown up. And older structures are altered. They add a few passages to their histories, usually towards the end of each warm period, but it's substantially the same culture. They're not reinventing the wheel each time." Not, of course, that there are wheels here, but we know what he means. "So where are they now? In between times? I mean, yes, human history had similar phases but people were still around. Just fewer of them, living in smaller communities. Tell me which of the *things* out there built all this, and then gave it up, but somehow remembers what it was, ready for the next time. Or..." He actually has Rasmussen by the collar of the new overalls I stole for her. "Was it us?" he demands. "You said, 'absent human interference.' Have we killed them somehow? Just from being here? Our radio signals, our biochemistry?"

I separate him from Rasmussen. I'm feeling a terrible weight inside, because I understand what she's going through right now. I can lend my support, but there's nothing I can do. She's the mirror of the millennia-long process she's talking about. The flowering of the new means the extinction of that other form, which just clung on.

"This is where things shift from your field to that of biosciences," Rasmussen says in a whisper. She looks more gaunt now than she did when we ushered her in here. Consumed from within by all the cryptic microfauna that were sheltering in her, awaiting a new spring. I feel every transition and decomposition that's going on inside her, and Vessikhan can't ever know. It's all I can do not to break down, to lament, tear my hair, beat my breast. Ylse Rasmussen's long stasis is thawing.

"The Kilnish ecology is an order of magnitude more complex than that of Earth," she whispers. "And Earth's was more complicated than we ever appreciated, before we destroyed most of it. By the time we understood the science enough to study it, there was so little left. Everything on Kiln is part of a network that includes everything else. Even the most hostile interactions, predator and prey, are still working to a pattern of mutual benefit. A biosphere that expands and complicates itself to the limits of its environment. You've seen nothing, none of us have. I only wish I could have. In the warm phase of the world, there'd have been ten times the number of component species, a hundred times the number of combined forms. Incredible specialism, webs of inter-relations..."

"The builders," Vessikhan snaps, a man who thinks he's been robbed. "Where are they?"

Rasmussen chuckles. "Well they're here. But they're not anywhere. Absent human interference. Where is the tangle in the string when you pull it taut? Gone."

I see his eyes goggle through the mask's lenses.

"Everything is the builders," she says at last, and it doesn't help because he can't get his head round it.

She sags back against the wall, and she's already been sagged back as far as I thought she could go. I can see the contours of her body slowly falling in on themselves. Skin and bone, that's all they left of her, but what was within her kept her manic, active and alive, like a device constantly searching for a signal. Now I am the signal, and I will carry what's in her to the wider world. Where will Ylse Rasmussen herself be, after that? The knot after the string is pulled. There's no such thing as ghosts, and I have never believed in the soul, yet it seems to me that something of her will survive and be scribed into a curved wall somewhere, to be remembered. To be a part of the world for ever.

I take her hand. "Everything is the builders," I echo, and Vessikhan rounds on me. He thinks we're mad, that we're a cult. And he now worries he's committed professional, and perhaps actual, suicide for nothing.

"The builders are an emergent property of the Kilnish ecosystem," I say. "When there is sufficient interconnection, sufficient complexity, the world wakes, and knows itself." It's mystical nonsense, and if someone had told me this when I'd first arrived on Kiln, I'd have the same aghast expression that Vessikhan doubtless sports now. "The Kilnish civilization is like a fungus. It exists *in potentia* during the dry periods, a million components in contraction, jigsaw pieces in the box. When the world blooms, they reconnect—never the same way twice, but that's okay because they left notes for themselves, from the last time. What builds the ruins, Vessikhan? Everything does. From each microscopic assemblage of molecules to creatures bigger than you can imagine, reaching high to lift things into place or smooth them over. A whole ecosystem of things living and dying and eating one another, that together make a mind which knows itself. Can you imagine?"

He shakes his head. He can't imagine it. *I* can't imagine and I'm in it. What must it be like, to be that world-entity? Was it subdivided into linked individuals, the way I am with Keev and Rasmussen and the rest? Or was it truly one great ocean of thought, surging around the globe? Vast, immeasurable, yet not superhuman. Not a godlike power. A thing that knew itself and speculated about the universe around it, and left the impression of its mind on the walls of the structures that its various component parts had raised up. A thing that understood it had a duty to the *it* of the future, and knew its place in the cycle of growth and decline which created and dismantled it. Leaving its sandcastles on the strand every time the tide went out, so that it would be able to rediscover them the next time the waters rolled back.

He's on the point of giving us up, I know. He's close enough to the true revelation that I can smell it on him. He's going to rush out and shout for Security, claim I overpowered him, disavow his actions. Maybe that would work, maybe it wouldn't. Except then we actually hear Security coming along the gantry, finally realizing there's one last place they haven't looked for us. Working their way through every nook and shadow along the back of the commandant's sanctum. They might not be so very diligent as to search this grimy corner behind the fan hoods, but probably they will. Vessikhan has his moment to call out but doesn't take it, frozen, agonized.

"Please," he whimpers. "Tell me."

"We've told you." I watch Rasmussen, gripping her hand, hoping they give us enough time that she can just go in peace, the candle finally gone to a twisting, ascending cord of smoke.

"This is nothing," he says. "This isn't *science*." He jabs me hard in the shoulder. "You with your high horse about Mandate orthodoxy, Daghdev. This is worse than Primatt's goddamn humanoid Kilnie. Mystic bullshit. Is that what this place does? Rots your brain until you have visions?" I can hear the weeping in his voice, the despair at what trash he's sold himself for, but it's all right.

"The inter-relation of Kiln life doesn't lend itself to complex central brains," I tell him. It's not actually a non sequitur, though it must seem like one. "It is very good at making connections, though. From the moment we arrived here, the biosphere has been working at the puzzle we represent, all those weird molecular combinations it never saw before. Various Kilnish species have been working out ways to bridge the gap between us and the world."

"That's what she always said. When she was mad." He nods at Rasmussen. " 'Bridge the gap.' "

"It bridged the gap, to her. And they locked her away from it," I say. Our voices are growing lower and lower as the search grows closer. Our moment of spring growth looks to be a brief one. "Then we got stuck out there, and had to walk back. And it already had the tools by then. It just needed to fit the key in the lock and turn it. Open us up. To the world."

I remember what it was like, on the march. Terrifying, hard, maddening. Knowing something was going wrong with the others, waiting for Ilmus to go so irrevocably mad that we'd have to leave them. Waiting for it to start on me. But the worst never happened, the madness never came. Instead, I experienced an alienation from my fellows, because I was one of the very last to succumb, along with Keev and Primatt. My innate stubbornness; I was always my own worst enemy.

"We're the product of a line of Earth evolution that led to big, complex brains. Isolated, solitary intellects. No single species or symbiosis on Kiln ever produced anything as convoluted as the human mind," I tell Vessikhan. "And now we're part of the Kilnish biosphere. Linked to each other and linked to the world at large. The Mandate's dearest wish has come true. The builders of Kiln are out there again, out of season and a thousand years before schedule, walking around on two feet and looking just like humans. Because we presented the ecosphere with the complexity to rediscover itself through us. We gave it the processing power to remember what it is. That's how I know all this. I know it because I'm a part of it now. We all are."

Finally Security see us. For a moment they look straight at us and don't process what's there because it's so unexpected, but then they're shouting for us to surrender—I mean, what is there we could honestly do? As they point their guns at us, I wait for Vessikhan to erupt in excuses and finger-pointing.

Instead, he reaches up and slowly pulls his mask up off

his face. Underneath he's the pinkish colour of cooked salmon, his scalp slick with sweat. He takes a deep breath.

Rasmussen is still with us, stick-thin, her overalls hanging off her like a tent. I gently help her to her feet before the impatient truncheons of the guards. Her eyes are fever bright. I wonder if she'll put on a final show for them, a little ranting just for old time's sake.

They bring us out into the open. Security is out in force down at the rails. I look for the commandant and don't see him. He'll be sealed off in his office, but he'll have electronic eyes on me, I'm certain. I hunt for a camera and stare into it, searching for that moment of connection. But there's nothing. Too much distance between us for us to ever see eye to eye.

"No superpowers, then?" Vessikhan says faintly. The connection is growing in him, but it seems unlikely that he'll live long enough to find what he's been looking for for so long. "Shrug off bullets? Tear down steel beams?" Perhaps he thinks I'll sprout tentacles and go romping around the camp pulling off limbs. But even though I'm part of something so much greater, I'm still just Arton Daghdev, and a professorship isn't much use as a shield or a weapon.

The commandant joins us then, at least virtually. His voice over a speaker, and of course the speaker is set up a pole on high because he wants us looking *up* at him.

"Doctor Vessikhan," he says. "I can't stress how disappointed I am in you." He sounds ragged. And why not? Everyone's abandoning him. He's a tinpot dictator with a handful of toy soldiers and almost nobody left to lord it over. But perhaps that's unfair. He's also someone with a puzzle he can never solve, because the people who were supposed to crack that nut for him won't play any more. It's not even the criticism from back home, if he returns empty-handed, that bothers him. Like Vessikhan, it's that he won't *know*. Except he can never know, because that would mean stepping out of those tight boots, that antique uniform, that rigid doctrine. It would mean becoming someone else, and Commandant Terolan won't ever do that.

I wonder what his next play will be. Hang us from the gantry as a warning to the others? Use us as bargaining chips? Appeal to our scientific rigour? In the yawning gap that follows, I realize that he doesn't actually know. He's out of plans and can't see any way to bridge from this current disaster back to a properly behaved, working camp, where people do what he tells them. How long will he even keep control of Security? All he can do is wait for the next fragmentation barge and then somehow take the handful of survivors and build a new camp off them. How carefully he'll have to treat them, each one of them a precious resource! And yet it's not in him, I think, to make that leap. To see he has more in common with the convicts under his jurisdiction than his masters back on Earth. Just as they'll soon have more in common with the busy world of Kiln than with him.

Rasmussen laughs. She throws back her head and cackles madly, like the thing we always thought she was. I feel it rack her body, grinding the ends of her bones together, in pain, save that she's past pain. Fragmentation, but in a way that conserves the pieces, rather than scattering them to the void.

Still, that laugh comes as a surprise and I almost drop her. A moment later I catch up. Even as the first shouts come from the handful in Security who are looking outwards. Then come the others, because there's a general groundswell of grass-roots activism from the bulk of my colleagues behind the printed barricades. It's not that they're coming for me. I really am not that important. They're coming for Terolan. He's made it plain that they can't just go off and wear flowers in their hair outside of the Mandate. So here's the answer they've been preparing.

I hear shots. Some of the Security around us are obviously desperate to gun us down. Others run from rail to rail to get a look at what's going on. But there are others who've seen something else. Shouts to look *outwards*, which get confused in the general rattle of orders and warnings as Keev's people—my people—make their move.

Vessikhan can see how they've fortified the gantry. To him it's a sign of strength, not an admission of defeat. He can only think of we poor peasants trying to storm the castle with our sticks and stones. Charging up the steps onto the wire in full view of the towers. A killing ground for any valiant charge by Keev and the others. Suicide. His eyes are wide as he shakes his head.

Then something impacts against the dome of the camp with an appalling sound of strained supports and snapping plastic. The entire gantry sways and shudders. We hear the cries of the guards.

"Maybe one superpower," I tell Vessikhan. Rasmussen keeps laughing.

32.

Something hits the side of the dome hard enough to grind its sections against each other. A fine sift of plastic dust falls on us. The commandant squawks excitedly over the speakers, while Rasmussen throws her skull's head back and cackles again like the wickedest witch there ever was. Vessikhan drops to his knees.

Across the dome, on the far side from the impact, something else snaps and we all see the lightning-crazy cracks racing up the clear shell. More than half the Security who've been holding us at gunpoint rush over to repel the boarders, but there's some confusion about what boarders they're repelling. Some are valiantly holding the stairs against an assault that isn't happening. A knot are over one edge, shooting down full auto in the direction of the trashed airlock. The handful who still have their weapons trained on us get shakier and shakier as further impacts shudder the very substance of the dome. That ineffectual shield which yet symbolizes the inviolable boundary between Mandate territory and the wilds they are so terrified of.

Inside I feel... transcendent. The sort of mad, exhilarated rush I only ever had from the most cutting-edge drugs. I can do anything, because I am the world. And, for that reason, I do nothing. I'm so full of potential that my little human body seems irrelevant. What can it possibly accomplish compared to the hammer that's being brought down on the camp right now? I don't even try to take cover, and Suiye, the lieutenant, is marching over with a pistol pointed directly at my forehead. I think I'm grinning at them, daring them. The builders of Kiln have woken. My mind, to the others' minds, to the biosphere, have pushed the local complexity past the point where that emergent, world-wide conscious-ness stirs. I'm still me, little Arton with his wounds and his pain, but I confess I'm more than half out of my head at this point. I'm in no position to be making decisions, but right then nobody's making the decisions. We're all together in the dream that Kiln is having, and the decisions just happen in the space between us.

Something strikes the cracked side of the dome one more time and abruptly the whole sky above us is a mosaic of jagged angles, one final shock away from shattering. In my sight, the nearest section is being levered up where it meets the ground, undermined and shouldered out of true, splin-tering where it's fixed to the girders of the gantry. Something …but I keep saying *something* and that's mendacious of me. I *know* what all those somethings are. They're me, and they're themselves, and they're all their component parts working in unison. They are the vast communion of this world. I say *something* just to put you into Vessikhan's head, perhaps, as he experiences it all. Soon enough he'll under-stand it as thoroughly as I do. If he can only keep breathing.

Keeping breathing is going to be a challenge. The lieutenant has the cool circle of the pistol barrel right up against my forehead. I can't hear what they say to me, past the apocalyptic sounds of the dome being breached, past the incoherent roar of the commandant's static-fuzzed orders, but the motion of their lips says, *Make it stop!*

I meet their gaze and mouth the word *No*. Not that I could stop it, but I don't want it to stop anyway. If they kill me then that's regrettable, but the greater purpose is more important. Kiln has finally been roused to oust these intruders who would not be a part of something greater. The closed minds of the Mandate are finally having their doors kicked in by our monstrous jackboots.

I can see Suiye's eyes, wide and mad, behind their goggle lenses. Then I can see them more clearly because Rasmussen reaches out, sinks her fingers into Suiye's mask beneath the chin, and pulls. I expect nothing, but the rubber tears across a rough seam and abruptly the lieutenant's metal-patched, terrified face is exposed to the infectious air. Those heavy-duty protective suits were fabricated in the same shoddy printers as everything else. It's all jackboot-and-fetishwear show, in the end, and short on substance.

Suiye screams, free hand clutching at their face. They actually claw gashes in the skin of their cheek, as though they can rid themselves of a million microscopic living things by brute force. And, of course, all they're doing is opening more doors for all that life to get into their system. But I skip the Epidemiology 101 because they're in no position to appreciate it. They recoil from Rasmussen, but the old bird has her fingers hooked into the rubber still and goes with them. Then she's actually leapt onto Suiye, limbs crooked around them like an arthritic spider, still cackling like a mad thing. She's found a new superpower, albeit a terminal one. It's the final stage in her life cycle, triggered by the rejuvenated world-awareness of Kiln. Humans aren't supposed to have a life cycle, not like that, but she was the first. She's been incubating this thing within her for longer than humans are even supposed to survive.

Her laughter turns to something else. A fog of spores begins to vent from her throat, clouding the air about her and Suiye. The lieutenant's shrieking goes an octave shriller and they push their gun beneath Rasmussen's chin and fire. What comes out of the wound is more of the same, the substance of her, broken down and carried across that bridge from Earth biochemistry to Kiln-stuff. Now it vents from all over her: cuffs, pores, eyes. She withers and deflates as the busy stuff within her performs its final evacuation plans, abandoning the old ship that had carried it for so long. I see there our fate, when our long lives are gone. Back to the soil of an alien world, nothing wasted. Crossing the bridge into that undiscovered country.

Suiye collapses, eyes bulging from their sockets, face going purple, tearing even more at their own skin with their nails. It's not the spores killing them, not poisoning, not infection, not even an allergic reaction. It's sheer terror, a horror of what they might become. An utter refusal to countenance that larger world. They collapse, their hands at their throat, with Rasmussen's husk still clinging to them. The first bullet skips past me like a wasp on a mission. The next would probably have done for me if Vessikhan hadn't hauled me to the ground.

The dome shatters at last. Great razor pieces of plastic rain down across the camp. Vessikhan's already been dragging me towards cover, and so I catch a gash across one calf but nothing worse. Several of the Security detail go down under the inclement weather, but honestly that's the least of their worries, because by then the Elephant's Dad is inside the camp.

The same one as before? I don't think so. The same general combination of features and species though. Skittering in on its three spiny legs, its tubular mouth-feet waving and gaping hungrily. And it isn't alone. As though tired of waiting for us to come and collect more specimens, Kiln's ecology has come to us at last. Frond-backed worms with flailing razor whips carried into battle on undulating rows of suckers; swarms of clawed umbrellas trailing tangles of barbed fishing line; hunchbacked beetle things the size of a torso, manoeuvring like little tanks and spitting out knuckles of stone with enough force to break bones. At the edge of the fractured dome, stone crabs push their way out from the earth, grappling with the gantry supports as though they're determined to take souvenirs before everything is erased.

And the others.

There's one guard in all this chaos who is absolutely determined to do their duty. Even as the Garden of Earthly Delights Re-enactment Society gets to work, this one determined servant of the Mandate runs over to Vessikhan and me with his gun levelled. They possibly think I can stop it, but I honestly believe it's more that we represent a human-level problem and they're only equipped with human-level solutions. Everything else is just too much to confront.

I realize I'm about to be shot. They are still in the shouting phase right now, but that's only one letter away. Then the shooting happens, and it isn't their gun at fault. Instead, the guard who'd been standing there in front of me, taking up a disproportionate amount of my attention, moves abruptly some distance to the right. As though they're a bad comedian who's been yanked offstage with a hook. I actually laugh at the incongruity of it, before my mind catches up. I look left and see Ilmus, who's never to my knowledge used a gun before in their life. They've made up for it right now, but perhaps the enhanced perspective helps. Pulling the trigger as though they were controlling someone remotely in a game. And judging the aim, because they can draw on my eyes as well as their own.

They're all coming up, then, out of that wash of monsters. Keev, Greely, Frith. The entire Labour Block, risen up to finish the war because the commandant hadn't been able to. Shooting down any guards who look like they're going to escape the vengeance of monsters.

Vessikhan's gone from hauling me around to clinging to me. Trusting me to save him from the wrath of an angry planet. I want to explain to him that it isn't anger. And it isn't even the planet. It's us. We, the people. We've had enough of the camp and its autocracy, and we have the means to do something about it. Because we represent a disproportionate amount of the emergent mind of Kiln's biosphere, which is piggybacking off our big Earth brains. The thing we've become a part of values its own existence and therefore wishes to preserve our participation in it for as long as possible. In short, what we want, right now, we get, and what we want is to wipe the Mandate off the face of Kiln.

I see Primatt riding up the steps atop a big stone crab, just like she did on the last days of the march, before we'd come close to camp and had to resume helping her along just to keep up appearances. Lurching atop her mighty steed and brandishing a staff like she's the druid queen of Kiln. Which she is, in a way. We all are. It's not that she guides her mount over to Vessikhan and me, more that it understands what she wants, and obliges.

"Nimell?" Vessikhan gets out, real awe in his voice. I can feel him at the very threshold, the doors of his mind being levered open inch by inch from where they've been nailed shut. One of us; one with the whole. The inheritor of Kiln's history.

The mind of Kiln. The builders or builder, because it's simultaneously one and many, and our human language isn't set up to deal with something like that. Its long history, in which it came to awareness of itself over and over, as the biological complexity reached that critical mass each time. In which it learned to encrypt its knowledge of itself in the structures that it raised, building a hundred different ways at once to sprout ruins like mushrooms across this part of the planet. Not dwellings, nor ritual sites, but memory. Preserved in temperature-controlled vaults, in stone, in perpetuity. And, just like a mushroom, we saw only those artificial fruiting bodies when we came to Kiln, and didn't perceive the vast unseen network waiting for its next age of sapience. We could have come and gone entirely within that dead zone in Kiln's civilization, departed baffled and unfulfilled, and never known what potential was waiting to re-emerge. Worse, we could have colonized and industrialized the world, if the Mandate had been of that mindset. We could have obliterated the very mind of the world in our search for builders who were just like us.

Instead, this.

In the end, the dome is reduced to potsherds which the soil of this world will reclaim, eventually working out a way to break down and reconstitute it into Kilnish biomass—a reclamation plant that puts the camp's noisy little engine to shame. The Elephant's Dad storms the last holdout of Security, letting their bullets tear through its rubbery flesh and then skewering them on its spiked limbs, feeding them to the inner beasts which have learned how to metabolize Earth proteins. And after all this, we are left with the commandant.

His office, a sealed metal box on the final rickety section of scaffolding. No way down, no power, no ventilation. But Mox Calwren is there, by then, the turncoat engineer. He re-establishes communication so I can have one last chat with my old nemesis.

And by "I," I mean everyone.

"You can just open the vents," I tell him, reasonably enough.

"You'd like that, wouldn't you," he spits back.

"Not particularly. It would bring you into what we have here. I would rather not have you as a part of it, even temporarily."

"Temporarily."

"You'd be judged," I tell him. "By everyone. You'd be able to see yourself the way we do."

His reply to that is scarcely printable.

"For what it's worth, I believe you were genuinely dedicated to the research here. Not even because it was your orders, but for yourself. You wanted to know," I say, into the silence which follows that. "And you can know. Just open a window. Before whatever happens to you, you can know it all. I can put Vessikhan on, if you want. Our newest recruit. He understands, now."

"You've brainwashed him with your spores," Terolan hisses. "That's what you mean. You're not Arton Daghdev any more. You're some...*thing*. You've been changed."

I want to tell him that I'm still me, because I am. But at the same time, yes, I've changed. Because who could possibly experience all this and not change? What would be the point of it, if the man who walked out the far end of these events was the same as the one who walked in? I want to tell him it's not alien mind control. That you can still be yourself, even as you become a part of something greater. There's no way I can describe what it's like without sounding like I've converted to some insane cult, though. We don't have the language. Only Kiln has the language, and it's written on the walls of all those ruins. The histories of the world.

The vines are already starting to recolonize the ruin at the heart of the shattered camp. They will start writing soon, the new history of this world. An unseasonal awakening, when all should have remained fallow for centuries. A new phase of both human and inhuman sentience.

I want to tell Terolan, "What's the worst that could happen?" but his mind is full of worsts that far exceed anything actually real. He is torturing himself in his sealed box with thoughts of how terrible it would be to lose his *self*. His inviolable, separate selfness that he cannot abide to share. He is consumed by the drive to *know*, but not at the cost of being *known* by others. He is the commandant, above it all. He will not be dragged down into the mud.

He never opens his box, and we do not tear down that last section of scaffolding. Let him perish in his tomb. We'd rather he wasn't part of us, in the end.

Peace arrives, and in that peace we come to terms with what we've become. Because we *are* changed, and that's hard. It's like therapy. Sometimes in order to escape the bad place you're in, you have to go through trauma and hardship. Sometimes letting go of the barbed wire means tearing your skin some more, before you're free. We talk, and information passes between us that is not talk. We try to understand what it is that we understand.

We all know what it is to be Ilmus now, a person who was always a stranger before, even to their friends. Everyone understands what had seemed, when we were all solitary humans together, to be inalienable contradictions in their nature. I feel their fear at the openness, and they feel mine. It runs through the herd of us and dissipates, insufficient concentrations to effect any significant change when spread across the mass of us.

"It just doesn't..." they tell me, "just doesn't *end*."

I know what they mean. We have our own minds, but where there were hard borders, censors, guards, now there is only a stretched-out grey area, crossable country linking *them* and *me*. And beyond our little network of polities, there is Kiln. The whole world, awake—a greater thing that we are an integral part of now. It's difficult to adjust to, each one of us being simultaneously many things. We could get lost easily. Perhaps the only thing that saves us from being washed away by that ocean of thought is the fact that, the moment we did lose ourselves, the greater mind would lose itself too. It relies on our individual complexity to exist in its active state. Without us it would be no more than sleeping seeds waiting for the rain.

And it goes further. We are the world and so we are the vines that creep about the ruins. We touch the records of a hundred past ages of this same mind, and reconnect not just with the planet of today but with its pasts. Because every wakening was different, the mind pulling itself together from whatever combinations of species were available. The introduction of human brains really isn't that much of a change.

Ilmus and I walk through the camp, hearing people weep and laugh as they try to process the information. As the vast tides of Kiln wash past us, we are the weed hauled this way and that by the undertow, but rooted still in ourselves. Feeling that we are part of a net, each knot an individual. But for better or worse, we will never be entirely what we were.

The vines creep higher up the camp's ruin, along with all the others we burned and despoiled for science. In their wake we are immortalized. The memory-structures of Kiln's distributed mind adapt to the new wealth of perspective we bring it. I run my fingers across the characters they grow, a whole new lexicon of molecular language. Kiln has learned about Earth. Kiln has raised a cenotaph to Ylse Rasmussen, the first. Kiln flexes its mental muscles and we, its neurons, cluster and eddy between options. Again, decisions form in the space between our individual brains.

There will be other ships. Other fragmentation barges are already on their way, a long chain of them across all the cold years to Earth. Calwren and the other more technically minded of us have rigged up the kit that will receive their signals and let us know when to gather, to intercept their cargoes. We will save everyone we can.

More staff are on their way too, although less frequently. Replacements for Science and Security who were to return home. A new commandant. Old news and scientific papers from Earth. At some point, the ship in orbit above us will be expected back. In its absence, concern will eventually germinate and grow. The mass-mind that is the Mandate will eddy and cluster and make a decision. To abandon the effort on Kiln, rewrite its histories to cover up the loss of life and resource, and focus on the other extrasolar camps instead. Erasing the most promising of all non-Earth worlds from its own collective memory, because it could not tame or contain it. Or else they might want to double down on their investment, sending more ships, more guards, more guns. A different approach. Colonists, perhaps. Who knows what the Mandate, or whatever succeeds it, will want to do with those living worlds it has discovered? So many years will have passed by then. They may send scientists, they may send a vast ark ship ready to disgorge thousands. Or they may send a bomb. We are not a part of them, so we can't know.

And so the decision coheres between us. We have a ship, after all. There is another living world out there. And we were sent here as convict labour, not colonists. But we were colonized, and we have become colonies, so now we will be colonizers in turn.

It must be Primatt or Vessikhan or Calwren, at the very least. None of them particularly want to go, but if we send an embassy it must have an acceptable face. They are staff. It's conceivable they would be on the ship back, for early retirement, invalided out, too much stress. Their presence should be enough to get the ship into Earth orbit.

And then we can take a tip from the fragmentation barges. We have the printers. We also have a human understanding of the technology married to the resources of a whole world willingly proffered. We can manufacture something considerably better than the lowest-bidder shoddiness which delivered us to this world. Kiln is curious about its faraway sibling. We have awakened the mind here to the concept of alien life. Although "alien" is only ever a transient state, to the biosphere of Kiln. It will always get to know you in the end.

Then in Earth orbit, while Primatt and her fellows talk through whatever gloss we decide to put on the situation, the ship will begin shedding itself into our homeworld's gravity well. From pieces of the microscopic, to be blown on the winds of the world, to a faint haze of spores, as well as durable eggs that can survive the rigours of re-entry, and even the human-sized. Men and women in one-shot capsules, plunging down like missionaries to bring the good word of Kiln. Ready to reach out to all the dissidents, subcommittees and free thinkers. To bring them the gift of knowing one another. To root out the informants and agents provocateurs, bringing people together to crack open the dome of the Mandate, in whatever form it might exist. And to free people by teaching them new ways to know themselves. I say these words, and a part of me is screaming at them. The *me* from before, who was terrified of the frothing madness of Ylse Rasmussen, whose name is being encoded even now in the walls of the ruin. I am Arton Daghdev still, and I know that what we will bring to Earth is the second greatest monstrosity ever perpetrated upon the human species. But the thought of what we might *become* is irresistible. Presented with the means, how could we not?

We brought Kiln back to an awareness of itself. Maybe we can do the same with Earth. Start with a waking, end with an awakening.

ACKNOWLEDGEMENTS

My thanks to everyone whose work has gone into this book, especially Simon and Oliver at the agency, and Bella, Charlotte, Gillian, Claire and everyone at Pan Macmillan.

extras

orbit

meet the author

Tom Pepperdine

ADRIAN TCHAIKOVSKY was born in Woodhall Spa, Lincolnshire, in the UK and headed off to university in Reading to study psychology and zoology. For reasons unclear even to himself, he subsequently ended up in law. Adrian has since worked as a legal executive in both Reading and Leeds and now writes full-time. He also lives in Leeds, with his wife and son. Adrian is a keen live-action role-player and occasional amateur actor. He has also trained in stage fighting and keeps no exotic or dangerous pets of any kind—possibly excepting his son.

Find out more about Adrian Tchaikovsky and other Orbit authors by registering for the free monthly newsletter at orbitbooks.net.

if you enjoyed
ALIEN CLAY

look out for

CHILDREN OF TIME

by

Adrian Tchaikovsky

Who will inherit this new Earth?

The last remnants of the human race left a dying Earth, desperate to find a new home among the stars. Following in the footsteps of their ancestors, they discovered the greatest treasure of the past age—a world terraformed and prepared for human life.

But all is not right in this new Eden. In the long years since the planet was abandoned, the work of its architects has borne disastrous fruit. The planet is not waiting for them, pristine and unoccupied. New masters have turned it from a refuge into mankind's worst nightmare.

Now two civilizations are on a collision course, both testing the boundaries of what they will do to survive. As the fate of humanity hangs in the balance, who are the true heirs of this new Earth?

1.1 JUST A BARREL OF MONKEYS

There were no windows in the Brin 2 facility—rotation meant that "outside" was always "down," underfoot, out of mind. The wall screens told a pleasant fiction, a composite view of the world below that ignored their constant spin, showing the planet as hanging stationary-still off in space: the green marble to match the blue marble of home, twenty light years away. Earth had been green, in her day, though her colours had faded since. Perhaps never as green as this beautifully crafted world though, where even the oceans glittered emerald with the phytoplankton maintaining the oxygen balance within its atmosphere. How delicate and many-sided was the task of building a living monument that would remain stable for geological ages to come.

It had no officially confirmed name beyond its astronomical designation, although there was a strong vote for "Simiana" amongst some of the less imaginative crewmembers. Doctor Avrana Kern now looked out upon it and thought only of *Kern's World.* Her project, her dream, *her* planet. The first of many, she decided.

extras

This is the future. This is where mankind takes its next great step. This is where we become gods.

"This is the future," she said aloud. Her voice would sound in every crewmember's auditory centre, all nineteen of them, though fifteen were right here in the control hub with her. Not the true hub, of course—the gravity-denuded axle about which they revolved: that was for power and processing, and their payload.

"This is where mankind takes its next great step." Her speech had taken more of her time than any technical details over the last two days. She almost went on with the line about them becoming gods, but that was for her only. *Far too controversial, given the* Non Ultra Natura *clowns back home.* Enough of a stink had been raised over projects like hers already. Oh, the differences between the current Earth factions went far deeper: social, economic, or simply *us* and *them*, but Kern had got the Brin launched—all those years ago—against mounting opposition. By now the whole idea had become a kind of scapegoat for the divisions of the human race. *Bickering primates, the lot of them. Progress is what matters. Fulfilling the potential of humanity, and of all other life.* She had always been one of the fiercest opponents of the growing conservative backlash most keenly exemplified by the *Non Ultra Natura* terrorists. *If they had their way, we'd all end up back in the caves. Back in the trees. The whole* point *of civilization is that we exceed the limits of nature, you tedious little primitives.*

"We stand on others' shoulders, of course." The proper line, that of accepted scientific humility, was, "on the shoulders of giants," but she had not got where she was by bowing the knee to past generations. *Midgets, lots and lots of midgets,* she thought, and then—she could barely keep back the appalling giggle—*on the shoulders of monkeys.*

At a thought from her, one wallscreen and their Mind's Eye HUDs displayed the schematics of Brin 2 for them all. She wanted to direct their attention and lead them along with her towards the proper appreciation of her—sorry, *their*— triumph. There: the needle of the central core encircled by the ring of life and science that was their torus-shaped world. At one end of the core was the unlovely bulge of the Sentry Pod, soon to be cast adrift to become the universe's loneliest and longest research post. The opposite end of the needle sported the Barrel and the Flask. Contents: monkeys and the future, respectively.

"Particularly I have to thank the engineering teams under Doctors Fallarn and Medi for their tireless work in reformatting—" and she almost now said "Kern's World" without meaning to—"our subject planet to provide a safe and nurturing environment for our great project." Fallarn and Medi were well on their way back to Earth, of course, their fifteen-year work completed, their thirty-year return journey begun. It was all stage-setting, though, to make way for Kern and her dream. *We are—I am—what all this work is for.*

A journey of twenty light years home. Whilst thirty years drag by on Earth, only twenty will pass for Fallarn and Medi in their cold coffins. For them, their voyage is nearly as fast as light. What wonders we can accomplish!

From her viewpoint, engines to accelerate her to most of the speed of light were no more than pedestrian tools to move her about a universe that Earth's biosphere was about to inherit. *Because humanity may be fragile in ways we cannot dream, so we cast our net wide and then wider...*

Human history was balanced on a knife edge. Millennia of ignorance, prejudice, superstition and desperate striving had brought them at last to this: that humankind would beget new sentient life in its own image. Humanity would no longer be alone. Even in the unthinkably far future, when Earth itself had fallen in fire and dust, there would be a legacy spreading across the stars—an infinite and expanding variety of Earthborn life diverse enough to survive any reversal of fortune until the death of the whole universe, and perhaps even beyond that. *Even if we die, we will live on in our children.*

Let the NUNs preach their dismal all-eggs-in-one-basket creed of human purity and supremacy, she thought. *We will out-evolve them. We will leave them behind. This will be the first of a thousand worlds that we will give life to.*

For we are gods, and we are lonely, so we shall create...

Back home, things were tough, or so the twenty-year-old images indicated. Avrana had skimmed dispassionately over the riots, the furious debates, the demonstrations and violence, thinking only, *How did we ever get so far with so many fools in the gene pool?* The *Non Ultra Natura* lobby were only the most extreme of a whole coalition of human political factions—the conservative, the philosophical, even the die-hard religious—who looked at progress and said that enough was enough. Who fought tooth and nail against further engineering of the human genome, against the removal of limits on AI, and against programs like Avrana's own.

And yet they're losing.

The terraforming would still be going on elsewhere. Kern's World was just one of many planets receiving the attentions of people like Fallarn and Medi, transformed from inhospitable chemical rocks—Earth-like only in approximate size and distance from the sun—into balanced ecosystems that Kern could have walked on without a suit in only minor discomfort. After the monkeys had been delivered and the Sentry Pod detached to monitor them, those other gems were where her attention would next be drawn. *We will seed the universe with all the wonders of Earth.*

In her speech, which she was barely paying attention to, she meandered down a list of other names, from here or at home. The person she really wanted to thank was herself. She had fought for this, her engineered longevity allowing her to carry the debate across several natural human lifetimes. She had clashed in the financiers' rooms and in the laboratories, at academic symposiums and on mass entertainment feeds just to make this happen.

I, I have done this. With your hands have I built, with your eyes have I measured, but the mind is mine alone.

Her mouth continued along its prepared course, the words boring her even more than they presumably bored her listeners. The real audience for this speech would receive it in twenty years' time: the final confirmation back home of the way things were due to be. Her mind touched base with the Brin 2's hub. *Confirm Barrel systems*, she pinged into her relay link with the facility's control computer; it was a check that had become a nervous habit of late.

Within tolerance, it replied. And if she probed behind that bland summary, she would see precise readouts of the lander craft, its state of readiness, even down to the vital signs of its ten-thousand-strong primate cargo, the chosen few who would inherit, if not the Earth, then at least this planet, whatever it would be called.

Whatever *they* would eventually call it, once the uplift nanovirus had taken them that far along the developmental road. The biotechs estimated that a mere thirty or forty monkey generations would bring them to the stage where they might make contact with the Sentry Pod and its lone human occupant.

Alongside the Barrel was the Flask: the delivery system for

the virus that would accelerate the monkeys along their way—they would stride, in a mere century or two, across physical and mental distances that had taken humanity millions of long and hostile years.

Another group of people to thank, for she herself was no biotech specialist. She had seen the specs and the simulations, though, and expert systems had examined the theory and summarized it in terms that she, a mere polymath genius, could understand. The virus was clearly an impressive piece of work, as far as she could grasp it. Infected individuals would produce offspring mutated in a number of useful ways: greater brain size and complexity, greater body size to accommodate it, more flexible behavioural paths, swifter learning... The virus would even recognize the presence of infection in other individuals of the same species, so as to promote selective breeding, the best of the best giving birth to even better. It was a whole future in a microscopic shell, almost as smart, in its single-minded little way, as the creatures that it would be improving. It would interact with the host genome at a deep level, replicate within its cells like a new organelle, passing itself on to the host's offspring until the entire species was subject to its benevolent contagion. No matter how much change the monkeys underwent, that virus would adapt and adjust to whatever genome it was partnered with, analysing and modelling and improvising with whatever it inherited—until something had been engineered that could look its creators in the eye and understand.

She had sold it to the people back home by describing how colonists would reach the planet then, descending from the skies like deities to meet their new people. Instead of a harsh, untamed world, a race of uplifted sentient aides and servants would welcome their makers. That was what she had told the boardrooms and the committees back on Earth, but it had never been the point of the exercise for her. The monkeys were the point, and what they would become.

This was one of the things the NUNs were most incensed about. They shouted about making superbeings out of mere beasts. In truth, like spoiled children, it was *sharing* that they objected to. Only-child humanity craved the sole attention of the universe. Like so many other projects hoisted as political issues, the virus's development had been fraught with protests, sabotage, terrorism and murder.

And yet we triumph over our own base nature at last, Kern reflected with satisfaction. And of course, there was a tiny grain of truth to the insults the NUNs threw her way, because she *didn't* care about colonists or the neo-imperialistic dreams of her fellows. She wanted to make new life, in her image as much as in humanity's. She wanted to know what might evolve, what society, what understandings, when her monkeys were left to their own simian devices... To Avrana Kern, *this* was her price, her reward for exercising her genius for the good of the human race: this experiment; this planetary what-if. Her efforts had opened up a string of terraformed worlds, but her price was that the firstborn would be *hers*, and home to her new-made people.

She was aware of an expectant silence and realized that she had got to the end of her speech, and now everyone thought she was just adding gratuitous suspense to a moment that needed no gilding.

"Mr. Sering, are you in position?" she asked on open channel, for everyone's benefit. Sering was the volunteer, the man they were going to leave behind. He would orbit their planet-sized laboratory as the long years turned, locked in cold sleep until the time came for him to become mentor to a new race of sentient primates. She almost envied him, for he would see and hear and experience things that no other human ever had. He would be the new Hanuman: the monkey god.

Almost envied, but in the end Kern rather preferred to be departing to undertake other projects. Let others become gods of mere single worlds. She herself would stride the stars and head up the pantheon.

if you enjoyed
ALIEN CLAY

look out for

SHARDS OF EARTH
The Final Architecture: Book One

by

Adrian Tchaikovsky

The war is over. Its heroes forgotten. Until one chance discovery....

Idris has neither aged nor slept since they remade him in the war. And one of humanity's heroes now scrapes by on a freelance salvage vessel to avoid the attention of greater powers.

After Earth was destroyed, mankind created a fighting elite to save their species, enhanced humans such as Idris. In the silence of space, they could communicate mind-to-mind with the enemy. Then their alien aggressors, the Architects, simply disappeared—and Idris and his kind became obsolete.

Now, fifty years later, Idris and his crew have found something strange abandoned in space. It's clearly the work of the Architects—but are they returning? And if so, why? Hunted by gangs, cults, and governments, Idris and his crew race across the galaxy, hunting for answers. For they now possess something of incalculable value that many would kill to obtain.

PROLOGUE

In the seventy-eighth year of the war, an Architect came to Berlenhof.

The lights of human civilization across the galaxy had been going out, one by one, since its start. All those little mining worlds, the far-flung settlements, the homes people had made. The Colonies, as they were known: the great hollow Polyaspora of human expansion, exploding out from a vacant centre. Because the Architects had come for Earth first.

Berlenhof had become humanity's second heart. Even before Earth fell, it had been a prosperous, powerful world. In the war, it was the seat of military command and civilian governance, coordinating a civilization-scale refugee effort, as more and more humans were forced to flee their doomed worlds.

And because of that, when the Architect came, the Colonies turned and fought, and so did all the allies they had gathered there. It was to be the great stand against a galactic-level threat, every weapon deployed, every secret advantage exploited.

Solace remembered. She had been there. Basilisk Division, Heaven's Sword Sorority. Her first battle.

*

The Colonies had a secret weapon, that was the word. A human weapon. Solace had seen them at the war council. A cluster of awkward, damaged-looking men and women, nothing more. As the main fleet readied itself to defend Berlenhof, a handful of small ships were already carrying these "weapons" towards the Architect in the hope that this new trick would somehow postpone the inevitable.

Useless, surely. Might as well rely on thoughts and prayers.

On the *Heaven's Sword*, everyone off-shift was avidly watching the displays, wanting to believe this really *was* something. Even though all previous secret weapons had been nothing but hot air and hope. Solace stared as intently as the rest. The Architect was impossible to miss on screen, a vast polished mass the size of Earth's lost moon, throwing back every scan and probe sent its way. The defending fleet at Berlenhof was a swarm of pinpricks, so shrunk by the scale they were barely visible until she called for magnification. The heart of the Colonies had already been gathering its forces for dispatch elsewhere when the Architect had emerged from unspace at the edge of the system. Humanity was never going to get better odds than this.

There were Castigar and Hanni vessels out there, alien trading partners who were lending their strength to their human allies because the Architects were everybody's problem. There was a vast and ragged fleet of human ships, and some of them were dedicated war vessels and others were just whatever could be thrown into space that wasn't any use for the evacuation. Orbiting Hiver factories were weaponizing their workers. There was even the brooding hulk of a Naeromathi Locust Ark out there, the largest craft in-system—save that it was still dwarfed by the Architect itself. And nobody knew what the Locusts wanted or thought about anything, save that even they would fight this enemy.

And there was the pride of the fleet, Solace's sisters: the Parthenon. Humans, for a given value of human. The engineered warrior women who had been the Colonies' shield ever since the fall of Earth. *Heaven's Sword*, *Ascending Mother* and *Cataphracta*, the most advanced warships humanity had ever designed, equipped with weapons that the pre-war days couldn't even have imagined.

As Solace craned to see, she spotted a tiny speckle of dots between the fleet and the Architect: the advance force. The tip of humanity's spear was composed of the Partheni's swiftest ships. Normally, their role would have been to buy time. But on this occasion, the *Pythoness*, the *Ocasio*, the *Ching Shi* and others were carrying their secret weapon to the enemy.

Solace didn't believe a word of it. The mass looms and the Zero Point fighters the *Heaven's Sword* was equipped with would turn the battle, or nothing would. Even as she told herself that, she heard the murmur of the other off-shift women around her. "Intermediaries," one said, a whisper as if talking about something taboo; and someone else, a girl barely old enough to be in service: "They say they cut their *brains*. That's how they make them."

"Telemetry incoming," said one of the officers, and the display focused in on those few dots. They were arrowing towards the Architect, as though planning to dash themselves against its mountainous sides. Solace felt her eyes strain, trying to wring more information from what she was seeing, to peer all the way in until she had an eye inside the ships themselves.

One of those dots winked out. The Architect had registered their presence and was patiently swatting at them. Solace had seen the aftermath of even a brush with an Architect's power: twisted, crumpled metal, curved and corkscrewed by intense gravitational pressures. A large and well-shielded ship might weather a glancing blow. With these little craft there would be no survivors.

"It's *useless*," she said. "*We* need to be out there. Us." Her fingers itched for the keys of the mass looms.

"Myrmidon Solace, do you think you know better than the Fleet Exemplars?" Her immediate superior, right at her shoulder of course.

"No, Mother."

"Then just watch and be ready." And a muttered afterthought: "Not that I don't agree with you." And even as her superior spoke, another of the tiny ships had been snuffed into darkness.

"Was that—?" someone cried, before being cut off. Then the officer was demanding, "Telemetry, update and confirm!"

"A marked deviation," someone agreed. The display was bringing up a review, a fan of lines showing the Architect's projected course and its current trajectory.

"So it altered its course. That changes nothing," someone spat, but the officer spoke over them. "They *turned* an Architect! Whatever they did, they *turned* it!"

Then they lost all data. After a tense second's silence, the displays blinked back, the handful of surviving ships fleeing the Architect's renewed approach towards Berlenhof. Whatever the secret weapon was, it seemed to have failed.

"*High alert*. All off-shift crews make ready to reinforce as

411

needed. The fight's coming to us!" came the voice of the officer. Solace was still staring at the display, though. *Had* they accomplished nothing? Somehow, this secret Intermediary weapon had shifted the course of an Architect. Nobody had made them so much as flinch before.

Orders came through right on the heels of the thought. "Prepare to receive the *Pythoness*. Damage control, medical, escort." And she was the third of those, called up out of the off-shift pool along with her team.

The *Pythoness* had been a long, streamlined ship: its foresection bulked out by its gravitic drives and then tapering down its length to a segmented tail. That tail was gone, and the surviving two-thirds of the ship looked as though a hand had clenched about it, twisting every sleek line into a tortured curve. That the ship had made it back at all was a wonder. The moment the hatch was levered open, the surviving crew started carrying out the wounded. Solace knew from the ship's readouts that half its complement wouldn't be coming out at all.

"Myrmidon Solace!"

"Mother!" She saluted, waiting for her duties.

"Get this to the bridge!"

She blinked. *This* was a man. A Colonial human man. He was skinny and jug-eared and looked as though he'd already snapped under the trauma of the fight. His eyes were wide and his lips moved soundlessly. Twitches ran up and down his body like rats. She'd seen him before, at the council of war. One of the vaunted Intermediaries.

"Mother?"

"Take him to the bridge. Now, Myrmidon!" the officer snapped, and then she leant in and grabbed Solace's shoulder. "This is *it*, sister. This is the weapon. And if it's a weapon, we need to use it."

There were billions on Berlenhof: the local population as well as countless refugees from the other lost worlds. Nobody was going to get even a thousandth of those people off-world before the Architect destroyed it. But the more time they could buy for the evacuation effort, the more lives would be saved. This was what the Parthenon was spending its ships and lives for. That was what the Hivers would expend their artificial bodies for, and the alien mercenaries and partisans and ideologues would die for. Every lost ship was another freighter off Berlenhof packed out with civilians.

She got the man into a lift tube, aware of the wide-eyed looks he'd been receiving as she hauled him from the dock. He must be getting a far worse case of culture-shock; regular Colonials didn't mix with the Parthenon and before the war there'd been no love lost. Here he was on a ship full of women who all had close on the same face, the same compact frame. Human enough to be uncanny but, for most Colonials, not quite human *enough*.

He was saying something. For a moment she heard nonsense, but she'd learned enough Colvul to piece together the words. It was just a demand to wait. Except they were already in the lift, so he could wait all he wanted and they'd still get where they were needed. "Wait, I can't..."

"You're here...Menheer." It took a moment for her to remember the correct Colvul honorific. "My name is Myrmidon Solace. I am taking you to the bridge of the *Heaven's Sword*. You are going to fight with us."

He stared at her, shell-shocked. "They're *hurt*. My ship. We jumped..."

"This is your ship now, Menheer." And, because he was shaking again, she snapped at him. "*Name*, Menheer?"

He twitched. "Telemmier. Idris Telemmier. Intermediary. First class."

413

"They say you're a weapon. So now you have to fight."

He was shaking his head, but then she had him out of the lift and the officers were calling for him.

The battle displays formed a multicoloured array in the centre of the bridge, showing the vast fleet as it moved to confront the Architect. Solace saw that they were finally about to fire on it: to do what little damage they could with lasers and projectiles, suicide drones, explosives and gravitic torsion. But their goal was only to slow it. A victory against an Architect was when you made yourself enough of a nuisance that they had to swat you before they could murder the planet.

They got Idris in front of the display, though Solace had to hold him upright.

"What am I—?" he got out. Solace saw he didn't have the first clue what was going on.

"Whatever you can do, *do*," an officer snapped at him. Solace could see and feel that the *Heaven's Sword* was already on its attack run. She wanted desperately to be on-shift at the mass loom consoles, bringing that ersatz hammer against the shell of the Architect. She didn't believe in this Intermediary any more than she believed in wizards.

Still, when he turned his wan gaze her way, she mustered a smile and he seemed to take something from that. Something lit behind his eyes: madness or divine revelation.

Then their sister ship's mass loom fired and Solace followed the *Cataphracta*'s strike through the bridge readouts. It was a weapon developed through studying the Architects themselves, a hammerblow of pure gravitic torsion, aiming to tear a rift in their enemy's crystalline exterior. Operators read off the subsequent damage reports: fissuring minimal but present; target areas flagged up for a more concentrated assault. The *Heaven's Sword*'s Zero Point fighters were flocking out of its bays now and dispersing, a hundred gnats to divert the enemy's time and attention from the big guns.

The whole bridge sang like a choir for just a moment as their own mass loom spoke, resonating through the entire length of the ship. Solace felt like shouting out with it, as she always did. And kept her mouth shut, because here on the bridge that sort of thing would be frowned on.

Idris gasped then, arching backwards in her arms, and she saw blood on his face as he bit his tongue. His eyes were wider than seemed humanly possible, all the whites visible and a ring of red around each as well. He screamed, prompting concerned shouts from across the bridge, eclipsed when the Fleet Exultant in command called out that the Architect had faltered. Impossible that so much inexorable momentum could be diverted by anything short of an asteroid impact. But it had jolted in the very moment that Idris had yelled.

The mass loom sang again, and she saw the *Cataphracta* and the *Ascending Mother* firing too, all targeting the same fractures in the Architect's structure. Smaller ships were wheeling in swarms past the behemoth's jagged face, loosing every weapon they had, frantic to claim an iota of the thing's monstrous attention. She saw them being doused like candles, whole handfuls at a time. And then the Architect's invisible hands reached out and wrung the whole length of the *Cataphracta* and opened it out like a flower. A ship and all its souls turned into a tumbling metal sculpture and cast adrift into the void. And it would do exactly the same to Berlenhof when it reached the planet.

The Locust Ark was annihilated next, fraying into nothing as it tried to throw its disintegrating mass into the Architect's path. Then the *Sword's* loom spoke, but the choir was in discord now, the very seams of the warship strained by the power of her own weaponry. Idris was clutching Solace's hands painfully, leaning into her and weeping. The Architect had halted, for the first time since it entered the system, no longer advancing on the planet. She felt Idris vibrate at that point, rigid as he did *something*; as he wrestled the universe for control over the apocalyptic engine that was the Architect. Her ears were full of the rapid, efficient patter of the bridge reports: stress fractures, targeting, the elegant physics of gravity as a bludgeoning weapon. Damage reports. So many damage reports. The Architect had already brushed them once and Solace had barely realized. Half the decks of the *Heaven's Sword* were evacuating.

"It's cracking!" someone was shouting. "It's cracking open!"

"Brace!" And Solace had to brace for herself and Idris too. Because his mind was somewhere else, doing battle on a field she couldn't even imagine.

Follow us:

 /orbitbooksUS

𝕏 /orbitbooks

▶ /orbitbooks

Join our mailing list
to receive alerts on our
latest releases and deals.

orbitbooks.net

Enter our monthly
giveaway for the chance
to win some epic prizes.

orbitloot.com